For my great-niece, Evie Marian Jane Atchison.

Dilly Court

Ragged Rose

HARPER

Harper
An imprint of HarperCollins*Publishers*
The News Building,
1 London Bridge Street,
London SE1 9GF

www.harpercollins.co.uk

Published by HarperCollins*Publishers* 2016
2

Copyright © Dilly Court 2016

Dilly Court asserts the moral right to
be identified as the author of this work

A catalogue record for this book
is available from the British Library

ISBN: 978-0-00-813735-9

Set in Sabon LT Std 12/14.5 pt by
Palimpsest Book Production Limited, Falkirk, Stirlingshire

Printed and bound in Great Britain by
Clays Ltd, St Ives plc

MIX
Paper from
responsible sources
FSC™ C007454

Ragged Rose

Dilly Court is a *Sunday Times* bestselling author of 28 novels. She grew up in North East London and began her career in television, writing scripts for commercials. She is married with two grown-up children and four grandchildren, and now lives in Dorset on the beautiful Jurassic Coast with her husband.

To find out more about Dilly, please visit her website and her Facebook page.

www.dillycourt.com

/DillyCourtAuthor

Also by Dilly Court

Chapter One

Cupid's Court, Barbican, London 1875

'Do hurry up, Cora. We're on in a minute.' Rose edged past her sister, bending almost double to avoid knocking the sequin-encrusted gowns off the pegs in their tiny dressing room, which in reality was little more than a cupboard.

Cora patted a stray curl in place, making a *moue* as she studied her reflection in the fly-spotted mirror. The atmosphere was thick with the smell of burning lamp oil and greasepaint, with wafts of cigar smoke seeping under the door, and the ever-present odour of stale beer and spirits permeated every inch of the saloon. She stood up, smoothing the tight-fitting bodice of the daringly low-cut gown with a satisfied smile. 'I'm ready.'

Rose opened the door in answer to an urgent knock.

'On stage, girls.' Tommy Tinker, the boy who undertook all the odd jobs that no one else wanted to do, stuck his head into the room, eyeing the girls with a cheeky grin. 'Very nice too, if I might be so bold.'

'Little boys should be seen and not heard,' Cora said with a haughty toss of her head as she squeezed past him.

'Show a bit of respect for your elders, young Tinker.' Rose paused in the doorway, fixing him with a stony stare until he blushed and dropped his gaze.

'Sorry, Miss Sunshine,' he muttered, making way for her by flattening himself against the whitewashed wall of what had once been a coal cellar. This small space now served as general store, as well as dressing rooms for the acts who performed in Fancello's Saloon.

'It's Miss Perkins,' Rose said mildly. 'Sunshine is our stage name, Tinker.'

He frowned. 'Best hurry, miss. The patrons are getting restless.'

Rose bundled up her full skirt as she negotiated the steep, narrow staircase, taking care to keep the satin from brushing against the damp walls. With Cora following close behind she arrived in the wings just in time to hear Fancello's introduction.

'Ladies and gentlemen.' He raised his voice in order to make himself heard above the general hubbub in the bar room. 'I am proud to present for your delectation . . . the delicious and delightful

Sunshine Sisters.' He clapped enthusiastically and his brother, Alphonso, downed the last of his pint and thundered out the intro on the piano.

Ignoring the continuous chatter, the occasional bursts of raucous laughter, and with the odd salacious remark tossed in for good measure by someone the worse for drink, Rose and Cora performed 'Pretty Little Polly Perkins of Paddington Green' with appropriate actions, and then launched into their dance routine. This had the effect of largely silencing the rowdy element of their audience, as the men craned their necks in order to get a better view of ladies' legs, and the occasional glimpse of a garter.

Rose and Cora left the small stage to a tumult of applause, and were called back for an encore, but Fancello intervened.

'You have had sunshine brought into your lives, gentlemen. The young ladies must not be allowed to exhaust themselves, but they will perform again later in the evening.' He joined the sisters in the wings. 'Well done,' he said, twirling his waxed moustache, a nervous habit that Rose had noted several times in the past. 'We mustn't spoil them – always leave the punters longing for more.'

'Yes, Signor Fancello,' Cora said with a coy smile. 'You're always right.'

Rose eyed him suspiciously. 'We agreed one performance a night, signor. You just said we would be on again later – I take it that we'll be paid double?'

He released his moustache and it recoiled like a

watch spring. 'I'm paying you for a night's work, Miss Sunshine. Don't bring on the storm clouds. Fancello is a fair man, but you can be replaced.'

Cora laid a small hand on his arm, her large blue eyes misted with tears. 'Don't be cross, signor. We understand, don't we, Rose?'

Rose ignored the warning look that Cora sent her. 'We might not be as well-known as your *bambina*, but we have been popular amongst your clients, signor. I think we deserve to be paid accordingly.'

For a moment she thought that she had gone too far. Fancello's dark curly hair seemed to stand on end like the fur of an outraged feline, and his full lips quivered, but a sly smile spread across his face and he roared with laughter. 'You drive a hard bargain, Miss Sunshine. I will pay you extra if you perform again later. My little *bambina* has the voice of an angel, but she is delicate like her *mamma* and we are careful to protect her.' He cocked his head on one side, frowning at the sound of a slow hand clap from the saloon. 'Go out there and circulate, but don't allow the punters to get too familiar.' He cupped his hand round his lips. 'Tinker.'

Popping up like a jack-in-the-box, Tinker appeared at his side. 'Yes, guv?'

'Where is the *bambina*? Why is she not ready to go on stage?'

Tinker shook his head. 'Your lady wife says it's no go, guv. The little 'un ain't to appear on stage as she's took sick.'

'We'll see about that.' Fancello strode off towards the staircase.

'Is she ill?' Cora asked anxiously. 'It's not catching, is it? I was talking to her earlier and she seemed perfectly fine then.'

'Gin,' Tinker said, tapping the side of his nose. 'The *bambina* likes a drop of gin and water to give her Dutch courage.'

Rose pursed her lips. She was no prude but she had listened to enough of her father's sermons to know the difference between right and wrong. 'She's just a child, a defenceless little girl. She should be drinking warm milk with a little honey to help her voice.'

'Ain't you never had a close look at her?' Tinker said with a superior smile. 'Ain't you never smelled the gin fumes on her breath, nor the tobacco smoke what clings to her hair and clothes?'

Cora's eyes widened. 'What are you saying, Tinker? Is this one of your jokes?'

'I been with the Fancellos since they plucked me from the poorhouse, miss. I seen the way they encouraged little Clementia to smoke and drink. It means she don't eat much and she don't grow proper – like us kids from the backstreets. Why do you think me legs is bowed and me arms don't straighten out proper? Most of us kids suffered from rickets.'

Rose laid her hand on his bony arm. 'It's a terrible affliction, Tinker. I'm ashamed to think I didn't notice your infirmities before, and I'm equally shocked to learn the truth about little Clemmie.'

'Never mind her,' Cora said urgently. 'There'll be a riot out there if we don't put in an appearance. Besides which, I saw a really handsome young man seated at one of the tables. I'd swear that he had eyes for me and me alone.'

'Best do it, miss.' Tinker peered out through a gap in the curtains. 'The signora is coming this way. She's got that look about her like when she starts throwing things. I'm off.' He turned and raced off towards the stairs that led up to the Fancellos' private apartment.

Rose went to meet Signora Fancello, who did not look amused. 'Your husband has asked us to do another performance this evening,' she said boldly. 'We have agreed but we must be out of the saloon before ten o'clock.'

Graziella Fancello's winged eyebrows drew together in an ominous frown. 'You are in no position to make demands on us, Miss Sunshine. We pay you to perform, and perform you will, even if we ask you to sing and dance at midnight.'

'But, signora, our mama is unwell and we have to look after her. She will be worried if we're out late. The streets of Islington are dangerous enough in daytime, let alone late at night, and we are two young women on our own.'

Graziella's red lips hardened into a thin line. 'I'll think about it. Now go out there and socialise with the clients.' She headed towards the stairs with a determined set of her chin.

'Well done, Cora,' Rose whispered, smiling. 'You know how to handle the wretched woman.'

'I suppose she's gone upstairs to give poor Clemmie a piece of her mind.' Cora adjusted her costume, pulling the bodice up in an attempt at a semblance of modesty. 'We'd best go out and circulate. Who knows, I might catch the eye of a rich man and he'll sweep me off my feet, and marry me?'

'I'd settle for being spotted by the manager of the Pavilion Theatre or the Grecian. We could earn twice as much, and we wouldn't have to pander to gentlemen with roving eyes and wandering hands.' Rose braced her shoulders. 'But we must leave here by ten, or Aunt Polly will have locked the doors.'

Cora pulled back the curtain and stepped down from the stage to a rousing cheer from the clientele: mostly well-dressed men of means who had come slumming. She headed for the blue-eyed gentleman she'd spotted earlier, who leaped to his feet with a courteous bow. Rose followed more slowly, walking between the tables, acknowledging the flattering comments, and ignoring suggestive remarks that would have made a courtesan blush. There were familiar faces amongst the audience, some whom she knew it was best to humour and then move on. Just as Fancello erupted onto the stage to introduce his *bambina cara*, Clementia, Rose came to a halt at a table occupied by a distinguished-looking gentleman of military bearing. He was older than the usual punter, and he had a kind, fatherly look about him.

'You are on your own, sir,' she said, smiling. 'May I join you?'

He half rose from his chair, motioning her to take a seat. 'That would be delightful, but you must excuse me if I don't stand. I have a gammy leg – an old war wound, you understand.'

She sat down opposite him. 'I'm sorry to hear that, sir. Were you in the Crimea?'

Just as he was about to reply, Clementia began to sing in a sweet clear soprano that momentarily stilled and silenced the audience. Rose sat back, watching the small creature perform. Poor Clemmie was never allowed out unaccompanied, Rose knew that for a fact. Tommy liked to gossip, and his favourite subject was little Clemmie, who was virtually a prisoner of love; doted on and fiercely protected by adoring parents. Rose was unsure whether this was entirely out of parental devotion, or whether Clemmie's ma and pa had an eye to nurturing a valuable talent. Whatever the reason, the young girl had no life outside the walls of the smoky saloon.

Rose turned to the military gentleman with an encouraging smile. 'You were about to tell me of your exploits, sir.'

'Colonel Mountfitchet at your service,' he said gallantly.

Rose felt herself blushing. 'I'm Rose Sunshine. How do you do, Colonel?'

'My friends call me Fitch.'

'I – I couldn't.' Rose had a vision of her father's shocked face were he to hear her being disrespectful to a much older gentleman, let alone a war hero. 'That wouldn't be proper, sir.'

'I take it that Sunshine is not your real name, and I respect your right to anonymity.' He leaned towards her. 'What are you doing here, Rose? You're not the sort of girl who normally frequents places such as this.'

'My sister and I are here to entertain, sir. We don't fraternise with the customers, if that's what you are inferring.'

'Certainly not, my dear, and it's none of my business.'

Rose eyed him warily. This was not the usual way that conversations with patrons ran. There might be a little mild flirtation, but that was as far as it went. She had learned to slant her questions so that the gentlemen talked about their favourite topics, namely themselves, but the colonel was different. He seemed genuinely interested in her, and that was alarming.

He cleared his throat. 'You must forgive me, Rose. It's a long time since I was in the company of a beautiful young lady. I beg you to forgive an old soldier for his ill manners.'

'No, sir. I won't allow that,' Rose said hastily. She leaned forward, lowering her voice. 'My sister and I work of necessity, Colonel. We have our reasons, but I would ask you not to enquire further.'

He nodded and his pale grey eyes twinkled. 'You

have my word, Rose. Now will you allow me to buy you a drink? The signora has returned and she is looking this way. I imagine she expects to boost sales by sending the Sunshine Sisters behind enemy lines.'

Rose stifled a giggle. 'I would hardly call you the enemy, Colonel, but I must warn you that she serves us lemonade and charges for champagne.'

'I would expect nothing else from a business-woman like the signora.' He clicked his fingers to attract a waiter. 'Champagne for the young lady,' he said grandly. 'And a whisky for me.'

A somewhat half-hearted round of applause heralded the end of Clemmie's performance, and Rose was quick to note the frown on the signora's face. Poor Clemmie would come in for some fierce criticism when her mother joined her upstairs. The colonel was clapping enthusiastically, but Rose had a feeling that he was acting from chivalry rather than appreciation of Clemmie's pitch-perfect, but emotionless, render-ing of 'Come into the Garden, Maud'. She nodded to the waiter, who placed a brimming glass on the table in front of her. 'Thank you.'

He grinned and hurried away to serve a gentleman who was already the worse for wear. Rose sipped what indeed turned out to be lemonade. It had been a long day and she was tired, but it was not yet over.

The colonel added a dash of water to his whisky, and raised his glass to her. 'Here's to your lovely green eyes and russet hair, Miss Sunshine. May you continue to delight us for many an evening to come.'

'Thank you, Colonel.' Rose glanced over her shoulder and saw Cora beckoning to her. 'I think we're on again, so I must leave you.' She downed the sweet drink in one. 'I hope to see you here again, sir.' He attempted to rise, but she held up her hand. 'Please don't get up, sir.'

He subsided onto his seat. 'You've brought a little sunshine into an old man's life, Rose. I will definitely patronise Fancello's establishment again, and I will tell him so.'

Rose acknowledged his gallant remark with a smile before weaving her way through the closely packed tables to join her sister.

'It's nearly ten o'clock,' Cora whispered. 'We'd better go through this one double tempo.' She climbed onto the stage and waved to Alphonso, who had a full pint glass in one hand and a cigar in the other. For a moment it looked as if he were about to ignore her signal, but Fancello had reappeared and he clapped his hands.

'Ladies and gentlemen, I have pleasure to present, for a second time this evening, the superb, sweet and sensational Sunshine Sisters. Maestro, music, if you please.' With an expansive flourish of his arms he turned to face the girls. 'Smile.'

Alphonso rested his cigar on the top of the piano and took a swig of beer. With a rebellious scowl he flexed his fingers and began to play.

When they finally escaped from the stage, having taken several encores, Rose and Cora each did a quick change, crammed their bonnets on their elaborate coiffures and wrapped their shawls around their shoulders before leaving by the side door, which led into Cupid's Court. It was dark and there were no streetlights to relieve the gloom of a March night. The buildings around them were mainly business premises, vacated when the day's work came to an end. Their unlit windows stared blindly into the darkness, and homeless men and women huddled in doorways. The cobblestones were slippery beneath the girls' feet and gutters overflowed with rainwater. They had missed a storm, but a spiteful wind tugged at their clothes and threatened to whip their bonnets off their heads as they ran towards the relative safety of Golden Lane. Gas lamps created pools of light, and, even though it was late, there were still plenty of people about, although it was a different crowd from the housewives, office workers, milliners and stay makers who frequented the busy thoroughfare in daylight. Darkness brought out the worst in society, and the girls held hands as they hurried on their way.

The home for fallen women was situated on the corner of Old Street and City Road, directly opposite St Luke's Hospital for Lunatics and the City of London Lying-In Hospital. The sour smell from the vinegar works behind St Mark's church hung in a damp cloud, grazing the rooftops as it mingled with the fumes from the gas works in Pear Tree Street, and the odours belched out by the manufactories alongside the City Road Basin. Shrieks from the inmates of the asylum were indistinguishable from the screams of the women in labour in the building next door, and, in stark comparison, laughter and voices raised in drunken singing emanated from a nearby pub.

The door of the home opened just a crack in response to Rose's rapping on the knocker.

'Who is it?' The young voice sounded wary.

'It's Rose and Cora,' Rose said urgently. 'Let us in, please, Sukey.'

'You can't be too careful,' Sukey muttered as she let them into the dark hallway. 'There's one of them loonies escaped earlier today. We'll all have our throats slit while we sleep in our beds.' She closed the door and picked up an oil lamp.

Cora patted her on the shoulder. 'I'm sure that the poor person will be far away from here by now.'

'I imagine that the first thing people think about when they escape is to make their way home,' Rose said in her most matter-of-fact voice. 'So you need not be afraid.'

Sukey slanted her a sideways look. 'Yes, miss. I expects you're right.' She drew herself up to her full height, although her twisted spine gave her the look of a young sapling stunted in its growth. 'Shall I tell Miss Polly that you're here? Only she's up in the dormitory sorting out a fight.'

'It's all right,' Cora said hastily. 'We'll go to the parlour.'

'We can't stay long,' Rose added. 'We're late as it is.'

'Your duds are laid out for you. I done it meself, so I know it's done proper. You can't trust the servants to keep their traps shut or do things right.'

Rose kept a straight face with difficulty. 'We appreciate everything you do for us, Sukey. If you'd be kind enough to tell Miss Polly that we're here when she's free, that would be splendid.'

Sukey puffed out her concave chest. 'You can trust me, Miss Rose.' She scuttled off with her lop-sided gait.

'Poor thing,' Cora sighed. 'She'd be pretty if she didn't have such a terrible disability.'

Rose headed for the parlour. 'She copes very well, and she's lucky that she's got a good home here with Polly. She might have ended up in a circus or a freak show, poor soul.' She paused to glance at the steep flight of stairs, listening to the shouts and streams of invective that flowed with such fluency. 'I wonder if we ought to go upstairs and help.'

'I don't think so.' Cora hurried on ahead of her. 'I think Aunt Polly can handle the situation.' She opened the parlour door and went inside.

The warmth from the coal fire enveloped Rose like a comforting blanket as she followed her sister into Polly's inner sanctum, where nothing ever changed. Polly's theatrical past was evoked by the play bills that covered the walls, and framed photographs of her in her heyday hung from the picture rail. Mementoes of her brief reign as queen of the London stage covered the entire surface of a large mahogany chiffonier, and sheet music of her most popular songs lay on the piano stool. One of her stage costumes was draped over a tailor's dummy, standing proud between the two windows. It was faded, and moths had been feasting on the material, but Polly refused to pack it away. She clung to her memories, insisting that one day a theatre manager would come calling, and her star would shine again.

It was not an elegant room, but Rose had always felt more at home here than in the neat parlour at the vicarage, where the atmosphere was so often uncomfortable. It was Aunt Polly who had looked after the infant Rose and Cora when their mother was suffering from frequent bouts of illness. It was in this room that Polly had given the girls singing lessons and taught them dance routines, unbeknown to their strict father. It was to Aunt Polly they had come recently when news of their brother's troubles reached them in a letter that Billy had sent from Bodmin Gaol. It was Polly who had given the girls the courage to go out and earn money to pay for his defence lawyer, and now Polly was helping them to keep their mission secret.

Rose was overtaken by a sudden wave of nostalgia as she breathed in the lingering aroma of Aunt Polly's perfume, laced with the fumes of gin and overtones of brandy. She looked round the room with a feeling of deep affection. It was true that the furniture had been purchased in sale rooms and was well worn, but Polly said that gave each item a mystique and a history that was sadly lacking in anything brand-new. Polly's favourite piece was a chaise longue, which was draped with exotic shawls, although the only occupant at this moment was a fat tabby cat of uncertain nature. He had wandered in from the street one night and taken up residence, bringing with him his feral dislike of all humans with the exception of Polly, whom he tolerated.

Cora was about to sit down when she spotted Spartacus, as Polly had named the animal, and she moved to a chair by the fire. The cat opened one eye, stretched and exposed his sharp claws, and then went back to sleep.

Rose began to undress. 'Don't get comfortable, Cora. We've got to get home before Pa sends out a search party. I can't face an angry scene this evening.'

'I'm tired,' Cora complained bitterly. 'My feet are sore and I don't think I can walk another step.'

'We can't afford a cab. You'll have to make the effort.' Rose slipped off her blouse, sniffed it and shook her head. 'It reeks of tobacco smoke and stale beer,' she said, sighing. 'I wouldn't bother to change, but Ma would be sure to notice and demand an explanation.'

'Couldn't we say that the women here smoke and

drink?' Cora asked, smothering a yawn. 'Aunt Polly would back us up. I know she would.'

'Ma might be taken in, but Pa would know we were telling fibs. He has an uncanny ability to sniff out a lie. Neither you nor I have ever been able to look him in the face and fib.'

'That's not quite true,' Cora insisted. 'They think we spend our spare time helping the fallen women. Both Ma and Pa would have a fit if they knew what we were really doing. Especially Pa.'

'And they mustn't be allowed to find out,' Rose said firmly. She picked up a grey linsey-woolsey gown and tossed it to her sister. 'Come on, Corrie. Be a good girl and get changed. You know we're doing this for a good cause.'

Cora raised herself to her feet and began undoing the buttons on her cotton blouse. 'I know we're doing it for Billy, but I wish he were here now.' Her bottom lip trembled, but she sniffed and attempted a smile. 'I miss him, Rosie. He's the best brother a girl could have and I'll never believe ill of him.'

'Cora!' Polly erupted into the room. 'I've told you before not to mention William's name in this house. You never know who might be listening.'

'I – I'm sorry,' Cora said, hanging her head. 'But I do miss him and I want him to come home.'

'That's why we're doing this.' Rose slipped her gown over her head. 'It will be worth it in the end, and who knows, we might become famous along the way.' She turned to her aunt with a pleading look.

'Don't be cross with Cora, Aunt Polly. She's tired and her feet hurt. We had to do two shows tonight.'

Polly threw herself down on the chaise longue, pushing the cat out of the way, to his obvious annoyance. Spartacus hissed and took a half-hearted swipe at her before settling down again on one of the velvet cushions. 'Wretched animal,' Polly said crossly. 'I ought to throw you out on the street where you belong.' She glanced up at Rose, who was eyeing her with a wry smile. 'He's useful. He keeps the rodent population under control.' She leaned against the buttoned back rest. 'Pour me a glass of gin, Cora. I've just had a tussle with two women who would like to slit each other's throats.'

'I'll do it,' Rose said, moving to the side table where Polly kept a selection of decanters. 'You would think that they would support each other instead of falling out. They've all been abandoned by their husbands, and face the prospect of bringing up their children on their own. From what I've seen of the gentlemen who frequent the saloon, being married doesn't stop a man having a roving eye.'

'It's true that most of my women have wedding rings.' Polly stretched out her hand to take the drink from Rose. 'But knowing those two upstairs, they've probably filched them from corpses.'

'Why were they fighting?' Cora asked.

Polly swallowed a mouthful of neat gin. 'They've only just realised that they've been taken in by the same man, and he's turned his back on both of them.

They were at each other's throats. I think they would have killed each other had they had a weapon other than a hairpin and a teaspoon. I must tell Ethel to lock away the kitchen knives tonight.'

Rose picked up the much-darned woollen shawl that she had worn when she left home earlier that evening and wrapped it around her shoulders. 'Hurry up, Corrie. The sooner we set out the sooner you'll be tucked up in your bed at home.'

'I wish there was some other way for you girls to raise money,' Polly said, frowning. 'Heaven knows what your father would say if he knew about all this, and Eleanor would never let me hear the last of it. She was always the bossy older sister . . . in the old days, anyway.'

'I'm sure she will understand when Billy tells her the whole story.' Cora picked up her bonnet and rammed it on her head.

Polly's rouged lips curved in a wry smile. 'I don't know about that, Cora. Eleanor thinks the sun rises and sets in her first-born, and your father is convinced that William is following in his footsteps. How could you tell a man of the cloth that his precious son is in gaol, awaiting trial for killing his best friend? Especially when we've all kept up the fiction that Billy is a guest of the Tressidick family in Cornwall.'

'They must never know,' Rose said firmly. 'We won't allow their hearts to be broken. Come on, Cora Perkins. It's time we were home.'

*

19

It was less than a mile from the home for fallen women to St Matthew's church, and the walk was uneventful, notwithstanding a bunch of drunken youths who staggered out of The Eagle tavern on the corner of City Road and Shepherdess Walk. Rose grabbed Cora by the hand and marched past with her nose in the air, which seemed to work as the young men made no attempt to molest them, resorting instead to hurling insults and collapsing with drunken laughter. Rose came to a halt on the bridge over the City Road Basin, where the Regent's Canal came to a sudden end. A young woman was standing on the parapet and seemed about to throw herself into the murky waters, which were stained with indigo dye, coal dust and industrial effluent.

'Don't do it,' Rose said gently, ignoring Cora, who was tugging at her hand. 'He's never worth it, and you'll spoil that pretty frock if you fall into that filthy water.'

The girl turned her head and in the light of the streetlamp Rose could see that she was very young. Her face was pale and streaked with tears, and her lips worked soundlessly. Rose held out her hand. 'Nothing can be so bad that it can't be made better by a nice hot cup of tea and a warm fire.'

'Who are you? And what d'you want with the likes of me? I ain't going back into service, not for no one. He done this to me, and now he don't want to know.'

Rose and Cora exchanged knowing looks. They had both heard this story many times before.

'What is your name?' Rose kept her voice low, knowing that any sudden move or harsh tone could send the girl plummeting to her death.

'M-Maisie. Now you know, so leave me be.' Maisie held out her arms and raised herself on tiptoe, ready to jump.

Chapter Two

'Don't!' Rose and Cora cried out as one, but it was Rose who lunged at Maisie and caught her round the waist. She dragged her back onto the pavement and they fell in a heap.

'Rose, are you all right?' Cora cried anxiously as she attempted to help her sister to her feet.

'Yes, don't fuss, Corrie. Catch hold of her – don't let her run away.'

Cora seized Maisie by the scruff of her neck. 'You silly girl. He's not worth it, whoever he is, and you might have taken my sister with you.'

Rose scrambled to her feet. 'It's all right, Corrie. No harm done.' She helped Maisie to stand. 'Don't cry. We'll take care of you.'

'I don't need you, nor anyone.' Maisie wiped her nose on the frayed cuff of her sleeve. 'I can look after meself.'

'I'm sure you can,' Rose said, brushing the mud off her skirt. 'But we all need a little help now and then. Why don't you come to the vicarage with us? You can stay the night, and tomorrow morning you can decide what you want to do.'

Maisie looked from one to the other and her bottom lip trembled. 'I ain't religious. I don't want no sermon.'

'I promise you that won't happen,' Rose said, holding out her hand. 'You'll just have to trust us, and let's face it – anything is better than drowning in filthy water.'

'Yes, do come with us,' Cora pleaded. 'I'm so tired that I could sleep on the cold pavement and my feet are aching.'

Maisie nodded dully. 'All right, but just for tonight. I ain't a charity case.'

'Of course not.' Rose started off in the direction of St Matthew's church, leading Maisie by the hand.

The vicarage was situated close to the church in a respectable middle-class area. The wide streets were lined with terraced houses built in the Georgian era, and the dwellings were well maintained. Unlike some of the surrounding streets, this part of Islington exuded an air of comfortable prosperity.

Rose guided Maisie through the garden to the back of the house and Cora rapped on the kitchen door. It was opened almost immediately by their cook-housekeeper, Mrs Blunt. She was ready for bed, wearing a long robe, and her nightcap sat askew on her head.

'Where have you been, young ladies? Your pa has waited up for you.' She glared at Maisie. 'Who is this?'

Cora stepped inside. 'We're so sorry to have kept you up, dear Mrs Blunt.'

'But we were helping Aunt Polly,' Rose added hastily. 'And we came across this young girl who is in desperate need of warmth and comfort.'

Mrs Blunt stood arms akimbo, looking Maisie up and down. 'Runaway servant, I'd guess. We can't take in all the waifs and strays in the city, Miss Rose.'

'It's just for tonight, and I rather think it's up to Pa to decide,' Rose said firmly. She tempered her words with a persuasive smile. 'A nice hot cup of tea wouldn't go amiss, and a slice of your seed cake would go down well, I'm sure.' She turned to Maisie without giving Mrs Blunt a chance to refuse. 'You have never tasted anything as good as Mrs Blunt's caraway cake. She is the best cook in Islington.'

'The best in London,' Cora said, smothering a yawn. 'Might I have a cup of warm milk, please? I'm ready for bed.'

'Miss Day works you girls far too hard. That's my opinion and I don't mind saying so.' Mrs Blunt hurried over to the range and moved the kettle to the hob. She turned to Maisie. 'You can make yourself useful, child. Fetch the milk jug from the marble slab in the larder, and bring the cake as well.' She pointed to the cupboard on the far side of the room. 'Chop chop.'

Maisie stood like a statue, as if her limbs had suddenly turned to marble. 'I'll help you.' Cora took her by the arm and guided her as she might a sleep-walker.

Rose could see that her sister had the situation in hand. 'I'll go and tell Pa that we're home.' She left them and made her way down the gaslit passage that led into the entrance hall of the draughty, rambling vicarage. The front parlour was to the right of the wide staircase, and it was where the family gathered in the evenings, and after church on Sundays. Rose entered the room to find her father pacing the floor.

'Pa, I'm so sorry we're late.' She could tell by the strained expression on his deeply lined face that he had been angered by their lengthy absence, and for the first time she felt guilty even though she and Cora were carrying out their deception for the best of reasons. 'I'm afraid it was unavoidable.'

Seymour Perkins glowered at his elder daughter. 'It isn't safe for you girls to be walking home un-escorted at this time of night. Polly ought to know better than to keep you so late, and I will tell her so in no uncertain terms next time we meet.'

'It wasn't Aunt Polly's fault,' Rose said quickly. 'She had some trouble with two of the women, it's true, but that didn't hold us up.' She moved to her father's side, laying her hand on his arm. 'Do sit down. You look worn to the bone, Pa. You work too hard.'

He subsided onto a chair by the fire, which had

25

burned down to a few glowing embers. 'The end of winter seems to accelerate the death rate amongst the frail and elderly. I've been attempting to comfort the dying and take care of the bereaved since dawn this morning.'

'I know, Pa.' Rose looked into his face, experiencing a surge of tenderness that made her throat constrict and her eyes sting with unshed tears. Her father seemed to have aged suddenly, or perhaps she had not noticed the passing of the years. The man who had been a strict disciplinarian when she, Billy and Cora were children had grown old, although he had not mellowed with age. 'I'm truly sorry that we added to your worries.'

'I applaud the fact that you and your sister work so tirelessly with the unhappy women in Polly's care, but I cannot have you neglecting the poor of this parish. Your mama is too frail to undertake the duties my calling thrust upon her.'

A wave of shame made Rose look away. She could feel the blood rushing to her cheeks and she could not look her father in the eye. 'There's another reason we were late, Pa. We came across a young girl who was about to hurl herself off the City Basin bridge. Cora and I persuaded her not to jump, and we've brought her home. I was hoping she could stay tonight and perhaps we could take her to Aunt Polly in the morning.'

Seymour's lips hardened into a thin line of disapproval. 'I suppose it's the usual story.'

'I fear so. Maisie hasn't told us much, but no doubt the whole sorry tale will come out as she begins to put her trust in us.'

'She must remain here, where she is safe from temptation. It's probably best if you make her comfortable for the night and I'll see her tomorrow when she's rested.'

'I'll do that, and you must get some sleep, too. You look exhausted.' Rose kissed him on the cheek, but the sudden look of suspicion on her father's face made her withdraw hastily as she realised her mistake.

He gave her a reproachful look. 'Have you taken up smoking, Rose? I can smell it in your hair.'

'No, certainly not, Pa.' She struggled to think of a convincing reason for her exposure to such a substance. 'It must have come from the home, Pa. Polly allows the women to smoke if it calms them down. They have little enough enjoyment in life.'

'It seems to me that they've had a little too much enjoyment for their own good,' he said, frowning. 'I should have known better than to accuse you of such a thing. You have always tried to be a good daughter.'

She made a move towards the doorway. 'I'll see to Maisie, and then I'm going to bed. Things will look better in the morning.'

Maisie was seated at the kitchen table, devouring cake as if it were her last meal on earth, and in between each bite she swallowed a mouthful of hot tea. Cora looked up, meeting Rose's gaze with a shrug. 'Mrs Blunt will have to make another seed cake in the morning. I told her to go to bed; the poor old thing looked worn out.'

'Don't let her hear you calling her old,' Rose said, chuckling. 'Mrs Blunt is in her prime, or so she keeps telling me, but I think it has something to do with Mr Spinks, the butcher. Ma told me that he delivers the meat in person these days, instead of sending his boy. I think he's sweet on Mrs Blunt.'

'Or maybe he likes her cooking.' Cora put her cup of warm milk aside. 'I have to go to bed, Rose. I'm dead on my poor aching feet.'

'I'm sorry to put you to so much trouble,' Maisie said through a mouthful of cake. 'I can sleep on the floor by the range. It's what I'm used to.'

'Not while you're in our house.' Rose picked up the teapot and filled a cup, adding a dash of milk. 'You can have the boxroom. It's small but the bed is quite comfortable, and tomorrow we'll have a proper talk and decide what is to be done.'

Cora rose to her feet. 'Come with me, Maisie. I'll take you to your room and I'll lend you a nightgown. Everything will look brighter in the morning.'

Maisie stuffed the last few crumbs of cake into her mouth and drained her teacup. She stood up, covering her mouth in an attempt to quieten a loud belch. 'I'm sorry. I shouldn't have bolted me grub, but I ain't eaten since yesterday and that cake was bloody good.' She blushed and lowered her gaze. 'Begging your pardon for the bad language.'

'That's all right, Maisie.' Rose sank down on the nearest chair, overcome by a sudden wave of fatigue. 'Sleep tight and wake bright.'

Next morning Rose was up early as usual. She had taken it upon herself to be first in the kitchen, where she set about riddling the ashes in the range and encouraged the remaining embers to burst into flame with the addition of some kindling. In days gone by the Perkins family had employed a scullery maid, but economies had had to be made as Rose's mother's delicate state of health necessitated spending money on doctor's visits and medicines. Eleanor had continued her parish duties for as long as possible, but these days she relied more and more on help from her daughters. Rose loved and respected her mother, but she had seen her mother bend beneath her husband's strong will, and fade like a flower in the desert. Seymour Perkins was a good man, but he had had little sympathy for weakness in others, and, Rose thought privately, he reserved his compassion for this flock.

As she entered the kitchen Rose discovered Maisie sound asleep, curled up on the mat in front of the range, but she awakened with a start and snapped into a sitting position, staring round bleary-eyed.

'You give me a turn, miss,' she said, yawning. 'I couldn't think where I was for a moment.'

'Did you sleep here all night?' Rose asked curiously. 'Weren't you comfortable in your bed?'

'I'm sorry, miss. I didn't want to appear ungrateful, but I ain't used to such softness. I felt more at home here.' Maisie scrambled to her feet. 'Here, let me see to the fire for you. I can't pay for me night's lodgings so I should do something to help.'

Rose smiled and shook her head. 'That's very thoughtful of you, Maisie. Why don't you go outside and fetch some water? There's a bucket in the scullery and the pump is in the yard. You'll feel better for a wash. I'll put the kettle on, we'll have some breakfast and you can tell me all about yourself.'

Maisie clasped her hands tightly in front of her, staring down at her scuffed boots. 'There ain't much to tell, but I suppose you guessed that I got a bit of a problem.'

'I'm sure we can sort something out, so try not to worry.'

'Ta, miss. You're a good 'un and no mistake.' Maisie headed for the door that led into the scullery and Rose picked up the bellows. She applied them vigorously until flames licked around the coals. When she was satisfied with the result she followed Maisie out into the back yard, snatching a towel from the airing rack as she went past.

Maisie had taken her at her word and had stripped off the borrowed nightgown and stood shivering in her chemise as she doused herself in cold water. Rose handed her the towel. 'I was going to heat some water so that you could wash at the sink. It's a bit chilly out here.'

Maisie tossed her wet hair back from her face and patted herself dry. 'I'm used to it, miss. We had to wash outdoors even if it was snowing. The mistress was very strict about things like that.'

'You're soaked to the skin, Maisie. You'll need dry clothes and I can help you there.'

'Like I said before, I ain't a charity case, miss,' Maisie said through chattering teeth. 'I'll dry out in the warmth of the kitchen and me duds is wearable, thanks to you and the other young miss.' Maisie's lips curved in an irrepressible grin. 'They would have been covered in stinking mud if it hadn't been for you and your sister.'

'Mrs Blunt came down after Cora put you to bed and took it upon herself to put them in to soak. They were a little grubby and in need of a patch or two. But there's no need to worry, Maisie; we have a missionary barrel filled with perfectly good clothes.' Rose picked up the bucket and headed indoors. 'Kind-hearted people donate them for those in need, and at the moment you qualify without question. Let's see what we can find, and then we'll have some tea and toast.'

Under the mildly disapproving eye of Mrs Blunt, who had erupted into the kitchen ready to take control of her small empire, Rose sorted out a set of underwear from the overflowing missionary barrel, together with a cotton print frock and a woollen shawl. Maisie seemed to forget her troubles and pirouetted around

31

the kitchen like the child she was. Rose watched her, smiling indulgently, but was conscious of the fact that Maisie was a fourteen-year-old who would soon become a mother. The vexing question was whether or not the father would take any responsibility for her and the baby. Rose waited until they were seated at the breakfast table before she asked Maisie anything, starting with her early life, which turned out to be in a foundling home.

'I was left on the doorstep,' Maisie said, licking jam off her fingers. 'They told me I was about a month old, or thereabouts, but there weren't no note or anything that would identify me, so I don't know where I come from.'

'Some mothers deserve horsewhipping,' Mrs Blunt said in a low voice. 'I was never blessed with a child, and yet some women have them like shelling peas. There's no justice in this world.'

Rose sipped her tea, eyeing Maisie thoughtfully. 'So you have no one to turn to now?'

'No, miss. That's why I was ready to jump.'

'And the father isn't prepared to help?'

Maisie threw her head back and laughed, but it was not a humorous sound. 'Lawks, miss, that's why I got the sack. The mistress noticed me belly was getting bigger and she made me tell her the truth, but when I said it were the master what got me in the family way she boxed me ears and turned me out on the street. Mind you, I never expected nothing more. The tweeny told me about one of the housemaids who caught the master's eye. She ended up in the workhouse with her nipper. That's not going to happen to me.'

'It most certainly is not,' Rose said firmly. 'My aunt runs a home for girls who are in your unfortunate position.' She held up her hand as Maisie opened her mouth to protest. 'And she's very kind and understanding. If you want to keep your baby she will do her best to make it possible, or, if you cannot see your way to bringing up a child on your own, she will find a family who will give the infant a loving home.'

Maisie toyed with a piece of buttered toast. 'I wouldn't want me kid to grow up not knowing who its mother was. My ma dumped me like a bundle of washing and never give me another thought. I used to sit in the window of the foundling home wishing that she would come and get me, but she never did. I don't want that for my baby.'

Rose and Mrs Blunt exchanged worried glances. 'You'll have to do what's best for the child,' Mrs Blunt said sternly. 'You're young, Maisie. You'll get over it in time.'

Maisie pushed her plate away and her eyes filled with tears. 'But she won't. I know it's a little girl and I ain't going to desert her.'

Rose stood up, holding out her hand. 'Come with me, Maisie. I'm taking you to my aunt Polly. She'll take care of you and your baby. She's helped countless young women in your position.'

'I dunno,' Maisie said warily. 'She's not one of them women what—'

'No, she most certainly is not. Put that idea out of your head, because I wouldn't think of sending you to one of those backstreet practitioners. I'm going to fetch my bonnet and shawl and we'll be off.'

Rose and Maisie arrived at the house in Old Street and Sukey opened the door.

'You're early, miss.' She gave Maisie a knowing look. 'Another one, I suppose.'

'Is my aunt up yet, Sukey?'

'I don't think so, Miss Rose. I'll go and see.'

Sukey shambled off towards the staircase and Rose ushered Maisie into the parlour.

'Well, I never did,' Maisie muttered as she gazed around the room. 'I never seen nothing like this in all me born days.'

Rose was used to the somewhat bizarre collection of memorabilia, but seeing it through a stranger's eyes she had to admit that it was a little eccentric. 'My aunt was a celebrated performer in her day,' she said by way of an explanation. 'She sang and danced on most of the great stages in London.'

'Really?' Maisie's eyes widened and she stared at Rose open-mouthed. 'I'd give anything to go to a music hall. I've seen buskers singing on street corners, but I've never been in a proper theatre, have you, Miss Rose?'

'Well, I . . .' Rose was saved from answering by

the sudden appearance of Polly, who made a grand entrance wearing a diaphanous silk wrap and a frilled nightcap. She came to a halt, peering at Maisie through her lorgnette. 'Who is this child, Rose?'

'This is Maisie, Aunt Polly.' Rose turned to Maisie, raising her eyebrows. 'What is your surname? I'm afraid I forgot to ask.'

'I'm Maisie Monday, and before you enquire as to how I come by such a moniker, they give it me at the foundling home because it was on a Monday morning when they come across me on the doorstep.'

Polly shooed Spartacus off the chaise longue and took his place amongst the colourful cushions. The cat arched his back and his tail twitched angrily, but as if to show his independence he strolled over to Maisie and rubbed himself against her skirts. With a cry of delight she had scooped him up in her arms, before either Rose or her aunt could warn her that Spartacus bit and scratched, as the mood took him.

'You're a beautiful pussycat,' Maisie cooed, rocking him in her arms like a baby.

'I'd be careful if I were you,' Rose said hastily, but Spartacus, contrary to the last, closed his eyes and began to purr.

'Bless my soul, who would have thought it?' Polly threw up her hands. 'That creature can kill a rat with one bite, and now just look at him. You must have a way with animals, Maisie Monday. Can you charm the birds out of the trees?'

'I dunno, miss. I never tried.'

'Maisie is in need of your help, Aunt,' Rose said calmly. 'I'm sure she'll tell you her story in time.'

'First things first, Rose. Ring for Sukey, please. I'm in desperate need of sustenance. One of my girls went into labour after you left last night and it took three of us to get her over to the Lying-ln Hospital. Poor thing, she was convinced that they would take the baby from her and sell it to the highest bidder. Lord knows where she got such an idea, but she struggled back across the road at four in the morning with the child in her arms. One of the attendants from the hospital ran after her, trying to persuade her to return to her bed. It was quite a scene.'

Rose tugged at the bell pull. 'You must be fagged out, Aunt. I'm sorry I disturbed you but Maisie is in dire need of a place to stay until her baby is born. Her employer threw her out on the street, and when Cora and I came upon her last evening she was in a desperate state.'

'Quite so,' Maisie said emphatically. 'I were about to jump off the bridge when the young ladies come upon me and dragged me to the ground. Ever so kind, they was.' Her brown eyes filled with tears and she buried her face in Spartacus's fur.

Rose held her breath, hoping that Spartacus would not suddenly turn feral, but he was behaving like a pampered pet.

'I suppose it's the usual story,' Polly said, sighing.

'Yes, I'm afraid so.' Rose kept her gaze fixed on Spartacus and was ready to snatch him from Maisie's arms should he show signs of growing tired of her embrace, but the cat appeared to be completely relaxed and his purring echoed round the room. He did not even stir when a tap on the door preceded Sukey barging into the room.

'You rang, Miss Polly?' She caught sight of Maisie and the cat and her jaw dropped. 'Best put him down, girl. He'll have your eye out in a minute. Nasty beast . . . he's got an evil streak.'

Maisie cuddled him closer. 'No, you're mistaken, ma'am. He's a sweet little puss, and I love him already.'

'Has this one escaped from the lunatic asylum across the street?' Sukey turned to Polly with her hands outstretched. 'We've got enough trouble with the other harlots, miss. You aren't going to take a loony on as well, surely?'

Rose was about to protest but Polly waved Sukey's protest aside with a casual flick of her fingers. 'Maisie Monday has come to join us, and she is saner than you or I, if it comes to that.'

'That's a matter of opinion,' Sukey muttered, just loud enough for all to hear. 'What do you want, miss?'

'Coffee, Sukey. A large pot of coffee, and you can add a nip or two of brandy.'

'At this time in the morning, Aunt Polly?' Rose glanced at the clock on the mantelshelf, which was partly obscured by a large ostrich feather fan. However, she could make out most of the numerals, and it was only a little after half-past eight.

'As I said, Sukey, coffee and a touch of brandy to revive me.'

'Yes, Miss Polly.' Sukey hobbled out of the room, slamming the door behind her.

Polly turned to Rose with a bright smile. 'You might find yourself resorting to such tactics in time to come, my pet. I have a busy day ahead of me and I dare say that you have too. I suppose Eleanor has taken to her bed as usual.'

'I haven't seen Mama since yesterday afternoon,' Rose said quickly. 'She was quite well then.'

'My sister is a good woman, but she has always used her delicate constitution as an excuse to get her own way.'

'That's not fair,' Rose protested.

'I've known her a lot longer than you, Rose. It started when we were children and Eleanor discovered that illness was a useful tool when it came to dealing with our father, who was inordinately strict. His parishioners were terrified of him and his sermons could conjure up visions of hellfire that had them trembling in their seats.'

'He was a fierce old gentleman,' Rose said, chuckling. 'I was always very good when we were taken to visit him and Grandmamma, but Cora was his favourite.'

'Cora takes after your mother. You, alas, are more like me. I was the rebel who challenged authority and suffered the consequences.'

'I'm no rebel, Aunt.'

'Are you not?' Polly put her head on one side, eyeing Rose with an amused smile. 'I'll say no more on the subject.' She tapped the side of her aquiline nose, nodding in Maisie's direction. 'Little pitchers have big ears, as they say. Anyway, I won't keep you as I know you have a long day ahead of you. Leave the child with me. I'll look after her and I'll see you and Cora this evening.'

'You will, of course.' Rose moved to Maisie's side, but when she attempted to stroke his head Spartacus opened one eye and stopped purring. She withdrew her hand hastily. 'I'm leaving now, Maisie, but I know you'll be well cared for here, and I might see you this evening.'

'You're coming back just to see me?' Maisie stared at her in surprise. 'Really?'

'Of course. I want to make sure that you're happy and settled, but Cora and I usually call in to see Aunt Polly after work.'

'You work? What do you do? I thought you was rich.'

'It would take too long to explain now.' Rose looked to her aunt for help, but Polly shrugged. 'But we'll talk about it some other time.'

Maisie set Spartacus down on the floor. 'You won't just leave me here, will you, miss?' Her voice rose in panic as she caught Rose by the sleeve. 'I'm scared.'

'There's no need to be frightened,' Rose said, giving her a quick hug. 'Aunt Polly is the kindest person I know, and I come here often so you'll see quite a lot of me. I won't abandon you, Maisie.'

With obvious reluctance Maisie released her hold. 'All right. I believe you, miss.' She shot a sideways glance at Polly. 'If you're sure she's all right.'

'I may seem old to a child like you,' Polly said irritably, 'but I'm not deaf. Come and sit down, you silly girl, and I'll tell you what your duties will be.'

Rose hesitated in the doorway, giving Maisie an encouraging nod and a smile.

'I ain't afraid of hard work.' Maisie perched on the edge of a chair. 'I'm used to scrubbing floors and washing dishes.'

'That's as maybe, but we have all those jobs in hand. I think I will put you in charge of Spartacus. He's a grumpy old chap and most of my girls are scared of him, and Cook chases him with a carving knife when he steals food from the larder. It will be your job to take care of him and make sure he doesn't get into trouble.'

Maisie put her head on one side, eyeing Polly like an inquisitive robin. 'If he's such a pest why do you keep him?'

'Because he's a brilliant mouser and rat catcher. He earns his living, but he has to be kept in order. Can you do that? Speak up if it's too much for you.'

'It ain't much of a job. I'd say it was more a pleasure. I'll do it and more.'

Polly held out her hand. 'Then we have a deal.'

Rose was smiling as she left the house. Aunt Polly

had hit on the one thing that would make it easier for Maisie to settle into her new home. Coming as she did from a reasonably close family, Rose could only imagine what it must be like to be raised in an institution. She quickened her pace; this was the day when she and Cora visited the sick and the needy in the parish, taking jars of calf's-foot jelly and beef tea. If Mrs Blunt was feeling particularly generous she would add some of her small sweet cakes, which she said would tempt the most jaded appetite. Rose took charge of these in case Cora was tempted to sample a few during the long walk; a habit that had endured since childhood when their mother had been well enough to undertake parish duties.

She arrived home to find Cora alone in the dining room, yawning and seemingly half-asleep over a bowl of porridge.

'Have you seen Pa this morning?' Rose asked.

'He was called out to baptise a newborn that wasn't expected to live,' Cora said sleepily.

Rose reached for the coffee pot and filled a cup, adding a dash of milk and a lump of sugar. The walk in the chill of the early morning had sharpened her appetite, and, even though she had eaten earlier, she buttered a slice of toast. 'Is Ma up yet?'

'I don't think so.' Cora pushed her plate away. 'Mrs Blunt said you'd taken Maisie to Aunt Polly.'

'I did and you'll never guess what happened.' Rose bit into the toast, chewed and swallowed. She reached for the raspberry jam and spooned some on the side of her plate.

'I'm too tired to work out a conundrum, Rosie. I couldn't sleep for thinking of Gerard.'

Rose paused with the toast halfway to her lips. 'Gerard? Who is he?'

'The handsome young man I was talking to at Fancello's last night. Didn't you see him?'

'I saw dozens of men, but the only one I remember was the dear old colonel. He was such a gentleman.'

Cora sighed. 'Gerard is a gentleman. He's the Honourable Gerard Barclay, and he's the younger son of Lord Barclay.'

'For goodness' sake, Cora, show a little sense,' Rose said crossly.

'I don't know what you mean.' Cora's lips formed a sulky pout. 'You're just jealous.'

'Don't be silly. I can't even remember what he looked like, but he'll be a toff on the lookout for a pretty girl to flirt and amuse himself with.'

'You don't know that. He was perfectly charming.'

'I'm sure he was, but if he's there tonight you must ignore him. Don't allow yourself to be taken in. I don't know anything about him or his family, but what I do know is that they don't mix with the likes of us.'

'We're perfectly respectable girls. Pa is a clergyman. He speaks directly to God.'

Rose choked on a mouthful of coffee, unable to stifle a chuckle. 'Tell that to Lord Barclay and note his reaction. I'm sorry, Corrie dear, but you know the rules. We mustn't get involved with anyone at Fancello's. We have to carry on until we have enough money to hire a lawyer.'

'I hadn't forgotten. How could I forget? But I think sometimes you get carried away with being on the stage. I think you enjoy it.'

'I do. I admit that, and you do too, if you're being honest. I love the excitement and the applause, and there's nothing I'd like more than to perform at the Grecian or the Pavilion, but that's not going to happen.' Rose finished her slice of toast and drained her cup. 'Come on, Corrie. We've got to do our duty in the parish, but tonight we can put on our greasepaint and our costumes and make believe. Gerard comes into that category, and you must keep him there. He mustn't find out who you are.'

Cora rose from her seat. 'I know, and yes, you're right.'

'I understand it's hard, Cora,' Rosa said gently, 'but we're doing well so far.' She stood up, brushing crumbs from her skirt. 'I'm going to see if Mrs Blunt has finished packing the baskets and then we'll set off. At least it's not raining and the sun is trying to come out, so maybe it will be a nice day after all.'

Despite her cheerful words Rose could not help feeling anxious as she made her way to the kitchen. Cora was sweet-natured and affectionate, and she always saw the best in people. Gerard Barclay had obviously made a deep impression on her and it could prove disastrous. Rose loved her sister and she was determined to protect her, but they must not lose sight of their goal. She opened the kitchen door and was greeted by a flustered Mrs Blunt.

'Thank goodness you came. There's a messenger at the back door who refuses to go away unless he speaks to you in person. I tried to make him see sense, but he says he'll stand there all day if necessary.'

'Really? I don't know who that could be.' Rose frowned, thinking hard. 'I'll go and see what he wants.'

Chapter Three

Rose hurried through the scullery, wondering why a messenger would choose the back door over the front entrance. It seemed unusual for one of her father's flock to make a mystery of what would probably turn out to be a request to visit the dying or a plea for help. She opened the door and came face to face with a scruffy youth whose ragged clothes might have fitted him once, but were now too short in the arms, and his trouser legs ended an inch or so above his shabby boots where the uppers had come away from the soles, exposing muddy toes.

'Can I help you?' she asked warily.

'I got a message for you, miss.' The boy glanced over his shoulder, as if expecting to see spies lurking in the shrubbery.

'Well, what is it?'

'A certain gent what's been doing work for a

professional person in Cornwall has asked to see you, miss. It's urgent.'

'I'm not sure I understand,' Rose said carefully. 'You'll need to explain further.'

The boy snatched off his battered cap exposing a mass of wildly curling red hair. 'The gent what I speak of will be in The Eagle at noon. He begs you to attend, miss. He says it's of the utmost importance.'

'Has this man a name?'

'He give me tuppence to keep mum. Will you come, miss? I'll wait for you on the corner and take you there safe. You won't come to no harm when you're in the company of Bobby Lee.'

Rose thought quickly. If she managed to persuade Cora to hurry they might be able to do the rounds before midday, or at least they could visit the most pressing cases, although what Pa would say if he knew she was about to venture into a public house was something she did not choose to dwell upon. She had probably damned her eternal soul for ever by exhibiting herself on stage, so one more transgression was unlikely to make any difference. She nodded. 'All right, Bobby. I'll meet you on the corner just before noon.' She closed the door hastily and returned to the kitchen.

'It was nothing,' she said airily. 'Just a youth desperate to find work. I sent him on his way.'

'That's right,' Mrs Blunt said with a nod of approval. 'He was probably hoping to cadge food, but these people shouldn't be encouraged. There's plenty of work out there for those who are willing to look hard enough for gainful employment.' She sniffed and resumed kneading the bread dough as if she were beating it into submission.

'I'm off then. Will you tell Mama that I'll see her this afternoon? I didn't want to disturb her this early in the morning.' Rose picked up the heavy baskets and went to find her sister.

She discovered Cora preening herself in the hall mirror. 'You look very pretty as always, Corrie, but I doubt if we'll meet the Honourable Gerard Barclay where we're going this morning.'

'You are such a tease, Rose. Just wait until you meet the man of your dreams, although I can't imagine who could live up to your ideals. He would have to be a cross between Richard the Lionheart and Lord Byron.'

'What an imagination you have, to be sure,' Rose said, laughing at the vision Cora's words had conjured up in her mind. 'But I have to admit that it would be an interesting combination. Anyway, we'd best hurry or we'll never get done.'

All that morning, while handing out sympathy and nourishment to poor parishioners, Rose found it hard to concentrate on the task in hand. She let Cora do the talking, but that was not unusual as Cora had a way with people, especially those who were sick or aged. Rose was content to offer help, when required to do so, and give practical advice, should it be requested, otherwise she stood back and allowed her sister to shine. Everyone said that Miss Cora Perkins was a saint; Mrs Blunt had told Rose so with a smug smile, which confirmed Rose's long-held suspicion that their housekeeper was also one of Cora's many admirers. But jealousy had never been one of Rose's failings, and she could quite see why her sister won hearts and minds. Cora was an angel whose only failing was vanity, although Rose considered this to be perfectly justified in someone who had the delicate beauty of a snowdrop, and a smile that would melt the hardest of hearts. Rose was well aware of her own worth, and if she were not quite as lovely as her sister, she knew that she had a quick mind and a ready wit. Her looks, as she had often been told, were striking and she had inherited the dark auburn hair and green eyes from her father's side of the family. It was her brother, however, to whom she was especially close. When they were children she and Billy had often been mistaken for twins, and Rose felt his disgrace now as deeply as if it were her own. She missed him more than she could say, and she would do anything to bring her brother home, absolutely anything.

She was waiting on the corner of City Road and Oakley Crescent when Bobby Lee came swaggering along the pavement, hands in pockets. He greeted her with a cheery smile and she followed him at a discreet distance to The Eagle. It was the first time she had stepped inside a public house and she wrapped her shawl around her head, hoping that no one would recognise her. Bobby weaved his way between tables in the crowded taproom, and Rose was acutely conscious of the curious stares aimed her way. He led her to a settle by the fire where a man sat on his own with a pint tankard on the table in front of him. Through a haze of tobacco smoke that stung her eyes and made her want to cough, Rose took a good look at the person who had requested her presence in such a dramatic manner.

'This here is the gent.' Bobby indicated the man with a sweep of his hand.

'You must be Miss Rose. I'm Todd Scully.' He half stood and then sank back on the settle. His dark eyes scanned Rose's face as if he were memorising each feature in turn, but his expression gave nothing away. 'Take a seat, miss.'

Rose pulled up a stool and sat with her back to the rest of the drinkers. 'Please say what you have to say, Mr Scully. I'm not comfortable in a place like this.'

A tight little smile played around Scully's thin lips. 'That's not what I heard, Miss Perkins, or should I say Miss Sunshine?'

Rose glanced nervously over her shoulder, but the other customers were too involved in their own business to appear to be listening. 'I don't know where you got that piece of information, sir.'

'Come on, miss. Don't play games with me. I was hired by a certain someone in the county of Cornwall to find out all I could about the case in question, and, as you and your sister are related to the person at present incarcerated at Her Majesty's pleasure, it seems logical to start with you.'

'There's not much I can tell you, Mr Scully. I don't know the exact circumstances of the event.'

Scully leaned forward, fixing her with bright, beady eyes, oddly reminiscent of a blackbird about to snatch a worm from the soil. 'What do you know about the deceased? He was, I've been informed, your brother's friend. They knew each other at Oxford.'

Rose nodded dully. 'Yes, that's correct.' She had met the young man in question on a couple of occasions when Billy had brought him to the vicarage for supper, but she had not been favourably impressed. Gawain Tressidick had struck her as being too full of his own importance, and although Billy had assured her that his friend came from an old and respected Cornish landowning family, she had not considered this to be an excuse for bad manners. Gawain had monopolised the conversation at dinner, and his patronising attitude to her parents had annoyed her to the extent that she had been tempted to get up and leave the room, but good manners had prevailed. It was tragic that he had lost his life in what appeared to have been a barroom brawl, but Rose could not believe that Billy had been involved. She knew that her brother had gone through a wild stage at university, but after the initial excitement of being away from home and free from the strict upbringing they had all endured, Billy had finally settled down and applied himself to his studies.

Scully was regarding her steadily. 'Was there any bad feeling between them?'

'No. Not that I know of.' Rose felt a wave of resentment building up in her breast. What right had this man to call her brother's good character in question? She met his bold stare with a frown. 'My brother is the most good-natured, easy-going person you could wish to meet, and he was that person's friend. No matter what the provocation he wouldn't have stooped to violence.'

'But what about the victim? What do you know of his temperament?'

'Absolutely nothing.' Rose lowered her voice. 'I didn't like him, but then I hardly knew him.'

Scully leaned back against the wooden settle and sipped his ale. 'I need to ask these questions, you must understand that.'

Rose made as if to stand but he motioned her to remain seated. 'There is one other thing.'

'What is it?' She was growing impatient now. They were attracting unwanted attention and she was desperate to leave before someone recognised her.

'Money, Miss Rose.' He put his hand in his pocket and pulled out a crumpled piece of paper, which he spread out on the table in front of her. 'My services were engaged by the lawyer defending the case. He wanted you to be aware of the costs that you will incur, and he needs your permission to proceed on that basis.'

Rose scanned the figures and her heart sank. She and Cora had saved every penny of their earnings at Fancello's, but it would take months to raise such a large sum, if ever. She gulped and swallowed. 'I understand perfectly.'

'And you still wish to proceed?'

'Of course I do. My brother's life is at stake. If found guilty he will suffer the ultimate penalty, and I know he is innocent. I'd stake my own life on it.'

A slow smile spread across Scully's craggy features. 'That's all I need to know, miss. Rest assured that I will do my best.'

'Perhaps you would discover more about the person in question if you visited his college in Oxford.'

'That is next on my list, Miss Rose.' Scully beckoned to Bobby, who was warming himself by the fire. 'See the young lady home, boy.'

Rose folded the sheet of paper and tucked it into her reticule. 'I'll keep this, if I may, and then I can refer to it if need be.' She stood up. 'I know you will do your best, Mr Scully, but I beg you to double your efforts. You will be saving an innocent man from the gallows.'

Scully raised his tankard. 'I'll drink to that. Rest assured that everything that can be done will be done.'

Rose made her way out of the taproom, half blinded by smoke and fumes as well as the hot tears that burned the backs of her eyes. Scully's visit had made the threat to Billy's life a reality instead of a vague possibility, and now more than ever she knew she must raise the money to pay for his defence. She did not feel like going home to face a barrage of questions from Cora, and she needed to find out exactly how much they had managed to save. Aunt Polly had been entrusted with keeping the money safe as it was not possible for the sisters to open a bank account, and hiding the money in the vicarage was not an option. Rose set off for the house in Old Street, having forgotten that Bobby had been charged with her safety, and it was not until she was on the doorstep that she realised he had followed her. She hesitated with her hand on the doorknocker. 'Thank you, Bobby. You can go now.'

His freckled features creased in a worried frown. 'But I was told to see you home, miss. This ain't the vicarage.'

'It's my aunt's house, so you need not worry.'

'I got to see you home,' he said with a stubborn set to his jaw. 'That was me instructions from Mr Scully, and I don't get paid unless I tell him I done so.'

Rose knocked on the door. 'I'm afraid you'll have to wait a while.'

He leaned nonchalantly against the railings. 'That's all right, miss. I got nothing else to do, and I need the money for me night's lodgings.'

'Haven't you got a home to go to?'

'I doss down wherever I can.'

Rose was about to question him further when Maisie opened the door. 'Good afternoon, miss.' She grinned and threw herself at Rose, almost knocking her off the step as she wrapped her in a warm embrace. 'I ain't half pleased to see you. I was afraid you might not come again.'

'Here, you be careful, like.' Bobby leaped onto the step and steadied Rose, who had staggered backwards and was in danger of toppling over. 'Watch your manners, nipper.'

Maisie stepped away, glaring at him with narrowed eyes. 'And who might you be?'

He snatched his cap off his head with a flourish and bowed from the waist. 'I'm this lady's protector, just for today, you understand. Anyway, who's asking, if I might be so bold?'

Rose suppressed a chuckle. 'Behave yourselves, both of you. Let me in, Maisie, I want to see my aunt.' She turned to Bobby. 'Thank you, but you're free to go. I might be a little while.'

'I was told to see you home,' he insisted. 'And see you home I shall.'

'Then you'd better step inside because it's starting to rain.' Rose glanced up at the darkening sky. Large spots of rain had begun to fall and the gathering clouds promised a sharp downpour. 'Maisie will take you to the kitchen where I'm sure Cook will find you something to eat and drink.'

Bobby bounded into the hall and closed the door. 'Ta, miss. I wouldn't say no to a bite to eat. Come to think of it, nothing has touched me lips since last evening when I bought a baked tater from a cart. Very good it were, too.'

Maisie gave him a cursory glance. 'You could do with a wash, boy. You're very dirty.'

Rose could see that this might turn into a squabble but she left them to sort themselves out and went in search of her aunt. At this time of day Polly was usually to be found in the small cubbyhole she called her study, where she pored over the accounts. As Rose had expected, Polly was seated at her desk with a pair of steel-rimmed spectacles balanced on the bridge of her nose.

She looked up. 'Is anything wrong, Rose?'

'I've just been speaking to a private detective, a Mr Scully. Billy's lawyer hired him to find out what he could about Gawain Tressidick.' Rose perched on the edge of the desk. 'I couldn't tell him much.'

'Did he think you and Tressidick were close?'

Rose stared at her in horror. 'Good heavens, no. Why would he think like that?'

'If true, it could have been the reason for the fight between William and Tressidick.'

'I hadn't thought of that,' Rose said slowly. 'But I barely knew Gawain, and what I did know I didn't like. I told Scully that much, and now he's gone to Oxford to see if he can find out anything there.'

'So what is the problem, Rose?'

'It's money, or rather the lack of it.' Rose took the bill from her reticule and laid it on the desk.

'We have to find that much in order to pay Mr Scully, in addition to the lawyer's fee and expenses. I doubt if we have that much saved.'

Polly studied the figures. 'No, indeed. That's a hefty bill. I hope he's a good detective.'

'Billy's life depends upon it, Aunt Polly. We have to raise the money quickly.'

'I'd help you if I could, but we barely manage day by day and we rely entirely on charity.'

'You've done more than enough. It's up to Cora and me. Perhaps we can squeeze a few more performances in, if the pay is right. There has to be a way.'

Signor Fancello listened with his head on one side and a calculating gleam in his dark eyes. 'Two shows a night,' he said, twirling the waxed end of his moustache round his index finger. 'And that means every night of the week, shall we say for a month?'

Rose swallowed convulsively. 'We cannot work on Sunday, signor. It is impossible.'

'You ask me to give you more employment and then you try to bargain with me.' He threw up his hands. 'You English, you do not know what hard work is. How do you think I built up my business when I arrived in London?'

'We have to attend church on Sundays, signor. We cannot work on the Sabbath day.'

Fancello's beetle brows drew together in a frown. 'You want the money, you do the late show. It is not for you to dictate terms to me.'

Rose thought quickly. It would make life difficult, but she had no choice. There had never been any question of family members missing Sunday services, unless they were too ill to attend. Both she and Cora took Sunday school classes, and after evensong, at half-past seven on the dot, everyone gathered in the dining room to enjoy a cold collation as it was Mrs Blunt's evening off. Her preferred way of spending her leisure time was to sit in the rocking chair by the range, knitting shapeless garments for the poor, while Rose and Cora tackled the washing-up in the scullery.

Rose shook hands with Fancello. 'Very well, I accept. When do we start?'

'Two performances a night, every day of the week except tomorrow, which is Sunday, but I expect you here in time for the nine o'clock performance.' He gave her a wolfish smile. 'And you will need to broaden your repertoire. Alphonso will guide you; he knows all the popular songs. And you had better speak to my wife about new costumes. That is her department.' He wandered off, berating one of the waiters for breaking a glass.

Rose hurried to the tiny dressing room where Cora was struggling with her stays. She grabbed the laces and tugged on them until her sister gasped and begged for mercy.

'Stop. I can't breathe, let alone sing and dance.'

Rose loosened them a little before tying a bow. 'There you are, now you can help me with mine.' She slipped off her plain grey gown. 'Undo me, please.'

57

'What were you saying to old Fancello?'

'We were haggling over the amount of extra performances.' Rose breathed out with a sigh as Cora undid the laces. She reached for her wrap and flung it around her shoulders. 'We're going to do the late show tomorrow, as well as two performances a night.'

'On Sunday? That's not possible.'

'Fancello won't budge, and I've worked it out in my head, Corrie. We'll slip away after supper.'

'But it's Mrs Blunt's night off.'

'I'm going to ask Maisie to come and do the washing-up. After all, we used to have a scullery maid and a housemaid before Mama became ill, and I'm sure that Maisie could do with the money.'

'How will you explain it to Pa?'

'I don't know yet, but leave it to me. I'll think of something. We have to do it for Billy.'

Rose began to apply her stage make-up, which was laid out on the narrow shelf that had to suffice as a dressing table. Each time she went through this routine she could see her mother's face gazing reproachfully at her from the fly-spotted mirror.

Cora, however, did not seem to have such reservations. She was humming a tune and smiling as she rouged her cheeks and lips. 'I do hope he's here tonight.' She made a *moue* at her reflection. 'We'll have more time to make friends with the patrons; that's the good thing about doing two performances a night.'

'Yes,' Rose said doubtfully. 'But don't get too

involved, Corrie. It's all part of the entertainment, as far as the audience are concerned, so you mustn't take it too seriously.'

'Ten minutes, ladies,' Tommy Tinker bellowed through the keyhole. 'We've got a full house tonight.'

'Thank you, Tommy.' Rose and Cora spoke as one, exchanged amused glances and giggled. Tommy Tinker might pretend to be a man of the world, but he had burst into the dressing room on one occasion to find them both in a state of undress. He had blushed to the roots of his hair, turned and fled. He had always assumed a cocky air since then, but he never looked them in the eye.

Rose pinned a silk gardenia in her hair. 'That will have to do. I've only got to put on my dancing shoes and I'm ready.'

Minutes later they were waiting in the wings, and Fancello was going through his usual patter as he introduced them to enthusiastic cheers and clapping from the largely male audience. Rose peeped through the curtains, noting that there were only a few women present, and without exception they were gaudily dressed persons who would not warrant an invitation to tea at the vicarage. Mama would consider them past redemption, and Papa would try to save their souls, but Rose had become acquainted with some of them and she was no longer judgemental. Each of them had her own story, and virtually all had suffered abuse and hardships that Rose could never have imagined. It was ironic that she and Cora were now teetering on the brink of respectability, and one little nudge was all it might take to send them tumbling into the abyss of ruined reputation and disgrace.

'Stop daydreaming, Rosie,' Cora said urgently. 'We're on.'

They pirouetted onto the stage, came to a halt with their hands clasped demurely in front of them, and launched into 'The Daring Young Man on the Flying Trapeze', followed swiftly by their dance routine, with 'Come into the Garden, Maud' as an encore. They swept off into the wings, returning gracefully to loud applause, but Fancello was waiting for them this time. He had his arm around little Clementia, who was scowling ominously.

'Don't try to upstage my little girl,' he said through gritted teeth. 'Remember who pays your wages.' He gave his daughter a hug. 'You are on next, *cara mia*.'

Clementia curled her lip as she glared at Rose. 'I'm the star,' she muttered. 'You're just the chorus.' She stomped off, leaving Rose wondering what could have upset Fancello's pampered child prodigy.

'Go out into the audience and do your bit, girls,' Fancello said, jerking his head in the direction of the saloon. 'I don't pay you to laze around back stage.'

'Yes, signor,' Cora said meekly as she made her way down the steps. She paused. 'I've seen him, Rosie. He's all alone and he waved to me.'

'Be careful.' Rose followed her more slowly as

Cora sashayed between the closely packed tables, acknowledging compliments with a sunny smile. Rose looked for the colonel but there was no sign of him and she was suddenly at a loss. A sea of expectant faces greeted her and she felt a moment of near panic. Physical contact with the patrons had never previously been part of the bargain and she almost envied Cora, who Rose guessed by the delighted look on her pretty face was being showered with compliments. Gerard Barclay was undeniably handsome and urbane, and, although Rose was suspicious of his motives, he seemed to be behaving like a perfect gentleman. She turned with a start as someone tugged at her skirt and found herself looking down at a person who was leering at her in a drunken manner, which was quite unnerving.

She managed a tight little smile. 'Excuse me, sir. Would you be kind enough to unhand me?'

His answer was a loud guffaw as he pulled her onto his lap. 'Now, now, darling. That's no way to treat a paying customer.' He slid his hands around her waist, holding her in a surprisingly strong grip. 'You're here to entertain me, so what about a kiss?' His breath reeked of cigar smoke and brandy, and she noted in disgust that his white evening shirt was stained with wine and what looked suspiciously like gravy.

'This is no way to behave,' she said, forcing herself to remain calm.

'Don't be a spoilsport, young lady. Give him a

kiss.' One of his companions at the table leaned over and poked her in the ribs. 'I know Carter of old. He won't give up until you do.'

Rose was close to panicking. Clementia was warbling like a skylark, with Alphonso hammering out the tune, and all around her the cacophony of sound grew louder, filling her head with noise, while her attempts to get free from Carter's clutching hands only seemed to excite him more. The tinkle of glassware and popping of champagne corks together with raised male voices and raucous laughter echoed in her head until she thought she could stand it no longer. She felt sick and suddenly everything went dark and she was falling . . .

Chapter Four

'Are you all right?' A voice from far away brought Rose back to consciousness, and she opened her eyes, focusing with difficulty on the stranger's face.

'You fainted,' he said calmly, 'but you're all right now.' He held a glass of water to her lips. 'Take small sips. You'll soon feel better.'

'I never swoon,' she said shakily. 'It must have been the heat.'

'It was just a bit of fun.' Carter shifted uncomfortably on his chair. 'If the girl can't take a joke she shouldn't be working in an establishment like this. I'll call Fancello over and tell him so.' He raised his hand but the stranger caught him by the wrist and forced his arm to his side.

'I don't think that's a good idea. I saw what occurred, and if I make a complaint you will find yourself barred from this saloon.'

Rose glanced over her shoulder, but Cora had eyes only for Gerard and he had the appearance of a man who was spellbound by a pretty face and winning ways. The other patrons were intent on their own pleasure and none of them was paying any attention to the drama being enacted at Carter's table. His friends were trying to placate him, but Carter himself was too drunk to see sense. He staggered to his feet. 'I should call you out, sir. You can't talk to me in that insolent tone. Who are you, anyway?'

The stranger had been kneeling at Rose's side, but when he stood up he was a good head taller than Carter, and although not heavily built he had the look of a man who knew how to handle himself. His winged eyebrows drew together in an ominous frown. 'My name is Bennett Sharpe, barrister-at-law.'

Carter's florid features paled visibly and he puffed out his cheeks. 'What do I care what profession you follow, sir? You insulted me.'

'You took advantage of this young lady.' Bennett's deep voice held a note of authority that did not seem to have been lost on the people seated around them, and they shifted uncomfortably in their seats, exchanging wary glances.

Rose clutched his arm. 'It's all right, sir. I'm truly grateful for your intervention, but I'm perfectly fine now. It must have been the heat. I beg you not to trouble yourself any further.'

Bennett silenced her with a single glance. 'I know what I saw, and I dislike bullies.' He turned to Carter.

'You are in the wrong, sir. An apology to this young lady is required and then we'll consider the matter closed.'

'For God's sake, say you're sorry, old man.' Carter's vociferous friend slapped him on the back.

Out of the corner of her eye Rose had seen Fancello making his way towards them, and she held her breath. If Carter made a complaint against her it would not bode well. She tugged at Bennett's sleeve. 'Please say no more.'

He followed her gaze. 'Is that the proprietor of this establishment?'

'Yes, it is,' Carter said angrily. 'And I intend to complain about your behaviour, Mister Lawyer. Let's see whose side Fancello takes. I am a regular and valued patron.'

Rose was about to release her hold on his arm, but Bennett forestalled her by laying his hand on hers. A smile transformed his stern features as he greeted Fancello. 'A bottle of your best champagne, please, mine host. This pretty lady has agreed to share it with me.'

Fancello's frown was wiped away in an instant. 'Of course, sir. At once.' He signalled to one of the waiters.

'I say,' Carter protested as Fancello chose to ignore him. 'Deuced cheek.'

Bennett led Rose to a table on the far side of the room. 'You will be more comfortable here,' he said, pulling out a chair. 'Take a seat, Miss Perkins.'

Rose stared at him aghast. 'How do you know my name? Who are you, sir?'

'Please sit down and try to look as though you're enjoying yourself. Signor Fancello is staring at us even as he decides how much to overcharge me for a bottle of inferior quality champagne.'

Rose sank down on the spindly gilt chair. Her mouth was dry and her heart was racing. 'You told me your name, Mr Sharpe, but you have the advantage over me.'

'I have accepted the brief to defend your brother.' Bennett took the seat opposite her. 'I wanted to find out as much as I could of his background, and it was William himself who advised me to seek you out.'

'Of course I'll do everything I can to help my brother, but how did you find this place? No one knows that Cora and I work here.'

'Todd Scully is one of the best private detectives in London. I believe you are acquainted with him.'

'I've met him only once, and that was today.' Rose lowered her voice. 'Are you telling me that he has been spying on us?'

'That's a bit harsh. I prefer to call it gathering information in order to make a good case for your brother.'

'If you're defending Billy you must believe that he is innocent.'

'What I believe or don't believe is immaterial. My job is to convince a judge and jury of his innocence.'

Bennett leaned back in his chair, his dark eyes intent on her face, as if he were capable of reading her innermost thoughts. 'This case interests me. I would normally leave it to a solicitor to provide me with the facts, but this is no ordinary brief. I find it hard to believe that a young man like William would kill a dear friend.'

'He is a good man. I'll never believe ill of my brother.' Rose returned his intense gaze stare for stare, but was the first to look away. There was something about Bennett Sharpe that was unsettling.

'He is lucky to have two such devoted sisters,' Bennett said in a low voice. He looked as though he was about to say more but at that moment the waiter arrived with their champagne.

He uncorked the bottle with a theatrical flourish and filled two glasses, but then in answer to a summons from another client he scurried off with his tailcoat flapping like the wings of an agitated crow.

Bennett handed a glass to Rose and raised the other in a silent toast before taking a sip. He shook his head. 'As I thought. A poor vintage being sold at a ridiculous price. However, that doesn't matter. I came here tonight in the hope of meeting you and your sister.'

'Wouldn't it have been easier to visit us at my aunt's house? I'm sure you already know the reason for our keeping this from our parents. What I don't understand is why you felt it necessary to see us here.'

'When Scully told me that two such respectable

young ladies were prepared to risk their reputations by performing in a third-rate saloon, I wanted to see for myself.'

'We're working here to raise money to pay you for defending our brother, which, as it happens, will also pay for this bottle of champagne.' Rose swallowed a mouthful and pulled a face: it was sharp and slightly bitter, and the bubbles tickled her nose.

'You are not what I expected, Miss Perkins.'

'Please don't use my real name. Cora and I go by the name of the Sunshine Sisters.'

'I'm sorry, of course you're right, Miss Sunshine.'

She eyed him curiously. 'What were you expecting?'

His eyes were alight with amusement, and his lips twitched. 'I dare say you would be offended if I told you that my idea of a clergyman's daughter was as unlike you and your sister as could be.'

'I'm not sure whether that's a compliment or an insult.'

'It was certainly not intended to be an insult, but I imagined you and your sister to be prim and proper young ladies who had been brought up to fear the Lord and serve the community. I was worried that my presence might be too much for such delicate sensibilities.'

'You must have been terribly disappointed,' Rose said, trying to keep a straight face and failing.

'An illusion shattered for the better, I can assure you.' His appreciative smile faded and his eyes darkened. 'But this isn't the sort of place for you and your sister. Have you tried to raise the money from family members or friends?'

'There is no one we can ask, and Papa doesn't know anything about this. It would break his heart if he discovered the truth.'

'Where does he think his son is, if I may ask?'

'He thinks that William is staying with the Tressidick family in Cornwall until Trinity term begins next month.'

'So your parents know nothing about William's arrest?'

'No, and they mustn't know. Papa would be devastated, and Mama is recovering from a bout of ill health. A shock like that might set her back weeks, if not months.'

'It's not a secret you can keep for ever. If the case goes against William he will face the death penalty.'

His words struck her like a knife to the heart. 'Don't say that.'

'But it's a possibility. All the evidence points to a drunken brawl, and there are witnesses who will testify that William struck the fatal blow.'

'My brother is not a violent man. I don't know what happened on that fateful night, but Gawain was Billy's best friend and I know that my brother would never have hurt him intentionally.'

'That is what I hope to prove. I'll be in London for the next few days, and it would be helpful if we could meet again. I want to find out as much about William's background as I can.'

Rose nodded eagerly. 'Of course. I'll do anything – absolutely anything – to help free Billy.'

'I can see that.' Bennett glanced over her shoulder. 'But I think you are wanted, Miss Sunshine. I see Fancello advancing on us with a purposeful look in his eye.'

'I'll have to go,' Rose said, rising to her feet. 'When will we meet again?'

Bennett opened his mouth to reply, but was forestalled by Fancello. 'I'm sorry to interrupt, sir, but Miss Sunshine has another performance. We must not disappoint her other admirers.'

'I'm coming, signor.' Rose smiled and nodded in Bennett's direction. 'Thank you for the champagne, sir.'

'That's enough of that,' Fancello hissed in her ear. 'I pay you to keep all my customers happy, so don't think you can pick and choose.'

'No, signor. I understand.'

Holding her head high, Rose swept past him and made her way to the wings where Cora was waiting for her. She could tell by her sister's heightened colour and the sparkle in her blue eyes that Gerard had proved to be an exciting companion.

'I've had such a lovely time,' Cora whispered. 'He's such a gentleman and he wants to take me driving in the park one afternoon. Do you think Papa would allow it?'

'Are you mad?' Rose grabbed her by the wrist. 'You can't tell anyone about this, least of all Pa.'

'But that's not fair.' Cora's eyes brimmed with unshed tears. 'He likes me, Rose. He really likes me.'

'I'm sure he does. Don't cry, Corrie. There's our intro – we're on stage, so smile.'

As they emerged from the smoky atmosphere of Fancello's saloon into the darkness of Cupid's Court, Rose was immediately aware of a tall figure loitering at the far end of the alley. He was silhouetted against the light of a streetlamp, but he appeared to be wearing an opera hat and cloak. Her conversation with Bennett had put all thoughts of Carter out of her head, but now she was nervous.

'What's the matter?' Cora demanded. 'Why have you stopped?'

'It's nothing,' Rose said quickly. The last thing she wanted was to worry Cora, but her heart was thudding against her ribs and she was scared. 'We must hurry or Aunt Polly will have retired for the night.' Rose walked on, hoping that the man would go away, but it became obvious that he was waiting for them. He turned to face them and she saw to her relief that it was Bennett Sharpe.

'Who is that man?' Cora demanded breathlessly. 'Do you know him?'

'It's all right, there's no need to be scared,' Rose said hastily. 'I met him in Fancello's. He's a friend.'

'And you thought I was being forward,' Cora whispered. 'At least I didn't arrange an assignation with Gerard.'

'It's not like that. Trust me, Cora. This man is to defend Billy in court and he's here to help us.' Rose greeted Bennett with an attempt at a smile. 'I didn't realise you were waiting for us, Mr Sharpe.'

'I thought it best if I were to escort you home.'

'I recognise you now,' Cora said slowly. 'You're the gentleman who put that dreadful man in his place. I was going to come over myself, but I could see that you had the matter well in hand. I'm Cora, by the way. The other half of the Sunshine Sisters act. How do you do, sir?'

Bennett's expression softened and he bowed over Cora's hand. 'Bennett Sharpe. How do you do, Miss Sunshine?'

'It sounds so odd when you say it that way, Mr Sharpe,' Cora said, laughing.

Rose was accustomed to seeing strangers falling under her sister's spell, and it was clear that Bennett was no exception, but it was getting late. 'We have to call in at our aunt's establishment in Old Street, and we need to get there before she locks up for the night.'

Cora tucked her hand in the crook of Bennett's arm. 'I expect Rose has told you everything, Mr Sharpe. The things we get up to might be the plot of a penny dreadful, but we have to go to great lengths to keep our secret, and we couldn't do it without Aunt Polly's help.'

Bennett proffered his free arm to Rose. 'Anything that either of you can tell me will be of great value, and if you don't want me to speak to your parents it might help if I can talk to your aunt.'

Polly was ready for bed and did not bother to disguise the fact that their late arrival was an annoyance. Her expression hardened when she saw Bennett.

'Who is this? Why have you brought a man to my house? This is unacceptable behaviour for which there is no excuse, girls.'

'It's not what you think, Aunt Polly,' Rose said hastily. 'Mr Sharpe is the barrister who has been hired to defend Billy. He came to the saloon tonight to talk to us, and he's going to see us home.'

'You'd better come in.' Polly showed them into her parlour. 'You're very late. I was about to go to bed.'

'We're so sorry. We didn't know we were expected to do two shows this evening.' Cora laid a hand on her aunt's arm. 'Don't be cross, Aunt Polly.'

Polly shrugged, refusing to be pacified. 'Your father would be horrified if he knew what you girls were up to. Quite honestly I'm beginning to regret my part in all this.'

'Pa will be even more horrified if he discovers that his only son is awaiting trial for murder.' Rose had not meant to speak so sharply, but it had been a long and exhausting day. 'I'm sorry we've caused you to worry,' she added apologetically. 'But events have moved rapidly, and Mr Sharpe thinks we might be able to help.'

Polly clutched her robe around her, eyeing Bennett with suspicion. 'I suppose you're trying to justify a huge fee, sir? We're poor people and these girls are risking more than their reputations in an attempt to raise the money for William's defence.'

Bennett inclined his head. 'As I discovered this evening, ma'am.'

'I can't talk to you now.' Polly glared at him, refusing to be soothed by his apologetic smile. 'It's late and my nieces should be at home in bed. I'll ask you to wait in the hall while they change into their street clothes, and then you may walk them home.'

'I understand perfectly, ma'am. I hope you will excuse this intrusion and will allow me to call tomorrow at a more suitable hour.'

'I'll see you at noon. Don't be late, I detest bad manners.'

'I will be here on the dot, ma'am.' Bennett left the room, closing the door behind him.

'He's trying to help us, Aunt Polly,' Cora said mildly.

'And he's Billy's only hope.' Rose took off her bonnet and shawl. 'I'm very sorry I couldn't let you know that we would be late.'

'Don't be angry, Aunt Polly. I will cry if you scold us.' Cora's bottom lip trembled ominously. 'I am so very tired.'

Rose stepped into her plain grey gown, fumbling with the tiny buttons on the bodice in her haste to get dressed. 'We'll be gone in a few minutes, and tomorrow we'll have time to talk properly to Mr

Sharpe and discover exactly how he plans to help Billy. You do want to help him, don't you, Aunt?'

'Silly girl, of course I do.' Polly moved to a side table and poured a generous tot of brandy into a glass. She collapsed onto the sofa, took a sip and sighed. 'I doubt if I'll sleep a wink tonight. All these comings and goings are too much for me.' She seized one of the many fans that were scattered about the room and used it vigorously.

Rose experienced a pang of guilt. Aunt Polly was not a young woman, and she worked hard to keep the unfortunates in her care from ending up in the workhouse. 'You must say if our visits are too much for you. I know you are up at the crack of dawn every day.'

'Are you insinuating that I'm too old to be of any use?'

'No, of course she isn't.' Cora slipped her shawl around her shoulders. 'You weren't, were you, Rosie?'

'Certainly not, but we don't want to take advantage of your good nature, Aunt Polly.' Rose moved to her aunt's side and leaned over to brush Polly's powdered cheek with a kiss. 'You are a wonderful woman and we love you dearly. We couldn't raise the money to save Billy without your help, and I know you will work your considerable charm on Mr Sharpe tomorrow. He'll be eating out of your hand, just as the gentlemen used to when you were the toast of the London stage.'

Polly drained her glass of the last drop. 'It's true.

I had my devoted following, but those days are long gone.'

'I'm sure you could dance all night if you chose to do so, but you've taken a different path, Aunt. You look after women who are in desperate need, and I admire you for that.' Rose patted her aunt on the cheek. 'I think you are a heroine, Aunt Polly.'

'Stuff and nonsense, girl.' Polly's pale cheeks flooded with colour, but despite her harsh tone she was smiling. 'We agree on one thing, and that is the need to do everything we can to clear Billy's name.'

'That's the only reason we're appearing on stage, and now we have to work tomorrow night as well.'

'But tomorrow is Sunday,' Polly said, patently shocked by such a notion. 'Your father wouldn't like that.'

'I hope he won't find out, and that's where we need your help, Aunt. Mrs Blunt has Sunday afternoon and evening off, so Cora and I do the washing-up. If we could have Maisie to do that for us we could get away without anyone being the wiser.'

'I'm not sure that I ought to collude in such behaviour, but you can have Maisie. Heaven knows, she's not much use here. She faints if she sees a cut finger, let alone a woman in labour. On occasions we can't get an expectant mother across the road to the Lying-In Hospital, and sometimes they simply refuse to be moved. I don't know how she will cope when her time comes.' Polly flapped her hands at them. 'You girls need to hurry home. It's very late, but at least you have a capable-looking man to see that you get there safely.'

'I love you, Aunt Polly,' Rose said, blowing her a kiss as she opened the door. 'Come on, Cora, don't waste time primping in the mirror. It's too dark outside for anyone to notice you.'

Bennett was waiting for them in the entrance hall. 'What is this place?' he asked, frowning. 'I've heard screams coming from a room upstairs, and a baby crying.'

'This is a home for fallen women,' Cora said shyly. 'Aunt Polly helps unfortunates who have nowhere else to turn in their time of greatest need.'

'Papa thinks that we come here to help look after the poor souls.' Rose grimaced at the sound of a fierce argument upstairs. 'We wouldn't be able to perform at Fancello's were it not for Aunt Polly.'

'Yes,' Cora added. 'We change our clothes here, and then we go on to Fancello's. We do this in reverse on our way home.'

'I'm not sure I understand why you feel the need to complicate matters in this way.' Bennett looked from one to the other, frown lines furrowing his brow.

'Because the lingering smell of tobacco smoke and the fumes of alcohol would be noticed at home,' Cora said earnestly. 'We would have difficulty in explaining that away.'

'I admire the way you've thought things through, but I have to agree with your aunt. You're exposing yourselves to enormous risks.'

'Our brother's life is at stake,' Rose said coldly. 'Would you have us sit at home and do nothing?'

'That's a question you should be asking William, not me.'

'I wish I could see Billy,' Rose said passionately. 'I would tell him that we're doing everything in our power to secure his release.'

'Poor Billy . . .' Cora's voice broke on a sob.

Bennett opened the front door and ushered them out into the cold night air. He walked on with lengthy strides. 'Gawain Tressidick is dead. He was a young man with a promising career ahead of him.'

Rose had to quicken her pace in order to keep up with him. She held her sister's hand, towing her like a small, tired child. 'He was Billy's best friend. I'll never believe that our brother struck the fatal blow.'

'Nor I,' Cora said faintly. 'Billy abhorred violence of any sort.'

'But I understood he was something of an expert in the noble art of pugilism.' Bennett came to a halt, facing Rose with a steady look. 'He was, wasn't he?'

Rose gulped and swallowed. It was a question she had been dreading. 'He regarded it as a science as well as a sport. Billy would have defended himself, but he would never start a fight. I'd stake my own life on it.'

'He was a southpaw,' Cora said proudly. 'He told me so, although to be honest I'm not exactly sure what that means.'

'Billy is left-handed?' Bennett's dark eyes glinted

with the golden reflection of the gaslights as he met Rose's questioning look with a triumphant smile. 'Is that correct?'

'It is,' she said slowly. 'But I don't see what that's got to do with anything.'

'This piece of information might have a huge bearing on the case.' He smacked his hand on his forehead. 'Why didn't I think of that before?'

Rose and Cora exchanged baffled glances. 'I don't understand,' Rose said, frowning. 'What difference does it make?'

'I can't be certain, but it might be the one fact that has been overlooked. I have to return to Cornwall first thing in the morning.'

'So soon?' Rose stared at him in surprise. 'But you said you needed to know more about Billy.'

Bennett started to walk, hands clasped behind his back. 'This could be just what I was searching for. I couldn't understand how a young man who was destined for the clergy could suddenly turn into a vicious killer, which is why I accepted the brief in the first place.'

Rose forgot that her feet hurt and her throat was sore from singing in a smoky atmosphere. A glimmer of hope had been ignited in her breast and she wanted to know more. She caught him up, leaving Cora to stumble along behind them. 'Why is it so important, Mr Sharpe? Don't keep me in suspense.'

'I don't want to raise your hopes too high. You will have to trust me in this. I'll leave a message for

Scully and he'll keep you informed as to my progress, or the lack of it.'

'Stop here,' Rose said breathlessly. 'This is where we live.'

Bennett came to a halt, staring at the vicarage as if committing every brick and tile to memory. 'Then I'll say goodbye for now. Will you explain my absence to your aunt, and ask her to accept my apologies?'

'I will, but I know she'll be overjoyed to think that there is hope.' Rose held out her hand. 'Thank you from the bottom of my heart.'

Bennett raised it to his lips. 'I promise you I will do my utmost for Billy.'

'Are you leaving us, Mr Sharpe?' Cora caught up with them, holding her side and panting. 'We'll see you tomorrow.'

'I'm afraid not, Miss Cora. Rose will explain everything, but I hope to see you when I return to London.'

'When will that be?' Rose asked anxiously. 'Please don't leave us in suspense.'

'I don't know. Everything depends on what I discover when I return to Portmorna.'

A shiver ran down Rose's spine. 'Billy was staying at Portmorna House.'

Bennett slipped his hand into his breast pocket and took out a deckle-edged calling card. 'This is the address of my chambers in Lincoln's Inn. If you need help they will put you in touch with Scully.'

Rose took the card from his outstretched hand, and it was still warm from his touch. She tucked it into her reticule. 'I'd like to see Billy. He's so far from home and I can't imagine what he must be feeling.' She slipped her arm around Cora, who had begun to sob. 'Don't cry. Mr Sharpe is doing everything he can for Billy.'

'I promise you that I'll do my utmost to bring this sorry situation to a satisfactory end.' Bennett backed away. 'I have to leave you now, but next time we meet I hope it will be under happier circumstances.'

'Thank you.' Rose stood very still, watching Bennett until he was out of sight. A chill wind whipped her hair from beneath her bonnet and a feeling of exhaustion threatened to overcome her. They were alone again, with nothing to sustain them other than hope.

'Let's get you indoors, Cora. You'll feel better in the morning.'

'It's too hard,' Cora sobbed. 'I felt better when Mr Sharpe was here, but now he's gone it's just the same as it was before.'

'Not quite,' Rose said gently. 'We know he's on our side, and I trust him.' She was about to open the gate that led to the tradesmen's entrance when the clattering of a horse's hoofs and the rumble of wheels echoed down the quiet street. She hurried Cora into the garden and waited for the vehicle to pass, but it slowed to a halt at the kerb. She peeped out from behind a laurel bush and her breath hitched in her throat.

'It's Dr Grantley, Cora, and he's calling here. Something awful must have happened. Go inside, quickly.'

Chapter Five

The kitchen was deserted, but the kettle singing on the range was a sure sign that Mrs Blunt had not retired for the night. Rose helped Cora to a chair. 'Sit down and dry your eyes. I'll go and find out what's happening.'

'It must be Mama.' Cora raised a tear-stained face. 'We shouldn't have left her.'

'I'll find out. Stay there and try to keep calm.'

Rose discarded her bonnet and shawl as she hurried from the room, making her way to the entrance hall where Dr Grantley and her father were deep in conversation. The sound of their deep tones echoed through the otherwise silent house.

'What's wrong, Papa?' she asked anxiously. 'Has Mama been taken worse?'

Seymour's thin features were sharply outlined by the shadows cast by the flickering gaslights, and his face was ashen. 'I'm afraid so. Mrs Blunt is with her now.'

'I'll go up, shall I, Vicar?' Dr Grantley moved to the foot of the stairs without waiting for a response. 'I know the way.' He lumbered up the staircase and the treads creaked beneath his considerable weight.

'Why are you home so late, Rose?' Seymour demanded angrily. 'I'll have words with Polly for keeping you girls out until all hours. She will have to hire more help if she cannot run her establishment without you and Cora.'

'It wasn't Aunt Polly's fault, Pa. We lost track of the time.'

'Well, it isn't good enough. I don't want my daughters roaming the city streets late at night.'

'I'm truly sorry that you were worried, Pa.' Rose could see that her father was upset and unlikely to be mollified by excuses. 'Shall I go upstairs with the doctor? I'll ask Mrs Blunt to make you a cup of tea or a tisane to calm your nerves.'

He seemed to shrink before her startled gaze, and his shoulders stooped as if burdened by an unbearably heavy weight. He dashed his hand across his eyes. 'Yes, Rose, that would be for the best. I think I might go to my study and rest for a while.'

The temptation to put her arms around him and give him a hug was almost irresistible, but Rose knew that her father was not the sort of man who welcomed personal contact. Even as a child she could not remember any outward demonstrations of affection on his part. As far as she was concerned, Papa had always been a slightly aloof figure of authority. Billy had always been his favourite, and no matter how hard Rose tried to please her father it had never seemed to be enough, but it was a shock to see him bowed and bent like a gnarled tree battered by a gale. She made a move to follow the doctor. 'I'll take care of Mama, and I'll send Mrs Blunt to you.'

'Where is Cora?' Seymour demanded anxiously.

'She's in the kitchen, Pa.'

'You must take care of her, Rose. She's delicate, like your mother, and I worry about her health. Going out in the night air isn't good for anyone with a weak constitution.'

'Cora is perfectly well, Papa. I wouldn't allow her to do anything that might compromise her wellbeing.' Rose waited until her father went into his study before continuing upstairs to her parents' bedroom.

Mrs Blunt was standing by the bed with a doleful expression on her face. She gave Rose a reproachful look. 'Your ma was taken ill an hour or more ago. She was calling for you.'

Rose approached the bed, keeping a respectful distance from the doctor, who was using a stethoscope to examine his patient. Eleanor lay amongst the pillows like a broken flower, her long hair spreading out around her head in a halo of pale gold. Seeming to sense her daughter's presence, she opened her eyes and her bloodless lips curved in a hint of a smile. 'Rose,' she whispered. 'Where were you?'

'No talking, please, Mrs Perkins.' Dr Grantley shot a warning glance at Rose before continuing his examination.

'I'm sorry, Mama,' Rose said softly. 'I was delayed, but I'm here now.' She turned to Mrs Blunt. 'My father looks very tired. I'm sure a cup of tea would revive him, or one of your excellent camomile tisanes.'

'Yes, of course, Miss Rose.' Despite her meek response Mrs Blunt managed to convey her reluctance with a twitch of her shoulders and a loud sniff as she left the room, but Rose was too concerned with her mother's health to worry overmuch about offending their housekeeper's sensibilities.

Dr Grantley folded the stethoscope and replaced it in his medical bag. 'Your mother needs rest and quiet, Rose.' He leaned over the bed, fixing Eleanor with a stern gaze. 'I'll give you some laudanum, which will help you to sleep, Mrs Perkins, and I'll call again in the morning.'

He took a small glass bottle from his bag and handed it to Rose. 'One or two drops diluted in water will ease the pain.' He snapped the lock shut and headed for the door, beckoning Rose to follow him. 'Your mother is very unwell. She has a delicate constitution and I'm afraid that the polluted air in the city has taken its toll on her health.'

'What can we do to make her better, Doctor?'

'I would advise good food, country air and above all rest, but I fear that is out of the question.' He stroked his beard, frowning. 'Unless, of course, you have relatives who dwell in the countryside, or a family friend who lives out of town and would care for Mrs Perkins during her convalescence?'

'I don't think so, Dr Grantley. My grandparents died several years ago and Mama has only one sister, but she lives in Old Street.'

A grim smile curved Dr Grantley's thin lips. 'Ah, yes. I know Miss Day very well. A good woman, despite her colourful past. I attend her establishment on a fairly regular basis.'

'And Papa was an only child. As far as I am aware, he has no living relatives.'

'What about William? I believe he is at Oxford; would it be possible for your mother to stay with him for a few weeks?'

Rose hesitated, caught unawares by the mention of Billy's name. 'I'm afraid that's out of the question. My brother is staying with friends in Cornwall until the beginning of the next term. He has rooms in college.'

Dr Grantley shook his head. 'A great pity. However, I will come again tomorrow. We can only do so much and the rest is in God's hands.'

Rose returned to the bedside and measured out two drops of laudanum into a glass, topping it up with water. She helped her mother to a semi-recumbent position and held the glass to her lips. Eleanor drank thirstily and fell back on the pillows, exhausted by the effort.

'I'm sorry to be such a nuisance to you all,' she murmured.

Rose replaced the glass. 'Don't talk like that, Mama. You know that's not true. We'd do anything to make you better, anything at all.'

'I feel so useless,' Eleanor whispered. 'I spend more time confined to my bed than I do looking after my family, or helping to care for the poor of the parish.'

'You do more than enough, and that's partly why you keep falling ill. You wear yourself to the bone looking after the sick and aged, but you mustn't worry. Cora and I will do more to help Papa, and you must concentrate on getting well.' Rose leaned over to kiss her mother's pale cheek. 'I promise you that we'll take care of everything.'

'You're such a comfort to me, Rose.' Eleanor's eyelids fluttered and closed and within minutes she was sound asleep.

Rose went straight to her father's study. Her mother's fragile condition could no longer be put aside as being a temporary indisposition. She knocked and entered the room without waiting for a response. 'Pa, I need to talk to you.'

Seymour put his cup back on its saucer, eyeing her with a worried frown. 'What is it, Rose? Has your mama taken a sudden turn for the worse?'

She sank down on the chair in front of his desk. 'Mama is asleep. The laudanum has done its work, but it isn't a cure. Dr Grantley said that she needs rest and country air. You must get her away from London before it's too late, Pa.'

Seymour peered at her over the top of his steel-rimmed spectacles. 'Don't you think I would have done that months ago had it been possible, Rose?'

'I don't think there is a choice now. There must be something we can do.'

'I can't abandon my duties as parish priest.'

'Joshua is in his fourth year as curate, Papa. Surely he could take over for as long as need be? If you could take Mama to the seaside it would be beneficial to her health.'

'I can't afford it, Rose. It's as simple as that.'

Rose was not going to give up easily. 'There must be a way.'

'I have to trust in the Lord, my dear.' A tired smile lit Seymour's grey eyes. 'Wearing yourself out with worry isn't going to help, Rose. You're a good daughter and I'm proud of the work you do, but you must take care of yourself or you might fall ill and then what would we do?'

She glanced at the clock on the mantelshelf and rose to her feet. 'I didn't realise it was so late. I'll say good night, Papa, but we'll talk about this again in the morning. I'm not giving up so easily.'

Rose barely slept that night and was up early next morning. She washed in cold water and dressed in her Sunday best. She left the house without disturbing the rest of the family and made her way to the church. As she had hoped, Joshua Hart was in the vestry preparing for the services that would begin with Holy Communion. He turned with a start and a slow smile spread across his plain but pleasant features, making it impossible to respond in any other way. Rose had taken to Joshua from the moment they first met when he had come to St Matthew's as a newly ordained cleric. He was one of the few people she knew who was unfailingly cheerful and courteous, with a kindly nature and a genuine desire to help those less fortunate than himself. His quiet sense of humour saved him from becoming over-serious, but early on Rose had discovered his one weakness; Joshua Hart was hopelessly in love with Cora, who barely acknowledged his existence.

'You are up and about early, Rose.' Joshua replaced the chalice he had been polishing in readiness for communion. His smile faded. 'Is anything wrong?'

'I need your help, Joshua.'

'You know that I'm always ready to do anything I can. What is it?'

'I'm worried about my parents. Mama is very unwell and the doctor says she needs rest and fresh air. I think Papa is wearing himself out with work as well as worry.'

'Just tell me how I can help. You know I'll do anything for you and your family.'

'I want you to persuade Papa that you are ready

and willing to take over the parish so that he can take Mama somewhere to recuperate.'

'Of course I'll try to convince him that I'm capable of filling his shoes, but I'm not sure he'll believe me.'

'If I can find somewhere for them to stay that doesn't cost too much, and if you can persuade him that the world won't come to an end because he isn't here for a while, we might make him see sense.'

'I won't put it quite like that, but I'll have a word with him and see what I can do.'

'You are a good friend, Joshua. I have every faith in you,' Rose said, smiling.

'Will you go with them? Your father might not think it proper for you to remain in the house on your own.'

'Cora and I can look after ourselves, and we'll still have Mrs Blunt. We'll stay at home and carry out Mama's parish duties to the best of our ability, so there's no need to worry on that score.'

'Leave it to me, Rose. I'll do my very best.'

She thanked him again and left him to finish his task, safe in the knowledge that Joshua could be trusted to keep his word, but finding somewhere for her parents to stay might prove an insurmountable problem. She decided not to mention anything to Cora until she had a definite plan in mind.

Later that morning, Rose left on her own for Old Street and it was Maisie who answered her knock on the door.

'You're early, miss.' Maisie eyed her curiously. 'Is something up?'

Rose stepped inside. 'You're just the person I wanted to see. I need your help.'

'I'll do anything, miss. You know that.'

'You know the situation,' Rose said carefully. 'I don't have to explain everything, but Cora and I have to work this evening, and it's our housekeeper's night off.'

'And you need some help in the kitchen,' Maisie said, grinning. 'That's right up my alley, as you well know. Of course I'll help out, but I'll have to ask Miss Polly first.'

'Ask me what?' Polly emerged from the parlour. 'Rose, what are you doing here at this time of day?'

'Cora and I have to perform at the saloon tonight and we need some help at home. Maisie has said she's willing, as long as it's all right with you.'

'Yes, of course.' Polly turned to Maisie. 'Off you go. I'm sure you have chores to attend to.'

Maisie bobbed a curtsey. 'Yes'm. It is all right for me to go to the vicarage this evening, isn't it?'

'Haven't I just said so?' Polly waited until Maisie had trotted off towards the back stairs. 'I need to talk to you, but not out here in this draughty hall. I don't know why I keep this house on. I'd be better off living alone in a small cottage than trying to keep this place going.' She ushered Rose into the parlour and threw herself down on the chaise longue, disturbing Spartacus, who opened one yellow eye, stretched and extended his claws, and, having made his feelings clear, went back to sleep.

Rose took a seat by the fire, holding her hands out to the blaze. Spring might be in the air, but it was cold outside, and a fitful sun had not yet managed to burn off the thick haze of pollution from the gas works, and the pall of smoke from manufactories and coal fires.

'What did you want to say to me, Aunt?'

'That girl cannot remain here much longer. It's not her fault, but she's mixing with women twice her age, and the majority have got into trouble by selling their favours on street corners. They're not bad souls for the most part, but it's no place for an innocent like Maisie.'

Rose stared at her aunt, puzzled by her sudden change of heart. 'Surely she'll learn something from her experience here? I know that her employer took advantage of her, but she will have to go out into the world and earn her own living at some stage.'

'Maisie trusts everyone – I realised that from the start – and she's very impressionable. She might have the body of a young woman, but in her head she's still a little girl. We need to find her somewhere permanent.'

'I've asked her to help out at home this evening. Maybe I can persuade Papa to take her on as a scullery maid. Mrs Blunt has more than enough work to keep her occupied.'

'That would be a kindness to the girl, otherwise

I can see her ending up in a brothel, or the workhouse. A fate that most of my girls will suffer, alas.'

'I've never seen you like this, Aunt Polly. You're usually so positive and forthright.'

'We lost one of the younger mothers last night, Rose. I took her across the road to the Lying-In Hospital, but they couldn't save her or the child.' Polly dashed her hand across her eyes. 'Don't take any notice of me, my dear. I expect I'm just tired. I'm getting too old to be up all night. When I was the toast of the East End I could give my best on stage and go on to dine and dance, staying out until the small hours without any adverse effects.' She forced her lips into a smile but her eyes were lacklustre and red-rimmed. 'Now tell me what is bothering you.'

'It's Mama. She was taken ill again yesterday, and the doctor says she needs to get away from the city. I'm hoping I can persuade Papa to take her to the country, or the seaside, although I'm certain he will say that it would cost too much.'

'I suppose you could use some of the money you've saved. It's all there in my strong box.'

Rose shook her head. 'No. I can't do that. Billy's life depends on having the best barrister I can afford. Billy has chosen Sharpe and I have to trust his judgement. By the way, Mr Sharpe won't be calling this morning as he's had to return to Cornwall.'

'Then I am at a loss, for the moment at least.' A glimmer of humour lit Polly's blue eyes. 'Which is unusual for me, you must admit.'

'I do freely, Aunt,' Rose said, chuckling. 'I've never known you to be lost for words before.'

'I will think about it very carefully.' Polly sat up straight, as if struck by a sudden thought. 'There is one possibility.'

Rose sat on the edge of her seat. 'Really? What is it?'

'Eleanor had a friend who lived near us in Islington until she married, and then she moved to the south coast. She is your godmother and I believe my sister corresponded with her for many years. You could ask your mother if she remembers Isabel Harman. If they are still in touch perhaps she could stay with Isabel, and then your father wouldn't need to leave his flock. Although I know he thinks he's irreplaceable.'

'Papa needs a rest too. I've asked Joshua if he would be prepared to take over, providing Papa agreed, and there was no objection from the diocese.'

'Then I suggest you go home and speak to your mother, or even Mrs Blunt. I don't think there's anything that woman misses. I suspect that she listens at keyholes, and I wouldn't put it past her to read any correspondence she found lying around.'

'That's not fair,' Rose said, suppressing a chuckle. 'Mrs Blunt has been with us for ever.'

'My point exactly.' Polly stroked Spartacus absent-mindedly and he began to purr. 'Now go home, Rose dear. I'm going to take a nap before luncheon.' She closed her eyes. 'And take Maisie with you. Her endless chatter grates on my nerves.'

'Yes, Aunt. Of course.' Rose jumped to her feet. She was eager to get home and find out more about Isabel Harman.

Eleanor was propped up on pillows, sipping a cup of warm milk, when Rose entered the bedroom. 'You're looking much better, Mama,' she said softly. 'How do you feel now?'

'I hate hot milk.' Eleanor held the cup out to her. 'Please take it away, and don't let Mrs Blunt see you tip it down the sink.'

Smiling, Rose took it from her. 'I won't tell on you, Mama. Although I'm sure it's good for you. Can I get you something else?'

'No, thank you, my love. I'm not hungry. All I want to do is sleep.'

Rose hesitated. 'I was talking to Aunt Polly and she told me that you have a friend who is my godmother. I didn't realise we had anyone close to us.'

A faint smile hovered around Eleanor's pale lips. 'She must have meant Isabel, who was my dearest friend. She moved away from town when she married for the second time. Her new husband didn't like London.'

'Aunt Polly said you've kept in touch with her.'

'Why the sudden interest?' Eleanor's thin hand plucked at the coverlet. 'What has Polly been saying?'

'That's all she told me. I was just curious, because I thought it might be nice to have someone for you to visit occasionally. I dare say you would like to see her again, wouldn't you?'

'I'm too ill to travel,' Eleanor said pettishly. 'I need to rest now, Rose. Go away like a good girl.'

'Of course, Mama. I'm sorry if I've tired you.' Rose walked to the door. 'Mrs Harman moved to Brighton, so Aunt Polly said.'

Eleanor's eyes opened wide. 'Polly never could get anything right. Isabel lives in Lyme Regis. Brighton, indeed!'

'Of course,' Rose said smugly. 'I must have made a mistake.' She was smiling as she left the room.

'Why are you looking so pleased with yourself?' Cora demanded when Rose entered the dining room.

'I think I might have found the answer.'

Cora placed the last spoon and fork on the dining table and stood back to admire her work. 'The answer to what?'

'We have to pay attention to what Dr Grantley said last evening. Mama is only going to get worse if she remains in London. He recommended the country or the seaside, and I might have found a place where she can recuperate.'

'Go on.' Cora pulled up a chair and sat down. 'I hope you realise that apart from attending Holy Communion, which you missed, I've spent all morning doing the chores that we're supposed to share.'

'I'm sorry, but I had to make sure we have Maisie to help out this evening, and I wanted to speak to

Aunt Polly. What's more, I've discovered that Mama has a friend, my godmother, called Isabel Harman who lives in a place called Lyme Regis.'

'I don't see how that helps.'

'Wouldn't it be wonderful if she were to invite our parents to stay for a while? A little holiday for them both.'

'Rose, you are so devious.'

'You don't think it's a good idea?'

'No – I think it's a marvellous idea. With our parents away we can work at Fancello's without fear of being found out.'

'And Mama will get well again.'

'Yes, of course,' Cora said hastily. 'That goes without saying.'

'You're late,' Fancello said crossly. 'This is not a day of rest for you, young ladies.'

Rose bit back a sharp retort. She would have liked to spend the evening quietly at home, sitting by the fire in the parlour with a good book, or attending to the heap of mending that awaited her attention. Instead she and Cora had braved the cold and rain to walk to Cupid's Court, only to be greeted by a scolding from their employer.

'We are so sorry, signor,' Cora said apologetically. 'It won't happen again.'

'It had better not.' Fancello looked them up and down, shaking his head. 'You look like two drowned sparrows. Go and change at once. Make yourselves look beautiful for the patrons.'

'Yes, signor.' Rose drew back the curtain just far enough to get a view of the saloon. 'It's very quiet out there. Is it always like this on Sunday nights?'

Fancello bridled visibly. 'More will arrive soon.' He stomped off in answer to an urgent summons from his wife.

'Don't take any notice of him, Rose,' Cora said, slipping her arm around her sister's shoulders. 'I suspect that he's had a row with Graziella, and he was taking it out on us.'

'You're right. I'll just think of the money we're adding to the amount in Aunt Polly's strong box, and ignore his bad temper.'

Cora peered through the gap between the heavy velvet curtains. 'Gerard isn't there. I wonder if he'll come tonight.'

'I know I've said it before, but be careful, Cora. He might have a wife and children waiting for him at home, or at the very least a fiancée. Men like the Honourable Gerard Barclay don't marry girls like us.'

'That is so mean,' Cora whispered. 'You don't know him, Rose. He's a gentleman and he wouldn't lead me on. I know he wouldn't.' Cora hurried off in the direction of the dressing room.

'I hope you're right,' Rose said in a whisper, but Cora was already out of earshot. Rose caught up with her as Cora squeezed into the tiny dressing room. 'I didn't mean to upset you.'

Cora sniffed and turned away. 'I know what you think. You don't have to keep telling me, Rose. I'm not a child.'

'I'm sorry. I care about you, Corrie. I don't want you to end up broken-hearted.'

'I'll take that chance.' Cora stepped out of her dress and slipped her costume over her head.

Rose was about to close the door when she heard the sound of shouting from the upstairs apartment and the sound of breaking glass. 'Another family squabble,' she said, chuckling. 'Thank goodness we don't throw things when we get cross.'

'Their fights used to worry me, but I'm getting used to them.' Cora turned her head. 'Will you tie my laces, please, Rose? As tight as possible.'

Another loud crash from above made them both jump, and then there was silence. Rose did as Cora asked and then concentrated on getting herself ready.

She was just adding the finishing touches to her stage make-up when Tommy stuck his head round the door. 'You're wanted upstairs, Miss Perkins.'

She stared at him in astonishment. 'Upstairs?'

'The signora is in hysterics. The signor wants you.'

'Shall I come with you?' Cora asked anxiously.

'I'll be all right. I expect it's something and nothing.' Rose stepped into the corridor. She could hear Fancello's raised voice, and, as she climbed the narrow stairs, the sound of Graziella's hysterical sobs grew louder. The door to the Fancellos' flat was ajar and she pushed it open.

The sight that met her eyes made her gasp with shock and her hand flew to her mouth. 'Oh, my goodness.'

Chapter Six

'Don't you dare breathe a word of this to anyone.' Fancello grabbed Rose by the arm, dragged her inside and slammed the door.

The sight that met her eyes was so shocking that she could only stand and stare.

'What are you gawping at?' Clementia was naked except for a small towel tied around her waist, and then she braced her shoulders exposing a flat chest covered with a soft, downy fuzz of hair.

Graziella had been cowering on the sofa, but her child's words seemed to galvanise her into action and she sprang to her feet, throwing her shawl around Clementia's shoulders. 'You have killed me, my son,' she cried. 'You have stuck a knife into your *mamma*'s heart.'

'Y-you're a boy.' Rose felt the blood rush to her cheeks and she hastily averted her gaze.

Fancello clenched his fists. 'You are a wicked boy, Clementino.'

'I don't understand.' Rose looked from one to the other. 'Why have you made your son pretend to be a girl?'

'Are you mad?' Fancello demanded angrily. 'The patrons would not pay to hear a choirboy sing. They want to see pretty girls on stage.'

'But I am not a girl,' Clementino protested. 'I never wanted to be a girl. You have turned me into a freak.'

'You are an ungrateful child,' Graziella stormed, clutching her hands to her breast. 'Haven't we given you everything?'

Rose looked Clementino in the eye and experienced a sudden surge of sympathy. 'What's the matter? Don't you want to perform any more?'

'Don't put ideas into his head.' Fancello glowered at her. 'He is our little star.'

'I'm not your little star,' Clementino's voice deepened. 'You hear this? I can no longer be a girl. I am a man now.'

'You are not yet fourteen.' Graziella held her hands out to him. 'You are my baby still.'

'I am growing up, Mamma.' Clementino dropped the shawl to the ground, flexing his biceps. 'You cannot force me to wear a dress and sing like a girl.' He fingered his chin. 'I have to shave twice a day. Do you want to put me in the circus as a bearded lady?'

Rose picked up the shawl and laid it on the arm of the sofa. 'You must listen to him, signor. Can't you see how unhappy he is?'

Fancello turned on her. 'I didn't send for you so that you could give me a lecture. I want you to persuade this bad son to honour his parents and do as we say. He might listen to you because he will not listen to his *mamma* or me.'

'Clementino is right,' Rose said slowly. 'You are making a show of him and it isn't fair. He just wants to be himself.'

Clementino pointed a shaking finger at Rose. 'She speaks the truth. She understands me, but you don't. I will kill myself if you make me go on that stage tonight.' He reached for a bottle of gin and held it to his lips.

'No!' Graziella leaped to her feet and snatched it from him. 'What will we do, Alessandro?'

'I am ruined.' Fancello subsided onto a chair. 'Ruined by an ungrateful child. The show will close tonight. I cannot go on.'

Clementino threw back his head and laughed. 'It is a punishment for the way you have forced me to live these past five years, wearing dresses and bows in my hair. I will do it no longer.'

'Where will we find another act to compare with our dear child?' Graziella moaned.

'Where will you find someone who works for next to nothing?' Clementino reached for a shirt and slipped it on. 'I intend to go home to Naples where

I hope to join the opera buffa, and train to be a basso buffo. You have used me long enough.'

Fancello held his head in his hands. 'We will have to close.'

'We cannot let our patrons down tonight,' Graziella said, rising from the sofa. 'Sing for us just once more, Clementino? Just once more, for your *mamma*.'

'No. Never again.' Clementino tossed his long dark locks and stalked out of the room.

'I know the words to most of his songs.' Rose looked from one bleak face to the other. 'So does Cora. We could do Clementino's act just for one night, but we would expect to be paid extra.'

'It would be a travesty.' Fancello threw up his hands. 'I won't allow it.'

'Yes, you will, Alessandro.' Graziella moved to a side table and unlocked a tin box. 'Do what you can, Rose. Here is your pay, including extra for tonight. We will not be requiring you again.'

Rose accepted the money. 'What will you do, signora?'

Graziella's full lips twisted into a semblance of a smile. 'We will return to Italy. We have family in Naples, and I wish to be close to my son. Perhaps one day he will forgive us for what we have done to him.'

'I hope he will, signora.' Rose left the room. As she made her way slowly down the stairs, she noticed for the first time that the treads were worn and plaster was flaking off the walls. She must, she thought, have had stars in her eyes when she first came to Fancello's saloon, and if she were to admit the truth she had enjoyed every minute of each performance. Papa would be horrified and Mama might never speak to her again, but she had loved the limelight and revelled in the applause. Now it had come to an end, and the distress she felt was not entirely due to the shortfall in the amount they needed to free Billy. She would miss the excitement of leading a double life, and the ever-present danger of discovery, but she could not help feeling sorry for Clementino and his parents. She went to give Cora the bad news.

Both their performances went down well, and the audience did not seem to notice the absence of the child star, but as they took their final bow and exited from the stage Rose found herself embraced by Clementino. It was the first time she had seen him in male clothing and he was every inch a handsome youth.

'Thank you, Rose,' he said, kissing her on both cheeks. 'You have saved my life.'

Cora stared at him in amazement. 'Well,' she breathed. 'Who would have thought it?'

'Good luck, Clementino. I hope everything turns out well for you.' Rose watched him walk away with a feeling akin to envy. His metamorphosis was complete, and now he could fly away like a butterfly emerging from its pupa: there was no such escape for a young woman like herself. This adventure was over, and now she must return to a life of duty and diligence, at the beck and call of her father and then the man she might ultimately marry. Her brief stab at independence, albeit for a just cause, had come to an end. How they would find the money to pay for Billy's defence was a problem yet to be solved. She turned with a start as Cora tugged at her sleeve.

'Stop daydreaming, Rose,' Cora said impatiently. 'I've seen him. Gerard is seated at his usual table and he is on his own. I must speak to him.'

'It's over, Corrie. You won't see him again after tonight.'

Cora tossed her head. 'We'll see about that.' She pulled back the curtain and ran down the steps to join Gerard. His handsome features dissolved into a charming smile as he stood to greet her. Rose turned away. She had seen enough to realise that there was more to her sister's relationship with the young aristocrat than she had at first suspected. It was another complication in an already difficult situation. She went to their dressing room and began taking off her stage make-up.

It was almost midnight when they returned to the vicarage, having first stopped to change their clothes at Polly's establishment. It had been decided that Maisie should remain at the vicarage until morning, as it was unsafe for her to walk home alone at this hour of the night. Even as Rose opened the scullery door she sensed that all was not well, and, as she entered the kitchen she heard the sound of groaning. A single candle guttered on the table leaving the room in deep shadow, and she almost tripped over Maisie, who was lying on a mat by the range. She was curled up in a ball, clutching her belly and moaning piteously.

Rose went down on her knees beside her. 'What's wrong? Are you ill?'

Cora lit a lamp and held it over them. 'What's the matter?'

Maisie raised a pale, tear-stained face and her mouth contorted with pain. 'I dunno, miss. I got collywobbles. It don't half hurt.' She grimaced and clutched her hands around her belly.

Rose looked closer and saw a tell-tale dark stain on the mat where Maisie lay. She exchanged worried glances with Cora. 'We'll need towels and hot water.' She smoothed Maisie's hair back from her damp forehead. 'It will be over soon. Don't be scared, we helped once when a woman miscarried at Aunt Polly's, so we know what to do. It's probably for the best.'

A thin sliver of daylight filtered through the kitchen window as Rose and Cora sat down to drink a well-earned cup of tea. Maisie had survived her ordeal, and was sleeping peacefully in Billy's old room.

Cora added two lumps of sugar to her cup. 'I suppose if the worst comes to the worst we could seek employment as midwives.'

Rose sipped her tea. 'As Papa would say, losing

108

the baby this early is a blessing in disguise, but I can't help feeling sorry for the poor girl.'

'She's little more than a child herself.' Cora stifled a yawn. 'I'm so tired, Rose. I must get some sleep.'

'Go to bed. I'll finish clearing up.'

Cora stood up, gazing anxiously at her sister. 'You must be exhausted, too.'

Rose shrugged and smiled. 'Oddly enough I'm not at all tired. It will probably catch up with me later, but when I've finished in here I'm going to Papa's study to get pen and paper, and I'm going to write to Mrs Harman.'

'But you don't know where she lives, other than that it's a place called Lyme Regis.'

'I spoke to Mrs Blunt before she went off duty yesterday afternoon, and she remembered posting letters to Isabel Harman at Beehive Cottage. She might still be living there so it's worth a try.'

'I suppose so, but I'm too worn out to think. Wake me up in time for breakfast, Rose. We don't want Papa to suspect anything.'

'I agree. I'm hoping that Papa will agree to take Maisie on as scullery maid. He knows her situation, and I'm certain he would consider it unchristian to turn her away in her hour of need. I'll be sure to point that out to him should he refuse.' Rose finished her tea and stood up. 'Go to bed, Corrie. Leave everything to me.'

Having banked up the fire in the range and tidied away all signs of the night's events, Rose went to her father's study and sat down at his desk to compose a letter to her mother's old friend. She was reading it through when her father walked into the room. He came to a halt, staring at her in surprise.

'Rose? It's six o'clock in the morning. Why are you up so early, and to whom are you writing?'

She smiled apologetically. 'I'm sorry, Papa. I should have asked you first, but I'm composing a letter to Mrs Harman.'

Seymour pulled up a chair and sat down. 'Why are you writing to your godmother?'

'Dr Grantley said that Mama needed rest and fresh air, and Mrs Harman lives by the sea in Lyme Regis.'

'I think I follow your line of thought, Rose, but this is a matter for your mother and myself to decide, not you.'

'I realise that, of course, but there's no harm in finding out if my godmother still resides in Beehive Cottage.'

Seymour regarded her steadily. 'Your mother had a restless night, and I've barely slept at all.' He stood up again, and began to pace the room. 'Perhaps you're right, Rose. Maybe I haven't been willing to face the fact that Eleanor's condition is worsening.'

'You look exhausted,' Rose said softly. 'You could go with her.'

'And leave my flock? No, I couldn't do that.' He came to a halt by the desk. 'Finish your letter and post it. If Isabel invites your mother to stay I'll make sure that she accepts, and you will travel with her.'

'But surely you ought to accompany her, Pa.'

'I can't leave Joshua to cope alone. He has almost completed his training, but this is not an easy parish to run. No, I will remain here, and, all things being equal, you will take your mother to Dorset. Cora can stay with me, and keep house while you are away.'

Rose could see that he had made his mind up and she knew that to argue would be futile. She seized the opportunity to mention Maisie. 'That sounds an excellent plan, Pa. But Cora and Mrs Blunt would need extra help. It just so happens that Aunt Polly has no further need of Maisie's services. Perhaps she could stay on as maid of all work . . . for a while, anyway.'

'I suppose so. I know you will give me no peace unless I agree.'

'We rely so much on Mrs Blunt. I'm sure she will be glad of an extra pair of hands.' Rose signed the letter with a flourish and blotted the ink dry. 'I'll post this after breakfast, if you'll be kind enough to give me a penny for the stamp.'

He smiled and nodded. 'You are so like your dear mama was when I first met her. If she had made up her mind to a certain course of action, she would allow nothing to stand in her way. I believe I might have remained a dry old bachelor had she not seen something in me to love.'

'I'm sure you sent many hearts aflutter, Pa,' Rose said smiling.

111

'I would not claim such a thing even if it were true. I'm afraid I was a dull dog, but Eleanor didn't seem to think so. I've been much blessed with a wonderful wife and three healthy and handsome children. I'm proud of you all, and with William about to follow me into the ministry I couldn't ask for more.'

Rose had to bite her lip to prevent herself from crying. The thought of her parents learning the truth about their beloved son was too much to bear. She made an excuse to leave the room, and instead of going to the kitchen to see if Mrs Blunt needed any assistance in the preparation of breakfast, she crossed the hall to the drawing room and let herself out into the garden through the French doors.

It was cold and there was a faint hint of frost icing the lawn, but the birds were singing their spring song and daffodils bowed gracefully in the gentle breeze. The air still smelled of soot, smoke and the effluent pumped out of the factories that lined the Regent Canal, but it was quiet and peaceful in the garden and she needed time on her own to think. The money they had saved so far would pay a little more than half the legal fees, but now there was no prospect of earning more at the saloon. Billy's life and liberty hung in the balance, and there was no one to whom she could turn for help.

She folded her arms in an attempt to keep warm as she walked through the shrubbery, carefully avoiding small clumps of violets and golden celandines.

This town garden had been her retreat and solace since she was a child. The old swing hung limp and neglected from an overhanging branch of a sturdy oak tree, and the climbing rose planted on the day of her christening had rampaged up the trellis and had reached the eaves above her bedroom window. In summer it would produce small creamy clusters of sweet-smelling flowers, filling her room with heady perfume. She looked up and saw that Cora's curtains were still drawn. A fat pigeon was resting on the windowsill and its beady eyes stared down at her. If only she could fly like a bird, she would soar high up in the sky and head for the West Country. Perhaps a personal plea to Bennett Sharpe would persuade him to continue with Billy's case regardless of their finances. She felt sure she could convince him that to win such a difficult case would greatly benefit his career, but she needed to speak to him in person, and that in itself was a problem as she did not know where to contact him. Then it came to her in a flash. 'Scully!' she said out loud, causing the pigeon to fly to the relative safety of the oak tree. A glimmer of hope lifted her spirits. Sharpe had said that Scully would know how to contact him in Cornwall, and there was nothing she would not do in order to save Billy from the hangman's noose. She would visit Sharpe's chambers in Lincoln's Inn and leave a message for Scully to contact her as a matter of urgency. She hurried indoors and went to wake Cora. Everything must appear to be normal, she thought as she negotiated the stairs. No one must suspect that anything untoward had happened.

Eventually, after enquiring at the clerks' room at Sharpe's chambers, Rose found someone who was well acquainted with Scully. He had not yet returned from his trip to Oxford, but the clerk promised to pass on the message that Miss Perkins had need of his services. It was frustrating, but Rose had no option other than to leave and hope that Scully would contact her before too long. She called in at Polly's house on the way home and related in detail the events of the previous evening, including the sudden end to Maisie's pregnancy.

'It's just as well,' Polly said, nodding. 'The girl is far too young to be saddled with a child, as well as being not quite right in the head. She'll make a good scullery maid, but you'll need to keep an eye on her. She was getting very friendly with young Bobby Lee, and you know what boys are, and men in general.' She rolled her eyes as if to labour the point. 'I have rooms filled with unmarried girls and women who have been led astray.'

'I'll keep an eye on her, Aunt Polly.'

'And you say you've written to Isabel?' Polly said thoughtfully. 'She is a good woman, although I don't think she quite approved of me. However, that's by the bye, and I'm sure she would be only too pleased to see my sister again. As I recall they were inseparable when we were young.'

'I'll feel so much happier when I know that Mama is on the mend, but I'm desperate to speak to Scully. I'm afraid that Mr Sharpe will refuse to go any further with the case when he finds out that we've only raised half his fee.'

Polly leaned against the buttoned back of the chaise longue, idly stroking Spartacus, who was twitching his tail as if irritated by this casual show of affection. 'You know what you must do, Rose,' she said after a moment's thought.

'I'm not sure, Aunt. I've been racking my brains in an attempt to find a solution, and time is short. I don't know when Billy's case is due in court, but it must be soon.'

'There is only one thing you can do, Rose. You must go to Cornwall in person and speak directly to Sharpe. From my brief acquaintance with him I would say that he is a reasonable man, but I suspect he could be quite ruthless if the need arose. He knows how you have been raising the money and he will understand if you tell him why it has come to an end.'

'Do you really think I ought to travel to Cornwall? How would I explain that to my parents?'

'That is up to you, Rose. I can only make suggestions. You are the one who will have to carry them out.' Polly snatched her hand away as Spartacus took a spiteful swipe at her fingers. 'You wretched animal. I don't know why I took you in off the street.'

'You have a big heart, Aunt Polly,' Rose said, rising from her chair by the fire. 'And he is a spoiled beast. He thinks he can behave exactly as he pleases and he gets away with it.'

Polly sighed. 'He's a male, my dear. They're all the same under the skin, or the fur, it doesn't matter what species they are. Men rule the world.'

'Nonsense, Aunt. We have a queen on the throne and Britannia rules the waves; both are women.' Rose leaned over to kiss her aunt on the cheek. 'You are the best aunt and the most generous person I have ever known. You've given me hope, and now I know what I must do. When I've spoken to Scully I'll be able to make a plan, but until then I'll wait for a response to my letter to my godmother. I posted it on my way to Lincoln's Inn, so hopefully it will reach Isabel very soon.'

'I wish there was more I could do,' Polly said, sighing. 'I'm not a rich woman.'

'You've helped immeasurably, Aunt.' Rose reached for her shawl. 'I've left Cora to cope at home and she'll have Maisie to look after as well as Mama, so I'd better hurry.'

'I'll miss your nightly visits, child. But you must do what you think best, and if I can help in any way you must let me know.' Polly elbowed Spartacus out of the way as she raised herself from the chaise longue. 'I know I ought not to suggest it, as your father would not approve, but you might do well to pay a call on the manager of the Grecian Theatre. I don't think the Sunshine Sisters are finished yet.'

Rose tied the ribbons on her bonnet at an angle

beneath her chin. 'I'll do anything to earn the rest of the money to pay for Billy's defence, although I'm not sure that the Sunshine Sisters are quite ready for the Grecian.'

'Nonsense, my love. You have inherited some of my talent. It would be a shame to hide yourself away doing good works when you could be giving joy to so many.'

Rose kissed her aunt's leathery cheek. 'I don't think Papa would agree with you, but I'll bear that in mind.' She left the house, glancing up and down the street in the hope that Scully might turn up suddenly, but there was just the usual mix of people going about their daily business. The more affluent house-wives were out shopping, accompanied by their maids. Others, less fortunate, whose shabby clothes and down-at-heel boots defined their place in society, rubbed shoulders with bowler-hatted rent collectors, chimney sweeps, costermongers and errand boys. Rose hurried home.

She spent the next few days waiting anxiously for word from her godmother and from Scully. Maisie recovered quickly and was put to work in the house, which she seemed to consider was a step up from being a humble scullery maid. Eleanor remained in bed, improving slightly each day, but she was still too weak to stand unaided and her appetite was poor. Mrs Blunt shook her head at the sight of untouched plates of food, although Maisie was only too pleased to polish them off.

On the fourth day, Rose had almost given up hope of hearing from Isabel and was beginning to wonder if Scully had received her urgent message. She was about to leave the house on a parish errand when the postman arrived bearing a letter from Lyme Regis, and at exactly the same moment Scully turned up outside the front gate with a big grin on his sallow features.

Rose ushered him into the parlour, safe in the knowledge that her father was in his study, fully occupied as he composed his Sunday sermon. Cora was upstairs sitting with their mother, and Maisie was in the scullery peeling potatoes. Mrs Blunt rarely ventured outside the kitchen during working hours and it was unlikely that they would be interrupted. She motioned Scully to take a seat by the fire, and she perched on the chair opposite him.

'I need to see Mr Sharpe,' she said firmly. 'Will you take me to him, Mr Scully?'

He held his hands out to the blaze. 'Good fire you have going there, miss. It was very cold up there in Oxfordshire.'

'I'd offer you a cup of tea, but I don't want to alert anyone as to your presence.'

Scully cast a quick look round the room and his mouth drew down at the corners. 'Something a little stronger would be of benefit to a man perished with cold, miss.'

Rose jumped to her feet and moved swiftly to a corner cupboard. She unlocked it and took out a bottle of brandy. 'My father keeps this for medicinal purposes.' She hesitated. 'I'd pour you a tot, but I'd have difficulty explaining a wet glass.'

Scully held out his hand. 'Give it here, miss. I can take it neat.' He snatched the bottle from her and held it to his lips.

Rose watched as his prominent Adam's apple moved up and down above his dirty cravat with each gulp of the fiery spirit. He licked his lips, belched and handed the bottle back to her. 'That's done the trick.' He wiped his mouth on his sleeve. 'Now then, let us have a talk.'

He left ten minutes later, having agreed to take Rose with him when he returned to Cornwall towards the end of the following week. They would meet at the station hotel in Exeter at midday, or thereabouts, on the Thursday. Quite how she was going to explain her departure to her mother, and what method of transport she might use to reach her destination, was a problem that she would meet when it arose, but as she saw him out of the house she experienced a feeling of near panic. Perhaps she had been too hasty making such an arrangement when she had not seen the contents of Isabel's letter. She returned to the parlour, closed the door and went to sit by the fire where she broke the seal on that letter with trembling fingers. She studied Isabel's copperplate writing, scanning through the pleasantries until she came to the last paragraph. The words danced about before her eyes and her breath hitched in her throat. If the response was negative she would simply have to think of another excuse to leave London. She crossed her fingers and read on.

> *Indeed, dear Rose, it would give me great pleasure to entertain yourself and Eleanor as my guests for as long as you wish to stay. Lyme Regis is particularly lovely at this time of year, subject to the vagaries of the English climate, but the air is clean and bracing. I am certain that a prolonged visit would improve my dear friend's health, and we will have much to talk about. I have advised my servants to make rooms ready, so please, please come as soon as you may. Send word of your travelling arrangements by return and I look forward to seeing you in the very near future.*
> *Your devoted godmother and friend,*
> *Isabel Harman*

'Thank you, Godmother,' Rose cried out loud. 'You don't know it but you might well have saved Billy's life.'

She took a deep breath and stood up. Everything depended upon her mother's agreement to go and take Rose with her, although she would keep her own travel plans thereafter to herself.

Chapter Seven

The screech of giant engines letting off steam only added to the cacophony of sound, as yet more trains thundered into Waterloo Bridge railway station. The rumble of trolley wheels and the clatter of booted feet added to the noise, and conversation was all but impossible.

Cora clutched Rose's arm. 'I wish I could come with you.'

'So do I, but it's going to be difficult as it is. I need you to smooth things over at home.' Rose lowered her voice to a whisper, placing her lips close to her sister's ear. 'You know what you have to do, Cora. I'm relying on you.'

Cora nodded, biting her lip. 'I'll do my best. You know I will.'

'Come along, girls. The train has just pulled into the platform.' Seymour tucked his wife's hand through the crook of his arm and marched off in the wake of the porter, who had their luggage piled up on his trolley. He helped her into the first-class carriage and saw her settled into a corner seat. 'I'll pray for your speedy recovery, my dear.' He brushed her cheek with a kiss.

Eleanor reached out to clutch his hand, her bottom lip trembled ominously. 'I hope to return home very soon.'

He smiled. 'I hope so too.' He turned to Rose. 'Look after your mother.'

'I will, Pa.'

'Give my regards to Isabel.' He climbed down to join Cora on the platform, and slammed the carriage door.

'Don't forget to write.' Cora's voice was almost drowned out by the shrill blast of the guard's whistle.

Rose leaned out of the window. 'I will, Corrie. I promise.' The train jerked and moved forward, and she waved until her father and sister were out of sight. She returned to her seat. 'We're fortunate in having the carriage to ourselves, Mama.'

Eleanor nodded wearily. 'This is the first time your father and I have been separated since we were married. I don't know how he will manage on his own.'

'He has Cora to take care of him, and you will be able to regain your health and strength at the seaside.'

'I haven't seen Isabel for ten years,' Eleanor said, sighing. 'I hope we still have something in common, as I believe she is childless. She can never know or understand a mother's feelings.'

Rose nodded silently. She could see that this was going to be a long journey, and she made herself as comfortable as possible as the carriage rattled and jolted its way out of the city. As it picked up speed the rhythmic clattering of the great iron wheels over the points had a hypnotic effect, and soon Eleanor was nodding off, leaving Rose alone with her thoughts.

It was early afternoon when they arrived in Axminster where Rose had planned to take a horse-drawn omnibus to Lyme Regis, but Isabel had sent her carriage to pick them up and they travelled the last five or six miles in style. Even so, Eleanor was pale and exhausted by the time they reached their final destination.

Beehive Cottage was situated on a clifftop over-looking Lyme Bay, and for a moment Rose forgot everything in the sheer delight of breathing the salt-laden air as she took in the view. The sun shone from a cloudless azure sky, its brilliance reflected in the ever-changing colours of the sea. White-crested waves danced and tumbled onto the shore and seagulls soared overhead, mewing and crying like souls in distress. Rose was enchanted and had almost forgotten why she had travelled so far from home, but a cry from the front door of the cottage brought her back to earth with a jolt. She turned to see her godmother running down the path with outstretched arms.

Eleanor, showing the first signs of liveliness for

months, seemed to forget her invalid state and hurried to meet her old friend. They hugged and then held each other at arm's length, laughing like excited schoolgirls. Rose stood back, allowing them time to greet each other while she studied her surroundings. The cottage, which to her mind was far too grand to have such a humble title, was round like a honeypot, but that was where its resemblance to a beehive ended. Sunlight glanced off the white stucco walls and was reflected in the small windowpanes, giving the house the appearance of being alive with light. The Gothic windows added to the eccentric design, and each one curved into an ogee arch. It was an odd building, set in a typically English cottage garden with flowerbeds overflowing with hyacinths, tulips and narcissi. Their heavenly perfume mingled with the scent of newly cut grass and the briny smell of the sea. Rose took deep breaths, feeling quite drunk as the clean air filled her lungs.

'Come into the house, Rose,' Isabel called from the front door. 'It might be sunny, but there's a cool breeze.'

Rose followed them indoors, leaving the coachman to bring their luggage.

'I'll show you your rooms,' Isabel said, smiling, 'and then we'll take tea in the parlour.'

'That would be delightful.' Eleanor gazed round the entrance hall with a rapt expression. 'You have a lovely home, Isabel.'

'Thank you, my dear. It suits me well enough.'

Isabel signalled to a housemaid. 'Tabitha, you may take the cases to the guest rooms.' She turned to her friend with a worried frown. 'Can you manage the stairs, Eleanor? If not I could have a bed made up for you in the music room.'

'I'm not an invalid, Isabel. I am a little tired after such a long journey, but I feel quite invigorated by the change of scene. I didn't realise how much I missed living in the countryside.'

'My dear, I understand exactly,' Isabel said, linking her arm through Eleanor's. 'We'll soon bring the colour back to your cheeks, and we'll have time for lovely long talks about the old days.' She glanced over her shoulder as she led Eleanor up the stairs. 'I hope we won't bore you too much, Rose, but your mama and I have known each other since we were children.'

'I think it's splendid,' Rose said earnestly. 'You obviously have so much to talk about.'

'Tabitha will show you to your room, Rose, while I take care of my dear friend.'

Rose followed the maid up the curved staircase to a sunny room overlooking the bay. It was small but comfortably furnished with a brass bed, a walnut dressing table, clothes press and washstand, and a chintz-covered armchair. Tabitha placed the valise on the floor. 'Shall I unpack for you, miss?'

'No, thank you,' Rose said hastily. 'I'll do it myself.'

'Very well, miss.' Tabitha bobbed a curtsey and left the room.

Left to herself, Rose went to the window and

gazed out at the ever-changing sea and sky. The clear air and the translucent blues and greens of the water dazzled her eyes, and she would have been content to stand there all afternoon, but she had a duty as a guest and she had a quick wash in cold water, tidied her hair and went downstairs to join her mother and Isabel. She followed the sound of voices and entered the parlour to find them laughing and chatting as if they had never been parted.

Isabel looked up and smiled. 'Do come and join us, Rose.' She picked up the teapot and filled a dainty china cup, added a dash of milk and passed it to her. 'Do try some of Cook's fruitcake, but not too much, my dear. We dine at six o'clock, which is unfashionably early, I know. However, we live a simple life here in the country.'

'We also dine early.' Eleanor eyed her friend over the rim of her teacup. 'Your husband is away on business, I suppose?'

'Mr Harman passed away two years ago,' Isabel said casually. 'It was a short illness.'

'I'm so sorry,' Eleanor murmured. 'How tragic.'

'Yes, indeed,' Rose added, nodding.

'Ah, well, these things happen,' Isabel said with the ghost of a smile. 'Now let's talk about something more pleasing. There are lovely walks along the clifftop, Rose, and I believe there are still fossils to be found, if one knows where to look. We are quite famous now, thanks to Mary Anning, although I myself am not very interested in old bones.'

'I'm not planning to stay long,' Rose said carefully. 'I've left Cora to cope with duties around the parish, but I should return to London before the end of the week.'

Eleanor put her cup down, staring at her daughter with a frown creasing her brow. 'This is the first I've heard of it, Rose. I thought you were to stay and keep me company.'

'I'm certain that you and my godmother will do very well without me,' Rose said firmly. 'I plan to leave for London on Thursday morning.'

'But it's Monday already. That means you will only have two days in this delightful house. It seems a little hasty, even for you, Rose.'

'I'm sorry, Mama, but I thought I had made it clear at the outset.' Rose prayed silently that the white lie would be forgiven, but she pressed the point home. 'You would not want Papa to suffer unnecessarily, I'm sure. He must be missing you.'

'That is true, Rose.' Eleanor turned to her friend. 'It is the first time that Seymour and I have been apart since our marriage. I can only try to understand how you must have felt when Mr Harman was taken from you.'

'Actually it was more of a relief than anything.' Isabel pulled a face, chuckling. 'Don't look so shocked, Eleanor. Not all marriages are made in heaven, and mine certainly was not.' She turned to Rose. 'More tea, dear?'

*

The next two days passed quickly and more enjoyably than Rose had thought possible. Her godmother was a considerate hostess, and her idle life seemed to suit Eleanor admirably. Isabel rarely rose before noon, and although she advocated long country walks she did not appear to follow her own advice. Having enjoyed a leisurely lunch her only exercise of the day seemed to be a stroll around the garden, after which she retired to the drawing room and reclined on the sofa. Rose left her mother and Isabel to their own devices and went out to explore the countryside and the small town. Although popular with summer visitors, out of season it was very quiet, and she was able to stroll in solitude on the beach and walk out unimpeded along the curve of the Cobb to watch the ships, some of them under sail and others steaming along at a rate of knots. At night, in her comfortable bed, she fell asleep listening to the waves lapping on the shore and the gentle sighing of the breeze. Each morning she had to remind herself that she was on a mission and this was not a pleasant holiday by the sea. She wished that she could confide in someone, but she soon realised that Isabel was a gossip who could not be trusted to keep a secret.

Early on Thursday morning Rose was packed and ready to leave. Her mother and Isabel were still in their rooms, which suited Rose very well as they had said their goodbyes after supper the previous evening. The coachman arrived on time to drive her to Axminster station where she boarded a train for

Exeter. At Isabel's insistence she travelled first class – though not in the direction Isabel had supposed – and had the luxury of having a carriage to herself. It was the first time she had ever travelled on her own, but she sat back in the seat and watched the lush green pastures flash past the window. The wooded valleys were dissected by rivers and the train passed through pretty villages, and in a little under two hours pulled into Exeter station, coming to a halt with a loud blast of steam. A porter opened the carriage door and picked up Rose's valise.

'Where be you bound, miss?'

'The station hotel.' Rose stepped down onto the platform. She was tempted to take her luggage from him, but she realised that she was attracting some curious looks from her fellow passengers and she decided that it would be worth the tip the porter would expect to be escorted through the station concourse.

Having given him what she thought was reasonable, and the man himself seemed satisfied, Rose went to the hotel lounge to await Scully's arrival. She ordered a pot of tea and a ham sandwich, and sat down to read a copy of *The Times* that had been left on the seat beside her. She was immersed in an article when she realised that someone was standing in front of her. Thinking it was the waiter with her order she looked up and was about to thank him when she realised her mistake. She let the paper fall into her lap.

'Mr Sharpe. I thought Mr Scully was to meet me here.'

Bennett pulled up a chair and sat down. 'He sent me a telegram informing me of your plans. I replied by return, telling him that I would meet you here as I have work for him in London.'

'I see,' she said slowly. 'It was you I wanted to see.'

He acknowledged this with a curt nod. 'I think I can guess why you're here.'

'You can?' She stared at him in surprise 'Really?'

'To fund a defence for a capital crime is not cheap. I imagine you are having some difficulty in getting the money together.'

'You're very direct, Mr Sharpe.'

'So I'm correct in my assumption?'

'Fancello's is closed.'

'I see.' He moved aside to allow the waiter to place a tea tray on the table.

'But we will find a way,' Rose said hastily. 'There are other places where Cora and I might find work.'

He gave her a searching look. 'That is unlikely to bring in the amount you will need to pay the court costs, let alone other expenses.'

'I know.' Rose stared at the plate of sandwiches that the waiter placed in front of her and her appetite deserted her. 'That's why I needed to come in person, but I see I have wasted my time.'

'No, you haven't.' He shook his head. 'If that had been the case I would have telegraphed Scully and told him to explain matters to you.'

She raised her eyes to meet his. 'I don't understand.'

'Your brother's case is due to be heard in Bodmin Crown Court next week. I've arranged for you to visit him.'

'I can do that?' Rose felt her mouth dry and her throat constricted. She reached for the teapot and filled a cup. 'I'm sorry, would you like some tea, Mr Sharpe?'

'No, thank you. I should prefer coffee this morning.' He raised his hand to attract the attention of a passing waiter. 'Coffee, please.'

'Yes, sir.' The waiter hurried off, his white apron flapping about his knees.

'I'd like to see Billy,' Rose said breathlessly. 'Do you think he has a chance?'

'I wouldn't have taken the case if I didn't think I could get him acquitted.' Bennett sat back in his chair. 'I've arranged for you to stay at Portmorna House.'

Rose choked on a mouthful of tea. 'But isn't that where Gawain Tressidick used to live?'

'Yes, it is. But you will find his brother is open-minded. He wants to see justice done as much as you or I.'

'Can you tell me more? I don't want to say or do the wrong thing. How can you be certain that Mr Tressidick won't object? I would have thought he'd hate anyone connected with the man accused of his brother's murder.'

'Bedevere Tressidick is my cousin and I know I can speak for him.'

'I don't understand,' Rose said slowly. 'You're saying that you are related to the Tressidicks, and yet you've taken on my brother's case. Why?'

'Because I won't stand by and watch an innocent man go to the gallows. It's as simple as that.'

'And I am to stay with the bereaved family?'

'It is the only place in Portmorna where you would be comfortable. You want to see Billy, don't you?'

'Yes, of course I do.'

He smiled. 'Then I suggest you eat your lunch and we'll be on our way.'

'How will we get to Bodmin?'

'We'll take the train to Plymouth and change there for Launceston. I've hired a carriage to take us the rest of the way.'

'Will it take long?'

'We'll be travelling for the rest of the day, but you'll see Billy tomorrow morning, I promise.'

Travelling by train was still a novelty to Rose, and she spent most of the time gazing out of the window. It was a largely silent journey as Bennett was occupied reading through a batch of documents and did not invite conversation. They changed trains at Plymouth and, after some delays, it was late afternoon by the time they arrived in Launceston, where a carriage was waiting to take them on to Bodmin. Dusk was dissolving the rocky tors into a magical and mysterious landscape as they crossed the moor. Gnarled trees were twisted into tortured shapes by the prevailing winds, and all too soon they were in almost complete darkness, with only the flickering lights of the carriage lamps to show them the way. Travelling in such proximity with a man who was little more than a stranger would, under any normal circumstances, have made her feel awkward and embarrassed, but Rose was tired to the point of exhaustion. She leaned back against the worn leather squabs and closed her eyes. The carriage rocked and swayed as it negotiated the rutted track, and eventually she fell into a deep and dreamless sleep.

She awakened to find that they had come to a standstill and light from burning torches flooded through the carriage windows. Outside she could hear voices and the sound of horses' hoofs on cobbled streets.

'Where are we?'

'The George and Dragon inn.' Bennett leaned across to open the door. 'We'll stay here tonight. I've booked two rooms and a private parlour.' He alighted from the carriage and held his hand out to her. 'It's all perfectly proper. Even for a clergyman's daughter.'

He sounded serious, but Rose was quick to see the humorous glint in his eyes and she smiled. 'I don't think anything I've done recently would be considered suitable behaviour for a respectable young woman.' With her feet once again on firm ground she took in her surroundings, but it was too dark to see anything outside the lights of the inn. She followed Bennett into the crowded taproom, which was hazy with tobacco smoke and the air was thick with the smell of beer and sweaty humanity. Bennett led her through to a private parlour at the back of the building where a table was laid for two.

'I ordered supper, and tomorrow we'll leave directly after breakfast.'

Rose took off her bonnet and mantle and laid them on a chair. 'This must be costing a great deal of money. I don't know how we'll repay you, unless you're prepared to wait.' She went to sit at the table. In the surreal world she felt she was inhabiting it did not seem strange to be dining alone with a man she barely knew. At this moment nothing would have shocked or surprised her.

Bennett shrugged off his greatcoat and took a seat opposite her. 'We'll forget about money for the time being. The main thing now is for you to see your brother. I'm just waiting for Scully to report his findings in Oxford, and then I'll have a good case for the defence.' He looked up as the door opened and a maidservant entered carrying a steaming bowl of what turned out to be a savoury rabbit stew. She retreated hastily and returned again with a basket of freshly baked bread and a jug of wine.

'Will there be anything else, sir?'

Bennett glanced at Rose, raising an eyebrow. 'Would you prefer tea or a glass of water?'

'No, thank you,' Rose said, not wishing to appear

gauche and unworldly. She rarely drank wine other than that sipped at communion, and even then Joshua had been instructed to take the chalice away before either she or Cora had had a chance to do more than moisten their lips.

'Thank you, that will be all for now, thank you.' Bennett gave the girl a charming smile that brought colour to her cheeks.

'Yes, sir.' The maid scuttled from the room, closing the door behind her.

To prove that she had meant what she said, Rose filled her glass with wine and took a sip. It was rich and red but slightly acidic, with a bitter aftertaste, and she tried not to wrinkle her nose. 'Perhaps I ought to return to London after I've seen Billy,' she said tentatively. 'I really do need to find work.'

Bennett ladled stew into a bowl and handed it to her. 'I've told you not to worry on that score, Rose.' He met her startled look with a smile. 'I think Billy would benefit greatly from the knowledge that you were close by. We'll talk about finances when we win.'

'Are you so certain of victory?'

'One can never be certain how a jury will react, but I have never yet lost a case and I don't intend to start now.' He reached across the table to pat her hand. 'Your visit will raise Billy's spirits and give him courage. It's not going to be easy to prove his innocence, but I will do everything in my power to save him from the noose.'

Rose gazed at his slim fingers as they covered her

own, and she had to conquer a sudden desire to cry. It had been a long day and despite her nap in the carriage she was mentally and physically exhausted. 'I'm truly grateful,' she said softly. 'But I will repay you, if it's the last thing I ever do.'

He withdrew his hand and raised his glass to her. 'Here's to success.'

Bodmin Gaol loomed over the town. Constructed entirely of cold, hard granite, it appeared stark and forbidding. The mere sight of it was enough to send shivers down Rose's spine, and as they entered the grim building she sensed the unease created by centuries of despairing souls who had been confined within its walls. Those who were currently incarcerated were vocal in their dissatisfaction, and she tried to shut her ears to the pleas for help and clemency as the warder led them through a maze of corridors. The light from the warder's lamp created monstrous shadows in the darkness, and the smell of burning paraffin mixed with stench of excrement became nauseating. Rose covered her nose and mouth with her handkerchief, but Bennett seemed unperturbed as he strode along at her side.

An icy draught whistled down the passage and she shuddered to think what it must be like in the confines of the prison when night fell. She had never believed in ghosts, but after five minutes inside the gaol she was beginning to think that the place was indeed haunted. She could feel the sadness and despair emanating from the stone walls, and she had to subdue the desire to turn and run.

Bennett took her by the arm, giving it a comforting squeeze. 'It's not a pleasant place, but then it wasn't meant to be. I've seen to it that Billy has a cell to himself and that he is fed regularly.'

'Thank you,' Rose whispered.

The warder came to a sudden halt, unlocked a cell door and stood aside to let them enter. 'Five minutes,' he said tersely.

Bennett took a coin from his pocket and pressed it into the man's hand. 'Ten minutes.'

'Aye, sir.' The warder closed the door and the key grated in the lock.

Rose blinked as her eyes became accustomed to the gloom and for a moment she thought that the dank cell was empty, but as she drew further in she could see a hunched shape lying on the bed, partly covered by a coarse blanket. Her breath caught in her throat and her heartbeat quickened.

'Billy,' she said softly. 'Billy, it's me, Rose.'

The body remained stiff and still and she experienced a feeling of panic. She turned to Bennett. 'He's not moving. What have they done to him?'

Chapter Eight

Bennett crossed the floor, leaned over the bed and shook Billy by the shoulders.

'Eh? What?' Billy snapped into a sitting position. 'Bennett, is that you?' He blinked and ran his hand through his tangled auburn hair.

Rose hurried to his bedside and threw her arms around his neck, sobbing with relief. 'I thought you were dead.' She released him only to slap him twice on the shoulder. 'You gave me such a fright.'

'Hold hard, Rose. Why are you here?' He glared at Bennett. 'Why did you bring my sister to this hellhole?'

Bennett leaned against the wall as there was nowhere other than the bed where a person could sit. In fact, as Rose was quick to notice, the only other furniture was a roughly made table on which was an enamel jug and washbowl. The flagstone floor was bare of anything that might hint at comfort and the wind whistled through the badly fitting barred window.

She reached up to stroke her brother's whiskery cheek. 'I hardly recognised you beneath all that fuzz,' she said with a shaky laugh. 'I'm so glad to see you, Billy.'

He wrapped his arms around her, burying his face against her shoulder. 'You shouldn't have come here, Rose. This is no place for a lady.'

'Don't talk such nonsense,' she said severely. 'I would have come sooner had it been possible, and I couldn't have done it without Bennett's help.' She looked up and met Bennett's gaze with a grateful smile. 'He's going to get you acquitted, Billy. We both know that you're innocent.'

Billy raised himself, dashing his hand across his eyes and sniffing. 'I didn't do it, Rosie. I swear to God I didn't kill Gawain. He was my friend.'

'I know you didn't,' Rose insisted. 'And Bennett is going to prove it. You mustn't worry about anything other than keeping yourself in good heart until we can get you out of here.'

'What does Father say to all this?' Billy grasped Rose's hand. 'Has he told Mama?'

'No one at home knows, apart from Cora and Aunt Polly. We've been doing everything we can to raise the money to fund your defence, so you mustn't worry about anything.' Rose held his hand to her cheek. 'You will be acquitted, I know you will.'

Billy's green eyes filled with tears and he blinked them away. 'I can't stand it in this place, Rose. If the case goes against me I'll kill myself. I'd rather die that way than at the end of a hangman's rope.'

Shocked and alarmed by his obvious distress, she held him close. 'Don't say things like that, Billy.'

He choked on a sob. 'This isn't the place for you, Rose. Don't bring her here again, Bennett.'

'I'll come every day until the trial, and nothing will stop me.' Rose passed him her handkerchief, close to tears herself. 'I'll bring you some clean clothes and a hairbrush. You look a mess, Billy Perkins.'

'Your sister has spoken, Billy,' Bennett said with a grim smile. 'I don't think either of us has much chance of deflecting her from her purpose.'

Billy opened his mouth to speak, but the sound of the key rattling in the lock preceded the appearance of the warder. 'Your time be up now, lady and gentleman.'

Rose kissed her brother on the cheek. 'You don't smell too good either. I'll bring some soap and a towel. They don't seem to provide such luxuries here.' She shot an accusing glance at the warder.

'This bain't be no hotel, miss,' he said stiffly. 'Time you was gone.'

'Please don't come again, Rose.' Billy threw himself down on the hard wooden bed. 'I'm done for and I know it.'

'Don't say things like that.' Rose cast an anxious glance at Bennett, but he shook his head.

'We will be back.' He slipped another coin into the man's hand, before turning to give Billy an encouraging smile. 'Until tomorrow, my friend.'

Rose hurried from the prison, stopping outside to gasp for breath, but the putrid stench seemed to have woven itself into the fabric of her clothing, and it clung to her despite the freshness of the clean country air.

Tears ran down her cheeks. 'That was worse than I imagined. Poor Billy, he was always such a cheerful person, with a kind word for everyone. I didn't think that he would be in such a state.'

Bennett proffered his arm. 'It's not pleasant, but Billy has the best of it, such as it is. The other poor wretches are crowded into cells without so much as a blanket between them.'

'I thank you from the bottom of my heart for all you've done for him, but I can't bear to see him like that.' Rose searched in her pocket for her hankie and then remembered she had left it with Billy.

'Here, take mine.' Bennett handed her a spotless white handkerchief.

'Thank goodness Cora and I have managed to keep the truth from our parents. I would walk barefoot over hot coals rather than let them know what's happened to Billy.'

A grim smile curved Bennett's well-moulded lips. 'That won't be necessary, but are you sure you want to visit again?'

'Of course, if it's at all possible. How far is it to Portmorna?'

'Eight or nine miles.'

Rose thought quickly. 'Perhaps I could hire a pony and trap. I wouldn't need to trouble you to bring me every day.'

'You are a determined woman, Miss Perkins.'

'I am a very determined woman, Mr Sharpe.' She met his quizzical look with a defiant lift of her chin. 'I will do anything to help my brother, and he ought not to go before the judge looking like a vagabond.'

Bennett tucked her hand in the crook of his arm. 'If you were trained in law you would make a good barrister. We'll return to the inn and collect our things and head on for Portmorna. Vere is expecting us.'

Portmorna House was situated on a wooded headland. Built by Thomas Tressidick, who had made his fortune from the mining and export of copper at the end of the previous century, the house had been designed in the Palladian style and constructed from granite. The grey stone glinted in the afternoon sunshine, reflecting the light like a jewel in its woodland setting. The trees were bursting into leaf and alive with birdsong and the stirrings of spring. Rose was impressed and a little overawed to think that she was to be a guest in such a grand house. It seemed unfair that she would be staying in such a beautiful place while Billy was confined to a dank prison cell.

Bennett leaped from the carriage and hallooed to a footman who stood beneath a columned portico. 'Is my cousin at home, James?'

'No, sir. He be down at the mine office. Shall I send word of your arrival?'

'That won't be necessary. Take the young lady's valise to the blue room, please, and ask Jenifry to bring tea and cake to the drawing room.'

'Aye, sir. It shall be done.' James seized the valise and hurried into the house.

Bennett stood aside to allow Rose to enter the square entrance hall. Her first thought was that you could fit almost the whole vicarage into this single space. The staircase rose in a gracious sweep to a galleried landing, and light flooded in through tall windows. Bowls filled with hyacinths filled the air with their heady scent and fluffy yellow catkins dangled from hazel twigs that someone had thought to place in a silver urn. It was as if springtime had been captured by loving hands and brought into the house. Rose was tempted to make a comment on her surroundings, but thought better of it as a housemaid came hurrying towards them.

'May I take your outer garments, miss?'

'Yes, thank you.' Rose took off her bonnet and mantle and handed them to her, but in doing so she was conscious of her crumpled and travel-stained gown, and she felt shabby and underdressed.

Bennett tossed his greatcoat and top hat onto a chair. 'Thank you, Jenifry. We'll take tea in the drawing room and then you can show Miss Perkins to her bedchamber.'

'Yes, sir.' Jenifry bobbed a curtsey and hurried off, her small feet pitter-pattering on the marble-tiled floor.

'You'll meet my cousin at dinner,' Bennett said as he led the way to the drawing room. He opened the door and ushered Rose inside.

Once again she was staggered by the size and elegance of the south-facing room, which was furnished tastefully, but with an eye to comfort. She took a seat by the fireplace, and sank into the cushioned depths of the armchair. Bennett tossed another log onto the glowing embers, prodding it into place with the toe of his boot. He glanced down at her. 'You'll feel better for something to eat and drink. It's been a long day.'

'I keep thinking of Billy in that dreadful place. I know I promised him fresh clothes but I've brought nothing of his with me.'

'Don't worry, there are chests filled with garments that will fit him, and I'll see that he has a razor and shaving soap. You mustn't bother yourself with details, the main thing is to keep his spirits up and I suspect you've done that already.'

'Why are you being so kind to us?' Rose asked curiously. 'You and your cousin have every reason to dislike my family.'

'Billy wasn't to blame.' Bennett took a seat opposite her. 'Gawain was a wild boy. He was always in trouble of some sort from the time he could toddle. He was born to die young, that's what my father used to say, and I think he was right. There are some people who invite disaster, and Gawain was one of them.'

'Are you saying that he deserved to die?'

'Certainly not, but if you believe in fate or destiny, whatever you like to call it, then Gawain was destined to come to a sticky end.'

'I don't understand,' Rose said slowly. 'How can you say a thing like that?'

'My cousin mixed with a bad lot. There are families in the village who seem to breed their sons for the single purpose of filling Bodmin Gaol. As a youth Gawain preferred their company to that of his peers. I'm convinced that I know the identity of the man who stabbed him, and I intend to prove it.'

'Can you tell me who it is?'

'It won't mean anything to you, but the Penneck family are well known in these parts, or should I say notorious? Gryffyn Penneck used to work in the quarry until he was caught in a rock fall and suffered a badly broken leg, which left him partially crippled. My uncle gave him work in the gardens, but he's a surly fellow and it's hard to know what goes on in his head. There's been talk of the family being involved in smuggling, and Gryffyn's sons, Day and Pasco, have been in and out of prison since they were boys.'

'And you think that one of them might have killed Gawain?'

'Pasco drinks too much. He was always jealous

of his brother's friendship with Gawain, and he and his father blame the Tressidicks for an accident that was nobody's fault. These things happen in the mining business.'

'So you think Pasco is the murderer?'

Bennett turned away and walked to one of the windows overlooking the harbour. He stood with his hands clasped tightly behind his back, staring at the view. 'Gawain and Billy came down from Oxford with two of their undergraduate friends. They were drinking in the pub when an argument started between them and the Penneck brothers. The landlord threw them out and a fight ensued. They were all very drunk but Gryffyn put a stop to the fracas and sent them all on their way, or so he says. Day and Pasco swear their innocence, as do Toby Wilkes and Edric Kenyon.'

'What happened then?'

'Gawain was found in the woods next morning. He'd been stabbed to death, but the knife was never found. Billy, Toby and Edric were discovered nearby in a drunken stupor. None of them remembered anything after leaving the Saracen's Head, but Billy's coat was covered in blood even though he had no wounds to show for it.'

Rose frowned, remembering a conversation they had had previously. 'You were very interested in the fact that Billy is left-handed. How does that affect the case?'

'I saw my cousin's body, Rose. I'm not an expert, but I'd swear that the fatal wound was inflicted by a right-handed person. I doubt if that would sway a jury, but it's a fact I might use if things don't go our way.'

'Is Pasco right-handed?'

'Yes, he is and so is his brother.'

Rose stood up and crossed the floor to stand beside him. She gazed out at the sweep of the bay. The sun was low in the sky now, bathing the ships in the harbour with its last golden rays, and casting long purple shadows on the lawn. A thin mist veiled the treetops, curling like fingers around the tree trunks. There was an aura of mystery, bringing to mind the legends of long ago that seemed to haunt the Cornish landscape. She could feel herself falling under its spell, but she dragged her thoughts back to the present.

'Do you think Pasco was responsible for the blood on Billy's jacket?'

'You're very shrewd. Do you always go straight to the heart of the matter?'

'I'm used to listening to people,' Rose said simply. 'My mother is an invalid and I've been helping in my father's parish since I was fourteen or fifteen. I visit people in their homes and they unburden themselves to me, but sometimes their true meaning is in what they don't say. It can become clear in their tone of voice or a look in their eyes, or simply knowing the family's circumstances.'

He turned to face her. 'I find that fact that you've been leading a double life intriguing. How do you equate the two?'

'I don't like deceiving my parents, but I don't feel guilt or shame for what I've been doing because it's for Billy, although I'd be lying if I said I didn't enjoy performing on stage.'

'Beauty, honesty and loyalty,' Bennett said, smiling. 'I never thought to find all three in one woman.'

Rose felt the blood rush to her cheeks, but she responded to the mischievous twinkle in his eyes with a chuckle. 'You make me sound like a pet dog.'

'I'm very fond of dogs.' He laughed and she noted that his eyes crinkled at the corners, softening the harsh contours of his face.

'You should laugh more often,' she said seriously.

He looked round as the door opened and Jenifry hurried in bearing a tray of tea and some small yellow cakes. 'Saffron buns.' Bennett nodded with approval. 'You're honoured, Rose. My cousin's cook keeps these for special occasions only.'

Jenifry placed the tray on a sofa table. 'Mrs Vennor says they be for the maid who has come to save Mr William from the hangman's noose.'

'Yes, thank you, Jenifry. That will be all for now, and thank Mrs Vennor for the saffron buns. They're a particular favourite of mine.'

'Yes, sir.' Jenifry curtsied and left the room.

Rose took a seat on the sofa and picked up the teapot. She shot an apologetic glance at Bennett. 'I'm sorry. I'm so used to pouring the tea. I suppose I should have asked you first.'

He held up his hands. 'Please do the honours, Rose.

I myself am not very domesticated. When I'm in chambers I have rooms in Star Yard and I always dine out.'

She poured the tea and handed him a cup. 'And when you are not in chambers, where do you live then?'

'I suppose this is my real home. I was born here and my mother died when I was two. My father was killed in a hunting accident when I was just seven, and my uncle took me in. He raised me as his own, and Vere and Gawain were like brothers to me, which is why I won't rest until I have his murderer brought to justice.' He sipped his tea. 'You must try one of Mrs Vennor's saffron buns. She'll be mortally offended if you don't.'

Rose took one and tasted it. 'Delicious,' she said, nodding. 'I've never tasted anything like it, but it's very good.'

'I think you'll be comfortable in the blue room,' Bennett said thoughtfully. 'If there is anything you need, just ask Jenifry. She'll look after you.'

Later, in her room Rose discovered that Jenifry had unpacked for her and had laid out fresh clothes. 'There's warm water on the washstand, miss. If you'll give me your gown, I'll rinse it through for you and hang it in the drying room.'

Rose nodded her head. 'Thank you, Jenifry. That's very kind of you. I'm afraid the smell of the prison still clings to the material.'

'Is it very bad there, miss?' Jenifry avoided meeting Rose's curious gaze. 'I wouldn't like to think of Mr William being treated like a common criminal.' Bright spots of colour flamed her cheeks. 'I mean, he be a nice gentleman and none of us believe that he killed Mr Gawain.'

'It is what one might expect a prison to be,' Rose said carefully. 'But it won't be for much longer. I'm certain that justice will prevail and my brother will be exonerated at the trial and released.'

'You might like to rest awhile, miss,' Jenifry suggested, turning her head to gaze out of the window while Rose took off her soiled gown. 'Dinner is served when the master returns from the quarry. I'll come and tell you when it's time – that's if you wish me to.'

'I do. Thank you, Jenifry.' Rose handed the garment to her. 'I would be grateful if it could be laundered as soon as possible. I travel light.'

'It shall be done, miss. I'd do anything to help free Billy, I mean, Mr William.'

Rose was suddenly alert. Intuition told her that there was something more than a casual acquaintance between her brother and Jenifry. 'Just a moment, please.'

'What is it, miss?' Jenifry paused in the doorway.

'You seem to care what happens to Billy, and yet you could only have met him briefly.'

Once again colour suffused Jenifry's face. 'Not exactly, miss. He's been here a good few times since Mr Gawain started at the university. They be good friends and got up to such larks, although it isn't my place to say so.'

'I get the impression that you like my brother, Jenifry.'

'It bain't my place to think good or bad of my betters, miss.' Jenifry opened the door. 'Is there anything else I can do for you?'

'No, thank you, but I would be grateful if you would show me to the dining room when dinner is about to be served . . . This is a very big house and I fear I might get lost.'

A wide smile transformed Jenifry's face, and in that moment Rose could see what might have attracted her brother to the maidservant. 'It will be my pleasure, miss.' Jenifry left the room, closing the door quietly behind her.

Rose sank down on the bed. 'Billy, what have you done?' she said softly. 'I hope you haven't been flirting with the poor girl.'

An hour later, washed, dressed and with her hair brushed and confined in a chignon at the nape of her neck, Rose was seated by the window as the last vestige of daylight faded into darkness. Pinpricks of light from the village and the vessels moored in the harbour twinkled merrily like dozens of tiny fireflies. She turned with a start at the sound of someone tapping on the door. 'Come in.'

Jenifry stuck her head round the door. 'The master is in the drawing room, miss. He requests the pleasure of your company.'

'Of course.' Rose stood up, smoothing the creases from her skirts. 'Lead on.'

She followed Jenifry downstairs, and was feeling apprehensive but also extremely curious as she entered the drawing room.

Bennett was seated by the fire, but he stood up and made the necessary introductions.

Vere Tressidick was younger than Rose had imagined. Compared with Bennett's dark, brooding looks and powerful personality, Vere seemed pale and slight. His clean-shaven face and small neat features gave him a boyish look, but his grey eyes were shrewd and calculating and his thin lips suggested a stubborn streak. He wore his light brown hair cropped short like a military man and he held himself erect, as if attempting to make himself appear taller.

'How do you do, Miss Perkins?' His voice was surprisingly deep and his tones clipped. 'It is a pity we meet in such dire circumstances.'

'How do you do, sir?' Rose inclined her head. 'I have great hopes for my brother's acquittal and I have great faith in Mr Sharpe.'

'Indeed.' Vere did not sound impressed. 'We will have to wait and see. One can never be certain of the outcome in a case like this.'

'But you don't think Billy killed your brother, do you, sir?'

'No, I do not, but I am neither judge nor jury, and the Pennecks are a slippery bunch.' He turned to his cousin. 'Are they not, Bennett?'

'They are, but they are also well known to the judiciary in these parts. I am confident that I can make a good case for Billy. The evidence is all circumstantial and there are no reliable witnesses. Scully might have some useful information when he arrives on Monday,' Bennett added casually. 'I sent him to Oxford to see if Toby and Edric can offer any more information. I am not beaten yet, Vere.'

Rose looked from one to the other, sensing tension between the two cousins. 'I'm truly grateful to you both and I am very sorry for your loss, Mr Tressidick.'

'Thank you, Rose.' Vere treated her to a hint of a smile. 'And you must call me Vere. We three have come together to prevent a miscarriage of justice.'

A knock on the door preceded James, who entered to announce that dinner was served. Vere proffered his arm to Rose. 'We don't employ a butler,' he said as if an explanation were needed. 'We live quite informally, as you will discover.'

'As do we,' Rose replied truthfully. 'I think your house is quite the most beautiful residence I've ever had the pleasure to visit.'

A genuine smile lit Vere's pale eyes. 'I think so too, even though I say so myself.'

Next morning Rose ate her breakfast in solitary state. Vere, so James informed her, had left early for the quarry and Bennett had gone to the stables. She was not very hungry and the silver serving dishes filled

153

with crisp bacon, devilled kidneys and buttered eggs might have tempted her at any other time, but she managed to eat a slice of toast, washed down with a cup of coffee. James stood in front of the laden sideboard, staring into space, but she could feel his silent disapproval. She finished her meal and stood up. 'My apologies to Mrs Vennor, James. I'm afraid I haven't done her excellent food justice, but I have little appetite this morning.'

He looked straight ahead. 'I'll pass the message on, miss.'

'I'll fetch my bonnet and mantle.' She was about to walk past him but he moved swiftly to bar her way.

'Jenifry will do that for you, miss.' He opened the door for her. 'If you'd like to wait in the hall I'll send her to you.'

'Thank you, James.' She realised that she had offended his sense of propriety, and that the servants had their own set of rules quite as rigid as those of their masters. She went into the hall and she did not have long to wait.

Jenifry appeared pink-cheeked and breathless from exertion. She set a portmanteau on the floor at Rose's feet. 'Mr Bennett packed this himself, miss. It contains clothes and such for Mr William.'

Rose shrugged on her mantle. 'Thank you, Jenifry. I'm sure my brother will be relieved to have some clean clothes at last.'

'I would have suggested it myself,' Jenifry said

shyly, 'but it weren't my place to say so. Gentlemen don't generally think of such things.'

'I know that Billy will appreciate the thought.' Rose put on her bonnet.

'The carriage is outside,' James announced, opening the double doors with a theatrical flourish.

Rose suspected that the servants were enjoying the drama of the occasion, which must be the talk of the village. She was about to pick up the case, but then she realised her mistake and stood back as James swooped upon it and carried it to the door. She stepped outside and was met by Bennett, who greeted her with a disarming smile.

'You're ready to go. That's excellent.' He handed her into the carriage and climbed in beside her. 'Tell me about Billy,' he said as the vehicle lurched into motion.

Startled, Rose stared at him. 'What do you want to know?'

'I've only met him on a couple of occasions, apart from visiting him in prison, and I know that Gawain thought a lot of him, but you can tell me what sort of son he is, and if he is a good brother to you and Cora. These are small details, but I want to build up a picture of Billy as a person when I defend him in court. A good son and a loving brother would have more appeal than a wayward, selfish sort of fellow. The fact that Billy is studying theology at Oxford, and is in his last year at university, should help, but he and his friends were involved in a drunken brawl, and that won't go down too well with the jurors. I'm afraid that Billy's friendship with the Penneck brothers will also go against him.'

Rose leaned back against the squabs. The full impact of the case against Billy hit her with the force of a physical blow. Until this moment she had thought that simply being there to cheer and comfort him was enough. It had not occurred to her that a jury might see a very different young man standing before them than the brother she knew and loved. Her mouth was dry and her heart was racing as she struggled to find the right words to describe him in the most favourable light. 'He might have fallen amongst bad company,' she said passionately, 'but Billy is a good man.'

Bennett's winged eyebrows drew together in a frown. 'That's just it, Rose. Billy is young and he is easily influenced. The Penneck brothers are his equal in years, but they've been in trouble since they were boys. Their story is that they staggered home immediately after the fracas, and their father is prepared to swear to that in court. I'm hoping that Toby or Edric might have some slight recollection of what occurred. If not, then it will be up to me and my powers of persuasion to convince the jury that Billy could not and would not have killed Gawain.'

Rose gulped and swallowed, turning her head away to gaze out of the window with unseeing eyes. 'I had hoped it would be more straightforward. Now I'm really scared.'

He reached out to take her hand in his. 'It's not going to be easy, but you have to trust me, Rose.'

The firm pressure of his fingers on hers was reassuring. She twisted her lips into a semblance of a smile. 'I do, Bennett.'

Billy was in a bullish mood, although Rose detected a feverish glint in his eyes that did not bode well. He seemed inordinately pleased with the change of clothes and the prospect of being able to shave, although the warder made certain that Bennett had the cutthroat razor in his possession when they left the cell. 'Can't be too careful,' he said, pocketing the silver coin Bennett had pressed in his hand. 'The rest of the Portmorna gang be in the gaol now.'

'What do you mean by that?' Bennett demanded angrily. 'My client isn't a member of a gang.'

'That's as maybe, sir. I only goes by what I hear.' The warder shifted from one foot to the other. 'The revenue men brought the Penneck brothers in last evening. Caught red-handed, they do say, and up before the judge on Monday, like your boy.'

Rose clutched Bennett's arm. 'I thought Billy was going to trial on Wednesday.'

The warder puffed out his chest. 'It's Monday for certain, maid. Date of the Assizes was changed.'

'Why wasn't I told of this?' Bennett demanded angrily.

'It bain't no business of mine, sir. You'd best speak to the Governor if you have a complaint to make.'

'Indeed I will. Take me to him now.'

'I doubt he'll see you, sir.'

'Nevertheless you will show me to his office and he will hear me out.'

The warder glanced anxiously at Rose. 'Bain't no place for a maid.'

'I'll wait in the carriage,' Rose said hastily. 'Do what you must, Bennett.'

The warder escorted her from the prison and she went to sit in the carriage. It was an anxious time and she could have cried with relief when she saw Bennett emerge from the gaol. She waited impatiently as he crossed the prison yard and the coachman leaped to the ground to open the door.

'What did the Governor say?' Rose asked anxiously, barely giving Bennet time to climb in and take his seat opposite her.

'It can't be helped. The Assize judge was taken ill and died of apoplexy, and his successor was already attending a session at Truro on Wednesday. The whole thing had to be moved at great inconvenience to everyone, especially to us.'

'Will Edric and Toby get here in time?'

'I believe a telegram was sent.'

'But it will be all right?'

Bennett leaned out of the window. 'Home, Yelland. We're done here for today.'

There was no visiting at the gaol on Sunday and Bennett shut himself away in the study, working on

Billy's case. Rose attended church with Vere and was aware of the curious glances she attracted from the villagers, although it was obvious that everyone knew exactly why she was in Portmorna.

Gryffyn Penneck was waiting outside when they left after the service. He stepped out in front of Vere and stood, cap in hand, staring down at his booted feet. 'I need your help, sir.'

Vere drew himself up to his full height. 'If it concerns your sons you must realise that you are wasting your breath, man.'

Gryffyn raised his head, and his lips trembled. 'They are but boys, sir. They will go to prison for a long time. It were a keg of brandy or two, that's all it were.'

'In days gone by they would have been hanged for such a crime or transported to Australia. Your sons have disgraced your name, and they deserve whatever punishment is meted out to them.'

'At least they weren't in the dock for murder.' Penneck curled his lip, turning his attention to Rose. 'Your brother will hang for what he done, miss. Be sure of that.' He turned his back on them and walked off.

'Don't listen to him,' Vere said, taking Rose by the arm. 'Justice will be done.'

Rose barely slept that night for worrying about the outcome of the trial next day. She was afraid for Billy, should the case go against him, and a feeling of helplessness made it even harder to bear. She was up early, but when Jenifry failed to arrive with her morning cup of tea and the hot water for the washbowl, she decided to get dressed. Bennett had reluctantly agreed that she could accompany him to Bodmin, and she was both excited and nervous as she went downstairs, but the sound of voices in the entrance hall made her stop and glance over the balustrade. The front door was open and Bennett was talking to a messenger.

'It isn't possible,' Bennett said loudly. 'You must have it wrong.'

'Indeed I don't, sir. I had it from the bailiff himself. I tell you it happened last night. There's no denying the facts.'

Rose descended the stairs at a run. 'What's happened, Bennett? What's wrong?'

Chapter Nine

The messenger vaulted onto his horse and rode off. Bennett stood motionless, staring after him.

'What's happened?' Rose asked anxiously. 'Tell me, please.'

He turned to face her, a deep frown etched on his brow. 'There was a breakout from the prison last night. The Penneck brothers and Billy escaped, by what means I have no idea, but it doesn't bode well for any of them. It will be seen as an admission of guilt.'

'Oh, no!' Her hand flew to her mouth. 'Why would he do such a thing?'

James had been standing to attention by the front door, but he stepped forward, clearing his throat nervously. 'Excuse me, sir. It may be nothing, but there be no sign of Jenifry this morning. Mrs Vennor wondered if she was took to her bed poorly, but she's nowhere to be found.'

'I thought there was something, at least on her part.' Rose cast her mind back to her conversations with Jenifry. 'Do you think she's involved in this?'

'She's the least of my worries.' Bennett nodded to James. 'Have my horse saddled and get some of the estate workers together. We'll go in search of them.'

'Begging your pardon, sir,' James said in a low voice, 'but if it were so well planned I dare say they be in France by now, or well on their way.'

'I'll take a chance on that. I'll ride into the village and speak to Jenifry's mother, and you can head a search of the woods. They might have gone to ground.'

'Aye, sir. It will be done.' James let himself out of the house and Bennett was about to follow when Rose caught him by the arm.

'What can I do?'

'Stay here. Scully will be arriving this morning. Keep him here until I return.'

'I'd rather go with you. I could reason with Billy and persuade him to return to prison and await his trial.'

He gave her a long look. 'I've no real hope of finding him, Rose. I'm going to talk to the local fishermen and try to find out if any small craft are missing. James is right. The most likely way of escape would be by boat, and the Penneck brothers are both experienced seamen.'

'I can't believe that Billy would run away like this.'

'You saw the state he was in. He knew that the odds were against him.'

'But you said you were confident of getting an acquittal.'

'I have to be confident of my own abilities, and I'm still of the opinion that it is possible, but Billy wasn't thinking straight. Prison does that to a man. I've seen it happen many times.' He laid his hand on her shoulder. 'I'll do everything I can. I promise you that.' He snatched up his top hat, gloves and riding crop and hurried out onto the carriage sweep.

Rose hesitated, undecided as to what to do next. She looked up and saw Vere making his way down the wide staircase.

'What's happened, Rose?'

'The Penneck brothers broke out of the gaol, and Billy's gone with them.' She took a deep breath. The desire to cry had left her and was replaced by anger. 'How could he be so stupid? He knew that Bennett would do everything in his power to secure his release.'

Vere moved swiftly to her side. 'Don't upset yourself, Rose.'

'This is a disaster. Everyone will assume that Billy is guilty.'

'There's little you can do, my dear. Come into the dining room and have some breakfast.'

'No, really. I've no appetite.'

'Starving yourself isn't the answer.' Vere took her by the arm. 'Come along, Rose. I insist.'

The last thing Rose wanted at that moment was to sit down to a formal breakfast with Vere, who at the best of times made her feel uncomfortable. Thoughts whirled around in her head like a swarm of angry wasps. Her main concern was for Billy, but she knew now that it would be almost impossible to keep the truth from her parents. They would have to know of their only son's disgrace, and his failure to stand up in court and defend himself would only add to their distress. She allowed Vere to lead her to the dining room and took a seat at the table.

He rang the bell and when no one came he rose to his feet and went to open the door. 'James.' His voice echoed eerily in the silent house. He returned to his place at the table. 'Where is he? And where is Jenifry? Has the world gone mad?'

'Bennett sent James to organise a search party in case Billy and the Penneck brothers are hiding somewhere on the estate. As to Jenifry, I fear that she has gone with the escapees. I suspected she had feelings for my brother, but I had no idea that they went so deep.'

Vere returned to his seat, pouting like a small boy denied a treat. 'I object to having my household turned upside down in this manner. I chose to believe the best of William, but now I see that I have been deceived. A guilt-free man would have fought to prove his innocence, and your brother has chosen to ally himself with criminals.'

'I'm so sorry,' Rose said softly. 'But you are wrong about Billy. I know he didn't do it, and had you seen him in gaol you might understand why he took such a desperate course.'

'I don't blame you, Rose. How could I? You have suffered too, and will have to bear the disgrace brought upon your good name.'

'Again, I'm sorry to disagree with you, but I will stand by my brother no matter what. Billy has been weak and foolish, but that doesn't make him a bad man. I'll never believe ill of him.'

Vere dismissed her argument with a wave of his hand. 'Please say no more. I don't want to hear William's name mentioned again, but you are still a welcome guest in my house. All I want now is my breakfast.' He picked up the bell and rang it vigorously.

Rose leaped to her feet. 'There doesn't seem to be anyone to hear you, sir. I'll go down to the kitchen and see what's happening.'

'No, you will not. I've never heard of such a thing.' Vere's offended tones followed Rose as she left the room, but she chose to ignore him.

The heat in the kitchen almost took her breath away, and the savoury aroma of frying bacon and hot coffee filled the steamy atmosphere.

Mrs Vennor looked up from the saucepan she was stirring and her mouth dropped open. She stepped away from the range and bobbed a curtsey. 'What can I do for you, miss?'

'Mr Tressidick would like his breakfast, but there doesn't seem to be anyone to answer the bell.'

'James should be in the dining room, miss. I'm afraid I don't know where Jenifry is.'

'You must be aware of what's happened,' Rose said, choosing her words with care. 'None of us knows exactly what occurred last night, but Mr Bennett has sent James on a mission.'

'Breakfast is ready, miss. I'll send Tamsin to the dining room, if you'd be kind enough to take my sincere apologies to the master.'

Rose picked up a salver filled with bacon and buttered eggs. 'I will, of course, and I'll take this. If Tamsin could bring the coffee and some toast I think that will be sufficient.' She ignored Mrs Vennor's protests and the startled looks from the young kitchen maid.

Vere looked even more surprised when Rose entered the dining room and set the salver on the table in front of him.

'I know this isn't done,' she said with a rueful smile, 'but this is far from being a normal day, so I hope you'll make allowances.'

He sat back in his chair, eyeing her with interest. 'What a surprising young woman you are, Rose.' He served himself from the dish. 'I insist that you eat something. It's a crime to waste good food.'

Somewhat reluctantly Rose took her seat at the

table just as Tamsin arrived with the coffee and a rack of toast. She placed them on the table and scuttled out of the room before either of them had a chance to speak.

Vere poured coffee for himself and for Rose. 'Mrs Vennor had better see about hiring a maid to take Jenifry's place. I have business to attend to, or I would stay and keep you company.'

'I understand.' Rose stared at the plate of food in front of her, but her thoughts were with Billy and she was growing more worried with each passing minute. If the fugitives had stolen a boat they could be in even more desperate trouble. A vision of them clinging to the hull of their craft after being capsized by stormy seas in the middle of the Channel brought her out in a cold sweat. She knew that her imagination was running away with her, and she made an effort to eat, but each mouthful tasted like sawdust and she was finding it difficult to swallow.

'Tell me about yourself, Rose.'

She looked up with a start. 'I'm sorry, sir?'

'I know nothing about you other than the fact that you are Billy's sister and your father is a clergyman.' Vere pushed his plate away, studying her with an intense look. 'You will have had a sheltered upbringing and yet you were prepared to come amongst strangers unaccompanied, risking more than your reputation. Apart from that, you do not strike me as a woman of means, so how did you propose to pay for your brother's defence?'

Rose sipped her coffee. She had been tempted to make up a convincing story, but there seemed little point in lying. 'Very well, since you ask, I'll tell you the truth. As a child I longed to follow my aunt onto the London stage. She taught me and my sister to dance and gave us singing lessons, in secret of course, because our father is very strict and would have forbidden such a thing. Then, when Cora and I realised that we had to find the money to pay for our brother's defence I saw a billboard inviting singers and dancers to audition at Fancello's saloon.'

Vere listened intently, his gaze never faltering from her face as she related the series of events that had brought her to Cornwall.

'I'm shocked, but I'm also amazed,' he said when she came to a halt. 'You are a redoubtable young lady, and you deserve better than a feckless brother who thinks only of himself.'

'That is very unfair, sir.' She pushed back her chair and stood up. 'You are entitled to your opinion, but I cannot remain here and listen to such talk. As soon as I know what has happened to my brother I'll return to London. Until then I will have to trespass a little longer on your hospitality.' She was about to leave when the door opened and Tamsin burst into the room. Her face was flushed and she hopped from one foot to the other.

'Please, sir. There's a gentleman at the door. He be from the newspaper and he says he won't go until he's spoken to you.'

Vere rose to his feet. 'I knew this would happen. Show him to my study, girl, and don't tell him anything, or you will be sent away without a character. Do you understand?'

'I do, sir.' Tamsin raced from the room, slamming the door behind her.

'Dealing with untrained servants makes me wish that I had a wife to sort out problems below stairs,' Vere said crossly. 'Keep out of sight, please, Rose. The fellow will never leave if he spots you. I'll deal with him.' He walked to the door, hesitated and turned to her with a hint of a smile in his pale eyes. 'You are more than welcome here. If I've said anything to make you feel uncomfortable I hope you will forgive me.'

'We are all suffering in our own way,' she said earnestly.

He acknowledged her response with a nod and hurried from the room. Rose sank down on her chair. There seemed little that she could do other than to await Bennett's return and hope that he would have some news of Billy. She jumped as the door opened again, but it was Tamsin who entered.

'I've come to clear the table, miss. If that be all right with you, so Mrs Vennor told me to say, and I very near forgot.' She attempted to curtsey and almost toppled over.

Rose had a sudden urge to laugh, but she managed to control herself. 'That's all right, Tamsin. You may do your work. I think I might go for a walk as it's such a lovely day.'

'The newspaper man give me a penny,' Tamsin said in a confidential whisper. 'He asked me if you was still here, but I never told him nothing, miss. He give me the penny anyway, and I shall spend it on toffee. I'll eat it all even if it do give I the belly-ache.'

Rose left the room wondering how she was going to fill in the time before Scully arrived. She was desperate to do something other than wander aimlessly round the garden. There were so many unanswered questions, and waiting patiently for news was simply not in her nature. She started off in the direction of the drawing room, where at least she would have a good view of the harbour, but found herself walking past Vere's study. The temptation to stop and listen was too great and she bent down, placing her ear against the keyhole.

'If you print this story I will sue your newspaper and put you out of business.' Vere's words rang out so loudly that she straightened up, glancing round anxiously in case anyone else was in the vicinity.

'You cannot stop me, sir. You can either give me your version of the truth or I will write what I think to be an accurate story. By tomorrow the escape from Bodmin Gaol will be in the London papers, no matter what you say.'

Rose clapped her hand to her mouth to stifle a cry of anguish. A vision of her father's face as he read the account of Billy's imprisonment for murder and subsequent escape flashed before her eyes, causing her physical pain. The sound of angry voices and the scrape of a chair on highly polished floorboards was followed by quick footsteps. She turned and ran. With no plan in mind she found herself outside on the carriage sweep. Her heart was pounding and she stopped to take deep breaths of clean country air perfumed with almond blossom and spring flowers. The faint sound of a horse's hoofs made her shield her eyes from the sun as she peered into the distance. She could not make out who was approaching at a gallop, but her heart beat even faster in the hope that it was Bennett returning with news. She did not hear the footsteps behind her until too late, and she spun round as someone tapped her on the shoulder. It was something of a shock to find herself looking into the face of a small, thin man with oily brown hair slicked back from his forehead. He had a knowing, arrogant look that made her want to back away.

'You must be the maid from London,' he said with a satisfied grin. 'My name is Enoch Frayne, of the *West Briton and Cornwall Advertiser*. I heard you were here, but Mr Tressidick denied all knowledge of you. I find that curious, don't you, Miss Perkins?'

'I have nothing to say to you.' Rose held her head high. 'Not a word.'

'Don't you want to defend your brother, Miss Perkins? Don't you think that breaking out of prison and running away is an admission of guilt?'

'My brother is innocent,' Rose said breathlessly. 'He is a good man.'

'Do you know where he is now?'

'Of course not.' Rose glanced over her shoulder, hoping against hope that it was Bennett who had just brought his horse to a halt, but it was Scully who dismounted. Even so, she greeted him with a cry of relief. 'Mr Scully, this man is a reporter from the local newspaper.'

'Scully.' Enoch Frayne took out his notebook and pencil. 'What connection do you have with this case?'

Without uttering a word, Scully seized Frayne by the scruff of his neck and marched him down the carriage sweep. Frayne's protests startled a clamour of rooks and they rose from a stand of beech trees, squawking loudly. Rose watched in awe as Scully reached the wrought-iron gates and pitched the unfortunate reporter through them. Frayne landed in an undignified heap on the dusty road. She could not hear what he was saying as he scrambled to his feet, but he did not look happy.

She ran to greet Scully. 'Thank you for that. He was determined to get a story no matter what I said.'

'He'll go ahead anyway,' Scully said, shrugging. 'I need to speak to Sharpe. Is he at home?'

Rose shook her head. 'No, he went down to the village to make enquiries. Have you heard the news?'

'It's all over Bodmin.'

'The estate workers are searching the woods in case Billy and the Penneck brothers are hiding there.'

Scully took off his battered bowler hat and wiped his brow. 'I travelled from Oxford last night, together with the two witnesses. They're staying at the inn, but I hired this nag in Bodmin and rode here.'

'You must be hungry and tired.' Rose led the way into the house. She hesitated, not knowing whether to treat Scully as a guest or a servant, but she was saved from making the decision by the sudden appearance of Vere.

'If you're another reporter I'll have you thrown out,' he said angrily.

'No, Vere, this is Todd Scully. You may remember Bennett mentioned him when we first arrived. He's been making enquiries in Oxford and he needs to speak to Bennett,' Rose explained hastily. 'He's just ridden all the way from Bodmin.'

Vere gave Scully a cursory glance. 'See to his needs, Rose. I'm going to the quarry.'

'What shall I tell Bennett?'

'I don't have to explain my moves to my cousin. I'll be back in time for dinner, but he knows where to find me.' Vere picked up his top hat and cane as he left the house, heading in the direction of the stables.

Scully met Rose's worried look with a chuckle. 'Don't worry about me, miss. I'm used to all sorts. Just point me in the direction of the kitchen and I'll wheedle some grub out of the cook. I'm used to taking care of meself.'

'I can do better than that,' Rose said firmly. 'I'll

173

come with you and introduce you to Mrs Vennor. Then you can tell me everything you know. I'm so worried about Billy and I don't know what to do.'

Bennett returned at noon. Rose had been waiting and watching in the hope that someone would come bearing news of Billy. She hurried to meet him, but he shook his head.

'I've been everywhere and asked all those who might be able to help, but none of them are admitting to any knowledge of what went on last night. Jenifry's mother is quite distraught, the girl being her only surviving child, and it was impossible to comfort her. Gryffyn Penneck swears that he had nothing to do with the escape, and the police had already spoken to him, but he sticks to his story.'

'Mr Scully is here. He's having a nap in the morning parlour.'

'Did he get anything out of Billy's friends from Oxford?'

Rose shook her head. 'I don't know. He won't tell me anything, which is very frustrating. James returned an hour ago and said they'd combed the woods, finding nothing.'

'I think James might have been right, and the Pennecks had a boat waiting in one of the coves. They're probably safe in France by now.'

'It does look bad for Billy,' Rose said slowly. 'Worse still, a reporter from the local newspaper came here this morning. He spoke to Vere and I overheard him say that the whole sorry story will be in the London papers by tomorrow.'

'I'm sorry, Rose. I wish there was more I could do to help.'

'I have to return home. Cora and I tried so hard to keep Billy's plight from our parents, and now this . . .'

'I'd come with you, but I still have some business to attend to here. Scully will accompany you. He'll see you safely home.'

'Thank you.' She hesitated, not knowing quite what to say. 'I'll find the money to pay you what we owe. You need not worry about that.'

He held up his hand. 'I wouldn't hear of it. The case hasn't gone ahead so I won't claim a fee. It would be very unfair.'

'But you've worked so hard to prove Billy's innocence.'

'Sometimes things don't work out as they should, but I refuse to take a penny from you. Go home, Rose. Go back to the life you know, and I don't mean dancing on stage in front of louche men, slumming in the East End.'

'Things will never be the same,' she said sadly. 'I dread to think how my parents will react. I was hoping to go home with the news that Billy had been falsely accused and had been acquitted. Now it will be splashed all over the newspapers and everyone will know. My father might even lose his living because of it.'

'Now you're jumping to conclusions. Give your

father credit for being an intelligent and forgiving man. I'm sure those to whom he answers in the Church will have more wisdom than to condemn him for the misdeeds of his son.'

'I hope you're right. Thank you for everything, Bennett.' Rose's emotions were raw, and she could feel her whole world teetering on its axis. 'I doubt if I'll ever see you again, but I'll always be grateful for what you did for Billy.' Her voice shook and she averted her gaze, unable to look him in the eye. She waited for him to speak, but he remained silent, and she walked away.

The journey home next day was uneventful. Scully was not the most entertaining companion, and he fell asleep as soon as the train left the station, but he was an experienced traveller and knew exactly what to do and where to go when they changed from one train to another. He insisted on seeing Rose home, and they parted on the vicarage doorstep.

'Good luck,' he said tersely. 'I think you'll need it, girl.' He tipped his hat and strolled off, whistling.

Rose knocked on the door and waited. The moment she had been dreading had come. Scully had bought a copy of the *Daily Telegraph* from a stand at the station, and, although it was not headlines, the story of the gaol break featured largely on the second page. The fact that a clergyman's son was involved in a murder, and had escaped from prison, was in bold print and would have been hard to miss.

The door opened and Cora's wary expression dissolved into a wide smile as she threw her arms around her sister. 'Rose, you've come home at last.'

Rose held her at arm's length. Cora's pallor and the dark smudges beneath her blue eyes bore witness to the fact that the news had reached home. 'You've seen the newspapers then?'

'Come inside quickly.' Cora glanced nervously up and down the street. 'We've had reporters on the doorstep all day. I thought you were yet another of them.'

Rose hefted her valise over the threshold and stepped inside, closing the door behind her. 'So you know the whole story?'

'Only what we've read. Papa has taken it very badly.'

'I was hoping to tell him before it became common knowledge,' Rose said wearily. 'We left Portmorna House early this morning, but there were delays along the way. I saw Billy, but the news isn't good.'

'Leave your case,' Cora said firmly. 'Maisie will take it up to your room. Come into the parlour and tell me everything.'

'Let me take off my things.' Rose laid her bonnet on a chair and unbuttoned her mantle. 'Tell me what's been happening here. Have you heard from Mama? Is she recovering well?' She hung her garments on the oak hallstand and followed Cora to the parlour.

'I've rung for Maisie.' Cora took a seat at the small table where their mother used to preside over afternoon tea. 'Mama is doing very well in Lyme, but

Papa has only just received her letter saying that you left there several days ago, and now Billy's disgrace is public knowledge. All this has been a terrible blow to Papa, Rose. I've never seen him so distraught.'

'We must keep it from Mama at all costs,' Rose said firmly.

'Let's hope she hasn't seen the newspapers—' Cora broke off mid-sentence as the door opened.

Seymour stood motionless, staring from one to the other. 'So you've come home, Rose.'

'Papa, I'm so sorry you found out like this.' She made a move towards him, but his stern expression made her hesitate. 'We were going to tell you.'

'You were going to tell me,' he repeated dully. 'My own daughters decided to keep me in ignorance of the fact that my son had been accused of murder and imprisoned. Were you going to mention the fact that he consorted with common criminals and had escaped from prison without going to trial? Am I a child to be treated thus?'

'No, Papa. It wasn't like that.' Cora's voice broke on a sob. 'We wanted to tell you, truly we did.'

He fixed his stern gaze on Rose. 'You left your mother in Lyme Regis. She thought you had returned home, and the first I heard of your desertion was in a letter I received this morning. So where were you, miss? What part did you play in all this?'

She had expected him to be upset, but this cold, angry man seemed like a stranger. 'I couldn't tell Mama that I was going to Cornwall. I had to see Billy and tell him that we were doing everything we could to prove his innocence. I hired the lawyer Billy had chosen to represent him.'

'A lawyer?' Seymour stared at her in amazement. 'You, a girl without a penny to her name, employed a barrister to defend my son in court?'

'I know it sounds preposterous when you put it like that, Papa, but that's what I did. It was all perfectly proper. I stayed at Portmorna House and when I visited Billy in Bodmin Gaol I was accompanied by his lawyer, Mr Sharpe.'

'You behaved in the most reckless, improper manner and you seem to think I should accept it without question. How do you intend to pay for this man's services?'

'Mr Sharpe is an eminent lawyer, Papa. He has refused to accept payment because the case has not gone to court. He is a true gentleman.'

'And you, my girl, are a fool. You've not only deceived your mother and myself, but you've compromised your good name. I can't believe that a daughter of mine would behave in such a manner.'

'I was only doing what I considered to be my duty. I went to Cornwall to help my brother, and I kept it from you and Mama because I wanted to spare your feelings.'

'I don't know how I'm going to break this to the bishop.' Seymour clasped his hands together as if in prayer. 'My only recourse will be to tender my resignation. I will lose the living here and be forced

179

to retire, disgraced by my own flesh and blood.'

'You aren't being fair, Papa,' Cora protested. 'You mustn't blame Rose. She was trying to make things right.'

Seymour eyed her with a cold stare. 'And you are equally to blame. You kept the truth from me and you have behaved as no young lady should, let alone someone of your standing in the community.'

'What does he mean?' Rose demanded. 'What is all this, Cora?'

'Tell her,' Seymour's voice boomed out as if he were addressing his congregation. 'Confess.'

Cora blushed rosily and hung her head. 'It was just a walk, Papa. Nothing untoward happened.'

'I don't understand.' Rose looked from one to the other, confused by the sudden turn of events.

'Your sister crept out one evening to meet a man,' Seymour said through gritted teeth. 'The foolish girl allowed her head to be turned by a person of higher social standing, whose motives for dallying with a girl of Cora's class were highly suspect.'

'Gerard was not dallying with me,' Cora whispered. 'He is a gentleman in every sense of the word.'

'If he were such he would not have arranged a clandestine meeting. He was amusing himself at your expense, you silly girl.' Seymour held up both hands as a sign that the conversation was ended. 'You two are a great disappointment to me, and as to your brother, I never want to hear his name mentioned again.'

'That's so unfair, Papa,' Rose said angrily. 'Billy is innocent and he needs our help and support.'

'An innocent man would not have run away. I had high hopes of my son, but he has destroyed them with his drunken, loutish behaviour. I don't want to speak of this again.' He turned his back on them and was about to leave the room, but Rose was too angry to allow him to simply walk away.

'What are you going to do, Papa?'

'I'm going to see the bishop, and then I plan to leave for Lyme Regis. Your mother needs me, and I'm done with this life and with the children who have brought disgrace upon me. I won't be able to hold my head up in front of my congregation, and I blame you most of all Rose.'

'That is so unfair, Papa.' Rose forced herself to sound calm, although inwardly she was seething. 'Are you going to abandon us because Billy is in trouble?'

Seymour paused in the doorway. 'You girls seem to have all the answers. I have none.'

The door swung on its hinges and slammed shut.

'Oh, Rose.' Cora choked on a sob. 'What will we do now?'

Chapter Ten

Events moved so fast that Rose was beginning to think she was in the middle of a bad dream from which she might one day awaken, but for now she had to contend with a heart-broken sister, disgruntled servants and an uncertain future. What passed between the bishop and her father remained a mystery, but Seymour left for Lyme Regis next day and Joshua Hart took over the parish until such time as a permanent replacement could be found. Rose and Cora were given a month to find alternative accommodation, although Joshua assured them that he was quite content to remain in his lodgings until they were ready to leave.

Mrs Blunt threatened to retire to the country to live with her bachelor brother, although she had to admit that his cottage was tiny and he shared it with three large dogs, which according to her were nasty, hairy brutes. She assumed the air of a martyr about to be burned at the stake, and it took Joshua a whole afternoon to persuade her to stay on and look after him until they knew the identity of the next incumbent.

Cora was deeply distressed and when Gerard called one afternoon, inviting her to take a carriage ride and tea at Gunter's with him, Rose put her misgivings aside and encouraged her sister to accept.

She waited until Cora had gone to fetch her cape and bonnet. 'You will bring her home immediately after tea, Mr Barclay?'

Gerard inclined his head, smiling. 'Of course, Miss Perkins. I wouldn't dream of compromising your sister's good name.'

Rose eyed him suspiciously. Gerard Barclay was undoubtedly handsome and extremely charming, but he had been brought up in a world of wealth and privilege, and she suspected that he lived by a different set of rules from those he considered to be of the lower orders. He seemed sincere, but there was a mischievous twinkle in his blue eyes, and a twist to his full lips that made him seem to be permanently on the brink of laughter. She was Cora's sister and not her keeper, but regardless of what was considered proper, Rose's main concern was for Cora's feelings. She did not want to see her breaking her heart over a romance that was doomed to failure from the start. Gentlemen like Gerard Barclay did not marry girls from more humble backgrounds.

'We are in a difficult position, sir,' Rose said, choosing her words carefully. 'I don't know how much Cora has told you.'

Gerard's smile faded. 'She has been perfectly frank, Miss Perkins. I pay little heed to what the newspapers say. Dashed inconvenient, but forgotten in days. My ancestors lived through no end of scandals and yet here I am today, unbeaten and unbowed. You have nothing to fear from me.'

'I hope not,' Rose said with feeling. 'I do hope not.'

'Why are you both looking so serious?' Cora rushed into the room with the ribbons on her bonnet flying and her cape over her arm. 'I'm ready, Gerard.'

He stepped forward and before Rose could offer her assistance he had tied a bow, securing Cora's bonnet with the expertise of a lady's maid. He draped the cape around her shoulders. 'Now you're ready. It's lovely outside, but the breeze is chilly.'

Cora's smile was radiant and she blushed rosily. 'You take such good care of me, Gerard. I'm not made of glass.'

He raised her mittened hand to his lips. 'You are to me, my love.' He placed his top hat at a jaunty angle on his head before tucking her hand in the crook of his arm. 'Goodbye, Miss Perkins.'

'Goodbye, Rose.' Cora paused as they reached the door, turning her head to give her sister a worried glance. 'Are you sure you're all right? I mean, I could stay with you and help if you need me.'

Rose shook her head. 'Go and enjoy yourself. I

think I'll pay a call on Aunt Polly, and I'll see you at supper.'

When Rose told Polly all that had happened over the past few days she exploded like a firecracker. 'I always knew that man was a sanctimonious hypocrite. I warned Eleanor. I told her not to marry Seymour and I've been proved right. He bullied the life out of her and now he's turned his back on his children.' She threw up her hands in despair. 'And he had the gall to criticise me for taking up a career on stage. I could wring the wretched man's neck.'

'He had cause to be upset, Aunt Polly, but I can't condone his reaction.' Rose took a seat at a safe distance from her aunt's flailing fists, and out of reach of Spartacus and his unsheathed claws. He had been sleeping on the chaise longue, and was awakened from his nap by the pitch of his mistress's raised voice. He arched his back and hissed.

Polly flopped down beside him and stroked his ruffled fur. 'There, there, old chap, it isn't your fault. I blame it all on Seymour.' She looked up, frowning. 'So you will soon be homeless, and Billy has fled to foreign parts. A pretty kettle of fish, I must say.'

'What's done is done,' Rose said calmly. 'I was very angry with the way Pa behaved, but now there's little point in being so. I have to work out how Cora and I will support ourselves and where we will live.'

'Well, that's one problem I can help you with. You'll come here, of course. You can stay with me

185

for as long as you like. It's my duty to look after you, but it would also be my pleasure. I've missed your evening visits when you were working for that Italian fellow. Your accounts of performing on the stage brought back happy memories.'

'Are you sure, Aunt Polly?' Rose asked anxiously. 'Have you room for us? I feel obligated to bring Maisie, too. Mrs Blunt has made it plain that she disapproves of the poor girl, and I doubt if Joshua could afford to pay her a wage.'

'I'm sure we could make up a bed for her in one of the attics. I don't go up there these days, but I'll ask Ethel to make arrangements. Maisie got on well with her when she was here, and for all her foibles I wouldn't want to lose Ethel. She's a good cook, even if I do have to keep money and valuables out of reach of her sticky fingers. She can't help pilfering; it seems to be part of her nature, no matter how hard she tries to reform.'

'If you knew she was a thief, why did you give her employment?'

'I came across her one wintry night. She was scantily clad and barefoot, and had been badly beaten. Despite the fact that she was stick-thin I could see that she was with child and close to her time and so I brought her here. The babe died but Ethel survived, although she was close to death for a number of days. When she recovered she was too afraid to go out onto the streets in case her man found her and finished off what he had started, so

I gave her a job in the kitchen. It was as simple as that.'

'And now you're offering to take us in.' Rose studied her aunt's flushed face. 'You're a good woman, Aunt Polly. But for you we wouldn't have earned the money to pay Mr Sharpe. As it is, he wouldn't accept any money, but I still consider that it's a debt I have to repay.'

Polly nodded. 'I understand, and I would feel the same. Never be beholden to anyone, that's my motto.' She continued stroking Spartacus and he repaid her by purring and kneading the velvet uphol-stery of the chaise longue, digging up minute tufts of thread with his claws.

'We will find work,' Rose said firmly. 'You won't have to support us, Aunt Polly. We're young and healthy and we'll do virtually anything to earn our living.'

Polly's thin lips twisted into a smile. 'I hope Cora agrees with you. That young lady has ideas above her station, if you ask me. She always wanted to marry a rich man, and from what you say she seems to have one in tow at this moment.'

'I don't know . . .' Rose said cautiously. 'I'm not sure about Gerard. In spite of his fine words I have a horrible feeling that he will grow tired of Cora and that will be the end of her dream. I don't want him to break her heart.'

'She'll have to get used to that if she's to find the right fellow for her. My poor heart was broken so many times that I doubted if it would ever mend. The last time was the worst, but Sandro was married, and divorce was out of the question.'

'But you survived.'

'After a fashion, I suppose. Anyway, I'm still here and when I see what my poor sister has been through I'm glad I remained single. Your mother was once a bright and beautiful young girl. Cora is exactly like her, and I wouldn't want to see her light dimmed by a bullying husband.'

'Are you trying to say I'm like my father?' Rose could not resist the temptation to tease her aunt.

'No, dear, you are exactly like me. You won't take second best, and you have the courage to stand up for what you believe in. You have backbone, Rose. Never allow anyone to change you.'

'Thank you for everything,' Rose said, rising to her feet. 'We will take advantage of your kind offer, at least for the time being, but we won't impose on you any longer than necessary.'

Polly dismissed this statement with a wave of her hand. 'Don't mention it, dear. You'll be doing me a favour. I love having you girls around. You're the daughters I never had.'

'I must go now. I have to pack up everything in the house. Joshua has agreed to store the furniture until such time as the new vicar is appointed, but I'm hoping that he'll get the living. He's a decent man and he deserves it.'

'Is he now?' Polly raised an eyebrow.

Rose leaned over to kiss her on the brow. 'Don't get any ideas, Aunt Polly. I'm fond of Joshua, but not in that way, and I believe he has a soft spot for Cora, although she barely notices him. However, I refuse to be a matchmaker. I've other things to do.'

'And what about Billy? Are the police looking for him?'

'I don't know, although if he has left the country I assume they will leave it at that. He won't be able to return unless we can prove his innocence. That's partly why I don't want to touch the money we've saved so far. When Cora and I are settled I intend to contact Mr Sharpe and maybe he'll put Scully to investigating the case again.'

'Indeed.' Polly nodded wisely. 'And keeping in touch with Sharpe appeals to you, does it?'

Rose hurried to the door. 'It does, but it's purely business. Sorry to disappoint you again, Aunt Polly.'

Two weeks later Rose was packing the last of their mother's best china in a wooden tea chest when Joshua entered the kitchen. 'I'm sorry to intrude,' he said awkwardly. 'I just wondered if there was anything I could do to help.'

Rose smiled. 'Thank you, no. I've packed the last cup and saucer. It's very good of you to store them for us, Joshua.'

'Not at all. It's the least I can do and I hope perhaps when all this dies down that Mr Perkins might return. I'm sure the bishop would welcome him should he change his mind.'

'Papa won't do that,' Rose said with conviction. 'I hope the bishopric see sense and give you the living, Joshua. You've earned it.'

'Of course that would be wonderful, but I wouldn't want to profit at the expense of others.'

'You must take the opportunity should it be offered to you.' Rose wiped her hands on her pinafore, leaving smears of printer's ink from the newspaper she had been using to wrap the china. 'If you don't, someone else will. I'd like to think of you here, bringing up your family as we were in this lovely home.'

His pale face flushed to a warm pink. 'If there's nothing I can do to help I'd better go about my parish rounds, but if you or Cora should need anything, don't hesitate to ask.'

'Thank you.' Rose watched him leave with a feeling of regret. She was very fond of Joshua and she knew that Cora liked him, but she could not help wishing that her moonstruck sister could see the difference between Gerard's dashing good looks, money and position, and Joshua's kindly nature and good heart.

Gerard had called almost every evening since their father departed, and had taken Cora for numerous carriage rides and trips to the theatre, followed by intimate suppers in expensive restaurants. To his credit he brought her home at the end of the evening and parted with a chaste kiss on the cheek, but despite his exemplary behaviour, Rose had to agree with her father: the Honourable Gerard Barclay might be fond of Cora, but he would never marry her. She had discovered, having made discreet enquiries, that his family owned a large house in Russell Square and an estate in the West Country. In all probability his parents had an heiress earmarked for him, and he would be unlikely to defy them in favour of a clergyman's daughter, especially one whose family was tainted by scandal.

It was now common knowledge that the vicar had resigned because his son was a murderer and had broken out of prison before his trial. Rose heard whispers as she went about her daily routine; people turned their heads away as she walked down the street, and even those she had known since childhood were openly embarrassed to be seen in her company. Cora kept as much to the house as possible, living for the moment when Gerard came to take her away from her unhappy home. Joshua did all he could to dispel gossip, but the tittle-tattle had gone too far and wild stories went round, growing more outrageous and shocking with every telling. Rose tried to ignore them, but Cora wilted and refused to be comforted.

Rose had hoped that Bennett Sharpe might put in an appearance, but he was not an easy man to reach. She visited his chambers on several occasions, each time to be told he was either in court or out of town. She was beginning to think that he was avoiding her, but she had not given up, and she would not rest until her brother was cleared of Gawain's murder.

There was no word from Billy, which was hardly surprising, although it would have been a huge relief to know that he was safe. There had been no contact with her parents either, apart from a brief note from Isabel, informing her that both Eleanor and Seymour were well and had found a small cottage on the edge of the village where they intended to live. Rose was saddened, but not surprised by her father's attitude. Her initial angry reaction had faded into acceptance of the inevitable.

She abandoned an attempt to lift the tea chest, realising too late that she ought to have asked Joshua to take it up to the attic. She made a pot of tea and took a laden tray to the parlour where Cora was resting after a particularly upsetting session going through their childhood mementoes. They had discarded many of their old possessions, and this had left Cora in floods of tears. Rose was not sentimental about broken toys or dolls with missing limbs, but Cora clutched her tattered rag doll, Hephzibah, to her bosom, refusing to let her go even though one leg had been eaten by mice and the embroidered left eye had come unstitched, making the doll look as though she was winking. They had ended up with a large box filled with Cora's treasures and one less than half the size that contained items Rose thought might come in useful.

Cora had been dozing on the window seat. The spring sunshine turned her fair hair into a golden halo around her head and her flushed cheeks gave her the look of a sleeping cherub. Rose felt a stab of sympathy for her sister. Cora would always follow her heart, but that was not always a good thing. She turned away to pour the tea.

Cora opened her eyes with a start. 'I must have dropped off,' she said apologetically. 'I'll come and help you now, Rose.'

'No matter. It's done. It didn't take long.' Rose handed her a cup of tea. 'We should be ready to move into Aunt Polly's tomorrow or the next day.'

'It seems so unreal.' Cora sipped her tea. 'I can't believe this is happening to us. How will we live?'

'We will have to work. Papa can't afford to keep us now, and it looks as though he and Mama intend to make their home in Dorset.'

'But we have money, Rose. There's the sum we saved for Billy's trial. You said that Mr Sharpe refused to take it.'

'I don't want to touch that unless it's absolutely necessary. Bennett earned it and he should be paid.'

'We were good as the Sunshine Sisters and it was nice to have money, even if we didn't keep it for ourselves.' Cora almost spilled her tea as the sound of the doorbell echoed round the room. 'I wonder who that is.'

'If it's reporters I'll give them a piece of my mind,' Rose said angrily. She marched out of the room and across the hall. She wrenched the door open. 'Oh!' The angry words that had been on the tip of her tongue went out of her head. 'Signor Fancello. This is a surprise. You're the last person I expected to see.'

He stood on the doorstep, clutching his top hat in his hands. 'Might I come in, dear lady?'

Rose could see that he was genuinely distressed, and although her first instinct was to send him away, she took pity on him and stood aside. 'Of course. Come into the parlour. My sister and I were about to take tea, if you would care to join us.'

'I don't drink tea,' he said apologetically. 'It is an English habit to which I have not grown accustomed.' He followed her into the parlour.

'Signor Fancello.' Cora stared at him in amazement. 'What a strange coincidence. I was just speaking of our time as the Sunshine Sisters when you rang the doorbell.'

'Take a seat, signor,' Rose said, indicating a chair by the fireplace. 'You look upset. Perhaps a drop of brandy would soothe your nerves? I think there is some left in the cupboard.'

'That is kind. I don't deserve such generosity.' He produced a grubby handkerchief and blew his nose. 'I have had a run of bad luck since my little Clementia returned to Italy.'

'Don't you mean Clementino?' Cora asked gently.

'His mother and Alphonso went with him. I am left alone in London with no one to support me in my old age.'

Rose found what was left of her father's brandy and poured it into a glass. 'Sip this, signor. It will revive you.'

He drank it down in one greedy gulp. 'Thank you, *cara*. I am sorry to burden you with my sorrows.'

'You haven't told us anything,' Rose said, taking a seat opposite him. 'Why didn't you return to Italy with your wife and son?'

'At home they think I am an important impresario in London. How could I return and admit that I am a failure?'

'You have the saloon in Cupid's Court.' Cora stared at him, her face alight with curiosity. 'Surely you could find other acts?'

He shook his head. 'I could not pay the rent. I had to close down.' He looked from one to the other with a sly smile. 'All I need is one good act to get me back into the business.'

Rose eyed him thoughtfully. This was not the larger-than-life Fancello she remembered. He seemed to have shrunk both physically and mentally. His clothes hung on him and his dark curls were flattened to his head, and even his moustache had lost its spring.

'Are you offering us work, signor?'

'Er, not exactly, but you are thinking along the right lines.' Fancello's eyes brightened. 'I am offering to become your manager. I no longer have a premises, but I would find you employment, and make sure that you were treated with due respect, for a small fee, of course.'

'How much?' Rose fixed him with a hard stare.

'Ten per cent.' He cleared his throat nervously.

'That is a modest sum to take if I am to get you top billing.'

Cora opened her mouth to speak but Rose held up her hand. She concentrated her attention on Fancello. 'How much do you think we would earn for each performance?'

'You are interested then?'

'Only if you come up with a reasonable proposition, signor. It would have to be worthwhile financially.'

Fancello stood up and seemed to grow in stature as he puffed out his chest. 'You are talking to one of the best in the business. I am not an amateur, ladies.' He moved towards the doorway. 'I have already spoken to the manager of the Grecian Theatre, and he is very interested. You have an audition at ten o'clock tomorrow morning. Meet me at the stage door.'

'We haven't got our costumes,' Cora protested.

Fancello tapped the side of his bulbous nose and his moustache quivered with excitement. 'I kept them all. They are in a trunk in my lodgings.'

'You were taking a huge chance,' Rose said slowly. 'How did you know we would be interested in your proposition?'

'I read the newspapers, Miss Rose.' He opened the door. 'Tomorrow morning, ten o'clock, stage door of the Grecian.' He left them staring after him in stunned silence.

*

The Grecian Theatre was situated in Shepherdess Walk at the back of The Eagle tavern. It was within walking distance of the vicarage, and Fancello was waiting for them as arranged. He had brought a large carpet bag filled with their stage costumes, which he thrust into Rose's hand as they made their way to the dressing rooms. 'Start with "Long, Long Ago",' he said in a low voice. 'Then, if they like that, do something lively, like "A Life on the Ocean Wave" or "Little Brown Jug". Let them see how versatile you are, and don't forget to smile.'

Cora tossed her head. 'You don't have to tell us how to perform, signor.' She pushed past him and flounced into the dressing room. 'Wretched man,' she said when Rose closed the door on him. 'As if we need to be told how to do our act.'

'A lot depends on this.' Rose stepped inside and was gratified to find that it was twice the size of the dressing room in Cupid's Court. 'We have to be practical if we're to earn enough money to support ourselves.'

Cora started to undress. 'Let's get it over with, Rose. Gerard is taking me to the zoo this afternoon.'

'You must take this seriously,' Rose said firmly. 'You can't rely on Gerard.'

'I don't know what you mean.' Cora shook out the costume they had selected for their audition. 'Tighten my stays, please, Rose.' She glanced at her sister's reflection in the mirror. 'And don't look so disapproving. Gerard's intentions are strictly honourable,

197

like his title.' She giggled. 'I must tell him that. He thinks I'm funny as well as adorable. He's always telling me so, Rose. I don't think it will be long before he proposes.'

Rose tugged at the strings, drawing them in until Cora's waist was little more than a handspan. It was on the tip of her tongue to tell her sister that she was living in a dream world, but that would be too cruel, and besides that, she did not want to upset her just before they went on stage. 'You know him better than I,' she said mildly.

'I'm happy to say I do.' Cora stepped into her costume. 'His family own a town house in Russell Square and an estate on Bodmin Moor. It has a lovely name – Rosewenna Hall. Don't you think that sounds sweet and romantic? Gerard said he'd take me there one day.'

'I wouldn't count on it too much, Corrie.'

'Stop worrying about me. I can take care of myself, Rose. I just wish you could meet someone who made you feel like this. I'm truly happy in spite of everything.'

Rose struggled into her own costume. 'Do me up, and then I'm ready. The Sunshine Sisters are back in action. Fingers crossed.'

Fancello was waiting outside smoking a cheroot. He dropped it onto the floor and ground it out on the bare boards. 'Splendid,' he said, grinning. 'You will charm them, of that I am certain. Smile.' He led the way through the maze of corridors to the wings.

The audition seemed to go well. The pianist was

a professional and played with true feeling, unlike Alphonso's enthusiastic clattering on the keyboard. The theatre manager and his underlings seemed impressed with the Sunshine Sisters' performance, and Fancello descended upon them afterwards, beaming happily. 'You were splendid. Now I go to negotiate.'

Rose and Cora retreated to the dressing room and left him to earn his ten per cent.

'It's a beautiful theatre,' Rose said enthusiastically. 'It's so different from Fancello's seedy little saloon. I would love to perform here.'

'I'd almost forgotten how good it feels to hear applause.' Cora stepped out of her frothy costume. She paused, studying her figure in the full-length mirror. 'I don't think I've ever seen the whole of me in a mirror,' she said, giggling. 'It's always been one bit at a time. I really think I have quite a nice shape.'

Rose smiled benevolently. 'You are beautiful, Cora. You surely don't need me to tell you that.'

'Papa would be disgusted if he saw me now. Perhaps what we're doing is sinful, Rose. Have you thought of that? Maybe we are condemning our souls to eternal fire.'

'Nonsense. I don't believe that for a moment. We're not doing anything wrong. In fact, we'll be giving people pleasure and making them happy. That's if the theatre manager decides to give us a part in their show. We mustn't assume that we've been accepted just because they seemed to like us.'

They dressed in silence, waiting for Fancello to come and give them the news, good or bad.

Rose was adjusting her bonnet in the mirror when Fancello rapped on the door. She rushed to open it. 'Well?' she said eagerly. 'What did he say?'

Chapter Eleven

'It's a start, Aunt Polly.' Rose put down the heavy carpet bag she had carried all the way from the vicarage. 'We didn't expect to be top of the bill at the beginning. The Grecian isn't anything like the saloon.'

'Leave your case, dear. Tommy will take it up to your room,' Polly said with a careless wave of her hand. 'Come and sit down, Rose. You look exhausted. You should have allowed me to hire a carter to bring your things here.'

'You've done enough for us already. Besides which, we've had Joshua to help with the heavier cases and Maisie has done her bit. I can't thank you enough for agreeing to take her in. The poor girl was afraid we would abandon her.'

'I can use another pair of hands,' Polly said airily. 'There's always work to be done here. She can assist

Ethel in the kitchen and Tommy sometimes needs a helper.' She turned to him with a smile. 'You'd appreciate that, wouldn't you, boy?'

He had started up the stairs with Rose's case clutched in his hand. He looked back, nodding vigorously. 'I'd do anything for you, miss. I'd have been living on the streets if you hadn't taken me in when Fancello give me the boot. Me and Maisie get along fine. She's a proper caution.'

'I'm sure she is,' Polly said wryly. 'You can show her what to do, but let her settle in first.'

'Yes, miss.' He scuttled up the stairs, and Rose was surprised to see how fast he could move, even allowing for his odd crabwise gait.

'I'd better go back to the house and make sure we've left everything as it should be,' she said, sighing. 'Mrs Blunt has agreed to stay on, and Joshua is moving in tomorrow.'

'When do you start at the theatre, Rose?'

'Early next week, Aunt. We have just a few days to polish up our act and then we're on. It's exciting and it's scary.'

Polly smiled benevolently. 'You have inherited my talent, Rose. I'm not so sure about Cora. She's pretty and she has a sweet voice, but you have spirit and the push needed to go far. I have great faith in you, my girl. Don't let me down.'

'I'll try not to.' Rose kissed her on the cheek. 'I must go. This will probably be the last time I'll set foot in my old home.' She opened the front door to find Joshua, Cora and Maisie standing outside surrounded by bags and suitcases. 'Come in.'

'Where are you going?' Cora demanded crossly. 'We've only just arrived and you're going out.'

'I'll be back before you know it, and ready for a nice cup of tea, so don't eat all the cake, Cora.' Rose set off along the street without waiting for a response.

The sun was high in the sky and it was warm for the beginning of May, but ominous grey clouds crouched above the chimney tops, ready to empty a shower on the unwary. Rose quickened her pace and had just reached the garden gate when rain spilled from the sky in a sudden downpour. She ran up the path and used her key to open the front door. The house where she had been born and raised seemed suddenly alien and unwelcoming. Stripped of the small touches that had made it home, it was just four walls and a series of empty rooms. She had meant to check each one thoroughly, but memories of childhood came flooding back, and when she reached Billy's old room she was overcome with a feeling of sadness and loss. The patch of wallpaper behind the door was scuffed and the marks indicating their ages and height were fading, but they were still there. Billy had always been the tallest and she herself had outstripped Cora at an early age, but her sister had grown suddenly and now there was less than an inch between them. She ran her finger over the pencil lines and her eyes stung with unshed tears. She hurried from the room and closed the door, but then as if her presence had conjured up echoes from the past she heard a male voice.

Her heart did a sudden leap and she started down the staircase, hoping against hope that Billy had returned home, but as she rounded the curve of the stairs she realised it was not her brother who was talking to Mrs Blunt.

'Mr Tressidick?' Rose said, descending at a more sedate pace.

Vere turned his head. 'Miss Perkins. I'm sorry to intrude.'

'I just told this gentleman that you'd moved out, Miss Rose.' Mrs Blunt's tone was laced with disapproval. 'I didn't know you was upstairs.'

'I was just checking to make sure we hadn't left anything behind, and I wanted to be certain that you were satisfied with the arrangements.'

'It doesn't please me, miss. This is a sad day for St Matthew's and for the whole community. I never thought I'd live to see such goings-on.'

'Perhaps I could trouble you one last time for some tea?' Rose said tactfully.

'It's quite all right,' Vere said hastily. 'I called on the off chance of seeing you, Miss Perkins. I can see this is not the best time.'

'I'll bring tea to the parlour. My legs aren't as young as they used to be, but it's no trouble.' Mrs Blunt hobbled off in the direction of the back stairs, holding her hand to her hip as if to demonstrate that each movement was acutely painful.

Rose led the way to the parlour, which looked strangely denuded without the familiar things that had made it home. There were ghostly shapes on the wallpaper where pictures had been removed, and the mantelshelf was bare of ornaments and the black slate clock that had ticked away Rose's childhood. The empty grate made the room seem chilly and unwelcoming, and their footsteps echoed on the bare boards.

'I'm sorry that you've caught us at such an inopportune moment,' Rose said hastily. 'We had no choice but to find other accommodation.'

'I'm sorry.' Vere glanced at the shabby, threadbare sofa and chairs. 'What brought you to this, if I may ask?'

Rose sat on the sofa, folding her hands in her lap as she made an effort to sound calm and unruffled. 'The shock of Billy's downfall was too much for our father. He decided to retire and join Mama, who was recuperating from an illness in Dorset.'

'And he left you and your sister alone in London?' Vere's sharp response echoed off the bare walls. 'That seems harsh treatment and quite unfair.'

'Perhaps, but Papa has strong views and he was extremely upset.' Rose motioned him to sit. 'Please make yourself comfortable. Mrs Blunt will bring tea shortly.'

He perched on the edge of an upright chair. 'Presumably he has given up his living, so where will you and your sister go now?'

'We're not children, Mr Tressidick. Cora and I are quite capable of looking after ourselves. We're in the process of moving in with our aunt, who lives not too far from here.' Rose shot him a sideways glance. She did not know why he had chosen to visit them, but there was little point in lying. 'Aunt Polly takes care of women who are less fortunate than others.'

Vere raised an eyebrow. 'Does your father know you intend to live in such a place?'

'You make it sound disreputable. I can assure you that it is a charitable institution and perfectly respectable.' Rose stood up at the sound of footsteps and went to open the door for Mrs Blunt, who marched in and placed the tray on a table with a loud thud.

'Will you be staying long, Miss Rose?'

'No. I'll be off very soon. Thank you for the tea.' Mrs Blunt sniffed and retreated.

'Your cook seems unhappy,' Vere said drily. 'I can't say I'm surprised. Does Bennett know that you have lost your home?'

'It's not his concern.' Rose poured the tea and handed him a cup. 'I've tried to contact him because I hoped he might help me to find out what has happened to Billy. Maybe his man, Scully, could investigate on my behalf. I'm working now so I can pay.'

'You're working?'

'Cora and I will be appearing at the Grecian Theatre from next week onwards.' Rose met his disapproving glance with a straight look. 'I'm not ashamed to admit it.'

Vere abandoned his tea and stood up. 'Rose, I can't sit here and pretend that none of this matters.'

She stared at him in astonishment. 'I don't understand.'

'I'm not an emotional man. I don't display my feelings, but this is an unacceptable situation.' He gazed at her, apparently at a loss for words.

'I don't see that it's any of your business, Mr Tressidick. You were kind enough to allow me to stay in your home and for that I am very grateful.'

'Let me have my say. I know it must sound odd, but I came here because I had to see you again, Rose. I thought that once you had left Portmorna things would go back to how they were before you arrived, but I was mistaken. I've been a bachelor for so long that I couldn't imagine any other way of life, but your presence in my home changed everything. It was as if the house awakened from a long sleep, and I can't get you out of my mind, no matter how hard I try.'

'I don't know what to say.' Rose was suddenly nervous. This was not the same, self-assured man she had known only briefly in Cornwall. She glanced at the door, preparing to make a quick escape.

'I'm not mad,' he said as if reading her thoughts. He paced the floor. 'Well, perhaps it is a form of insanity.' He came to a halt in front of her and grasped her hands. 'In my clumsy way I'm trying to tell you that I have missed your company more than I would have thought possible. Your presence turned a mausoleum into a home, and without you my life seems strangely empty.'

Rose snatched her hands free. 'Please stop, Mr Tressidick. I'm not sure what it is you want of me, but please don't go any further.'

He hung his head. 'I'm sorry. I'm putting it very badly, but I've never asked a woman to marry me before.'

'This really is madness,' Rose said shakily. 'You don't love me. You don't even know me.'

'I know all I need to know, and if this isn't love I don't know what is.' He made a move towards her, but she held him at arm's length.

'I'm very flattered, but my answer has to be no. I'm sorry, Vere. I don't have any feelings for you. I'm not sure I even like you.'

'I don't think that matters, Rose. We could live together amicably, of that I am certain.' He hesitated, as if considering the matter in more depth. 'As far as I can see you are in need of a home, and I am in need of a wife.'

'I understand that, but my answer remains the same.' She stood up and edged towards the door. 'Now, if you'll excuse me I have things to do.'

'I should not have sprung it on you like this,' Vere said hastily. 'I don't know how to woo a woman. My life has been devoted to business matters and little else. Won't you at least think about my offer?'

She hesitated. 'I don't want to hurt your feelings, and I'm very flattered by your proposal, but even if I were so inclined I don't think I'm the right person for you. I like the country but I love London. Cora and I are the Sunshine Sisters, and we'll be appearing nightly at the Grecian Theatre. We're doing it because we must earn our living, but I have to admit that I love entertaining people. When I step out on the stage I'm the real me.'

Vere stared at her, frowning. 'You can't mean that, Rose.'

'But I do.'

'Then it seems that there's nothing else to say.'

'I'm truly sorry.'

His expression brightened. 'I am not so easily put off. I've come this far and I've laid my soul bare before you. The least you can do is to give yourself time to think things over, Rose.' He held up his hand as she opened her mouth to protest. 'I intend to stay in London for a week or two. I have some business to attend to in the City, and with your permission I will call on you in a day or so.'

'I'm afraid I'll be very busy.'

'I'll call anyway, and I'll come to the theatre to watch you and your sister perform.' He made a move towards the door. 'I am prepared to enter your world, Rose. The least you can do is to give me a fair chance.'

She remained in the room long after he had gone, his parting words ringing in her ears. She was in a state of disbelief, although in her heart she knew that what he had proposed was the basis of many marriages, some of them successful. If she married Vere she would have a position in society and a secure future. Portmorna House was a desirable residence, large enough for Cora to live with them if she wished. If she married into the Tressidick family it would be Bennett's duty to clear Billy's name. She came back to earth with a jolt: Bennett would work just as hard if she approached him as a paying client. It was easy to imagine how he would react if she accepted Vere's offer of marriage. A vision of his cynical smile made her blush, even though there was no one to witness her embarrassment. She gathered up the cups and placed them on the tray, and was about to take it downstairs to the kitchen when Mrs Blunt burst into the room.

'I'm sorry, Miss Rose. I heard the front door shut and I thought you must have left.'

'I wouldn't have gone without saying goodbye and to thank you for all the years you've cared for me and my family.'

Mrs Blunt took a hankie from her sleeve and blew her nose. 'There, there, miss. I was just doing my duty. It's a sad day for me.'

'I'm sure Mr Hart will be a good employer, and I hope he secures the incumbency on a permanent basis.' Rose placed the tray in Mrs Blunt's outstretched hands. 'Goodbye, dear Mrs Blunt.' Rose leaned over to kiss the cook's ruddy cheek. She left before either of them had a chance to break down in tears.

Rose decided not to tell Aunt Polly or Cora about Vere's unexpected arrival and even more surprising proposal of marriage. She could only hope that he would realise the futility of his quest and return to Cornwall. Overnight she convinced herself that a convenient marriage was not for her. Better to starve on the street than to live the rest of her life with a man she did not love. She would, she decided, devote herself to her new career and use all her resources to prove Billy's innocence and bring him home safe and sound.

She ate a hasty breakfast, served by Maisie, who was clearly delighted with her new position. Rose knew only too well that Mrs Blunt had disapproved of Maisie, but Ethel had lived a hard life and she had suffered a similar loss. It might not make her overly sympathetic but she seemed to know how to get the best out of the girl, and Rose was pleased to see Maisie reverting to her old, cheeky self. She suspected that Tommy had something to do with bringing the smile back to Maisie's face, and Sukey seemed pleased to have someone to help her in the general running of the house. Cora was happy in her own way, but Rose suspected that Gerard Barclay was the main reason for the sparkle in her sister's eyes. Cora seemed unperturbed by their change in circumstances, leaving Rose to wonder if she herself was the only one who missed their parents and the old way of life, dull though it might have been. She rose from the table, intent on going out before anyone was up.

Polly was still in bed and Cora had not yet put in an appearance, which suited Rose very well as she intended to call on Bennett. There was little point in involving them in her plans until she was certain that there was a definite possibility of clearing Billy's name, and she set off for Lincoln's Inn, telling Maisie that she was going shopping for ribbons and a new bonnet.

It was still early when she arrived at Bennett's chambers and his clerk, Frostwick, was not particularly forthcoming. Rose suspected that the clerk saw everything from a financial point of view, and that he doubted she had the wherewithal to pay Sharpe's fee. It was a fine May morning and she decided to wait in the square. The London plane trees were in full leaf, and the elegant buildings in the old square exuded a quiet air of permanence. She sat on a bench beneath a tree and prepared to wait all day if necessary. The sun was warm and the birds were in full song. Her night's sleep had been disturbed by the wailing of babies. She had lain awake in the small hours, her mind filled with Vere's unexpected proposal and worries for Billy's safety, and now she was tired. She was drifting off when she heard someone speak her name. At first she thought she was dreaming, but then a hand on her shoulder jolted her wide awake. She looked up and saw Bennett staring down at her.

'What are you doing here, Rose?'

'I came to see you. Your clerk didn't seem to want me to wait in your chambers so I thought I'd enjoy the sunshine.'

'What did you want to see me about?'

'I should have thought it was obvious.'

'I suspect it has to do with your brother.'

'Of course it does. I've tried to see you several times and you're never here, or you're tied up in court. You're a hard man to track down.'

He sat down beside her. 'As a matter of fact I went to Oxford to see Gawain's friends. I wasn't satisfied with what they told me in Cornwall.'

'Do you think they were lying?'

'I don't know if that was the case, or whether it was a memory pushed to the back of Toby's mind by the shock of finding Gawain murdered.'

'So what did he say? Don't keep me in suspense.'

He gave her a long look. 'Are you seriously considering Vere's proposal?'

She recoiled, shocked by the sudden change in the conversation. 'How do you know about that?'

'He came to my lodgings last evening. I've never seen him in such a state. He told me what he'd done and asked my advice.'

'What did you tell him?'

'I told him not to rush you into making a decision that you might both regret.'

'Spoken like a lawyer,' she said, turning her head away.

'That's because I am a lawyer. What would you have had me say?'

'You could have told him that I know my own mind. He didn't seem to believe that I was serious when I refused his proposal.'

'He's a wealthy man, Rose. You would live in comfort for the rest of your life, and he's not a bad fellow, once you get to know him.'

'Why are we speaking of this? I don't wish to be rude, but it has nothing to do with you, Bennett. You were going to tell me more about Gawain's friend.'

'Yes, of course.' He stared straight ahead, frowning. 'Edric remembered nothing, but Toby had a vague recollection of momentarily regaining consciousness. He said he saw someone bending over Gawain's inert body, and the fellow had a blood-stained knife in his hand. Toby could not be sure who it was, but he's certain that Billy was lying beside him, dead to the world. He thinks he must have lapsed into unconsciousness because he remembers nothing until he came round to find the police examining the body.'

'Then that proves it wasn't Billy. He'll be exonerated as we hoped.'

'It's not that easy, Rose.' He met her anxious gaze with a glimmer of sympathy in his dark eyes. 'Billy is still on the run. We have to find him and bring him home for his trial, and that isn't going to be easy.'

Rose leaped to her feet. 'I don't care,' she cried passionately. 'I'll find my brother even if I have to swim to France and walk the length and breadth of the country.'

'I was going to suggest that we might employ Scully to that effect.'

'You're right, of course, and I'll soon be in a position to hire his services.' She shot him a sideways glance. 'Signor Fancello had to close his saloon in Cupid's Court, and now he's acting as our manager. Cora and I will shortly be appearing at the Grecian Theatre for an indefinite period.'

'You surprise me. Do you really trust this man to look after your best interests when his own business was a total failure?'

'It wouldn't have happened if his family hadn't deserted him. He depends upon us as much as we depend upon him.'

'Be careful, that's all I can say. If he offers you a written contract I suggest you might like to show it to me before you sign.' He stood up and proffered his arm. 'Scully will probably be loitering in one of the public houses in Fleet Street, where he gathers information from some of his more nefarious contacts.' His lips curved in a quizzical smile. 'Would it be an insult to ask a vicar's daughter to accompany me? We might have to visit one or two such dens of iniquity before we find him.'

Rose slipped her hand through the crook of his arm. 'You're forgetting that I performed on stage in

Fancello's saloon. My education has been broadened considerably, and I expect it to expand even more when working at the Grecian.'

His smile faded. 'There must be other ways for you and Cora to support yourselves until you decide to wed.'

'Cora will marry one day, but I'm not sure marriage is for me. I saw my mother dominated by my father until she became a mere shadow of herself.'

'It doesn't have to be like that, Rose. I don't remember my mother, but I've been told that she and my father were happily married, and well-matched.'

'I'm sorry. It must have been very hard on you to lose both your parents at such a young age.'

He shrugged, staring straight ahead, his expression carefully controlled. 'I can't complain about my childhood. I was happy enough, and Vere, Gawain and I were like brothers, which is the main reason I intend to see that justice is done.'

'I understand,' Rose said gently. 'It was for a similar reason that Cora and I became the Sunshine Sisters. We were desperate to help Billy, but if I'm honest I was doing it for myself as well. I can't speak for Cora, but I love singing and dancing, and the applause from the audience makes me feel special. I suppose you think that's vain and frivolous.'

'No, as a matter of fact I admire your honesty. I can't see anything wrong in entertaining people and making them happy. Life is hard enough as it is, and happiness is an elusive emotion.'

'Bennett,' she said, laughing, 'you sound like a poet, and I thought you were a hard-headed lawyer dealing only in facts.'

'I have a heart and a soul just the same as you or my cousin Vere. I just don't wear it on my sleeve.' He came to a halt outside a pub. 'We'll try this one first.'

Rose followed him into the smoky interior, blinking as her eyes grew used to the dim light. The drone of male voices was interspersed with bursts of raucous laughter, and the smell of ale and spirits mingled with tobacco smoke and the odour of sweating humanity. Bennett appeared to be well known, and was greeted in a friendly manner by some, while others turned their backs on him. Rose waited by the door while he went to the bar to question the potman. He returned almost immediately. 'Scully hasn't been here for several days. I know he frequents the George, so we'll try there next.'

Eventually, after calling in at all the pubs and coffee houses in Fleet Street, they found Scully in a dark back room in Ye Olde Cheshire Cheese, situated in Wine Office Court. He was deep in conversation with a scruffy fellow wearing a battered top hat and a scarlet neckerchief. It was difficult to make out much else in the light of a single flickering candle, but when the man saw Bennett he leaped to his feet and barged past them. Rose had to dodge him or she would have been bowled over in his haste to leave.

'What sort of company are you keeping, Scully?' Bennett demanded, chuckling.

'The sort what gives out useful information for the price of a jug of ale, guv.' Scully raised himself from the wooden settle, acknowledging Rose with a nod of his head before sinking back on his seat. 'It was to do with the case of Roper versus Roper. Luckily I got what I needed out of him before you turned up and scared him off.' He shot a curious glance at Rose. 'What can I do for you, miss?'

Bennett pulled up a chair for Rose. 'It concerns her brother, Scully. I discovered some useful information when I was in Oxford. We need to find Billy Perkins and bring him home to face trial.'

'But we don't know where he went, guv. He might have fled the country or he could be hiding out on them godforsaken moors.' He turned to Rose with an apologetic grin. 'Begging your pardon, miss.'

'It's quite all right. I've heard much worse.' She sat down with a sigh of relief. They seemed to have been walking for miles, although they had covered only a short distance. Nothing seemed straightforward when it came to helping Billy. 'I just want to find my brother so that he can prove his innocence.'

'So what part do I play now?' Scully looked from one to the other. 'Am I to go to Cornwall, or to France?'

Bennett took a seat beside Rose. 'I think it might be worth going to Portmorna and having another word with Jenifry's mother. I doubt if the girl would go far without contacting her family to let them know she was safe, although I can't say the same for the Penneck brothers. Even if he had some information, Gryffyn Penneck wouldn't let on. I know him of old.'

'But we can't prove that it was one of his sons who killed Gawain,' Rose said thoughtfully.

'No matter. If I can persuade the judge and jury that Edric is telling the truth, the court will have to acquit Billy of all charges. I'm not concerned with Day and Pasco. They'll end up in prison again one way or another, of that I'm certain.'

Scully drained his tankard. 'Give me the necessary and I'll be off, guv.'

'Frostwick will attend to it, Scully.' Bennett stood up again, holding his hand out to Rose. 'We've done all we can for now.' He gave her a searching look. 'We'll find a cab to take you back to Old Street.'

'I'm not tired, Bennett. I can walk.'

'You look exhausted,' he said bluntly. 'I'll hail a cab and give you the fare.' He helped her to her feet. 'And you can pay me back out of your first week's wages, so don't look at me like that.'

She did not choose to argue. Rehearsals were due to start at one o'clock and she needed to be home in time to change into something more suitable. If all went well at the theatre she would be solvent again.

Bennett stepped outside and hailed a passing cab. 'I'll let you know as soon as I hear from Scully,' he said as he handed her into the waiting vehicle. 'I might even come to the theatre to watch your show.'

She settled herself on the seat. 'Who knows, you might even enjoy yourself.'

Chapter Twelve

Rose paid the cabby and was about to mount the steps outside Polly's house when she heard someone calling her name. She turned to see Fancello lumbering towards her, his face was flushed and his moustache quivered with emotion.

'Rose, wait. I need to speak to you.'

'Whatever is it, signor? You look upset.'

He came to a halt, holding his side as he struggled to catch his breath. 'Might I ask for a glass of water? My heart, it is beating so fast that I cannot hear myself think.'

Rose knocked on the door. 'Are you ill?'

He leaned his hand on the jamb. 'No, not ill. But badly done by, Rose. Very badly done by.'

Sukey opened the door and her smile froze when she saw Fancello. 'No gents allowed,' she muttered. 'You know that, miss.'

'It's all right, Sukey. This is Signor Fancello. He is a business associate and it's quite all right to let him in.'

Sukey clung to the door, refusing to budge. 'I dunno. He don't look right.'

'Let us in, please.' Rose edged past Sukey. 'Signor Fancello is a friend. I'll make it all right with Miss Polly. I'd be obliged if you'd fetch a glass of water.'

'I could ask Cook to make a pot of tea. That's what Miss Polly wants when she has a visitor, but I dunno about him. Shall I call a copper?'

Rose slipped her arm around Sukey's hunched shoulders. 'A pot of tea would be lovely. If Maisie is in the kitchen you can ask her to bring a tray to the parlour.'

'I can't carry a tray,' Sukey said sadly. 'I can manage a jug or even a pitcher, as long as it ain't too heavy, and I'm growing stronger every day. You should have seen me when I first come here, miss. I were a sorry sight, and that's the truth.'

'Well, you're a picture of health and happiness now, Sukey.' Rose gave her a gentle push towards the back stairs. 'Ethel speaks very highly of you and so does Miss Polly.'

Sukey's plain face was transformed by a smile that seemed to light her from within. 'Does she, miss? No one ever thought highly of me afore.' She hobbled off talking to herself and chuckling.

'The girl is a halfwit,' Fancello said crossly. 'I am close to fainting and she is chattering like a lunatic.'

'Come with me.' Rose crossed the hall to open the parlour door. 'You need to sit down, signor. I'm not sure if Sukey will remember the instructions I gave her, but in the meantime perhaps a tot of rum or brandy would help calm you.'

'Brandy, if you please. My nerves are shattered.' Fancello staggered past her and slumped down on the chaise longue, narrowly missing Spartacus. The cat leaped up, arched his back and spat at him before launching himself onto the floor, tail wagging.

Rose poured the brandy and gave it to Fancello. 'What has happened to get you in such a state?'

'My wife has married my brother,' he said, downing the drink in one swallow. He held the glass up for a refill.

'How is that possible? Are the laws in Italy different from those in England?'

'Of course not,' he said, puffing out his cheeks. 'We were married in the eyes of God, but I neglected to make it legal. I trusted my brother and this is how he repays me. I trusted him with our finances, too, and he has taken all my money. I am now a poor man.'

Rose poured more brandy into his glass. 'I am so sorry. I don't know what to say.'

'What's going on?' Polly burst into the room with Spartacus in her arms. 'Sukey tells me that a man has forced his way into my house.' She came to a sudden halt, staring at Fancello. 'Sandro, is that you?'

Fancello jumped up, spilling brandy down his crimson velvet waistcoat. 'Paloma, is it really you?'

Rose looked from one to the other. 'I don't understand. Do you know each other?'

Bright spots of colour emphasised Polly's high cheekbones and her eyes sparkled. 'We were on the same bill many times in the past, Rose.'

'You performed on stage together?'

'No, dear, not together. I was the top of the bill, a soloist in my own right, but Alessandro and Graziella were close behind me.'

Fancello seized Spartacus and dropped him unceremoniously on a pile of cushions. He wrapped his arms around Polly and kissed her on both cheeks. 'You haven't changed a bit, Paloma.'

Polly pushed him away, blushing to the roots of her hair. 'Stop that, you silly man. We are too old to behave like this.'

He folded his hands over his heart. 'Never, *cara mia*. We had many good times, you and I, Paloma.'

'Why do you call her that?' Rose sank down on the window seat, feeling as though she were watching a play.

'Paloma means dove,' Fancello said dreamily. 'Your aunt was the most beautiful lady on the London stage. She was my beautiful dove.'

'Where was Graziella in all this?' Rose looked from one to the other in astonishment.

'Graziella had to stop performing when she was with child,' Polly said primly. 'For a while, Sandro and I did a double act, but only until Graziella was well enough to perform again.' Polly moved to the side table and poured two tots of brandy. She handed one to Fancello. 'Where is your dear wife, Sandro? I would love to see her again, and your little boy.'

Fancello clutched the glass in his hand and his eyes filled with tears. '*Cara mia*, I have such a sad tale to tell you.'

'I think I'd better go and find my sister,' Rose said hastily. 'We have to be at the theatre at one o'clock.' She stood up and made for the doorway. 'Are you coming with us, signor?'

'I think not. Your aunt and I have much to talk about.'

'Yes,' Rose said pointedly. 'I'm sure you do, and perhaps you ought to start by explaining why you and Graziella never married.' She left them staring blankly at each other, and went to look for Cora.

She found her in the kitchen helping Ethel to cook the midday meal. Flushed and with a dab of flour on the tip of her nose, Cora looked up from making dumplings to add to the mutton stew. 'Is it that time already, Rose?'

'Your sister ain't half useful.' Ethel thumped the lid back on the pan that she had been stirring. 'I been teaching Maisie to cook but she's more interested in helping with the babies upstairs. I dunno, I sweat me guts out cooking for them women and not one of them ever comes down to give us a hand.'

'Maybe we should organise a rota,' Rose suggested

tactfully. 'I'm sure that most of them know how to cook their dinner. That's if they're well enough to work.'

'Dunno about well enough,' Ethel said, curling her lip. 'They're lazy bitches, most of 'em. Never done a hard day's work in their lives.'

'We'll see about that.' Rose beckoned to Cora. 'I'm afraid we have to leave you now, Ethel. We've got a rehearsal at the theatre.'

Ethel brightened visibly. 'I don't suppose you could get us a ticket for the show, could you? I ain't been out nowhere for months. In fact I've forgot the last time I went anywhere other than the blooming market, let alone did anything what was enjoyable.'

'I'm sure we can arrange something. Come on, Cora, we don't want to be late for our first rehearsal.' She waited until they were out of the kitchen. 'You won't believe what I have to tell you.'

With their dancing shoes slung over their shoulders, Rose and Cora set off for the theatre. 'I can't believe it,' Cora said excitedly. 'Do you think that Fancello is Aunt Polly's long-lost love?'

Rose slowed her pace. 'I hadn't thought of that. It all happened so suddenly, but they were definitely very good friends. He calls her his dove.'

'How romantic. I wish Gerard would give me a pet name.' Cora shot a sideways glance at her sister. 'He's taking me out to tea after the rehearsal. You don't mind, do you?'

'I'm not your mother, Corrie. You don't have to ask my permission, but, as I keep telling you, don't get too involved.'

'I know what you're saying, but I don't understand why you're so against Gerard. He might be a gentleman, but then so is Vere, and he asked you to marry him.'

'And I refused, Corrie. Anyway, Vere hasn't any living relatives to disapprove of me.'

'Bennett is his cousin. What do you think he would say?' Cora's mischievous smile was not lost on Rose.

'Bennett wouldn't care one way or the other.'

'But you like him, don't you, Rosie?'

'I can't think what gave you that idea. My interest in Mr Sharpe is purely business. He's supposed to be the best lawyer in London, or that's what Scully told me, and he has no reason to lie. Bennett is a means to save Billy from the hangman's noose, or have you forgotten the threat that still hangs over him?'

'No, of course not. But Billy ran away, and I don't see what we can do now.'

'Scully is going to Cornwall to see if he can discover any clues as to Billy's whereabouts. Bennett thinks that Jenifry's mother might know something more than she's been telling us.'

'When did you see Bennett?'

'I went to his chambers first thing this morning. Someone has to do something, Cora. We can't just sit back and let things happen.'

Cora opened the stage door and stepped inside. 'Billy was a fool to run away. I love him – of course I do, he's my brother – but at this moment I could cheerfully strangle him. He's the reason that Papa abandoned us and we lost our home.'

Rose followed her into the theatre. 'I know it's hard, Cora, but Billy was caught up in circumstances beyond his control. You must see that.'

'All I know is that because of Billy we're having to live in a home for fallen women, and we have to work whether we want to or not.' Cora flounced off in the direction of the dressing rooms. 'It's just not fair, Rose. It's not fair.'

'You're talking like a spoiled child,' Rose said angrily. 'Do you think I wanted any of this?'

Cora came to a sudden halt. She turned on Rose, her face white with anger. 'I think you enjoyed the excitement of dashing off to the country. You left me with Papa and you went on a big adventure.'

'Someone had to try to help Billy. You didn't see him in that terrible prison, but I did. I know he's innocent and I'm going to prove it.'

'There you go again,' Cora said sulkily. 'It's all about Billy. Never mind poor Cora. It was always the same. I was the youngest and always left out of your games when we were children.'

'Oh, for goodness' sake stop feeling sorry for yourself.' Rose marched past her. 'I'm not continuing this conversation. You do what you want to do, Cora, but remember that we're the Sunshine Sisters and smile.' She entered the large dressing room and was almost bowled over by the fug of tobacco smoke, cheap scent and perspiring bodies. In the warm glow of the gaslights it was possible to make out at least six young women, all of whom were in various states of undress.

'Close the door, dearie. You're causing a draught.' One of the girls nearest the door reached out and slammed it, narrowly missing Cora, who managed to slip in before it shut in her face.

The chattering stopped for a moment. 'You're the new act.' The woman who had closed the door struggled into her wrap. 'I'm Florrie. What's your moniker, dearie?'

Rose held out her hand. 'I'm Rose and this is my sister, Cora. We've come to rehearse for the show.'

'Look out, girls, we've got a couple of toffs in our midst.' A plump girl with a mop of alarmingly red hair made a mock curtsey. 'Please to meet you, your highnesses.'

'Shut up, Nell. Give 'em a chance.' Florrie plucked a lit cigarillo from a saucer and put it to her lips. She blew a plume of smoke over Rose's head. 'What's your act, love?'

'We're the Sunshine Sisters. We used to perform at Fancello's in Cupid's Court, but it closed down.'

Sympathetic murmurs rippled round the room.

'We've all been there, ain't we, girls?' Florrie stubbed the cigarillo out. 'Cheap tobacco tastes filthy. One day I'm going to make enough money to afford some of them handmade Turkish cigarettes they sell up West.'

'You'll be too old to enjoy it by then.' Nell's remark was met with groans and grunts of assent.

'You don't have any baccy on you, do you, Rose?' One of the older girls sidled up to her. 'I'm Dolly, by the way, dear. I wouldn't ask but I'm broke until pay day.'

'I'm sorry,' Rose said apologetically. 'I don't smoke.'

'What do you do, dearie?' Nell demanded, tossing her head so that her curls bobbed like watch springs.

Rose was fast losing patience. 'We work hard to earn our living, just like you do.'

'Then you'd best put your dancing shoes on and get on with it.' Florrie shrugged. 'Watch out for Slippery. That's the stage manager, in case you don't know. He's a misery at the best of times and he has wandering hands.' She winked and lit another cigarillo. 'All right, Dolly, don't look at me like that. You can have a few puffs if you'll promise to stop nattering.'

Cora had been hiding behind Rose while she undressed down to the skimpy stage costume. She tugged at Rose's sleeve. 'I'm ready.'

'You can leave your duds here,' Florrie said, grinning. 'We don't steal off each other.'

'Unless it's blokes or baccy,' Dolly added, chuckling.

Rose stepped out of her grey gown. 'It's all right then, we've neither of those.' She unlaced her boots and put on her dancing shoes. 'Thank you for warning us about the stage manager.' She hesitated in the doorway. 'What's his real name? I can't call him Mr Slippery.'

'Slattery,' Nell said, curling her lip. 'Jim Slattery. Keep on his right side, but don't let him get you in a corner.'

'I hope they're exaggerating,' Cora whispered as they made their way to the stage. 'This isn't like Fancello's.'

'It's our chance to prove ourselves,' Rose said softly. 'We've come this far, Corrie. We can do it. We'll make Aunt Polly proud.'

'But our parents will never speak to us again. I'm not sure it's worth all the heartache.'

They arrived in the wings to find a troupe of acrobats just coming to the end of their act. Rose handed their music to the pianist and they waited for their intro.

'That's it,' Rose said eagerly. 'We're on, Cora. Smile.'

At the end of their performance the manager clapped enthusiastically. 'Very nice, ladies. The juggler will be on first and then you two. You'll follow him in the second half after the interval in the same manner. Any questions?'

The limelight was dazzling and even when she shielded her eyes Rose could not see him clearly, but she nodded. 'I understand.'

'Next.' He sat down again, leaving Rose and Cora no option other than to leave the stage.

'Well done, girls.' Jim Slattery met them with a broad grin, exposing a row of pointed yellow teeth.

'Thank you, sir.' Rose kept her tone neutral and was about to walk on, but Slattery moved a step closer, transferring his attention to Cora.

'I have a soft spot for golden-haired girls, Miss Sunshine.' He laid his hand on her arm. 'I can be very helpful or I can be extremely difficult.'

Rose stepped in between them. 'My sister is spoken for, Mr Slattery.'

His eyes narrowed. 'I'm not interested in that way, Miss Sunshine. I suggest if you want to keep your job you mind your manners and curb your tongue.'

'My manners are perfect, Mr Slattery. I can't say the same for yours.' Rose knew she was making an enemy but she was not prepared to let him get away with such behaviour.

Cora's worried expression melted into a welcoming smile. She pushed past Slattery. 'Gerard, you came.'

He held her hand and raised it to his lips. 'Cora, how enchanting you look.' He smiled and acknowledged Rose with a bow. 'I saw the whole thing. The manager is an old friend and he allowed me to watch.'

Slattery's belligerent jaw slackened visibly. He twisted his features into an ingratiating smile. 'I am sure that the Sunshine Sisters will grace our stage for many weeks to come, sir.'

'I'm sure you have work to do, Slattery,' Gerard said with an urbane smile. 'You mustn't allow us to detain you.'

Slattery's mouth worked silently as he seemed to

struggle for words. 'I'll be seeing you ladies.' He walked off, gesticulating angrily at a stage hand who happened to be in his way.

'I don't trust that fellow.' Gerard turned to Rose with a persuasive smile. 'I would like to take Cora out for tea. You would be very welcome to join us, Rose.'

She shook her head. 'That's very kind of you, but I have things to do. Maybe another time.'

'I'll hold you to that. Perhaps I could take you both to supper after your first show. I've booked tickets for the front row of the stalls so I shan't miss a thing.'

Rose had mixed feelings as she left the theatre. Gerard seemed to be genuinely fond of her sister, but although she tried to be happy for Cora she could not convince herself that the romance would turn out well. She was so deep in thought that she almost bumped into Vere, who was standing outside the stage door.

'Are you waiting for me?'

He doffed his hat. 'Of course. Surely you don't think I make a practice of loitering outside theatres.'

'I don't know you well enough to know,' Rose said carefully.

'That's what I intend to alter.' He proffered his arm. 'May I escort you home, Miss Perkins? After which I would like to invite you to dinner.'

Rose hesitated. 'I must be honest with you, Mr Tressidick. I don't move in your circles, and I have nothing suitable to wear to a smart restaurant. Besides which, I don't want to give you false hope.'

His smile did not waver as he took her hand and laid it on his arm. 'Your honesty is both refreshing and charming. You intrigue me, Rose, and I don't care if you wear sackcloth or silk. You are a beautiful woman and you have no need for fine gowns and jewels, although I would like to be in a position to buy them for you.'

She snatched her hand away. 'Please don't. I'm still of the same mind as when we spoke yesterday. You and I have nothing in common.'

'And that makes it all the more exciting.' His smile faded and he held her gaze with an intent look. 'Forget what I said before, and allow me to take you to dinner this evening. We can go to a chop house, if you would prefer such a place. I simply want to enjoy your company and get to know you a little better.'

'You make it very hard to refuse.'

'That's exactly what I intended. Now, may I see you safely to your door? And I would deem it an honour to meet your aunt.'

Rose could hear voices on the other side of the stage door and she recognised Dolly's shrill voice followed by Florrie's deeper tones. She could only imagine what they would say if they emerged from the theatre to find her in conversation with a toff. She took Vere's arm. 'I'll have dinner with you, Mr Tressidick.'

'Vere,' he said, smiling. 'It would make me much more comfortable if you would call me Vere.'

'I think it's going to rain, Vere,' she said hastily. 'Shall we walk a little faster?'

He quickened his pace. 'Of course, but I think it's just clouded over. This is turning out to be a very nice day.'

Sukey opened the door to let them in, and Rose stepped inside, hoping that there would be no fights or shouting matches while Vere was in the house, and that the woman who had refused to go into hospital to have her baby would now have been safely delivered. To her relief all seemed quiet, but as she opened the parlour door a wave of sound hit her forcibly. The sight that met her eyes made her wish that she had refused Vere's request to meet her aunt.

Fancello was playing the piano, hitting more wrong notes than right ones, and Polly was leaning against him singing one of the songs that had made her a success many years ago. Fancello joined in the chorus, belting out the words in a deep baritone that made the ornaments on the top of the instrument jump up and down. A strong smell of brandy pervaded the room and an empty bottle bore witness to the fact that the pair had consumed almost the entire contents. Rose was certain that it had been almost full that morning.

She turned to Vere with an apologetic smile. 'Perhaps this isn't the best of times . . .'

He ran his finger round the inside of his stiff collar. 'It does seem a trifle inconvenient.'

Polly did a twirl, ending in an artistic pose. 'I didn't know we had a visitor, Rose. Where are your manners?' She staggered towards Vere, holding out her hand. 'Charmed to meet you, sir. What is your name, dear?'

'Aunt Polly, may I introduce Mr Vere Tressidick from Portmorna? He was Billy's host in Cornwall.' Rose sent a warning look to Fancello, who stopped playing but kept his hands raised as if waiting to strike another chord. She turned to Vere. 'May I introduce you to Miss Day, my aunt?'

'How do you do, Miss Day? It's a pleasure to make your acquaintance,' Vere said gallantly.

Fancello stood up and moved towards him, swaying lightly on the tips of his toes. 'I am Alessandro Fancello,' he said grandly. 'I am an old friend of the family and I look after the business affairs of the Sunshine Sisters.' He grabbed Vere's hand and pumped his arm up and down.

'How do you do, signor?'

'Ah, you speak Italian. Splendid.' Fancello beamed at him. 'Alas, I have forgotten most of my native tongue during my many years of living and working in London.'

Rose shifted from one foot to the other. Despite his outward appearance of calm she could only imagine how Vere Tressidick must be feeling in what must seem like a madhouse, and to make things worse someone in the room above uttered a loud scream followed by a string of swear words that made Rose blush. The sound of pounding feet and slamming doors was followed by another voice raised in anger and yet more screams and groans.

Polly teetered to the door. 'It's nothing to worry about, Mr Tressidick,' she said with a sickly smile. 'It's just one of my women going into labour. It happens all the time.' She staggered out of the room, leaving the door to swing shut behind her.

Fancello cleared his throat and reached for his glass. 'That woman is a saint, sir. I tell you again, she's a saint. Who but my Paloma would take these poor souls into her home and look after them in their hour of need?' He held the glass up to the light. 'It's empty. Must have spilled my drink.' He held it out to Rose. 'Another tot would be most welcome, *cara mia.*'

Rose snatched it from him. 'I think you've had quite enough, signor. It's time you went home.'

'That's just the problem,' he said thickly. 'I have nowhere to go. Lost what remained of my money at the gaming tables last night.' He sank down on the piano stool, which creaked ominously beneath his weight. 'Broke. Bankrupt. Penniless.' He buried his head in his hands.

'I should go.' Vere made a move towards the doorway. 'I'll call for you at seven o'clock, Rose.

Don't worry, I'll see myself out.' He shot a wary look at Fancello as he opened the door and stepped out into the hall.

Rose placed the glass out of reach. 'You should be ashamed of yourself.'

He peered at her between his fingers. 'Don't shout at me. I had enough of that from Graziella when we were together.'

'I don't wonder that she shouted at you if you behaved like this. I've never seen Aunt Polly in such a drunken state. She likes a drop of brandy at the end of a hard day, but she never drinks to excess. It's your fault, Signor Fancello.'

'Paloma is my friend,' he said feebly. 'We were close many years ago and she said I can stay here until I sort out my problems.'

'You are the problem, signor. If you cannot handle your own affairs how can you expect to act as our manager?'

'I am a good businessman.'

'You are a failed businessman, and now you admit that you're a gambler. You've wheedled your way into my aunt's good books and you've got her drunk. I don't want you for a manager, signor.'

'I found you work.'

'You earned your money this once, but I'm not giving you a chance to ruin us. I'll honour our agreement and give your ten per cent when Cora and I get paid. I'm sorry, but that's an end to it. We'll manage on our own from now on.'

She was about to leave the room when the door opened and Maisie rushed in.

'Come quick, miss. There's ructions going on upstairs. That big woman has got a knife and she's holding it to Miss Polly's throat.'

Chapter Thirteen

Rose hurried after Maisie, who took the stairs two at a time. Agonised screams from one of the rooms almost drowned the sound of Polly's slurred speech, as she tried to reason with the woman who held her captive. Rose recognised her assailant as Big Bertha, a tall, rangy woman who had given birth several days previously.

'Let her go,' she said shakily. 'What has Miss Polly done to deserve such treatment, Bertha?'

'She took my baby from me,' Bertha snarled. 'She give him away, the bitch.'

Polly rolled her eyes nervously. 'I found him a good home. You agreed that he should be adopted, Bertha. You wanted it that way.'

'I weren't in me right mind. You took advantage of a sick woman and sold my boy.'

'No money changed hands. Your child will be

brought up by loving parents. He'll have a proper education and a secure future.'

Bertha tightened her grip, holding the knife dangerously close to Polly's throat. 'He needs his ma, and I want him back. You'll get him for me right now or I'll have your guts for garters.'

'Be reasonable, Bertha.' Polly was suddenly sober. 'It isn't as easy as that.'

'You got no choice. I wants him back now, or you die.'

Rose took a tentative step forward, holding out her hand. 'Bertha, please. You know you don't mean that. If you harm Miss Polly you'll go to gaol, and you'll never see your son again.'

'What's it got to do with you?' Bertha narrowed her eyes. 'Leave me to sort this out my way.'

'You'll get nowhere,' Rose insisted. 'If it were possible to get your boy back, how would you look after him? What sort of life could you offer a child?'

'I'm his ma. He belongs to me. I weren't in me right mind when I agreed to give him up.'

'But you *did* agree to it. You just admitted it, Bertha. I can't begin to imagine how you must be feeling, but you must see that it's the best thing for your son.'

'I lost my baby,' Maisie muttered. 'I knows how it feels.'

'You know nothing.' Bertha spat the words at her.

'Just because I'm young it don't mean I ain't got no feelings.' Maisie sniffed and wiped her eyes on her sleeve.

'Shut up,' Bertha snarled. 'Who asked you to put your oar in?'

'Let me go,' Polly gasped. 'You're choking me.'

'Please do as she says and we can talk this over like sensible people.' Rose slipped her arm around Maisie's shoulder, giving her a comforting hug while keeping a wary eye on Bertha. 'Harming Miss Polly isn't going to help. Let her go and—' She broke off at the sound of an agonised screech from one of the bedrooms.

'It's Lizzie. She's having her baby and she's going to die.' Maisie covered her head with her apron and began to sob.

'Go and check on her, Rose,' Polly said urgently. 'I can't do anything unless Bertha sees sense.'

Ignoring Bertha's stream of expletives, Rose left them and hurried into the darkened room. The stench of sweat was almost overpowering and one of the pregnant women was sitting by the bed, smoking a pipe. She glanced up, shaking her head. 'It ain't coming like it should.'

Rose pulled back the curtains and opened the window to ventilate the room, and waft away the thick pall of tobacco smoke. One look at the woman lying on the bed was enough to convince Rose that she was in dire need of help. 'She needs a doctor, Sal. I'll send Tommy to fetch him.'

Sal shook her head. 'No time for that. Get Big Bertha. She knows what to do. Although I dare say Lizzie's close to the end. I seen it all before. Heaven help me when my time comes. It's a case of taking my chances here or being a charity case over the road.'

Rose could see that there was no time to delay and she hurried from the room. 'Bertha. You're needed.'

'It's a trick.'

Maisie's wails were muffled by the apron she had covering her head and face. 'They'll both die.'

'It's true,' Rose said firmly. 'I don't know a great deal about childbirth, but Lizzie looks close to death, and the baby too.'

Bertha released Polly, who fell to her knees, just as Fancello arrived at the top of the stairs. He leaned against the banisters panting heavily. 'What's happened?'

'She's had a shock but she's unharmed.' Rose turned her attention to Maisie, who was sobbing quietly. She peeled the apron off the girl's face. 'It's all right. Bertha has gone to help Lizzie and Miss Polly isn't hurt.'

'I was scared, miss.'

'So was I, but it's over now. Go downstairs and ask Ethel to make a pot of strong coffee for Miss Polly and Mr Fancello. I think he'll be staying with us for a while.'

Having sent Maisie to the relative calm of the kitchen, Rose went back to check on Lizzie. Bertha now seemed like a different woman from the wild creature who had threatened Polly with a knife. She was calm and competent and was attending to Lizzie with the expertise of an experienced midwife. She glanced over her shoulder. 'The baby's the wrong way round. I'll have to turn it.'

Sal heaved herself off the chair. 'I'm gasping for a cup of tea.'

'Shall I send for the doctor?' Rose asked anxiously.

'I'm better at this than any man living.' Bertha glared at the woman with the pipe. 'Put that pipe out, Sal. I can't hardly breathe for the smoke. If you want to be useful go downstairs and get hot water and some clean rags, and don't hang about. If you don't come back straight away I won't help you when your time comes.' She shot a sideways glance at Rose. 'You can give us a hand.'

'Is she going to die?' Rose moved closer to the bed.

'Not if I can help it. You do as I say and if you're going to swoon make sure you fall onto the floor and not the bed.'

Two hours later Rose was on her way downstairs to the kitchen with a bowl of blood-stained rags in her hands when Sukey answered the door to Vere. He came to a halt, staring at her in surprise. 'Rose? What's happened?'

She had lost track of the time during the drama of helping a new life into the world. It had been a difficult birth, and she could only admire the expert way in which Bertha had dealt with the mother and the newborn baby girl, but a quick glance at the longcase clock in the hall reminded her that she should have been getting ready for her evening out with Vere. 'I'm sorry,' she said. 'I had to help upstairs. It was an emergency.'

'You amaze me, Rose. Each time we meet I see you in a new guise. Which one, I wonder, is the real Rose Perkins?' He put his head on one side, a glimmer of humour in his grey eyes.

She knew that she must present an odd sight. Her hair had escaped from the pins that were supposed to hold it in place and she had splashed water on herself as she helped Bertha clean up after the birth. 'I'm not nearly ready, Vere. Perhaps we ought to cancel our arrangement for this evening.'

'Certainly not. I wouldn't hear of it, Rose. I'm a patient man; I'll wait while you do what you have to do.'

'I'm surprised you came back after the performance you witnessed earlier.'

'It made me realise what a dull life I lead at home. Is it safe to wait in the parlour, or shall I stay here and wait for the next act?'

'You have no idea of the drama you missed, but you should be quite safe in there. I'll just get rid of this and then I'll change. I won't be long.'

'I look forward to hearing about it all over dinner, Rose.'

Stone's Chop House in Panton Street was situated close to Piccadilly Circus. Rose had rarely visited the West End, apart from an occasional shopping expedition to Oxford Street, but she did not wish to appear gauche and she refrained from making any comments that might betray her lack of sophistication. The temptation to remark on the elegant clothes worn by the ladies, and the relative opulence of her surroundings, was almost too great to resist, but she concentrated instead on the menu.

Vere ordered for them and the waiter brought a bottle of wine, which he uncorked and waited for Vere to taste before he filled their glasses.

Vere sat back in his chair while they waited for their food to arrive. 'Tell me, what happened after I left your aunt's house?'

Rose sipped the wine and found it rich and warming. 'It all happened so quickly. One of the women was in labour, as you probably realised. Aunt Polly went up to see what she could do to help and she was seized upon by Big Bertha, who held a knife to her throat.'

Vere almost choked on his wine. 'Good heavens! Why would she do a thing like that?'

Rose found herself telling him everything that had happened, although she left out the details of the birth itself. Vere listened with interest, interjected at times when he did not understand, and prompted her to talk about her old life in the vicarage. He was a good listener and Rose soon lost any last vestige of shyness she had felt in his company.

Over a dessert of spotted dick and custard she managed to turn the conversation around, asking him questions about his upbringing in Cornwall. He had been, he admitted, a serious child who was more interested in his studies than roaming the countryside with Gawain and Bennett. They had been privately tutored and Bennett had seemed to absorb his lessons without any noticeable effort, but Vere had had to apply himself to his studies. Gawain, on the other hand, had been far more interested in outdoor pursuits, which included carousing with the Pennecks, getting drunk, and having affairs with married women. Quite how he managed to fit in his studies at Oxford was a mystery. Rose absorbed this in silence. She was gradually building up a picture of how the cousins had grown up together, and beginning to develop an insight into their complex relationship.

At the end of the evening Vere handed Rose out of the hansom cab, telling the cabby to wait while he saw her to the door. 'I'm here for a few days more, and I've bought a ticket to see the first night of your show. Perhaps we could have supper afterwards.'

'I have enjoyed this evening,' Rose said carefully, not wanting to hurt his feelings. 'But I'm not sure it would be such a good idea.' She knocked on the door.

'You mustn't worry, Rose. My offer of marriage still stands, but I promise not to mention it again unless you have a change of heart.'

'I can't think about my future while Billy is a fugitive.'

He raised her hand to his lips. 'I understand, and we share a common aim. I can't rest until my brother's killer is brought to justice. We must work together, and we will discover the truth, no matter what it costs.' He stepped away as the door opened. 'Good night, Rose. I'll see you again very soon.'

Rose turned, expecting to see Maisie or Sukey but it was Cora who held the door open. 'What sort of time do you call this, Miss Perkins? I thought I was the one who stayed out late.'

Rose stepped inside and closed the door. 'Vere took me out for supper.' She glanced at the clock. 'And it's only half-past ten.'

'Papa wouldn't approve,' Cora said primly, but her blue eyes were sparkling mischievously. 'You were out with a gentleman, unchaperoned.'

'Isn't this the case of the pot calling the kettle black?' Rose gave her a hug. 'You are such a tease, Corrie. What time did you get home?'

'About ten minutes ago.' Cora pulled a crumpled letter from her pocket and handed it to her sister. 'This arrived earlier only I forgot to give it to you. It's from Papa and it's addressed to us both, so I opened it.'

'I can't read it in this dim light,' Rose said, handing it back to Cora. 'What does he say?'

'Very little. He obviously hasn't forgiven us. He's accepted the incumbency of a parish just a few miles from Lyme Regis. They won't be coming back to London, Rose. He doesn't say as much, but I fear that we are in fact orphans.' Her voice broke on a suppressed sob.

'Of course we're not,' Rose said stoutly, although she too was shocked by her father's decision. 'He'll come round eventually, and I'm sure that Mama must miss us as we miss her, but she'll have to agree with whatever he says.'

'We might never see them again.'

'You talk as though they're in a foreign country. There's nothing to stop us visiting them, and I intend to at the first opportunity, but in the meantime we have our own lives to lead.' Rose took off her bonnet and mantle and hung them on the hallstand. 'I'm tired. I'm going to bed. We'll talk about it in the morning.'

Cora followed her to the staircase. 'Gerard said his parents want to meet me, and he's bringing them to the first night of the show. I tried to dissuade him, Rose, but he said his father wouldn't listen to his protests, and it was out of his hands.'

'Let's hope he knows best, but I would have thought somewhere less public would have been more suitable.' Rose hesitated with one foot on the bottom step. 'Is Aunt Polly still up?'

Cora moved closer. 'I saw her go upstairs with Signor Fancello,' she added in a conspiratorial whisper. 'They were hand in hand and giggling like naughty children, but I can't believe that they would do anything improper, not at their age.'

'Nothing would surprise me,' Rose said wearily. 'It's best not to think about it, and anyway it's none of our business.'

'She's not proving to be a very good example to us.' Cora covered her mouth with her hand, stifling a giggle.

Rose had to bite her lip to stop herself from laughing as she climbed the steep stairs. 'What a day this has been. I doubt if anything will surprise me ever again.'

She was proved wrong next day when Bennett and Scully arrived on the doorstep shortly after breakfast. She took them into the parlour and closed the door so that Sukey, who had been hovering in the hallway on the pretext of dusting, could not hear.

'This is unexpected,' she said, taking a seat by the hearth. 'Why so early?'

'Scully is about to set off for Cornwall and he has some questions for you concerning William.' Bennett glanced at the table, which was littered with unwashed glasses and the remains of supper that had been abandoned, half eaten.

Spartacus had not yet taken up residence in the parlour or he might have attempted to dispose of a dish of sprats, even though it was mostly heads and tails. Rose tried to ignore the smell, curving her lips into a smile.

'How may I help you, Mr Scully?' She felt herself blushing with shame to think that her aunt and Fancello had left the room in such a state, and then she spotted one of Polly's satin slippers lying on the floor. The scene it conjured up in her mind was one she did not want to share with her visitors. She nudged the abandoned footwear with the toe of her boot until it was out of sight beneath her chair.

Scully slumped down on the chaise longue. 'It's just Scully, miss. It feels more professional, if you get my meaning.'

She did not, but she smiled and nodded anyway. 'Of course.'

'I just need a few details about the said William Perkins, miss. For example, would you know of any friends or acquaintances he might have in the West Country who would be willing to shelter him?'

'None to my knowledge.'

'We are working on the theory that they most probably headed for France. Might I ask a similar question about that particular place?'

'As far as I know Billy has never been abroad.'

'Would you know if he was partial to a bet on the horses, or if he likes to gamble on cards or perhaps other forms of gentlemanly activities?'

She shook her head. 'I've seen little of my brother since he went to Oxford, but he wasn't interested in gaming of any sort when he lived at home.'

Scully put his head on one side. 'Not likely he'd admit to such a thing when he lived in a vicarage, miss . . . if you'll pardon the liberty.'

'I think we've got a clearer picture of Billy's interests, Scully.' Bennett had been standing by the window, but he turned to him, frowning. 'It was my cousin who was the gambler, and a womaniser. Billy didn't seem to me to be the sort of friend my cousin would choose.' He shot an apologetic glance at Rose. 'I don't mean that in a derogatory manner. If anything it was a compliment.'

Rose clasped her hands tightly in her lap. 'I can't think of anything that would single Billy out from a crowd, apart from the fact that he seems to have had a relationship with Jenifry, one of the maids at Portmorna House. He was always a very caring brother, and if he is fond of this girl I'm certain he'll do everything in his power to protect her. I think if you find Jenifry, you'll find Billy, especially if they've gone to France. He wouldn't abandon her in a foreign country, no matter how difficult things were.'

'I thought as much.' Bennett nodded to Scully. 'There you have it. When you arrive in Portmorna make straight for the cottage where the girl's mother lives. She was very agitated when I last saw her, and I doubt if she is the type of woman who could hide her true feelings. If she has any news of her daughter it should be easy to persuade her to part with it.'

Scully stood up and jammed his battered bowler hat on his head. 'I'll be off then, guv.'

'Send me a telegram if you get word of Billy's whereabouts, and try the fishermen again and the men working in the docks.'

'Will you be joining me in Cornwall, guv?'

'If you find anything useful I'll be down on the next train.' Bennett shook Scully's hand. 'I'm relying on you, Scully.'

Rose jumped to her feet and held out her hand. 'As am I. Good luck, Scully. I pray that you'll find out something to set my mind at rest. I can't sleep at night for worrying about my brother.'

Scully grinned and tipped his hat. 'We can't have that, miss. Trust me, I'll do me level best.' He marched out of the room.

Rose turned to Bennett. 'I can't thank you enough for all this.'

'This has become as personal to me as it is to you. I don't want to alarm you, Rose, but if Billy has thrown his lot in with the Pennecks it won't be to his advantage, and if he has taken the girl to France he'll have to find work in order to support them both. Day and Pasco will resort to crime, and I just hope Billy has the good sense to get as far away from them as possible. Should he be arrested in a foreign country there's almost nothing I can do for him.'

'I understand, and I wish there was something I could do to help.'

'When we find him – and I won't rest until we do – he'll need somewhere to call home. I doubt if he would be welcome in your father's new parish.'

She stared at him in amazement. 'How did you know about that? I only found out last night myself.'

One of his rare smiles lit his eyes. 'Scully is a useful fellow, and he's training Bobby Lee to do some of the footwork for him. I don't enquire how they come by some of their information, but it's very useful.' His smile faded and his eyes darkened. 'I

253

also know that my cousin took you out for dinner last night.'

'It's true, but I don't see what business it is of yours.'

'He isn't a lady's man, Rose. Be careful how you treat him, that's all I can say.'

'I take that as an insult,' Rose said angrily. 'Are you insinuating that I've set my cap at him and that I'm leading him on?'

He moved towards the doorway, pausing to give her a searching look. 'Are you?'

'I won't dignify that with an answer. Just because my sister and I have to earn our living on the stage doesn't mean that we're gold diggers.'

'I'm glad to hear it. Vere and I don't always see eye to eye, but I wouldn't like to see him hurt.'

'I think it's time you left,' Rose said with as much dignity as she could muster. It would have been more satisfying to pick up any object that came to hand and hurl it at him, but that would have been childish.

'I know that Vere has bought a ticket for your debut. I will also be there to cheer you on, too.' Bennett opened the door and almost trod on Spartacus as he left the room. The cat narrowed his yellow eyes, arched his back and hissed.

Rose wished that she were a cat and could show her displeasure in such an obvious manner. She was both shocked and angered by his accusation, and she wondered what Vere had told his cousin. He had obviously refrained from admitting that she had turned down his offer of marriage.

She took a deep breath and wagged her finger at Spartacus as he strolled over to the table to sniff the remains of the meal. 'Men are arrogant fools. At least you know where you are with a cat.' She snatched up the plates, intending to take them to the kitchen, but she was met in the hallway by Fancello, who was still wearing his nightcap and dressing robe. She averted her eyes.

'Good morning, signor.'

He clutched his hands to his heart in a theatrical gesture worthy of Polly. 'What must you think of me, Rose?'

'It's none of my business. This is my aunt's house.'

'But you don't approve. I see it in your eyes. I have offended you and your sister.'

She turned to face him. 'I am not so narrow-minded, but if you want me to be honest I have to say that I think you are taking advantage of my aunt. You have lost everything and you need somewhere to live, so you've rekindled your romance with Polly. Shame on you.'

He hung his head. 'It must look like that, *cara*, but it is not so. Polly is the love of my life. She is the reason that I never made a marriage contract with Graziella. I am a weak man, but I am not bad.'

Rose shook her head. 'I just don't want you to break my aunt's heart for a second time. I believe that you are the reason why she never married, although she must have had countless offers.'

'I am humbled, Rose. I do not deserve such loyalty.'

'No, I don't think you do.' She was about to walk past him when he caught her by the sleeve.

'You will not say anything to my Paloma?'

'I doubt if she would listen to me anyway, but if you treat her well and make her happy, then I promise you I won't say a word.'

'You are an angel from heaven.'

'I don't think my father would agree with you, signor.'

'I had a daughter once.' Fancello's moustache quivered with suppressed emotion.

'No, signor, you had a son. Clementino is a boy. Had you forgotten?'

Fancello's eyes filled with tears. 'Not Clementino. Paloma had a beautiful baby girl but she only lived for a day.'

Rose almost dropped the plate she was carrying. 'Are you saying that you and my aunt had a child?'

'I would have married her then, but for Graziella and Clementino. I had not the courage to tell Paloma that I was in fact a free man. She sent me away, but I should have refused to go. I should have followed my heart.' He turned with a start at the sound of Polly's voice as she leaned over the banisters, her nightcap askew and her wrap billowing about her like a sail.

'Sandro, what are you doing downstairs in your night clothes?'

'Nothing, *cara mia*. I was on my way to the kitchen to get a pot of coffee for you.'

'You silly man. What do you think servants are for? Come upstairs and get dressed.' She glared at Rose. 'Don't stand there, girl. Tell Maisie to bring coffee and a glass of seltzer to my room. Coffee for two.'

Giving Rose an apologetic smile, Fancello bundled his long robe up around his knees and took the stairs two at a time. 'Coming, *tesoro mio*.'

In the kitchen Ethel had started preparing the soup for the midday meal while Maisie peeled onions with tears running down her cheeks. Through the open scullery door Rose could see Sukey standing on a box at the clay sink, up to her elbows in water as she washed the breakfast dishes. Big Bertha was leaning against the wall, drinking tea from a tin mug. She looked tired, with dark circles beneath her eyes, and her sallow skin seemed to sag beneath her high cheekbones.

'I was up all night,' she explained when Rose enquired as to her wellbeing. 'Lizzie had a bit of a problem after the baby come out, but she's on the mend now.'

'More washing,' Ethel said grimly. 'That copper in the wash house never gets a chance to cool down.' She shot a curious glance at Rose. 'I suppose they want breakfast in bed? Well, they won't get it. We're too busy.'

'My aunt would like coffee for two and a glass of seltzer,' Rose said calmly. She had known that trying to keep anything secret in this house would be impossible.

Maisie mopped her eyes on a dishcloth. 'I'll see to it, Ethel. It'll give me a rest from these blooming onions. My eyes are stinging something chronic.'

Ethel tossed a large beef bone into the pot. 'He was the one,' she said tersely.

'I beg your pardon?' Rose eyed her curiously. 'Do you mean Signor Fancello?'

'Don't matter what his name is, but he was the one what got her into trouble in the first place.'

'How do you know that?'

Ethel pursed her lips. 'Lost her nipper a couple of days afore she found me in the gutter. She nursed me through losing mine and we suffered our losses together. There weren't no one else to know what we was going through. I been here ever since.' She sliced through a chunk of stewing beef. 'If that macaroni man hurts her again I'll do for him.'

'That goes for me too,' Bertha muttered, slamming her mug down on the table. 'I keeps a chiv tucked in me boot, just in case I ever needs to defend meself. He'll get a taste of it if he don't play straight. I hates all men and him especially.'

Alarmed, Rose looked from one grim face to the other. 'I don't think it will come to that. I hope you'll give Signor Fancello a chance to prove himself.'

The loud ringing of one of the bells on the board above the door made them all turn with a start.

'It's her room,' Bertha snarled. 'I'll go and see what's up.'

Rose snatched the tray of coffee from Maisie's

258

hands. 'It's all right, Bertha. I'm going upstairs anyway. I'll take it.' She headed for the servants' staircase before anyone had a chance to argue. Polly needed to be warned of the unrest below stairs and, if Fancello were to stay for any length of time, he needed to win the trust of Polly's faithful friends. Rose had seen the look in their eyes and she was worried.

Chapter Fourteen

Fancello was contrite, but Polly was defensive. She insisted that it was her house, and what she did in it was her business and had nothing to do with her staff, or the women she cared for. Rose would have been even more concerned for her aunt's future wellbeing had it not been for worrying about Billy, and the prospect of appearing in front of a large audience at the Grecian.

On the morning of their debut she was up early and roused Cora. After a hurried breakfast they went to the theatre for a final rehearsal. Rose had expected to find just a few stage hands and cleaners there at such an hour, but they were only halfway through their routine when Jim Slattery strolled onto the stage. He had his shirtsleeves rolled up and his normally sleek brown hair hung lankly over his brow. He tossed it back with a grimy hand.

'Good morning, girls. Glad to see that you're keen.' He sidled up to Cora with a suggestive leer on his thin features. His hooded eyes feasted on her slender body as if she were a piece of carrion and he were bird of ill omen.

Cora's cheeks flamed and she sidestepped him. 'If you'll excuse us, Mr Slattery, we'd like to get on.'

'Yes,' Rose said hastily. 'We want our act to be polished and perfect for tonight.'

'I can make you a star, Miss Sunshine.' He laid his hand on Cora's shoulder, lingering too long for a casual gesture.

'Thank you, but we'll try to do that for ourselves.' Cora moved away from him. 'Where did we get to, Rose?'

Slattery's smile froze and his thin lips tightened into a hard line. 'Don't try to be clever with me, miss. I can make you or I can break you. Your future depends on me, so remember that this evening after the show.' He glared at Rose, who had opened her mouth to protest. 'And you can keep out of this. I intend to take your sister for a quiet drink and a bite of supper later on. We don't need a chaperone.'

'You won't get one,' Rose snapped back at him. 'Cora has a gentleman friend and he's coming to the theatre this evening, so I wouldn't advise you to get in his way.'

'Yes,' Cora added, 'and my gentleman is well-connected, so you'd better watch your step, Mr Slattery.'

'Well-connected. That's a laugh.' Slattery's smile would have curdled milk. 'He'll be after one thing and we all know what that is. I've seen it more times than I care to remember, and it never ends well. Stick to your own kind, love. Forget the toff, and I'll show you more than a good time.'

Cora turned away from him. 'You're disgusting.'

'Leave her alone.' Rose slipped her arm around her sister's shoulders. Cora had paled alarmingly and she was trembling, whether from fear or anger Rose could not tell, but she knew that Slattery was a real threat. 'If you continue in this manner I'll report you to the manager.'

He shrugged. 'You won't get nowhere. Him and me are like that.' He crossed his fingers as if to demonstrate their closeness. 'Get on with your rehearsal. You'd better be good tonight or you'll find yourselves out of a job.' He walked into the wings, muttering beneath his breath.

'I feel sick.' Cora covered her mouth with her hands.

'Don't let him see that you're upset.' Rose took her by the shoulders and gave her a gentle shake. 'Look at me, Corrie.'

Cora raised a tearstained face. 'He's hateful, Rosie. He makes me feel dirty.'

'He's all talk, and anyway I won't leave you alone for a second. After the show you'll have Gerard to take care of you, and I think some of Aunt Polly's girls are coming to see our opening night.' She wrapped her arms around Cora and gave her a hug. 'Just imagine Slattery faced with Big Bertha. She'd sort the wretch out.'

'She frightens me,' Cora said, giggling. She dashed the tears from her cheeks. 'You're right, Rosie. Let's go through our routine once more. I won't allow Slattery to put me off.'

'That's the ticket.' Rose hitched up her skirts. 'One, two, three . . .'

The dressing room was hazy with tobacco smoke. Gaudy costumes decorated with ostrich feathers and sequins hung from pegs like a flock of exotic, brightly coloured birds that had come home to roost, and the floor was littered with boots and shoes and a dusting of sequins. Rose examined her reflection in the mirror, adjusting the perky little hat she wore at a pert angle, while Cora added a touch of rouge to her pale cheeks.

'It went well in the first half,' she said with a nervous giggle. 'I hope I don't let you down in our last number, Rosie. Slattery keeps giving me the eye. If I happen to look his way he leers at me and winks. It's horrible.'

'You'll be fine, Corrie. I'm sure that Gerard will be in the audience, and I'm certain it was Bertha's raucous laughter I could hear when the tumblers were on. I think someone must have fallen badly and hurt themselves to amuse her so greatly. That woman has a rather cruel sense of humour.'

'I know what you're doing,' Cora said, smiling. 'You're trying to distract me, but I am afraid of Slattery. I don't feel safe when he's around.'

Rose tensed at the sound of footsteps clattering on the bare boards in the corridor.

'Five minutes, please.' The callboy banged on the door and hurried on.

'This is it, Corrie.' Rose opened the door. 'Come on. Let's give them an act they'll never forget. The Sunshine Sisters will go down in theatre history.'

They took their bows to resounding applause, and cries of 'Encore', which were ignored by Slattery, who shook his head when the conductor raised his baton and looked to him for guidance. Rose could see him standing in the wings, arms folded and a grim expression on his face. He did not look like a man who wanted to woo a girl with soft words. Her confidence ebbed away, and suddenly she was afraid for her sister. As they stood centre stage she could just make out the front row of the stalls. She spotted Gerard seated next to a well-dressed couple whom she assumed were his parents. They looked distinctly uncomfortable and out of place amongst the enthusiastic lesser mortals, who were stamping their feet, whistling and generally voicing their approval. They must, Rose thought, wonder what sort of place their son had brought them to, and be regretting their desire to meet the young lady who had won his heart.

The audience was restive, braying for an encore,

and Bertha was jumping up and down beside the startled Barclay family, while Ethel waved and hallooed as if she were at the head of the hunt and had spotted a fox. Maisie was there too, as were Polly and Fancello, who were still seated, but clapping wildly. Then, to Rose's surprise, at the very end of the row she saw Vere and Bennett, and just behind them she could make out the smiling face of Joshua Hart.

'They're all here,' she whispered to Cora as they scampered off the stage. Even then the audience were still calling for more, but the next act was announced and silence fell for the star, the beautiful Loribelle Le Grand, whose emotionally charged rendition of popular songs could have the audience in floods of tears or rocking with laughter.

Rose pushed past Slattery, dragging Cora by the hand. He was in no position to protest, and they escaped to the dressing room where the chorus girls were getting ready for the finale.

'You done well, my ducks,' Florrie said, allowing smoke from her cigarillo to escape from the corners of her painted mouth. 'We could hear the applause from here.'

Nell perched on a stool, showing an amount of leg that would have shocked Seymour Perkins to the core. 'Watch out for Slattery, Cora. He'll have his hands all over you given half a chance. We've all seen the way he looks at you. Fair gives me the shivers.'

'You should know, ducks,' Florrie said, grinning.

'I don't suppose you put up much of a fight when you was cornered by him. You never do.'

'I got a steak supper out of it, which is more than what you did, matey.' Nell shifted to a more comfortable position. 'Anyone got a nip of gin to spare? My plates of meat are killing me.' She reached out to take a hip flask from one of the girls who had it tucked into her garter. 'Ta, love. I'll return the favour when I gets paid.'

The door opened just enough for the callboy to poke his head into the room. He glanced round at the scantily clad girls. 'Line up for the finale, my beauties.'

Dolly threw a shoe at him, but he retreated quickly and it bounced harmlessly off the door as it closed. 'Cheeky little blighter. One day I'll fetch him a slap round the chops and see how he likes that.'

'He's just a kid,' Nell said, rising to her feet. 'If you want to slap someone, give Slattery a punch on the nose. He deserves it. Look out for him, Cora. He's got his eye on you and it's pay day. He'll have been in the bar at The Eagle during the interval and he'll have a bottle of blue ruin in his coat pocket, I don't doubt.'

'He don't need Dutch courage,' Dolly added. 'Take our advice and steer clear.'

'Don't worry,' Rose said hastily. 'I'm up to his tricks. I'll see she's all right.'

'My gentleman friend is in the audience.' Cora tossed her head. 'He won't stand for any funny business.'

Rose hurried her from the room. 'Just stick close to me. He's all talk, Corrie.'

The final curtain had come down, but in the general rush to get to the dressing rooms Rose lost sight of Cora. She retraced her steps to the wings and found Slattery had her sister pressed up against the wall.

'Leave her alone,' she cried angrily. 'Cora, come here.'

Cora's face was ashen against the black velvet curtain that separated this part of the stage from the steps leading down into the auditorium. 'He won't let me go, Rose.'

'We'll see about that.' Rose made a dive at Slattery, giving him such a hefty shove that he lost his balance, stumbled and fell against the curtains. He clutched at them wildly but they parted and he tumbled backwards down the steps, landing at the feet of Lady Barclay.

Gerard looked up and, seeing Cora, he leaped onto the stage. 'What happened?'

Cora shivered and her teeth were chattering so that her words were barely intelligible.

'He was taking advantage of her,' Rose said in an undertone. 'I only meant to get him away from Cora; I didn't mean to harm him.' She was uncomfortably aware that the audience near enough to have witnessed the scene were standing round watching, as if this was part of the evening's entertainment. 'He's been pestering her ever since we started here.'

Gerard placed his arm around Cora. 'Are you all right, my love?'

She nodded tearfully. 'I'm sorry. I'm b-being a b-baby, but he scared me.'

Gerard released her and took a flying leap onto Slattery, who had only just scrambled to his feet. They fell in a heap on the floor, arms and legs flailing.

'Stop this at once.' Lord Barclay made a futile attempt to separate them, but his wife caught him by the coat-tails.

'Freddie, please. Don't stoop to their level.' She glanced anxiously over her shoulder. 'Get me out of this dreadful place.' She uttered a cry of fright as Big Bertha waded into the fray, swinging punches at Slattery that would have been a credit to a bare-knuckle fighter. She was followed by Ethel, who danced about waving her hands and swearing volubly, while Maisie curled up as small as she could, almost disappearing into her seat.

Polly clutched Fancello's arm. 'Don't fight them, Sandro. I won't allow you to.'

It occurred to Rose, as she hesitated on the top step, that Fancello had no intention of joining in, but others had no such qualms. She held her breath as Bennett grabbed Slattery by the collar. He was joined by Vere, who helped Gerard to his feet, and Joshua pushed his way through the crowd in time to catch Lady Barclay as she fell down in a dead faint. He helped her back to her seat with the aid of Lord Barclay, who looked pale and shaken.

'Stay there, Corrie,' Rose said firmly. She lifted her skirt and took the steps carefully, not wishing to end up on the floor like Slattery. She moved closer to Bennett, keeping out of range of Slattery's flailing fists. 'That man is an animal,' she said in a low voice. 'He's been pestering Cora and he won't take no for an answer.'

Bennett twisted Slattery round to face Cora. 'You'll apologise to the young lady, or I'll call a constable. It's your choice.'

Slattery rubbed his chin where a dark smudge was turning into a large bruise. 'I'll have you up for assault.'

'No, you won't. You'll apologise and promise to leave Miss Perkins alone in future, or I'll have you arrested and you'll lose your job. I doubt if many theatre managers would want to hire you after that.'

Gerard helped Cora down from the stage. 'Are you sure you're not hurt?'

She shook her head. 'I'm fine, Gerard. I was scared, but I'm all right now you're here.'

Bennett poked Slattery in the ribs. 'What do you say?'

'Sorry.' Slattery spat the word at Cora.

'That's not good enough.' Bennett turned to his cousin. 'Call a constable, Vere. This fellow needs to be taught a lesson.'

'All right,' Slattery said hastily. 'I'm sorry, miss. It won't happen again.'

'I should jolly well hope not.' Gerard shook his fist at Slattery. 'I'll take pleasure in reporting you to your employer.'

'I said I'm sorry.' Slattery turned to Bennett, scowling. 'You've had your fun, now let a working man get about his business.'

Polly had taken a seat beside Lady Barclay during this altercation, with Fancello hovering in the background. She produced a vinaigrette from her reticule and wafted it under the unconscious woman's nose until she coughed and opened her eyes.

'What happened?' Lady Barclay stared round in horror. 'Take me from this palace of iniquity, Freddie. Take me home.'

Her husband leaned over to help her to her feet. He glanced up at his son. 'You haven't heard the last of this, Gerard. You should never have brought us to this vulgar show.'

'Hold on, guv.' Bertha towered over him. 'I don't like the tone of your voice. What d'you expect when you come slumming?'

'Who is this person, Gerard? Is she one of your new friends?' Lady Barclay leaned on her husband's arm. She peered at Cora through her lorgnette. 'You were on that stage wearing less than nothing. You should be ashamed of yourself, young lady. I understand that you are a vicar's daughter. What must he think of you?'

Cora's eyes filled with tears and her lips trembled, but before she could defend herself Joshua had managed to edge his way through the onlookers and he faced up to Gerard's indignant mother.

'The Reverend Seymour Perkins is very proud of both his daughters, my lady. I can tell you that for a fact. They have done nothing to disgrace the family name, as you would know had you taken the trouble to find out more about them.'

Lady Barclay staggered backwards, falling against her husband. 'I'm being castigated by a cleric, Freddie. What manner of establishment is this?'

'I don't know, my dear, but it's one we shall not be patronising again, and nor will you, Gerard.'

'I say, sir, that's a bit unnecessary. It was only a minor fracas, and it doesn't happen nightly.' Gerard glanced anxiously at Slattery, who was doing his best to appear invisible. 'Tell him, man. Tell my papa that this is not how one normally behaves in this theatre.'

'It ain't, your lordship.' Slattery touched his forelock, cringing like a whipped cur. 'It was an accident, your lordship. A misunderstanding, and it won't happen again.' He backed into the crowd and was lost from sight.

'It most certainly will not.' Lady Barclay adjusted her feathered hat as she turned to her son. 'Gerard, I forbid you to come here again, and you will put a stop to your relationship with this young woman.'

Rose had heard enough. She squeezed past Bennett, coming face to face with Lady Barclay. 'That is so unfair. You're blaming my sister for something that was beyond her control. She is a good person and she loves your son, and I believe he loves her.'

'Nonsense,' Lady Barclay drew herself up to her full height. 'This stops now. Gerard, you're coming home with us.'

'I'm a grown man, Mama.' Gerard lowered his voice. 'You can't order my life as if I were a boy.'

'You are not yet twenty-one. You will do as you are told.' Lord Barclay thrust Gerard's top hat into his hands. 'Defy me and I'll stop your allowance.' He gesticulated to the crowd of onlookers. 'Make way, we're leaving.'

Gerard hesitated. 'I'm sorry, Cora,' he said softly. 'I must go now, but this is far from over.'

'Don't leave like this,' Cora pleaded. She made to follow him but Rose caught her by the hand.

'Let him go, Corrie. If he truly loves you he'll find a way.'

Joshua placed himself between Cora and the departing Barclays. 'Allow me to see you home, Miss Cora.'

'I have to change out of my costume,' Cora said dully.

Fancello took off his opera cloak and wrapped it around Cora's shoulders. 'There you are, *cara mia*. Leave your things until the morning. You should come home and rest.'

Polly rose majestically to her feet. 'Come, ladies. I think we've had enough excitement for one night.' She took Fancello's arm. 'We will lead the way.'

They walked on, followed closely by Joshua and a distraught Cora.

Bertha shrugged her bony shoulders. 'I ain't had such an entertaining time since she found me drunk in the gutter, not that I remember too much about that night. I fancy a pint of porter. What about you, Ethel?'

'You took the words out of me mouth,' Ethel said, nodding. 'The only trouble is I ain't got a penny to me name.'

Bennett put his hand in his pocket and took out a handful of coins. 'Allow me, ma'am. That was an impressive display of fisticuffs. I'm glad you were on our side.'

Bertha blushed to the roots of her mousy hair. 'Ta ever so, guv. You're a real gent,' she said, tittering and fluttering her sandy eyelashes.

'Never mind him,' Ethel said gruffly. 'I was there too, so some of that's mine.'

Bennett pressed some coins into her hand. 'Of course. You were both splendid. It's good to know that Rose and Cora have such staunch friends.'

Still giggling, Bertha hurried towards the exit with Ethel trotting along behind her.

'I should go, too.' Rose hesitated. 'Thank you both for standing up for us. Slattery is a mean man.'

Vere frowned, shaking his head. 'I don't like the thought of you and your sister being exposed to such behaviour. This is not the place for well-brought-up young ladies.'

'We have to earn our living,' Rose said firmly. 'And this is something we're good at. Neither Cora nor I were brought up to do anything more useful.'

'Back me up on this, Bennett.' Vere turned to his cousin. 'You agree with me, don't you?'

Bennett met Rose's anxious gaze with a hint of a smile. 'Whether or not I agree is immaterial, Vere. From what I know of Rose she will do what she thinks is right for her and for her sister, and nothing that you or I might say will make the slightest bit of difference. Isn't that right, Miss Sunshine?'

'You seem to know me better than I know myself, but I have learned to stand on my own two feet. Or perhaps I should say that dancing on my own two feet has proved to be my salvation, and Cora's, too.' She glanced about the auditorium, which had emptied as if by magic when the fracas was over. 'I should go and change out of my costume.'

'I think it's rather charming,' Bennett said with a judicious nod of his head.

'But not the sort of garment a lady would wear off stage,' Vere added hastily. 'I was hoping you might allow me to take you out to supper, Rose.'

'Oh, I don't know about that. I am rather tired.'

'I'm returning home tomorrow. I would glad of your company this last time.'

Rose tried in vain to think of an excuse. The last thing she wanted was for Vere to repeat his proposal of marriage, and she knew instinctively that this was what he intended.

'We'll wait for you, Rose,' Bennett said before she had a chance to respond. 'I'm sure you wouldn't want to disappoint Vere, and I would very much like to join you.' He shot a sideways glance at his cousin. 'That's if you have no objection.'

'No, of course not.'

Rose could tell by his tone that Vere did care – very much – but she was relieved. 'All right. I'll be as quick as I can.' She hurried to the dressing room. The chorus girls had already departed, leaving a mess of rags soiled with stage make-up and saucers overflowing with ash and the stubs of cigarillos. Rose took off her make-up and changed out of her costume and into her day clothes, but she had second thoughts when it came to putting on her mantle, which was thin and offered little protection should it rain. She bundled it up with the rest of Cora's things and slipped on her sister's hooded cape. With a last quick look in the mirror she patted a stray lock of hair into place and set off to join her escorts.

They dined at the Gaiety restaurant in the Strand, and Rose began to relax. Perhaps the wine helped, and the food was excellent, but it was Bennett who put himself out to make her feel at ease. He was a surprisingly good host and seemed to know most of the waiters as well as the maître d'hôtel, who gave them an excellent table and hovered at a discreet distance, making sure that everything was to their liking. Rose was curious, having thought previously that Bennett was the type of man who kept himself to himself, but it seemed that she had been mistaken. It was Vere who appeared to be tongue-tied, only answering in monosyllables when asked a direct question. He ate his meal largely in silence and on several occasions she found him staring at her with a brooding expression that barely lightened when she spoke to him. More than ever she found herself drawn to Bennett, and laughing at the droll stories he told, although Vere did not seem to see humour in any of them.

They had finished dessert and were drinking coffee at their table when Vere found his voice. He cleared his throat, staring pointedly at Bennett. 'Perhaps you would give us a moment or two on our own, cousin. I have something particular to discuss with Rose.'

Bennett raised an eyebrow, glancing at Rose for her assent. She nodded and smiled. 'I'm sure it won't take long.'

'I'll be in the smoking room when you're ready to leave.' Bennett rose from the table and made his way through the tables.

Rose watched him go with a feeling of near panic. She had hoped that Vere would leave matters as they were, but it was obvious from his intense expression that this was not going to happen. He stared into his coffee cup. 'I think you know what I want to ask you, Rose.'

'If it's the same as before then I have to tell you that I am still of the same mind. Nothing has changed, Vere.'

He looked up and his face was pale and strained. 'Please reconsider, Rose. I dread going back to that large, echoing house alone.'

'You're hardly alone,' she said, attempting to lighten the mood. 'You have servants to wait on you, and outdoor staff to take care of your beautiful grounds. You're an important man in the town, and well-respected.'

He reached out to cover her hand with his as it rested on the pristine white tablecloth. 'But all that is nothing if I have no one to share it with. All these years I've been on my own, and I didn't realise how lonely I was until you came into my life. Now I find I can't live without you.'

'I'm sorry,' she said gently. 'I don't feel the same.' With an apologetic smile, she withdrew her hand. 'I am really sorry.'

'But you can't wish to remain here in London, living in that madhouse with your aunt and those rough women. Appearing on the stage with men ogling you isn't the sort of life I would wish for my wife or my daughter, or my sister, if I had one.'

'I am none of those, Vere. I am my own person, and, to be honest, I enjoy performing and entertaining people. I'm not the sort of person you need, surely you must see that. You deserve a wife who will be happy to stay at home and bask in your reflected glory. You're a good man, and a kind man. I wish I felt differently, but I can't make myself love you.'

'It might come in time. I've known couples who

were barely acquainted when they married and love came later. I would give you everything I have, and endeavour to make you happy.'

She stood up, unable to bear the sight of him pleading. 'No, Vere. It won't do. I'm sorry.' She held up her hand as he started to rise to his feet. 'I'll ask the doorman to hail a cab for me.'

'I can't allow you to go home unescorted.'

'You have no choice, I'm afraid.' She left him before he could protest and humiliate himself further. The success that she and Cora had enjoyed had been dimmed by Slattery's outlandish behaviour, and the pleasant meal had been marred by Vere's refusal to take no for an answer. She collected Cora's cape from the cloakroom attendant, and made her way to the front entrance where the doorman hailed a cab. She glanced over her shoulder as she was about to climb in, but there was no sign of Bennett. The cab pulled away from the kerb, and she settled back against the squabs with a feeling of relief tinged with disappointment. Bennett obviously cared more for his cousin than he did for her comfort or safety.

It was late when Rose arrived back at Polly's house and it had started to rain. She pulled the hood over her head as she stepped onto the pavement.

'That'll be one and six, please, miss.' The cabby leaned down from his box, holding out his hand. Rose opened her reticule and to her horror found that it was empty. She had left it in the dressing room during their performance and she knew for a fact that there had been two shillings in silver and coppers in her purse, but now there was nothing, not even a farthing.

'It seems that someone has stolen my money,' she said breathlessly. 'If you'll wait a minute I'll get the fare from my sister.'

'This had better not be a trick. I'm up to the games your sort plays.'

Rose might have been upset by this allusion to her being a woman of ill repute, but she was too anxious to worry about details. She ran up the steps and banged on the door, but the house was in darkness. She knocked again. The sound of horses' hoofs made her look round to see the cab driving off and a male figure looming out of the darkness.

'You got yourself into a pickle, didn't you, flower? You ain't so brave now you're on your own, are you, Cora?'

Rose uttered a gasp of dismay. She did not need to see his face – the gravelly voice was all too familiar.

Chapter Fifteen

She spun round to face him. 'It's Rose, Mr Slattery. You have the wrong sister.'

His expression hardened. 'You like playing tricks. Maybe I'll have you instead.'

'Touch me and I'll scream so loud that they'll hear me in the police station down the road.'

He took a step backwards. 'It ain't you I'm interested in anyway, you harpy. Tell Miss Cora that Jim Slattery will be looking to take her out for supper after the show tomorrow evening.'

'You're wasting your time. She won't go with you.'

'If she don't I'll need to have words with the manager and you'll find yourselves out of work, begging on the streets, or worse. Do you understand?' He leaned towards her, breathing heavily.

'Don't threaten me, Mr Slattery. I'll report your

behaviour to the manager and we'll see who comes off worst.'

The words had barely left her lips when he lunged at her, grabbing her by the throat. Pressed against the front door, she could scarcely breathe. She kicked and struggled but he was stronger than he looked, and her efforts to free herself seemed to add to his fury. His fingers tightened, but just as she felt herself slipping into a dark abyss she was pulled back from the brink by a pair of strong hands.

'You're all right now, Rose. You're safe.' Bennett's voice was oddly soothing, and she seemed to be moving through the air without having put a foot on the ground. 'She's all right, Miss Polly. A tot of brandy might be just the thing.'

Rose opened her eyes to find herself lying on the chaise longue in the parlour. 'What happened?' she demanded, making an effort to raise herself on her elbow. 'Where did he go?'

'He's sitting on the pavement outside, nursing a sore head.' Bennett leaned closer. 'Are you hurt?'

Polly thrust a glass of brandy under Rose's nose. 'Sip this, dear. It's lucky for you that Mr Sharpe arrived in time to save you from harm.'

Rose brushed the drink aside. 'No, thank you, Aunt Polly. I think a cup of tea would suit me better.'

Polly raised the glass to her own lips and drank it down in one gulp. 'Maisie, fetch tea for Miss Rose.' She turned to Fancello, who was hovering in the background, his nightcap askew and his face crumpled with concern. 'Take a look out of the window, Sandro. Is that man still there?'

Fancello moved to open the shutter just enough to peek outside. 'He's staggering off along the road. I don't think he'll bother us again tonight.' He turned to give Rose a worried look. 'Are you sure you are all right, *cara*? Perhaps we should send for the doctor?'

Rose struggled to a sitting position. Her throat felt sore and bruised, and she had skinned her knuckles in her attempt to escape Slattery's clutches. 'I'm all right.'

'Shall I fetch Cora?' Polly asked anxiously. 'You do look very pale, Rose.'

'I don't want her to see me like this.'

'That fellow should be locked up,' Bennett said angrily. 'You must report this attack to the police, Rose. He can't be allowed to get away with it.'

She frowned thoughtfully. 'I agree, but it's my word against his. He thought I was Cora and he would say that she led him on. He's a man, and his word would count more than either mine or my sister's. We're not in the most respected profession, as you must be aware.'

'It is all wrong,' Polly said, pouring herself another drink. 'It's scandalous, that's what I say.'

'I agree.' Fancello nodded vigorously. 'What do you think, Signor Sharpe? You are a man of the law.'

'Unfortunately I think that Rose is right. Slattery is a slippery character and it's unlikely that he would face arrest.' Bennett's expression was bleak as he gazed at Rose. 'I can't prevent you from going back to the theatre, but think carefully before you come to a decision.'

'Are you saying that we ought to give up our livelihood because of one man?'

'I know better than to tell you what to do, Rose. You've made an enemy there, and you have Cora to consider. Is she strong enough to put Slattery in his place?'

'He's right,' Fancello said earnestly. 'I've met men like him and they are no good.' He slumped down on the window seat. 'I was your manager, and I've let you down. I am not worth my ten per cent.'

'It's not your fault, Sandro.' Polly held her hand out to him. 'It's late, my dear. We should get some sleep, and that goes for you too, Rose. Things will look better in the morning.' She sent a meaningful look to Bennett. 'You'll be on your way now, Mr Sharpe. I'll bid you good night.' She sailed out of the room with Fancello in tow.

Rose sat up and swung her legs over the side of the couch. 'I'm grateful to you for turning up when you did, Bennett, but why did you follow me home?'

'My cousin is not very subtle. It wasn't hard to guess why he wanted to speak to you in private, and judging by the state of him when I returned from the smoking room, I knew you must have refused him a second time.'

'It would have been better had I declined your

invitation to supper. None of this would have happened if I'd come home with Cora.'

'A good lawyer's answer,' he said, chuckling. 'I've said it before, Rose, but you would make an excellent barrister.'

She smiled. 'Maybe one day there will be women lawyers. They might even have female police officers.'

Bennett helped her to her feet. 'I think that might be going a bit too far. I wouldn't want a sister or daughter of mine to have to deal with the ruffians who inhabit Seven Dials.'

She might have argued the point, but a wave of exhaustion swept over her and it was a relief to have a strong arm to lean on as he helped her from the room. They came to a halt at the foot of the stairs.

'By the way,' she said curiously, 'you haven't told me why you followed me home. You couldn't have known that Slattery would accost me.'

Bennett took his hat from the hallstand and put it on at a rakish angle. 'I knew that Vere must have said something to upset you, or you wouldn't have run off without a word. I just wanted to make sure you were all right.'

'It was time for me to leave, that's all.'

'Even so, my cousin is a good man, Rose. You could do a lot worse.'

'So you keep telling me, but when I marry it will be for love. Good night, Bennett.' She mounted the stairs and did not look back until she reached the top. When she did turn her head there was no sign of him. She heard the front door close with a thud that sounded like a final farewell. Her throat ached as she made her way to her room and it was not entirely due to the stranglehold applied by Slattery. She opened the door and was greeted by Maisie.

'I brought you a nice hot cup of tea and Ethel sent a slice of seed cake. She said she knows you got a liking for something sweet.'

Big Bertha emerged from the shadows clutching a tin mug filled with something hot and aromatic. 'My old mum used to give us nippers this for a sore throat,' she said gruffly. 'If I'd known what was going on outside I'd have come and given the bloke a good kicking.' She thrust the drink into Rose's hands. 'Cinnamon tea laced with honey. Drink it slowly and keep some by in case you get a dry throat in the night.'

'Thank you both.' Rose swallowed hard. Their kindness had brought tears to her eyes, but she did not want to break down in front of them. If she let her emotions take over she knew it would be hard to stem the flood.

Maisie hesitated, seeming unwilling to leave. 'I wish I'd taken a swipe at the brute when I saw him on the floor at the theatre. I was so scared I just sat there and watched, but Bertha give him what for.'

Bertha flexed her muscles. 'And I'd do it again, only next time I'll do it harder and better.' She grabbed Maisie by the arm. 'C'mon you. Miss Rose needs to rest.' She propelled Maisie out of the room and closed the door.

The house seemed oddly silent as Rose sat on the bed and sipped her tea. Her throat was too sore to allow her to eat the cake, and she drank some of Bertha's concoction before going to bed. She closed her eyes and made an effort to relax, but the events of that evening kept coming to mind and it was a long time before she finally went to sleep.

Next morning she awakened feeling remarkably well considering her ordeal the previous evening. She washed and dressed, put up her hair and went down to breakfast only to find the dining room empty. There was no sign of Poppy and Fancello, which was not unusual as they were late risers, but Rose thought it odd that Cora had not yet put in an appearance. She helped herself to a boiled egg and some toast, but swallowing still presented a problem, and she ate very little. Tea slipped down easily, however, and after two cups Rose decided to go upstairs and wake Cora, as they needed to discuss what tactics they would use at the theatre. The fracas after the show would not have gone down well with the manager. He had not been present at the time, but Slattery would be sure to put his side of the story, portraying himself in the best possible light.

Rose knocked on Cora's door and waited, and when there was no response she entered the room, to find it in darkness. She made her way to the window and drew back the curtains.

'Wake up, sleepyhead.' She was about to go over and give Cora a shake when she realised that the bed had not been slept in, and there was no sign of her sister. Even if Cora had risen early it would have been unlike her to make her bed and tidy the room before going down to breakfast. Rose moved swiftly to the clothes press and looked inside. Her worst fears were realised when she found it empty and Cora's valise was missing from the top of the cupboard.

It was only when she looked on the dressing table that she found a note written in Cora's neat hand.

Dear Rose

Don't be cross with me, but I cannot bear to be parted from Gerard. His parents will never accept me as their daughter-in-law and we are desperate to be together. Don't worry about me. I will be safe and happy with my darling boy. We are going where no one will find us.

Forgive me for breaking up the Sunshine Sisters, but I have no choice.

I will always love you.

Cora

Rose sank down on the stool, staring at her reflection in the mirror with unseeing eyes. 'Oh, Corrie,' she murmured softly. 'What have you done?' It took some moments for the full impact of her sister's elopement to register and then she leaped to her feet. 'Where would they go?' she demanded, gazing at the distraught young woman in the mirror. When nothing came to mind she hurried from the room and went to bang on Polly's door.

'Aunt Polly, I must speak to you urgently.'

The door opened and Fancello stood there, tousle-haired and bleary-eyed. His shirt hung open, exposing a tightly laced corset and his trousers were at half-mast, revealing his drawers.

Rose averted her eyes. 'I must speak to my aunt,' she said urgently.

'What is it, Rose?' Polly demanded sleepily. 'Can't it wait?'

'No, Aunt. It's Cora, she's eloped with Gerard.' There was no point trying to break the news gently. Rose took a deep breath. 'She left a note.'

'Come away from the door, Sandro. You're only half dressed.' Polly's bare feet padded across the carpet and she pushed Fancello aside. 'Are you certain of this, Rose?'

Rose handed her the note, and Polly held it at arm's length, squinting as she made out the words. 'The silly girl,' she said, thrusting the crumpled paper into Rose's hand. 'Give me time to get dressed and I'll see you in the parlour.' She closed the door.

'Where would they have gone?' Half an hour later Polly sailed into the parlour, fully dressed.

Rose glanced at the dainty ormolu clock on the mantelshelf. She had been pacing the floor while she waited, trying to think of the answer to just that question. She bit back a sharp retort. 'I really have no idea.'

Fancello sidled into the room with a half-eaten slice of toast in his hand. 'Perhaps they've gone to get her father's blessing.'

Rose and Polly stared at him in stunned silence. Rose was the first to recover. 'I'm afraid that's the last place Cora would go. Papa would be even more outraged than he is already, and Cora is well aware of that. He would send Gerard packing and heaven alone knows what he would say to Corrie.'

'You're right,' Polly said slowly. 'Do you think he would take her to Gretna Green?'

'He might, but we don't know for certain that he intends to marry her.' Rose sank down on a chair by the fireplace. 'I'm barely acquainted with Gerard, but what I saw of his parents makes me think that he would be unwilling to go against them.'

'Cora would be an asset to any family,' Polly said stoutly. 'But would that young swell make Cora happy? Personally, I doubt it.'

Fancello shook his head. 'It isn't up to us to make judgements. Who would have thought we would end up together, Paloma? Thirteen years ago it seemed like a wild dream.'

'This isn't helping,' Rose said angrily. They did not seem to understand that she had lost her brother, and now she was losing her sister. 'There must be something we could do.'

'You will be only half of the Sunshine Sister act.' Fancello took a small comb from his pocket. 'The manager at the Grecian might object.' He combed his moustache, curling the ends round the tip of his finger.

'Must you do that now?' Polly demanded angrily. 'This is important, Sandro.'

'After the scene last night we might have found ourselves out of a job anyway.' Rose clutched her throat. The mere thought of the theatre brought back memories of Slattery's hands around her neck.

'There is something I can do.' Fancello inspected his reflection in the mirror above the mantelshelf. 'I will visit the theatre and speak to that person. I will tell him what Slattery did to you. At least I can do something useful.'

'I suppose I could go on without Corrie. We really do need the money.'

'You have a better voice than your sister. You could do it, Rose.' Polly gave her an encouraging smile. 'You are so much like I was at your age. Is she not, Sandro?'

'You are the image of Paloma when she was a girl. You would go far as a solo artiste, *cara mia*. Take it from an old man who knows talent when he sees it. I will go to the theatre right away and prove that Alessandro Fancello is still a man to be reckoned with.' He bowed out of the room, as if acknowledging a round of applause.

The moment the door closed, Polly reached for a silver box. She took out a cheroot and struck a match. 'I don't normally indulge,' she said, exhaling a puff of smoke, 'but it's too early for a nip of brandy, and my poor nerves are shredded. Your sister has a lot to answer for, Rose. I won't forgive her for this.'

'I must do something.' Rose moved to the window and gazed out at the busy street. 'Of course,' she said, turning to Polly. 'Why didn't I think of it before? If there's anyone Cora might have spoken to it would be Maisie.'

'Ring the bell and we'll ask her.'

'No, I don't think that's a good idea. I'll speak to her in private.'

Maisie was reluctant at first, but after some gentle questioning she admitted that she had helped Cora to pack and had smuggled her out of the house through the tradesmen's entrance. Tommy had also been involved in Cora's romance, and had acted as go-between, taking messages to Gerard and returning with his responses.

'Then he knows where Mr Barclay lives,' Rose said eagerly.

'Yes, he does.' Maisie nodded. 'I doubt if they'll be at his lodgings. Miss Cora was scared of what Mr Gerard's parents would say if they found out, so he wouldn't take her home.'

'Even so, there might be someone there who knows where they've gone.' Rose clutched Maisie's hands in hers. 'You must ask Tommy to give me his address. I'll go there directly and, who knows, I might be in time to catch up with them before Cora's reputation is lost for ever.'

'I'm coming with you, miss.'

'There's no need. Tommy can show me the way.'

'I was a slavey in a big house up West. I know how them toffs carry on, and the young misses would always have their maidservant tagging along when they went out and about. You got to act like you're one of them or you won't get nowhere.'

Rose gazed at her in astonishment. She had always thought of Maisie as the desperate child they had plucked from the brink of suicide, but now she was seeing her in a new light. The girl had grown into a woman, seemingly overnight. 'I suppose you're right,' she said slowly. 'I hadn't thought about it like that.'

'You put on your best bonnet, miss, and I'll fetch Tommy. We ain't got no time to lose.'

Rose went to her room and changed into her Sunday best. She was ready for battle, whether it be with Gerard's parents or Slattery, it did not matter. She would take them all on in her efforts to save Cora from disgrace and despair.

The address in Duke Street turned out to be a select lodging house where Gerard had rooms. The landlady might have been a duchess, for all the airs and graces she assumed when the maid showed Rose into her parlour. Maisie had been told to wait outside the door, although Rose suspected that she would have her ear to the keyhole.

'What can I do for you, miss?' The landlady folded her hands in front of her, eyeing Rose up and down as if she were calculating the cost of her clothing, and finding her wanting in taste and style.

'Nothing for me personally.' Rose responded to her in a similarly haughty tone. 'I am a distant relative of Mr Gerard Barclay, and I'm recently up from the country so I thought I would call on him. This is the address he gave me.'

'A distant relative, you say.'

'Is my cousin at home, or is he not?'

'He is not. Mr Barclay left yesterday for an unspecified destination. I cannot help you any further.'

It was obvious to Rose that the woman thought the worst of her, which was humiliating although perhaps not unexpected, and there was no use continuing the conversation. She managed a weak smile. 'Thank you, ma'am. I won't trouble you further.'

'Who shall I say called?'

'It doesn't matter. I'm on my way to visit Lord and Lady Barclay in Russell Square. I'm sure they will tell me what I want to know.' Rose had the satisfaction of seeing a flicker of doubt in the landlady's eyes. 'Good day to you, ma'am.' She let herself out of the room, causing Maisie to leap to safety.

'What did she say?'

'I would have thought you heard most of the conversation.'

'You didn't get anything out of the stuck-up old bitch.'

'Hush, Maisie. She might hear you.' Rose hurried her to the front door, where the maid was waiting to show them out.

Rose stood on the pavement outside, wondering what to do next. She took a deep breath of the air that was considerably sweeter and cleaner this side of town.

'So did she say anything useful?' Maisie demanded.

'No, I'm afraid I'm none the wiser.'

'But I am, miss.' Tommy Tinker emerged from a doorway, grinning from ear to ear. 'I collared the boot boy. He told me that he'd taken Mr Barclay's luggage to Waterloo Bridge station where it was to be sent by train to Cornwall.'

'To Cornwall?' Rose clutched his sleeve. 'Where in Cornwall, Tommy?'

'I dunno, miss. I think he said it were going to the Barclay family estate, wherever that is.'

'You silly boy,' Maisie said crossly. 'You should have asked.'

Tommy's face flushed a dull red and his freckles seemed twice as large. He hung his head. 'Sorry, miss.'

'It doesn't matter,' Rose said hastily. 'I think I know where it is. Cora mentioned it once but I didn't take much notice. I had too many other things on my mind. You did well, the pair of you. Now let's find a cab and go home.'

*

'I have to travel to Cornwall, Aunt Polly.' Rose took off her bonnet and dropped it on a chair in the parlour.

'Cornwall?' Polly stared at her wide-eyed. 'Are you going to accept Vere Tressidick's proposal?'

'Good heavens, no. It has nothing to do with Vere. I think I know where Cora has gone.'

'Where is she? Where has that cad taken her?' Polly was suddenly alert. She had been relaxing on the chaise longue, stroking Spartacus, who was being unusually docile, but she sat up straight, dislodging him from his comfortable position. She patted his head absent-mindedly and he gave her a resentful look, closed his eyes and went back to sleep.

'Gerard's luggage was sent to the family estate, which Cora once told me is on the edge of Bodmin Moor. Tommy extracted that information from the boot boy in Duke Street.'

Polly's jaw dropped. 'What is this fascination with Cornwall? I'd never heard of these places until Billy got himself involved with the Tressidick family. Why couldn't they have had an estate in Surrey or Berkshire?'

'I can't answer that, Aunt Polly. Anyway, I'm getting the next train to the West Country. I don't care how long it takes, but I'm going to find Corrie and bring her home.'

'You can't go alone, dear. That wouldn't do at all.'

'I travelled to Cornwall from Dorset on my own, but if it makes you happy I'll take Maisie with me.

According to her, no respectable young woman would travel without her maid.'

'I suppose that will have to do,' Polly said reluctantly.

'I'll have to let the manager at the Grecian know that I won't be performing tonight.'

'I'm sorry, dear. You've lost your job anyway. Sandro returned not half an hour since with the news. Slattery got in first and told the manager a pack of lies, making out that you were to blame for the disturbance last night. Sandro tried to tell him that you were the innocent victim, but Slattery was believed and we were not. It's a sad fact, but you're better off staying away from there as things are.'

'I suspected as much,' Rose said, shrugging. 'The most important thing now is to find Corrie. The Sunshine Sisters aren't finished yet, you'll see.'

Less than an hour later Rose and Maisie were waiting on the platform at Waterloo Bridge station. Their train was due at any moment and the porter had their luggage stacked on a trolley, waiting to take it to the guard's van. Maisie's youthful face was flushed with excitement and her brown eyes were alight with wonder as she took in the busy scene. It was nothing new to Rose, but she could see that Maisie was drinking it all in. Her eyes widened as an engine let off steam, the loud screech reverberating from the rafters and the glass roof. She uttered a muffled shriek, covering her ears with her hands as the great beast of an engine roared into sight. It slowed down with a loud grating sound of iron wheels on iron tracks, and came to a halt with a burst of steam. The smell of hot oil, smoke and burning coals mingled with the industrial odours of the lead works and the local brewery. Rose was beginning to feel like a seasoned traveller, but Maisie appeared to be overcome by the experience.

'Follow me, if you please.' The porter trundled his trolley along the platform and Rose grabbed Maisie by the hand as he led them to a first-class carriage. Polly had insisted that they must travel in comfort and relative safety, and Rose had not had the heart to argue. Left to herself she would have saved the money and travelled third class, but Polly had taken the funds from her safe and had made Rose promise to do as she asked.

The porter opened the carriage door and Rose was about to get in when she heard someone call her name.

Maisie tugged at her sleeve. 'Look who it is, miss. What a coincidence.'

Chapter Sixteen

'Vere.' Rose had recognised his voice and her heart sank. She did not relish the thought of travelling all the way to Bodmin in his company. 'I didn't expect to see you.'

'I told you that I was returning home today. Perhaps you forgot.' He assisted Maisie into the carriage and climbed in after her. 'This is a most pleasant surprise. Might I dare to hope that you've changed your mind? Are you on your way to Portmorna?'

Rose settled herself in a corner seat. 'No, it's rather more complicated than that.' She frowned at Maisie, who seemed to have difficulty in choosing where to place herself. 'Do sit down, please. The train will be leaving soon.'

'I'm sorry, miss. I ain't never been on one of these things afore. I'm afraid of sitting close to the window in case I gets sucked out.'

Vere's normally serious expression melted into a smile. 'I wouldn't worry about that. This is a very safe way to travel. Might I suggest that you take a seat next to your mistress? I'll sit opposite, so if anyone gets sucked out of the window it will be me.'

Maisie sank down beside Rose. 'Ta, sir. You're a gent.'

Vere made himself comfortable and the sound of the guard's whistle and the slamming of carriage doors announced the train's imminent departure. The noise of the engine building up steam filled the compartment, making conversation impossible for a while. Maisie buried her face in her hands, apparently terrified by the noise, and she uttered a muffled scream when the train began to move. Rose sighed inwardly; it was going to be a long journey.

'May I ask where you're going?' Vere gave her a searching look.

'Cora has run away with Gerard Barclay.' She had not meant to blurt it out in such a manner, but there seemed little point in dissembling. Short of a miracle, it would be common knowledge soon enough. She could imagine how the newspapers would love to print a lurid story of the elopement of a baron's son and the girl from the music hall.

Vere frowned. 'I'm sorry, although after the debacle at the theatre it would seem inevitable.'

'Why would you say such a thing?' Rose demanded, bristling. 'My sister is a sensible young woman.'

'Perhaps, but people seem to act very differently

when they are besotted. It was obvious that Barclay's parents were intent on forbidding the match, which left the young couple with very little choice.'

Rose stared at him in surprise. 'You sound as if you approve of Cora and Gerard's actions.'

'Perhaps I do, in a way. I am not always as hidebound and prudent as you seem to think, Rose. My cousin Bennett is the one with the calculating mind. I, on the other hand, am inclined to be impetuous.'

At any other time Rose might have laughed at such a notion, but she was seeing Vere in a different light. She had expected him to be shocked and disapproving, and he was neither.

'I'm hoping to persuade Cora to return to London with me,' she said stiffly. 'If this becomes public knowledge her reputation will be ruined. They are both under age and would need parental consent in order to marry. I know that my papa would never agree to such a match, and it's obvious that Lord Barclay feels the same.'

'Perhaps you ought to inform your father, Rose. Cora is, after all, his responsibility.'

'I couldn't do that. Papa had to leave the parish he had nurtured and loved for twenty years because of Billy, and our mother is in a delicate state of health. I think another scandal would be too much for her to bear.'

'It ain't natural to travel so fast,' Maisie cried as the train picked up speed. She pulled her shawl over her head. 'We're going to crash. I knows it.'

'The faster we go, the quicker we'll get there,' Rose said calmly.

It was early evening when they finally arrived at Bodmin station, having parted company with Vere at Plymouth where they changed trains. He had once again extended an open invitation for Rose to visit him at Portmorna, extracting a promise from her that she would turn to him for help if matters did not go well.

'I'm too tired to go any further, miss,' Maisie said wearily. 'I could sleep on a bed of nails.'

'I'm tired too, but there is still an hour or two of daylight before dark. I really wanted to get to Rosewenna Hall tonight.'

Maisie shrugged her thin shoulders. 'They was together last night. The harm's already been done, miss.'

'We've come this far, Maisie. I'm not giving up now.' Rose beckoned to the porter who had been hovering at a discreet distance with their luggage. 'We need a carriage to take us to Rosewenna Hall.'

He edged closer. ''Tis a fair way, miss. 'Tis seven mile or more, and you'll not find anyone wanting to venture onto the moor after dark.'

'But it's still light.'

'Night's coming. You'd best put up at the inn.'

'Do you know where I could hire a pony and trap? I need to get to my destination tonight.'

He pushed his cap back on his head, scratching

his scalp while he gave this some thought. 'Maybe I do.'

'I'd be obliged if you would find one for me as soon as possible, and I need directions to Rosewenna Hall.'

''Tis a difficult place to find, especially at nightfall.'

Maisie tugged at Rose's sleeve. 'Perhaps we should stay at the inn and start off in the morning.'

'No, my mind is made up. If there's a vehicle for hire we'll travel on.'

The porter dumped their bags at their feet and ambled off, muttering to himself.

The wait seemed interminable, but at last he reappeared followed by a burly lad holding the reins of an aged nag. The contraption it pulled had also seen better days and was some kind of farm cart, covered in bird droppings, straw and a good helping of mud.

'That'll be a shilling.' The porter held out his hand.

Rose glanced at the boy, but he smiled vacantly and said nothing. She took a shilling from her purse and was about to give it to him when the porter snatched it from her. 'Don't give it he. He bain't all there, miss. He's a good boy, but a bit simple.'

The boy nodded and grinned.

Rose was suddenly assailed with doubts. The vehicle looked decidedly rickety, and the animal in the shafts should have been put out to pasture long ago, but she was desperate to find Cora. She took the reins from the boy. 'Thank you.'

He backed away, chuckling as if she had said

something hilarious. 'Thank you,' he repeated. 'Thank you, kindly.'

'Don't pay no heed to him, miss,' the porter said hastily. 'Not quite right in the head.'

Rose climbed onto the driver's seat. 'Get in, Maisie.'

'Are you sure about this?' Maisie hesitated, wrinkling her nose. 'It's dirty, miss.'

The porter slung their bags in the foot well. 'Do you want a hand, maid?'

Maisie shook her head. 'No, ta. Keep your hands to yourself, mister.'

'The boy has gone,' Rose said hastily. 'I was going to ask him for directions to Rosewenna Hall.'

'He'd send you a merry dance, miss. You'd end up in a bog if you followed young Sammy Nanpean's advice. Just follow the road eastwards till you come to Warleggan. Follow the lane for another mile or two and you'll see Rosewenna Hall. That's if you get there afore dark.'

'Then we'd best be off. Good day to you, sir. Thank you for your help. I'll return the trap tomorrow.' Rose spoke with more conviction than she was feeling. Until this moment she had never ridden a horse, let alone handled one that was harnessed to a cart. She had watched the cabbies in London and had a vague notion of how it all worked, but this was not the time to be faint-hearted. She clicked her tongue against her teeth. 'Walk on.' She flicked the reins and to her surprise the animal began to plod forward, albeit at a snail's pace.

'I didn't know you could handle a horse, miss.' Maisie sat beside her, clutching the seat with both hands.

'Neither did I,' Rose said with a nervous giggle. 'Let's hope the horse doesn't realise I'm a complete novice.' She urged the tired creature into a slow trot as they left the town behind and headed towards the moors.

The lanes were narrow and soon they were surrounded by dense woodland. The sound of tinkling streams and rustling leaves accompanied the clip-clop of the horse's hoofs, and the rumble of the wheels. It was cool beneath the green canopy and when they emerged from the wood the sun had finally set, leaving the pale blue sky streaked with purple and crimson. The puffy grey clouds were edged with gold from the sun's dying rays, and birds were flying home to roost as the shadows lengthened. Rose shivered as a cool breeze whipped her cheeks and tugged at her bonnet, but she kept her eyes steadfastly on the road ahead. The lane was narrow, too narrow for any vehicles to pass, and she could only hope that they did not meet any traffic on the way. The high hedgerows obscured most of the view, but as they passed through the pastures filled with sheep and cows, the land grew steadily wilder. Lush grassland gave way to scrub and bracken. Gorse bushes were crowned with yellow flowers, and small trees, made wedge-shaped by the prevailing winds, stood like twisted old men, watching over the vast expanse where wild ponies roamed free. Slabs of granite, exposed by centuries of soil erosion, looked as though a wayward child had piled them randomly on the landscape and then gone off to play with another toy. Rose could not but be impressed by the wild beauty, but darkness would soon be upon them and after they left the small village of Warleggan the narrow road became little more than a track.

'I don't like this,' Maisie wailed as one of the wheels hit a rock and they almost tipped over. 'We should have put up for the night at the inn.'

'It can't be far now,' Rose said hopefully. 'We've left the village and we should see the lights of the house very soon.'

'But there's nothing out there. It's a wilderness, like in the Bible. I never believed there could be such a place until now. We're going to die out here, I knows it.'

'Don't be silly.' Rose spoke more sharply than she had intended. 'We'll be all right, Maisie. We must be getting near.' But as the words left her lips the cart gave a lurch and one of the wheels came off with a sickening sound of splintering wood, and they were pitched onto the ground. Rose was winded, but her concern was for the poor animal who was trapped between the traces. She struggled to her feet, gasping for breath. 'Are you hurt, Maisie?'

'I don't know, miss. Everything aches something chronic.'

'I must see to the horse.' Rose went to the animal's

head and spoke to it gently. 'Whoa, there. You'll be fine. I'll get you out of this.' She gazed at the complicated harness, wondering where to begin.

'I knows how to do that.'

Rose turned to see Maisie had risen and was standing at her side. 'You do?'

'I seen the grooms do it in the mews behind the big house,' Maisie said proudly. 'I used to go round there often because the head groom had a daughter same age as me. She was the scullery maid and we shared a bed. Her pa used to give us hot cocoa when it were bitter cold outside and he let us sit by the fire in the tack room.' She set to work unbuckling leather straps as if she had done it all her life. 'I like horses,' she added happily. 'But I ain't keen on riding in that old cart. Me bum's so sore I won't be able to sit down for a week.'

Within minutes the animal was free and Rose took hold of the reins. 'We can't leave him here. We'll have to go the rest of the way on foot. Bring the bags, Maisie. We'll follow the track and hope for the best.'

Maisie hesitated, but the sudden cry of a dog fox made her move closer to Rose. 'What makes a noise like that?'

'I don't know,' Rose said nervously. 'It sounded like someone screaming.'

'What was that?' Maisie glanced up as a white shape flew overhead.

'I think it was an owl.' Rose remembered reading

about barn owls in one of her father's books, although her experience of the countryside had been limited to her brief stay in Lyme Regis and then at Portmorna. She suppressed a shiver. The gentle beauty of the Dorset landscape was far different from the wildness that surrounded them now. She started walking, holding the reins with the horse plodding after her and Maisie muttering as she followed on, carrying the valise and the carpet bag.

Rain clouds obscured the moon and they were enveloped in darkness. A thin veil of mist rose from the damp ground creating ghostly shapes that twisted and moved around them like tormented spirits of the long dead. Rose peered into what seemed like an abyss, hoping to see a pinprick of light in the distance. There was nothing they could do other than keep going forward, despite stumbling into potholes and snagging their clothing on encroaching brambles. Then, suddenly, as the track veered to the left, Rose spotted a light, and as the clouds scudded across the sky like a coven of witches on broomsticks, a fractured beam of moonlight revealed the shape of a large house.

'That must be Rosewenna Hall.' Her voice broke on a sob of relief. 'Look over there, Maisie. I'm not imagining it, am I?'

Maisie staggered up to her and dropped the cases on the ground with a sigh of relief. 'I hope so, miss. I doubt if I can walk another step.'

Rose pointed a shaky finger at the flickering light,

but the moon was now hidden behind a bank of clouds and they were once again in pitch-darkness. 'There must be an entrance somewhere close by, or a path that will lead us to the house. We've come this far, don't give up now.'

Maisie groaned as she hefted the valise in one hand and the carpet bag in the other. 'This is like a bad dream. Maybe I'll wake up any minute now.'

Rose tugged at the reins. 'Come on, horse. Let's hope they've got a nice warm stable for you.' She led him on, each step more painful than the last. Her feet were blistered and every bone in her body ached, but the end was in sight and that gave her a much-needed spurt of energy. They followed the track, but to Rose's horror she realised that it was leading away from the house and she came to a halt by a wooden gate set into a stone wall. 'We'll take a short cut,' she said firmly.

'But it's moorland, miss. There might be bogs and the like.'

'We'll allow the horse to lead us. He's a sure-footed animal bred in these parts. We'll put our trust in him.' Rose opened the gate and slackened her hold on the reins. 'Lead the way, horse. We're relying on you.'

Maisie scurried after them, complaining volubly as she tripped over tussocks of grass, but Rose had her sights set on the light, which seemed to come from a ground-floor room in the house. She kept hoping that the clouds would part and allow them to proceed by moonlight, but it had started to rain in earnest and there was nothing for it but to forge ahead. The horse seemed to sense that rest and shelter were close and their pace increased, although it was still slow going over the rough terrain. Rose lengthened her stride, but as Maisie attempted to keep up with them she tripped and fell. The carpet bag containing her things landed just a couple of feet away and as she stopped and turned her head, Rose saw it sink slowly into the bog.

'Don't move, Maisie,' she cried, but her warning came too late.

Maisie had scrambled to her feet and was attempting to pull her bag from the morass when she too began to sink. She uttered a terrified shriek. 'I can't move, miss. It's sucking me down.'

Rose took a tentative step towards her, but the ground was spongy beneath her feet and she knew that to venture any further would be fatal. She held out her hand, but Maisie was just out of reach, and she was already up to her knees and sinking fast. Rose slipped off her mantle. 'Catch this, and hold on. I'll pull you to safety.'

After several attempts Maisie managed to grab a sleeve, but she was now up to her thighs and panicking. With each frantic movement she sank a little deeper.

'Help me, miss.' Her voice was a thin wail carried away on the wind that had sprung up, chilling Rose to the bone. She tugged with all her might but she soon realised that she was not strong enough to save Maisie from being swallowed up in the bog. The horse whinnied and rubbed his head against her shoulder, as if understanding her plight.

'Good boy,' she breathed. 'Steady.' She looped one sleeve of her mantle around his breast collar and tied it as tightly as she could. 'Hold tight, Maisie. We'll soon have you out of there.'

Maisie's answer was lost as she fell forward, her arms stretched out and her hands entwined in the material. Rose backed the horse slowly, praying that the stitching would not give way beneath the strain. 'That's the ticket, Maisie. Don't let go, whatever you do.'

Gradually, inch by inch, Maisie slithered across the surface of the bog. The moment she was within reach Rose leaped forward and helped to drag her free. She collapsed beside her, laughing and crying with relief. The horse whinnied, as if in agreement, and Rose clambered to her feet. She untied the mantle that had saved Maisie's life, but was now beyond repair.

'Good boy,' she said, patting the horse's neck. 'Well done.' She turned to help Maisie to her feet.

'I lost all me things,' Maisie said tearfully. 'I got nothing left.'

Rose gave her a hug, getting even wetter in the process. 'You're alive. That's all that matters.'

Maisie stroked the horse's nose. 'Ta ever so, horsey.' She wiped away her tears, leaving streaks of mud across her cheeks. 'He's a hero. He ought to have a name.'

Rose shivered. The night was cold and she was soaked to the skin. 'We'll think about that tomorrow. We'd best make our way to the house as quickly as possible, or we'll both go down with lung fever.'

'I got nothing to change into.'

'Bring my valise. You can have one of my gowns, Maisie. It's the least of our problems. Keep close behind me and we'll let Hero find the way.'

'Hero,' Maisie said softly. 'I like that. A real hero he is.'

Rose had nothing to add to this. She gritted her teeth in an attempt to stop them chattering and put her trust in the horse, hoping that he could get them to the house without any further mishaps. Their pace was slow and Rose was hampered by her damp skirts. She knew that Maisie must be struggling even more as she was even muddier, but she was unusually quiet and that in itself was a worry. They needed to get into the warm and out of their wet garments as soon as humanly possible. Rose stopped, turning to speak to Maisie and found her slumped to her knees. She dragged her to her feet.

'Come along, now. Look, you can see the lighted window. There'll be a lovely big fire blazing up the chimney and a nice hot cup of tea will set you to rights.'

Maisie was shivering convulsively. 'Can't go another step.' Her knees sagged and it took all Rose's strength to keep her on her feet.

'Then you must ride the rest of the way.' Rose

tugged gently on Hero's reins and the horse ambled up to them. 'I'll help you to mount and we'll get there twice as fast.'

It was not as easy as Rose had hoped. Maisie was not exactly a dead weight, but she came close. She made a feeble attempt to help herself, but she was exhausted and chilled to the bone. Rose was close to giving up when with a last effort she managed to get Maisie sitting astride Hero's broad back. Rose handed her the reins. 'Just hold them loosely. He knows the way better than we do.' She picked up her valise. 'Walk on.'

It was raining hard by the time they reached the house. It was impossible to make out the exact size and shape of the building in the darkness, but a sliver of light illuminated the gravel path that led to the front door. Maisie slid from Hero's back and walked the last few steps. 'I thought we'd never make it.'

Rose raised the iron knocker and let it fall. They waited, whipped by rain and deafened by the wind that had come up and was howling like a banshee as it roared around the house, rattling windows and ripping tiles off the roof. Rose waited for a few seconds and then knocked again. This time she heard footsteps and the door opened. In the dim light of an oil lamp held in his hand, a small ragged boy with jam smeared around his mouth stared up at her.

'What d'you want?'

It was not the friendliest of welcomes and Rose had been expecting to see a housekeeper or a manservant. She forced her chilled lips into a smile. 'Is this Rosewenna Hall?'

'What if it be? What be it to you?'

'Will you please let us in? Can't you see we're wet and cold and we've travelled a long way to come here?'

'Ma said travellers bain't welcome.'

Ignoring the child's protests, Rose stepped inside, dragging Maisie by the hand. 'Take us to your mother, little boy, and I'd be grateful if you would stable our horse for the night.'

'You'm in trouble now!' He thrust the lantern into Rose's hand and ran away, calling for his mother.

'You can't shut Hero out in the cold,' Maisie cried passionately as Rose was about to close the door.

'I can't very well bring him inside.' Rose held the lamp high, gazing round at the square hall with its granite floor and low-beamed ceiling. The only furniture was a heavily carved oak table where chamber candlesticks were set out in a neat row. Draughts whistled through the mullioned windows and it was almost as cold inside as it was outdoors. 'It's not what I expected. I thought it would be a grand house.'

Maisie said nothing. Even by lamplight Rose could see that her pallor was alarming. She was about to go in search of the housekeeper when a woman appeared, holding the child by the hand. She was barefoot and her calico gown was much darned.

Her mop of dark hair was only partially confined beneath a mobcap. She looked like a drudge, but she held herself with pride and she met Rose's curious stare without blinking.

'What can I do for you, miss?'

The speech that Rose had been rehearsing mentally since they left London deserted her completely. 'I want to see my sister. I believe she's here.'

''Tis a bad night to make such a mistake. I'll have to ask you to leave, miss.'

'I told you so.' The boy stuck his tongue out at Rose and received a clip round the ear from his mother.

'There be no cause for rudeness, Jory.'

His brown eyes sparkled with unshed tears and his bottom lip stuck out. 'I only did what you said, Ma.'

'I won't leave without seeing my sister or Mr Barclay,' Rose said stubbornly. 'I know they're here, and we've come all the way from London to see them.'

'It's all right, Derwa. Leave this to me.'

Rose turned her head to see Gerard coming down the wide oak staircase. He was casually dressed as if he had spent the day on the moors, and he had the appearance of a country gentleman, quite different from his man-about-town image. He walked slowly towards them, looking Rose up and down with a hint of admiration in his blue eyes.

'Do you mean to tell me that you crossed the moors without a guide?'

'I want to see my sister.' Rose cast an anxious glance at Maisie, who looked about to drop. 'My maid is in dire need of a change of clothes and a hot drink. We haven't eaten since midday and our horse needs to be stabled.'

'Of course.' Gerard nodded to his housekeeper. 'See to it, please, Derwa, and send someone to take care of the animal. We'll be in the parlour.'

Derwa bobbed a curtsey. 'Yes, sir.' She shot a resentful look at Rose as she hurried away, but her son lingered, staring at them curiously.

Gerard turned to Rose with a boyish grin. 'There's a fire in the parlour. This old house is virtually impossible to heat.'

'Perhaps we could go somewhere to change our clothes?' Rose said urgently. 'Maisie almost lost her life in a bog on the way here.'

'It is a hazardous journey for the unwary. Many a stranger has got himself into trouble out on the moors.' Gerard moved swiftly to collar Jory, who was about to follow his mother. 'Make yourself useful and take these ladies to Aunt Tabitha's room.'

'Your aunt lives here?' Rose said hopefully. An elderly relative might add a touch of respectability to her sister's visit.

'My aunt is long dead, but the room was hers from a girl, and tradition dies hard in this part of the world. Go with Jory and he can wait and bring you to the parlour.'

'And I'll see my sister?'

'Of course. I'll go now and tell her that you're here.' He was about to mount the stairs but he paused. 'If your intention is to take her back to London, I'm afraid you will be disappointed. Cora knows her own mind.'

Chapter Seventeen

Aunt Tabitha's room was just as Rose might have imagined it had she been reading one of Cora's Gothic novels, an indulgence they both kept hidden from her parents. *The Castle of Otranto* by Horace Walpole, and Mary Shelley's *Frankenstein* had enlivened many a winter evening in the vicarage, and at this moment Rose felt as though she had stepped into the world as described in these works of fiction. The windows shook as if unseen hands were tapping on the small panes, like the ghost of Cathy Earnshaw in *Wuthering Heights* begging for admittance to her old home. The room smelled of damp and mildew, with just a faint hint of orris root and the scent of violets, as if the old lady was still in residence.

Although what the former resident would have made of the housekeeping was another matter. Even by candlelight it was possible to see the fluffy layers of dust on the old-fashioned furniture. The grate was empty, except for the remains of a bird's nest, and the bed hangings crumbled to the touch. The bedding itself was cold and damp, but Maisie was in a state of collapse and barely able to co-operate when Rose helped her to undress. She sent Jory to the kitchen with instructions to bring a cup of tea or better still some cocoa, laced with plenty of sugar, and a stone bottle filled with hot water to put at Maisie's feet. He disappeared into the darkness, and Rose could only hope that he would remember at least part of the message by the time he reached the kitchen.

With Maisie tucked up in bed Rose changed out of her wet gown and hung it over the back of a chair in the hope that it would be dry by morning. She treated Maisie's linsey-woolsey skirt and cotton blouse with the same care and had just finished when there was a thud on the door. She went to open it and Jory pushed past her with a mug of cocoa in one hand and a stone hot-water bottle wrapped in a scrap of cloth tucked beneath his arm.

'It's heavy,' he complained as Rose took it from him.

'Thank you, Jory. You've done well.' She took the mug and placed it on a side table.

He eyed her warily. 'Ma said you'd give I a tip.'

Rose lifted the coverlet and placed the bottle at Maisie's feet. 'And so I shall, but not now. You'll have to wait until morning.'

'You'll forget,' he muttered. 'You will, I knows it.'

'I will give you a penny, but only if you wait now and show me to the parlour.' Rose plumped up the pillows so that Maisie could sip the rapidly cooling drink.

'Don't leave me, miss,' she whispered, gazing nervously round the room.

'I'm going to see Cora and then I'll join you.'

'It ain't right, miss.' Maisie swallowed another mouthful of cocoa. 'You should have the bed, not me. I'm used to sleeping on the floor.'

'Nonsense. I wouldn't hear of it.' Rose put the mug back on the table. 'We've beaten the moor together and we'll get through this somehow. We'll be on our way home tomorrow.' She smoothed Maisie's tangled hair back from her forehead. 'I'll leave a candle burning and I'll be back before you know it.'

Jory bounded along ahead of Rose and she had to quicken her pace in order to follow the flickering light of his candle. He stopped outside the parlour and held out his hand. 'A penny, you says.'

Rose had come prepared. She placed the coin in his hand and he scampered off, leaving her to enter the room unannounced. In the glow of the firelight she saw her sister huddled in a chair with a shawl wrapped around her shoulders and her feet resting on the brass fender. She looked up and her lips trembled into a half-smile. Rose had been expecting their reunion to be fraught with Cora triumphant and also defiant, but she had not expected to see her looking pale and tearful.

'Are you all right, Corrie?' She crossed the floor to kneel at her side. 'Are you unwell?'

Cora seemed to shrink even further into the depths of the wing-back chair. 'Why did you come here, Rose?'

'I came to bring you home, silly. What else would you expect me to do?'

Cora shot a wary look at Gerard. 'I can't go with you.'

'Of course not,' he said calmly. He was smiling but his eyes were like chips of granite. 'Your sister has chosen her fate, Rose. She belongs to me now.'

Rose leaped to her feet. 'Are you married?'

He threw back his head and laughed. 'Barclays don't marry women who flaunt their charms on stage.'

'You'll have to go home without me,' Cora said plaintively. 'I'm a fallen woman, Rosie. I'm no better than Ethel and Big Bertha.'

'You cad,' Rose cried angrily. 'You had no intention of marrying my sister.'

'Did you really think I would?' Gerard's mocking laughter filled the room.

Cora covered her ears with her hands. 'I can never look Papa in the face again. I believed Gerard when he said he loved me. I was a fool, Rose.'

'You took advantage of an innocent girl.' Rose faced him with her hands clenched at her sides. 'If my brother were here he'd make you sorry for what you've done.'

Gerard took a step towards her. 'Your brother is wanted by the police. He's a common murderer who broke gaol and ran away rather than face his trial. He'll hang for his crime.'

'I'm not stooping to your level,' Rose said with dignity. 'Say what you like, Gerard Barclay, but I'm taking my sister home tomorrow. We'll leave as soon as it's light.'

'You will leave in the morning, but Cora stays here.' His expression hardened. 'I will tell her when I've had enough of her, and then she may do as she pleases. Until then she remains here with me.'

Cora rose to her feet. 'You can't keep me here against my will, Gerard. You tricked me into running away with you.'

'You were a willing victim. You saw yourself as the future Lady Barclay, but that will never be.' He moved to a small table and picked up a decanter. 'I'd advise you to go to bed, Rose. Say your farewells now. You won't see Cora before you leave.'

Rose enveloped her sister in a hug. 'Be ready first thing in the morning,' she whispered. 'I'm not going without you.' She held her at arm's length. Cora's eyes were red and swollen and in the glow of the firelight Rose saw a livid bruise on her sister's cheek. She traced it with her fingertip. 'Did he do that to you?'

Cora's eyes filled with tears as she glanced nervously

at Gerard. It was all the answer Rose needed. She grabbed her sister by the hand and made for the doorway. 'Don't try to stop us, Gerard. We leave at daybreak.'

He poured himself a drink. 'We'll see about that, but you can have her company tonight. I don't enjoy the sight of her blotchy, tear-stained face on my pillow. I can get any woman I want.'

'You disgust me.' Rose hurried Cora from the room. 'I don't know what he did to you, Corrie, and I don't want to know, but this is the last night you spend under his roof.'

'He'll follow us to London,' Cora whispered as they made their way upstairs in almost pitch-darkness. 'I'm ruined and he knows it. No decent man will marry me now and I'll end up an old maid.'

'Better to be an old maid than a slave to a man like him.'

'He'll find me wherever I go. You don't know him, Rose.'

'You need some arnica for that bruise,' Rose said, ignoring Cora's tearful protest. 'I'll leave you with Maisie and find Jory's mother and have a quiet word with her.'

'No, Rose. She won't do anything to upset Gerard.'

'Will she not? We'll see about that.'

With Cora settled in the bed beside a sleeping Maisie, Rose went downstairs to the kitchen where she found Derwa seated by the range, sipping tea.

She turned her head to give Rose a suspicious look. 'What d'you want?'

'Something to eat wouldn't go amiss.' Rose stood her ground as Derwa jumped to her feet. 'And if you have some arnica that would be a great help. You must have seen my sister's bruises.'

Derwa stared down at her bare feet. 'It be nothing to do with me, miss.'

'I think it is,' Rose said gently. 'Why else would a young woman like you work in a place like this? I saw the way you looked at me when I first arrived. You thought that I came here at your master's invitation, didn't you?'

'It crossed my mind, miss.' Derwa raised her head slowly. 'They come and go, but in the end he comes back to me.'

'I saw the likeness between your master and Jory.'

A dull flush suffused Derwa's features. ''Tis common knowledge in Warleggan. I'm not welcome at home no more.'

'I'm sorry.'

'She's different from the rest,' Derwa said bitterly. 'Most of the women are loose in morals, but she was fresh and untouched until he had his way with her.'

'My sister believed that they would be married.'

A harsh laugh racked Derwa's thin body. 'They still fall for that one, miss. 'Tis hard to believe.'

'But it's true. Give me what I ask for and I promise you that we'll leave at dawn.'

'I can give you bread and cheese, and there's a salve I make of comfrey leaves for the bruises. Heaven knows, he's given me plenty in the past.'

'Why do you stay with him?'

'Where would I go?' Derwa hacked some slices from a loaf and cut some slivers of a heel of cheese. 'My family won't have me back and I got no money. I have to think of my son.'

'I'm so sorry.'

Derwa went to the pantry and brought out a small glass bottle. 'This will bring out the bruise and ease the soreness.'

'Thank you.' Rose took it from her with a grateful smile. 'If you could have our horse saddled and ready first thing in the morning I would be very grateful.'

'That I will, and Jory will see you across the moor. He might be a child but he knows every inch of the path between here and Warleggan.'

After a restless night in the bed occupied by her sister and Maisie, Rose was up before dawn. She dressed quickly before waking the girls, and was relieved to find that Maisie had seemingly recovered from her ordeal, but it was Cora who gave her cause for concern. She was pale and listless and quite unlike her normal self; even so, she did as she was asked and followed Rose meekly down to the kitchen with Maisie holding her hand and whispering words of encouragement.

Derwa was on her knees by the range, encouraging the flames to take hold. She stood up, brushing a lock of hair back from her brow with a sooty hand. 'Jory is waiting outside with the horse. Go quickly.'

Rose placed a silver sixpence on the pine table. 'That will pay for our food. We're in your debt.'

Derwa hurried to open the door that led out into the cobbled yard. Dawn was breaking with streaks of pale green light in the east, and soon it would be light. Jory was holding Hero's bridle as he waited for them to join him. Then, without waiting for permission, he sprang onto the animal's back. ''Tis best if I ride, miss. Follow I and the nag and you'll be safe enough, but don't step off the path or you'll be swallowed up in the bog.'

Rose was about to protest but thought better of it. Cora was scared of horses and Maisie was well enough to walk. It made sense for the boy and the animal to lead them safely across the moor. 'Very well, Jory. Lead on.' She linked arms with Cora. 'We'll be home by nightfall.'

'I can't go back to London, Rose.' Cora fell into step beside her with Maisie walking on ahead.

'That's silly. Where else would you go?'

'I can't face Aunt Polly. She'll tell me what a fool I've been, and I don't want to go back to the theatre.'

'You're wrong about Aunt Polly. She'll understand, and there are other theatres, Corrie. We're still the Sunshine Sisters.'

'Wherever I go I know he'll be there watching me.'

'You have to forget about what's happened. You can't allow a cad like Gerard Barclay to ruin your life.'

'But he has done that already, Rose. What respectable man would want me for a wife now?'

'Anyone half decent would understand.'

Cora lowered her voice. 'And what if I'm in the family way?'

'We'll worry about that when the time comes. Let's concentrate on getting away from here before Barclay wakes up and finds you gone.' Rose quickened her pace, taking deep breaths of the gorse-scented air. 'This is so much easier in daylight,' she added as the sun rose, drenching the wild moorland in a golden glow. 'In the dark it was quite terrifying, but now I can see the true beauty of this place.'

Cora stumbled and would have fallen if Rose had not held her. 'I've seen enough of the countryside to last me a lifetime. I long for the city, but I'm dreading our return. I don't expect you to understand. You're always so positive, Rosie. I think I must take after Mama.'

'Maybe a few days or even weeks in Lyme Regis would be good for you,' Rose suggested hopefully.

'No, definitely not. I couldn't face either of them after what I've done. Papa would never speak to me again if he knew the truth.'

'He's not speaking to us now,' Rose said, chuckling. 'He didn't approve of the Sunshine Sisters and he doesn't want to have anything to do with Billy, but I'm not giving up on our brother. Bennett has sent his man to Portmorna to see if he can discover any clues as to Billy's whereabouts.'

Cora shook her head. 'All this began because of Billy. We were a happy family until he fell in with the wrong crowd.'

Rose said nothing. There was an element of truth in what Cora said, but she could not find it in her heart to put all the blame on their brother. They had each of them made their own choices, and now they must live with the results. She concentrated her efforts on keeping up with Maisie, who was sticking rigidly to the path created by Jory and Hero. There would be no repetition of last night's near disaster.

By the time they reached the lane Rose's skirts were mud stained and her boots were leaking, but it was a relief to have put some distance between them and Rosewenna Hall, and there was nothing to suggest that they had been followed.

'I'll leave you now.' Jory leaped off Hero's back and held a grubby hand out to Rose.

She opened her reticule and took out a threepenny bit. She closed his small fingers around the coin. 'There you are, and thank you for your help.'

He grinned. 'I'll spend this in the village shop afore Ma gets her hands on it.'

Rose nodded absently. She was more concerned for her sister's wellbeing than for anything Jory might do that would get him into trouble with his mother. Cora was dragging her feet and it was clear that she was exhausted, in complete contrast to Maisie, who looked fresh and filled with energy.

'Are you all right, Corrie?'

'I'm hot and tired, Rose.'

Maisie eyed Cora warily. 'She's coming down with a fever. I dare say it were that cold house what done it. But if it's catching I don't want it.'

Rose laid her hand on Cora's forehead. 'You're right, Maisie. She's burning up.'

A shout from Jory made them both look round. 'I found your cart, miss.' He scampered up to them, leaving Hero to crop the grass in the hedgerow.

'Well, it's no good to us with a broken wheel.' Rose gave her sister an encouraging smile. 'Come on, Corrie. We're near the village and maybe we can hire a vehicle to take us to Bodmin.'

'No need, miss.' Jory tugged at her sleeve. 'Danny Gerrans and his brothers have mended the wheel.'

'If you're joking it's not funny.' Rose hurried after him as he ran on ahead, and as she turned the corner she saw four burly youths crowded round the cart.

'That be Dan'l,' Jory whispered as the tallest of them stepped forward.

'This be yours I'm thinking.' Danny stood arms akimbo.

Rose was not in a mood to play games. 'How much do you want?'

'How much have you got, lady?'

She did a quick calculation in her head. It was

nearly seven miles to Bodmin and Cora was unwell. They needed the cart, but paying the boys would mean that she did not have enough to pay for their return fare to London. 'One shilling,' she said hopefully.

'Not enough. The wheelwright would charge a lot more.'

A commotion in the lane behind them made Rose turn to see Maisie waving to her. 'Cora's fainted. Come quick.'

Rose took a handful of coins from her purse and thrust them into Danny's hand. 'Take that, but I need one of you to harness the horse to the cart.'

He signalled to his brothers. 'Do what the lady says, boys.'

'And you look strong. Come with me.' She hurried back along the lane to where Cora lay prostrate on the ground. 'Lift her gently, please, and carry her to the cart.'

Daniel held his hand out and she added a sixpenny bit. They would get home somehow, but the important thing was to take Cora somewhere she could be nursed back to health. There was only one place that sprang to mind.

The sight of Portmorna House lazing in the afternoon sunshine brought tears of relief to Rose's eyes. She had used the last of her money to pay for the extended hire of the horse and cart and her purse was now empty, but more importantly she knew that Cora would be safe and would be well-cared for. It had been a tedious journey. Hero had plodded along at his own pace but now, seeming to sense that a comfortable stable was within reach, he pricked up his ears and broke into a trot, coming to a halt outside the front entrance. Rose relaxed with a sigh of relief. This was not their home, but she was certain that Vere would not turn them away. She handed the reins to a groom who had come running from the direction of the stables.

'Look after the poor animal,' she said tiredly. 'He's served us well.'

She was about to climb down from the driver's seat when the front door opened and James hurried down the steps to offer his assistance. 'We weren't expecting you, miss.'

She allowed him to help her to the ground. 'Is Mr Tressidick at home, James?'

'No, miss. He's at the quarry office. Shall I send for him?'

'That won't be necessary. I'll go myself, but first I'd like to see my sister settled. I need to speak to Mrs Vennor.'

Maisie leaped from the cart, landing on the dusty gravel with a display of red flannel petticoats. 'Miss Cora needs a doctor,' she said breathlessly. 'She's burning up with fever.'

'It's just a chill,' Rose assured James, who had taken a step backwards. 'You can carry her into the house without fear of catching anything.'

'Just so, miss.' James lifted Cora in his arms and

carried her into the entrance hall. He hesitated. 'Where shall I take her now, miss?'

The sound of approaching footsteps made Rose turn to see Mrs Vennor coming from the direction of the back stairs. Her thin cheeks were flushed and she did not look too pleased. 'I wasn't told we were expecting guests.'

'I know, and I'm sorry to arrive unannounced and uninvited, but my sister was taken ill. We were supposed to travel back to London today, but as you can see she is not capable of undertaking a long journey.'

Her apology seemed to go some way to appease Mrs Vennor, but a deep frown was etched on her forehead. 'The guest rooms are not prepared and I haven't yet found a suitable replacement for Jenifry.'

'I don't want to put you to any trouble. If you would be kind enough to provide the bedding my maid will make a room ready for Cora, and we will share a bed. Maisie can sleep on the floor if necessary.' Rose crossed her fingers behind her back. She was banking on Mrs Vennor's pride as a good house-keeper to refute such a suggestion.

Mrs Vennor puffed out her cheeks. 'I've never heard of such a thing. Your rooms will be ready directly, even if I have to make up the beds myself. James, carry the young lady to the drawing room.'

'Thank you,' Rose said gratefully. 'That's most kind.'

'I'll have some refreshments sent to the drawing

room.' Mrs Vennor beckoned to Maisie. 'You will come with me.'

Maisie cast a sideway glance at Rose and she nodded. 'Yes, Maisie. Do everything you can to help.'

Mrs Vennor started in the direction of the back stairs, but she hesitated, glancing at Rose over her shoulder. 'Does the master know you are here?'

'Not yet. I intend to walk to the mine office and tell him in person.'

'The groom could do that for you, miss.'

'No, thank you,' Rose said firmly. 'That won't be necessary.' She followed James to the drawing room.

He laid Cora gently on the sofa. 'Will that be all, miss?'

'If someone could be sent for the doctor I'd be very grateful.'

'Yes, miss. Right away.' James seized the opportunity to leave them, closing the door softly behind him.

Rose kneeled beside Cora. Her eyes were closed and her breathing ragged. 'Cora, can you hear me?'

When there was no response Rose began to worry. Until now she had thought that the malady was a chill or an affliction of the nerves, but it was obviously more serious. If only Mama were here, she thought, taking Cora's hot hand and holding it to her cheek. Aunt Polly would probably know what to do, or even Big Bertha. Rose had never felt as helpless as she watched her sister struggling for each rasping breath. She stroked Cora's hand and kept talking, although it was mainly trivial nonsense. She said anything that came into her head in an attempt to bring her back to consciousness, but then she lapsed into silence. Perhaps a temporary release from the trauma that Cora had experienced at Gerard Barclay's hands would help to mend her bruised body and restore her spirit.

'We're the Sunshine Sisters, Corrie,' Rose whispered as the door opened and Maisie clattered in with a tea tray.

'Mrs Vennor is getting your bedchambers ready,' Maisie said importantly. 'She's put me in charge of the sickroom, if that's all right with you, miss.'

Rose perched on the edge of the sofa. 'Of course, you're the best person to stay with my sister while I go to find Mr Tressidick.'

Maisie grinned. 'He'll think you've changed your mind, miss.'

'Well, I haven't,' Rose said firmly. 'Which is why I must see him before anyone tells him that we're here. I don't want him to be under a misapprehension.'

Maisie poured the tea, slopping some of it in the saucer. 'This is a swish drum, miss. You'd live like a queen if you was to marry Mr Vere.'

'It's not all about money. I think Mr Barclay proves that.' Rose accepted a cup of tea but shook her head when Maisie offered her a slice of currant cake. She had eaten almost nothing that day but her appetite had deserted her. Uppermost in her mind was the need to see Vere and explain what had brought them to Portmorna House. 'You can have the cake, Maisie. I'll eat later.' She gulped the rapidly cooling tea. 'I must go down to the village, but I'll be as quick as I can.'

'Is it all right if I eat all the cake, miss? I don't think Miss Cora will want any.'

'Enjoy it, Maisie. Mrs Vennor will be offended if she finds a single crumb left on the plate.' Whether or not that was true it did not seem to matter. Rose had her mind set on catching Vere before the gossips had time to pass on news of their arrival.

Vere was seated at his desk with a pile of papers spread out in front of him. His clerk had been reluctant to let Rose disturb his employer but she had stood her ground, and he had given in.

'A young lady to see you, sir.' The clerk ducked out of the room before his employer had a chance to remonstrate, leaving Rose standing in the doorway.

Vere looked up, frowning at the interruption, but his expression changed when he saw her and he stood up, scattering papers onto the floor. 'Rose, this is a surprise. You're the last person I expected to see.'

'I'm sorry to turn up like this,' Rose said awkwardly. She was hot and the wind had whipped her hair into a mass of tangled curls. Her straw bonnet had been ruined by the rain the previous evening, and her clothes were travel-stained and creased. She knew she was not looking her best.

'Won't you take a seat?' Vere rounded the desk to pull up a chair. 'May I offer you some refreshment?'

'No, thank you.'

'What brings you here today, Rose? Didn't you succeed in persuading Cora to return home?'

She sank down on a hard wooden seat of the chair beside his desk. 'I hardly know how to tell you, Vere.'

'Take your time. I can see that it must be serious if it brought you here.' He leaned against his desk, his arms folded and his head on one side as he waited for her to speak.

She began haltingly at first but with growing confidence. He listened intently without interrupting. 'So you see, I didn't know where to turn. Mrs Vennor sent for the doctor and I fear we will have to trespass on your hospitality until Cora recovers.'

He leaned forward to clasp both her hands in his. 'Of course you must stay. You did exactly the right thing.'

'I wasn't sure whether we'd be welcome after what passed between us.'

'If you need me as a friend then that is what I will be. I'll do everything I can to help you, and Cora will have the best possible treatment. I'm truly sorry that Barclay turned out to be such a swine. The poor girl must be heartbroken.'

'She is in a terrible state.'

'Your father should be told.'

'No, that wouldn't do at all. He's virtually disowned

us all. We tried to keep Billy's trouble from him, but of course he found out, and he thinks that what Cora and I have done is unforgiveable. If he knew the rest I doubt if he would ever get over the shock.'

'If he is a man of God he should be more forgiving. I'm sorry, Rose, but if I were a father I hope I would treat my children with more understanding and kindness, and I am far from being a holy man.' He straightened up. 'Come, I'll take you home in my carriage. Portmorna House will be your sanctuary for as long as you need it, and you need not fear that it puts you under any obligation to me.'

Rose stood up, facing him with a heartfelt smile. 'Thank you, Vere. You are a true friend and a good man.'

He pulled a face. 'I hope I'm a good friend, but I don't claim to be a good man.'

Chapter Eighteen

Dr Quinn looked grave as he moved away from the bed where Cora lay mumbling incoherently.

'What ails her, Doctor?' Rose asked urgently. 'I've never seen her like this.'

'Your sister is undoubtedly a very sick young woman,' he said, shaking his head. 'I cannot be certain, but lung fever would seem to be the obvious diagnosis. Take away the cotton sheets and let her lie between woollen blankets to purge the fever. I'll call again tomorrow.' He closed his medical bag and left Rose to carry out his instructions.

She managed to accomplish the difficult task with help from Maisie, but their ministrations did not seem to make much difference and, if anything, Cora's condition seemed to worsen. Rose was unwilling to leave her side, but Maisie managed to persuade her to go down to dinner.

She joined Vere in the dining room and took her seat beside him at table.

'How is the patient?' he asked, filling her glass with wine.

'Not well at all, in fact I think she's getting worse.' Rose took a sip. 'She's burning up with fever.'

'Dr Quinn is a good fellow. He might be a bit old-fashioned in his ways, but he treated us as boys and saw us through the usual ailments. Bennett and I are still around to tell the tale.'

Rose swallowed another mouthful of wine. The mention of Bennett's name had caused her heart to miss a beat and she turned her head away to hide the blush that flooded her cheeks. 'I shouldn't have left her side.'

'You must look after yourself, Rose. If you fall ill you'll be no use to Cora.' Vere frowned as the door burst open and a young girl clattered into the room carrying a tureen, which she dumped on the table in front of him.

'Soup, sir.'

He frowned. 'Where is Tamsin? Don't tell me that she's been sent packing, too?'

The girl bobbed a curtsey, almost toppling over her crossed feet in the attempt. 'She be gone, sir.'

'I don't recall seeing you before.' Vere lifted the lid and sniffed the savoury aroma.

'I be Kensa Penneck, sir.'

'You're related to Day and Pasco?' Rose said eagerly. 'Has your family had word from them recently?'

'No, miss. I don't know nothing.' Kensa backed towards the doorway and fled.

Rose served the soup. 'I seem to have scared her.'

'I don't know what Mrs Vennor was thinking of, sending a girl like that to serve at table.'

'It seems to me that Mrs Vennor has too much to do, Vere. She's cook and housekeeper, which is all right in a small establishment like our old vicarage, but you need to have both to run a house this size.'

'I've never given it much thought. Normally we're quiet and she has only me to consider.'

'We're putting you to such a lot of trouble.' Rose gulped down the remainder of her wine. 'We'll leave for London as soon as Cora is well enough to travel.'

'It's no trouble,' Vere said quickly. 'You mustn't think that, Rose. Of course you must stay until Cora is fully recovered, and if there's anything I can do to help you must let me know.'

She smiled, emboldened by the wine. 'You could engage a housekeeper so that Mrs Vennor can concentrate on her excellent cooking. She needs more help, and I don't mean children like Kensa Penneck.'

'You're right about the need to take on more staff. I'll speak to Mrs Vennor in the morning.' Vere tasted the soup and nodded. 'She is a good cook. I'm afraid I've taken too much for granted. I really must mend my ways.'

'It's just a question of organisation. I imagine you have more than enough to think about with running the mine.'

'That's true, and of course the tragic business with Gawain is never far from my mind.' He paused with his soup-spoon halfway to his lips. 'I still don't believe that Billy was the culprit, but I'd like to see an end to all this.'

'Perhaps I could speak to Kensa. She might tell me something that she would be afraid to pass on to you.'

'As far as I can make out Scully has spoken to everyone in that family and has come up with nothing new.'

'I'm determined to clear Billy's name. With your permission I'll have a quiet word with young Kensa. I can't stand by and do nothing.'

'You have no need to ask, Rose. For as long as you are here I want you to treat this house as your home.'

His plain features were transformed by the sincerity in his smile and Rose was deeply touched. 'Thank you, Vere. Thank you for everything.'

After an excellent meal, despite Kensa's clumsy attempts at serving the food, Rose said good night to Vere and went upstairs to relieve Maisie. She sent her to the kitchen to have her supper and took her place at Cora's bedside, watching over her as the shadows lengthened. When it was too dark to see she stood up, stretched and went over to the window where there was a table with candles waiting to be lit. She was about to strike a match when her attention was caught by a movement on the gravel carriage sweep. A lone male figure was striding towards the stable block, and although it was too dark to make out the details she knew instinctively that it was not one of the servants. At first she thought it was Vere, but she could not be certain, and it seemed odd that he would be venturing out this late in the evening. Then, whoever it was disappeared into the deep shadow and the only movement was the sweeping flight of bats as they soared into the sky in their search for food. There was still a faint light in the sky to the north, but stars were beginning to appear overhead, and a silver pathway of moonlight stretched from the shore to the horizon. It looked, she thought, as though it were possible to walk across the Channel to France.

A faint moan from the bed brought her back to earth and she lit a candle. Cora was tossing about restlessly and gabbling senselessly. Rose felt her sister's brow and was alarmed. She sat by the bed, talking in a low voice in an attempt to calm her, but she doubted whether Cora was able to understand. Maisie came to see if there was anything she could do, but Rose sent her to bed. She kept up her vigil until at last she dozed off to sleep.

She was awakened suddenly, and it took her a few moments to remember where she was, but on checking Cora she found her to be sleeping fitfully. Rose sat upright in her chair, straining her ears for a repeat of the sound that had woken her. She stood up, moving stiffly to the window. It was still dark but there was a thin strand of light in the east and she realised with a feeling of pure relief that the night was almost over. The candle had long since guttered and gone out, but soon it would be the dawn of a new day.

She leaned her head against the cool glass window-pane, and it was then she saw him. Whether or not it was the same man was impossible to say, and this time he was coming from the direction of the stables. She craned her neck to see where he went next, but whoever it was disappeared from sight, and she thought for a moment that she had imagined the whole thing, or it could be one of the male servants returning from a tryst with a local woman. There could be all manner of explanations. She yawned and stretched before returning to her chair at Cora's bedside. Dr Quinn would come as promised and she much hoped he would see some improvement in her sister's condition. At least Cora seemed no worse. Rose leaned back in the chair and closed her eyes.

Someone was shaking her and calling her name. Rose opened her eyes and found herself looking into Maisie's young face. 'What time is it?'

'You was sleeping so sound I didn't want to wake you, miss.' Maisie handed her a cup of tea. 'Drink this and don't worry. I seen to Miss Cora. I washed her face and hands like you done to me when I lost me babe. You was so kind to me then. I'll never forget it.'

'Thank you,' Rose said softly. 'You're a good girl, Maisie.'

'That's not what your pa would say, miss.' Maisie covered her mouth with her hand to suppress a gurgle of laughter. 'Anyway, Miss Cora seems a bit better so why don't you go downstairs and have some breakfast? Mrs Vennor's been frying bacon and kidneys and something called hog's pudding. She give me some instead of porridge and it were ever so tasty. If I was rich like Mr Vere I'd have bacon and kidneys and hog's pudding every day for breakfast, dinner and tea.'

Her enthusiasm and obvious enjoyment of her food made the day seem brighter. Despite her harsh upbringing, and the physical abuse that had resulted in her pregnancy and attempted suicide, Maisie's spirit was not dulled. The loss of her baby when she was little more than a child herself had been a bitter blow, but Maisie had somehow recovered and retained her youthful enthusiasm. Rose stood up to give her a hug. 'What would I do without you?'

Maisie stared at her in astonishment. 'I dunno, miss. Why would I want to leave you is more the question.'

'One which I hope will never need an answer. You're a treasure, Maisie.'

'Well, I never did.' Maisie sank down on the chair, gazing up at Rose wide-eyed. 'I been called lots of names, but no one said I were a treasure.'

'They didn't know you as well as I do,' Rose said,

smiling. 'Now, I suppose I'd better put in an appearance at breakfast. I won't be long, but if Cora's condition alters in any way you must send for me. Just ring the bell and hopefully someone will come.'

'Don't worry. I knows what to do.' Maisie folded her arms and fixed her gaze on Cora as if willing her to recover.

Satisfied that her sister was in the best of hands, Rose made her way to the dining room and the first person she saw as she entered the room was Bennett. She came to a halt, staring at him in surprise. The shock of seeing him had taken her breath away and she was momentarily lost for words, but he was smiling as he stood and pulled up a chair.

'Good morning, Rose. How is the patient?'

Vere had half risen but he subsided back onto his seat. 'I told Bennett what had happened,' he said apologetically. 'I hope you don't mind, Rose.'

'No, indeed. It's no secret. I'm sure that Cora's elopement is giving the gossips in London something to talk about.' She sat down, casting a sideways glance at Bennett. 'Was it you I saw coming from the stables this morning? It was still dark.'

'It might have been,' he said casually. 'I did arrive early.'

'Or it could have been me,' Vere added hastily. 'I went to check on my horse. The poor animal had gone lame.'

Rose reached for the coffee pot and filled her cup. 'I see.' She was not convinced, but she was not in a position to challenge either of them. She took a slice of toast from the silver rack and buttered it.

'Is that all you're having?' Vere asked anxiously. 'You ate almost nothing last night, Rose. You must keep your strength up if you're to nurse your sister back to health.'

'Stop fussing, Vere.' Bennett leaned back in his seat, an amused smile curving his lips. 'I'm sure Rose knows what's best for her.'

'I can recommend the hog's pudding,' Vere insisted, ignoring him. 'And the bacon is particularly tasty, or I could ask Mrs Vennor to scramble some eggs for you.'

'Leave her alone,' Bennett said, chuckling. 'Rose isn't a child.'

A quick glance in Vere's direction was enough for Rose. He was staring straight ahead but Bennett's teasing had obviously embarrassed him, and she sensed his chagrin. 'As a matter of fact I think I will sample the hog's pudding,' she said, rising to her feet. 'I've heard so much about it that it would be foolish not to try some.' She went to the sideboard and lifted the lid of the silver breakfast dish, taking a small helping of the blood sausage and a slice of crispy bacon. 'It smells delicious,' she added as she returned to the table. 'And you're right, Vere. I need to be strong for Cora's sake.' She popped a slice of the hog's pudding into her mouth, chewed and swallowed. 'I have to agree. It's very tasty.'

'I'm glad we have that settled.' Bennett pushed

back his chair and stood up. 'I have business to do in the village, but I'll be back later.'

'Are you here on my brother's behalf?' Rose asked anxiously. 'If so I'd like to know what you've discovered.'

He gave her a long look, his dark eyes holding her gaze. 'I am still working on it. You will have to trust me.' He turned to Vere. 'I'll see you at the office later.'

He left before Rose had a chance to question him further and she pushed her plate away. 'There's something more, I can feel it. What is it that you're not telling me?'

Vere made a show of folding his table napkin and placed it on his unused side plate. 'You must understand that Bennett and I are doubly involved in this case. We've lost our brother and cousin, and Billy was Gawain's friend and a welcome guest in this house. Neither of us will give up until we've had justice for both.'

'Yes, I know that, and I'm with you, of course. I just wish that there was something I could do to help.'

Vere's expression softened. 'You're helping by just being here, Rose. I only have to look at you and it reminds me what I'm fighting for. I beg you to be patient a while longer.'

'I should go upstairs and check on my sister,' Rose said, rising to her feet. She left the room before he had a chance to respond. There was something going on that was being kept a secret from her and she was curious, but it was obvious that neither Vere nor Bennett was prepared to take her into their confidence. She heard Vere's footsteps behind her as he left the dining room, but she did not look back as she mounted the stairs and he did not follow her.

Dr Quinn came an hour later and he seemed pleased with Cora's progress. She was quieter now and her fever appeared to be abating. He left behind an elixir of his own making and said he would call again the next day, unless Cora's condition gave cause for concern, in which case he would return at any time of the day or night. Rose thought privately that Vere must be paying the doctor a handsome fee in order to warrant such attention, but she merely smiled and thanked him.

When he had gone she uncorked the bottle, sniffed and wrinkled her nose. The overpowering smell was of a substance suspiciously like the one that Mrs Blunt had given her when as a young child she had eaten some deadly nightshade berries. The taste was vile and it had made her very sick. Mrs Blunt swore by ipecacuanha as a cure-all and often mixed it with honey and lemon juice as a remedy for coughs. It had always seemed to work, but Rose and Cora had been convinced that the cure was worse than the illness. She put the cork back and hid the bottle on the mantelshelf behind the clock. Cora would have to be in a desperate state for her to administer such a punishing medication.

She returned to the bedside, laid her hand on Cora's forehead and was relieved to find her cooler than she had been the previous evening, but the blankets felt damp and the wool was scratchy to her touch.

'Maisie, would you be a dear and ask Mrs Vennor for some fresh blankets and bedlinen? I'm going to change the bedding, never mind what Dr Quinn says. I can't think of anything worse than feeling hot and sticky as well as itchy and uncomfortable.'

Maisie had been sitting by the window but she jumped to her feet. 'I agree. I never thought it were a good idea in the first place. I'm not sure that doctor knows what he's on about.'

'We'll try it and see.'

Cora opened her eyes, looking dazedly round the room. 'Rose.'

Rose hurried to her side. 'I'm here, Corrie. Are you feeling better?'

'I'm thirsty.'

With Maisie's help Rose managed to get Cora into a more upright position and she held a glass of water to her lips. 'Sip it slowly,' she said gently.

Maisie plumped up the pillows and piled them behind Cora. 'There you are, miss. Now you can see what's going on. You got a fine room here. You're like a princess in this big bed.'

'Where am I? I don't remember coming to this place.'

'We brought you to Portmorna House,' Rose said before Maisie could make it into even more of a fairy story. 'It belongs to Vere Tressidick and it was the nearest place I could think of to bring you.'

'I've been quite poorly.'

'You were, but you're on the mend.'

Cora's eyes filled with tears. 'You should have let me die, Rosie. I'm a ruined woman, just like the ones that Aunt Polly takes in.'

'Stuff and nonsense. You might have been naïve, but Gerard took advantage of you, just like Maisie's employer took advantage of her. You're not to blame.'

'But what will I do if I'm in the family way? I'll die of shame.'

Maisie grabbed Cora's hand. 'It happened to me, miss. And then the baby got took by the angels. Mrs Blunt said I must have a guardian angel looking out for me, although I couldn't see it at the time. If one of them angels bothers to look after a poor orphan just think what sort of heavenly being must be on your side, you being a vicar's daughter and all.'

'Yes, thank you, Maisie,' Rose said hastily. 'I'm sure you had the angels on your side, but we mustn't tire Miss Cora. She needs to rest.'

'And she should have some beef tea.' Maisie nodded sagely. 'Mrs Blunt gave me beef tea to build me up after you know what. She said it would do me the world of good, and look at me now.'

'You're a picture of health.' Rose patted her on the shoulder. 'Why don't you go downstairs to the

349

kitchen and ask Mrs Vennor to make some beef tea for Miss Cora?'

'I will. Of course I will. I wouldn't mind a cup of it meself.' She danced off, leaving Rose and Cora alone in the room.

Rose sat on the edge of the bed. 'You have to stop worrying, Corrie. No good will come of it. The main thing is for you to get better, and we'll deal with problems if and when they arise.'

'Thank you, Rosie. I'm sorry I've put you to so much bother.' Cora's eyelids closed and she uttered a deep sigh.

Rose pulled the coverlet up to her sister's chin. Cora was on the mend physically, but it would take more than a cup of beef tea to take away the memory of Gerard's betrayal.

Rose went to the window and opened it, relaxing on the window seat and taking deep breaths of the salty, blossom-scented air. Alerted by the sound of a horse's hoofs she looked out to see Vere astride his grey mare, heading towards the park gates. There was not a sign of lameness as the animal broke into a trot. Rose frowned thoughtfully. She had not believed his story in the first place and this confirmed that he had lied, or at the very least the animal's condition had not been serious, and would not have involved Vere in a midnight visit to the stables. The cousins were definitely up to something and she was determined to find out what was going on.

*

Cora had awakened for long enough to take sips of water and beef tea, but when she remembered her ordeal in Rosewenna Hall she had become distressed, and it had taken a hefty dose of laudanum to calm her down. She was sleeping peacefully now, and Maisie was dozing in a chair at her bedside. It was early afternoon and the sun was shining. Rose had a sudden desire to go for a walk. She needed to clear her head and she needed time to think. Cora would recover, but their future looked uncertain. The shadow of the hangman's noose still hung over Billy, and Cora's misplaced trust in Gerard might have implications for the future. A baby born out of wedlock would carry that stigma for the rest of his or her life, and the mother would bear the blame and the shame. The father would deny all responsibility and the mother would be branded a scarlet woman. Rose put on her bonnet, picked up her shawl and crept out of the room.

She had not intended to walk far, but it was a beautiful day and she found herself on the edge of the village. She stopped, and was wondering whether to proceed or to turn round and return to Portmorna House when she saw a familiar figure emerge from the inn a little further along the lane.

'Scully.' She called his name and he turned his head.

'Miss Rose?' He ambled towards her. 'I wasn't expecting to see you here.'

'My sister and I are just visiting.' Rose had no intention of going into a detailed explanation, but she was curious. 'Have you discovered any news of my brother's whereabouts?'

'I might have, but it's too early to say.'

'But you have an idea? Can you tell me more?'

'It's not up to me, miss. I have to pass any information I have to Mr Sharpe. I dare say as how he'll tell you when he's good and ready.'

He tipped his battered billycock hat, and was about to walk on when she caught him by the sleeve. 'Are you going to see him now? Might I accompany you, Mr Scully? I'm desperate for news of my brother.'

'I can't stop you from following me, miss. On the other hand, I won't encourage you to do so. I'm heading for the mine office.'

'As it happens I was thinking of going there myself,' Rose said eagerly. At last she might learn something. It was an opportunity not to be missed. 'Lead on.'

He strode off and Rose had to quicken her pace to keep up with him. She was aware that they were attracting curious looks from the villagers, but Scully seemed oblivious, or perhaps he was used to people staring at him. He certainly presented an odd figure in his tight black trousers, his coat-tails flying and his battered hat pulled down over his lank, greasy locks, quite different from the local men in their working clothes or fishermen's smocks. He barged into the mine office with Rose just a few steps behind him.

The clerk seated behind a tall writing desk peered at Scully through steel-rimmed spectacles. 'Oh, it's you again.'

'It is I,' Scully said grandly. 'And I wants to see your boss, mister.'

'It's Mr Mabyn to you, Mr Scully. I thought we'd settled that some time ago.'

'Well, Mr Mabyn, it don't alter the fact that I wants to see your boss. Now do you announce me, or do I walk in?'

Mabyn slid off his high stool and banged on the door behind him. He waited for a moment before entering and reappeared seconds later. 'Mr Tressidick will see you now.'

'Ta.' Scully headed for the open doorway with Rose close on his heels. He paused in the doorway, glaring at her. 'What I got to say is for his ears only.'

'I'm coming in,' Rose insisted.

'It's all right, Scully.' Vere stood up, beckoning to Rose. 'Come in, Miss Perkins.'

Scully looked to Bennett, who was standing by the window. 'She insisted on following me, boss.'

'Thank you, Scully,' he said calmly. 'It's quite all right. Miss Perkins should be kept up to date with our investigations.'

'Thank you.' Feeling vindicated and not a little excited, Rose walked past Scully with her head held high. At last they were taking her seriously.

Vere hurried round the large desk to proffer a chair. 'Take a seat, Rose.' He turned to Scully. 'Well then, what did you discover?'

'I've been following Gryffyn Penneck for over a

week. He's a crafty old fox and he's led me a merry dance, but it was worth it in the end.'

'Come on, man,' Bennett said impatiently. 'Get to the point.'

'He takes his boat out every night, which is natural seeing as how he's a fisherman, but on one or two occasions he came back with no sign of a catch.'

'That's not an unusual state of affairs.' Vere resumed his seat, leaning his elbows on the desk.

'We've been down at the harbour ourselves,' Bennett said thoughtfully. 'We haven't seen anything unusual, have we, Vere?'

'If you'll kindly allow me to finish, guv . . .' Scully dragged off his hat and clutched it in his hands, which Rose noticed for the first time were bandaged. He caught her looking at him and grinned. 'Yes, miss. My hands are red raw from rowing. I hired a boat and risked life and limb to go out in search of your brother.'

'I didn't know you were an oarsman, Scully.' Bennett moved closer, folding his arms across his chest. 'You're a man of many talents.'

'My pa was a lighterman, boss. I grew up in Limehouse, and as soon as I was old enough to hold an oar he took me with him on the river. I can handle a boat, but being on the sea ain't the same as working the Thames. Anyway, as I was about to say, your man goes across the bay and beaches the craft in a cove surrounded by near-vertical cliffs. It were too dark to see much, but I swear he was guided by the light of a lantern high on the clifftop. I saw it bobbing about, and he headed straight for it.'

'He might be a smuggler,' Rose suggested. 'I've read about the free trade in these parts.'

Vere smiled and shook his head. 'It's hardly worth the risk these days, Rose. Forty or fifty years ago smuggling was rife, but when the duty on tea, tobacco, brandy and such goods was reduced it put an end to much of the free trade.'

'Yes, that together with more better trained and equipped revenue officers,' Bennett added, chuckling. 'It put a great many people out of business, including our great-grandfather. If he hadn't started the copper mine with his ill-gotten gains he would have been in a sorry state.'

Vere nodded. 'And when copper was no longer profitable my father turned to china clay.'

'But how does all this help Billy?' Rose said impatiently.

'Yes, Scully.' Bennett was suddenly serious. 'Go on. What's your theory?'

'I visited the girl's mother again. She's a comely widow with a liking for a tot or two of gin. She lets slip that her girl is safe, although she was quick to try and cover up her mistake. A couple more drinks and she admits that Jenifry is still in Cornwall, and she begs me not to let on. Naturally I says that me lips are sealed.'

'I feel sorry for the poor woman.' Rose glared at Scully. 'You took advantage of her, Mr Scully.'

'What would you have me do, miss? Would you rather I gave a widow woman the benefit of me charms and was rewarded by some vital information, or would you rather I left her with her secret and let your brother remain an outlaw?'

'That's enough, Scully.' Bennett sent him a warning look. 'Miss Perkins understands the situation.'

'So what are you saying, Scully?' Vere said quickly. 'Do you think that Penneck was taking supplies to his sons?'

'That's what it would seem, sir. It's worth further investigation, if you ask me.'

'It seems strange that they have not gone far.' Vere turned to Bennett. 'What do you think?'

He frowned. 'Maybe we didn't give them credit for being smarter than taking off for the Continent. They wouldn't have been able to speak the language and would have had difficulty in earning a living. If old man Penneck has been supplying them with essentials they could remain hidden out in one of the coves for years.'

'Then we must go there,' Rose said eagerly. 'You have ships that carry the china clay. Couldn't we use one of them to go to this place?'

'Of course, it's a possibility, but we would want a smaller craft.' Vere drummed his fingers on the top of the desk. 'Our vessels are too recognisable and too large to get close enough to a rocky shore-line to make a safe landing.'

'We need a fishing boat, like the one Penneck owns,'

Bennett said thoughtfully. 'But we'd be up against Day and Pasco. Their knowledge of the waters round here is far better than yours or mine, Vere. If they got wind of what we were doing they'd make a run for it. We have to catch the boys and bring them to justice, or Billy won't stand a chance of acquittal.'

Rose clapped her hands. 'I can't believe it's really happening. When will we do this?'

'I'm afraid you won't be involved directly, Rose,' Vere said with an apologetic smile. 'It's far too dangerous.'

'Bennett?' Rose turned to him holding out her hands. 'You won't leave me out, will you?'

Chapter Nineteen

She had won. It was a small victory, but Rose felt triumphant, and slightly nervous, as she sat in the stern of the fishing boat Scully had procured for them. It was a moonless night, and the darkness was almost as suffocating as the oily smell of mackerel from the last catch. She covered her nose with her gloved hand, but refrained from making any comments which might set her apart as a fussy female. It had been a struggle to persuade Vere that she would make a useful contribution to their party. He had stressed the fact that the Penneck brothers were desperate men. Scully had backed him up wholeheartedly, giving Rose the impression that he had little respect for her abilities, or perhaps he disliked women in general. She suspected that he had been thwarted in love, but whatever had caused his antipathy it had now become personal. It was

358

Bennett who had been her champion, and for that she would be eternally grateful. He was the only man she had ever known who treated her as an equal. Vere obviously placed her on a pedestal, like a marble statue, but Bennett saw her as an intelligent, if slightly wayward, woman.

She huddled up in the boat cloak that Mrs Vennor had found in one of the cupboards at Portmorna House. Although it was May, it was cold on the water, and the lugger ploughed through the waves, enveloping them in a fine mist of salt spray. Scully was at the tiller while Vere and Bennett handled the sheets and trimmed the sails with surprising expertise. The small craft tacked across the bay, keeping within sight of land. As they drew nearer the cove, Bennett and Vere lowered the yard, unhooked the clew, and handed the sail round the front of the mast. They took the oars and rowed towards the shore, beaching the vessel stern first, and they both leaped overboard to haul the boat up the beach.

Rose was about to clamber after them when Scully scooped her up in his arms, and carried her onto the damp sand, setting her down just above the waterline. She opened her mouth to thank him, but he laid his finger on his lips and shook his head. She acknowledged the warning with a nod, and fell in behind Vere and Bennett as they headed for the cliffs.

They came to a halt at the foot of the cliff face, which towered above them, its craggy contours silhouetted against the star-studded sky. The clouds had parted and everything around them was blanched by moonlight. Bennett turned to Scully, lowering his voice to little more than a whisper. 'Where did you spot the light?'

Scully pointed to the right side of the clifftop. 'Might have been a signal or maybe there's a cottage up top, but that was where Penneck seemed to be headed. He weren't gone for more than half an hour, so it couldn't have been too far.'

'We'll go single file.' Bennett jerked his head in the direction of the steep path. 'No talking.'

Vere laid his hand on Rose's shoulder. 'You should stay here.'

'We need her,' Bennett said softly. 'The woman might pay heed to what Rose says. We want Billy to come without a fight. He won't harm his sister no matter how desperate he might be.'

'I'm coming with you.' Rose picked up her skirts and headed for the narrow gap where the path snaked up the steep cliff.

Bennett strode past her. 'I'll go first.'

There was little point in arguing, and Rose kept up with his long strides as best she could, although she was hampered by her petticoats and her thick, linsey-woolsey skirt. Scully and Vere caught up with her and Vere proffered his hand, but she shook her head and he continued along the path, pausing occasionally to look back, as if to make sure she was still following. Rose reached the top not long after them, but she was exhausted by the effort and her leg muscles were screaming in silent agony. The others were conferring in sign language, having spotted a faint spiral of smoke rising into the night sky, although there was still no sign of habitation. Scully and Bennett went on ahead, leaving Vere and Rose to follow at a safe distance. There was nowhere to hide as they trod a rough pathway along the clifftop, and the land shelved steeply as they crested the rise. Then, in a hollow surrounded by gorse bushes and a tangle of brambles, Rose saw a cottage. It looked like a tiny doll's house that had been wedged into a crevice, and a few feet from the front door there was a steep drop to the jagged rocks below. The shutters on the ground floor were closed, and a tell-tale plume of smoke from a single chimney was the only sign of life.

Bennett came to a halt. 'Vere, stay here with Rose. Scully, come with me.' He walked on, moving slowly and stealthily towards the building.

Rose clasped her hands, praying silently that this was where Billy and Jenifry were hiding out. The wind soughed around them, and the sound of the waves breaking against the rocks was loud enough to drown the crunch of booted feet on the stony path.

Vere placed his arm around her shoulders. 'I should go with them,' he whispered. 'Will you be all right if I leave you here?'

'I'm fine,' she said, nodding. 'Scully seems to be beckoning to you.' She had no intention of being left behind, and she waited until Vere was several paces ahead before following him. As she drew nearer, she could see that the cottage had quite literally been built into the cliff face, and there was only one way in, with no escape other than an upstairs window. She held her breath as Bennett tried the door. Finding it locked, he took a step backwards and kicked it in. He barged into the cottage followed by Scully and Vere.

Angry shouts and the sound of a scuffle echoed round the cove. A woman screamed, and a broken chair flew through the open door, landing with a splintering crash at Rose's feet. She sidestepped it and edged towards the entrance, but she had to leap for safety as two men, locked in combat, tumbled out of the cottage and landed on the patch of turf. Flailing arms and legs and flying fists were accompanied by grunts and groans, as punches hit home. She stood motionless, unable to do anything other than look on in horror as blood flowed freely. A final blow rendered one of them unconscious, and she realised that Scully was the victor. She hurried forward to help him to his feet. 'Are you hurt?'

He brushed a grimy sleeve across his bleeding nose and lips. 'Never felt better, miss.' He staggered back into the building, leaving Rose alone with the prostrate figure. She did not recognise the young man, but with his shaggy, blood-stained beard and long hair she doubted if his own mother would know him. She stepped over him and went inside to find Vere and

Bennett standing over a second man, who was lying on the flagstone floor, groaning. It was not Billy.

'Are they the ones you were looking for?' she asked anxiously.

'It's the Penneck brothers all right,' Bennett said with a satisfied smile. He flexed his bruised fingers. 'I haven't had such a satisfying bout of fisticuffs since I was at university.' He slapped his cousin on the back. 'You did well, Vere. It's quite like old times.'

'But what about Billy?' Rose protested. 'You two might have enjoyed a fight, but where is my brother?'

'He made a run for it.' Jenifry's tearful voice from the narrow staircase made them all turn to look at her. 'He jumped out of the window. I told him to stay, but he wouldn't listen.' She collapsed on the bottom step, burying her face in her hands.

Rose went to comfort her. 'Where would he go?'

'The young idiot.' Bennett rushed out of the cottage and disappeared into the darkness.

'Why did you follow us?' Jenifry sobbed. 'We were getting on well enough, and Billy had just got himself work on a fishing boat. We could have stayed here for ever.'

'And what about them?' Rose jerked her head in the direction of the semi-conscious man. 'Did you want to spend the rest of your life protecting two villains?'

'They're not bad,' Jenifry sobbed. 'They done nothing wrong.'

Pasco opened his eyes and swore loudly, as Vere

hefted him onto a chair. 'This man murdered my brother, and he allowed Billy to take the blame.'

Jenifry sniffed and hiccuped, wiping her eyes on her nightgown. 'I don't believe it. Pasco is our friend. He wouldn't do such a thing.'

'We have a witness who will swear it in court,' Rose said gently. 'Pasco is the killer, but don't you see that it proves Billy is innocent?'

Vere produced a pair of handcuffs from his coat pocket and clipped them around Pasco's wrists. 'I had the forethought to borrow these from our local police constable,' he said with a wry smile. 'I hoped they'd come in useful.'

Rose glanced at a familiar pair of shoes that had been put to dry on the hearth. 'Those are Billy's. He won't get far barefoot.'

'And he's only wearing his drawers.' Jenifry clapped her hand to her mouth, eyes wide with horror. 'What will folk say?'

At any other time, Rose might have smiled at Jenifry's overt fear of public censure, but she kept a straight face as she helped the trembling girl to her feet. 'Why don't you go upstairs and get dressed? We're taking you home.'

'I'm going nowhere without Billy.'

'Bennett will bring him back, you may depend on that.'

'If he don't, I'm staying here. You can't make me go, if I don't want to.' Jenifry raced upstairs and slammed the bedroom door.

'Here's the other one.' Scully gave Day Penneck a shove that sent him staggering into the room. 'This one confessed to witnessing the murder, boss,' he said, grinning widely. 'He's going to speak up in court, ain't you, mate?'

Day blinked and swallowed hard, keeping a wary eye on his brother. 'He forced me to say it, Pasco.'

'We'll deny everything,' Pasco said, curling his lip. 'You can't prove nothing. It be your fellow's word against ours. And there's two of us.'

'I wouldn't count on it.' Vere moved a step closer, fixing Pasco with a hard stare. 'The word of a well-known scoundrel against that of an educated gentleman is not going to impress a judge, Pasco. You've had your chances, and you've proved yourself worthless. You'll take the consequences.'

Rose snatched a crust of bread from the table and tossed it at Pasco. He caught it, staring at her in astonishment. 'I ain't a monkey in the zoo, miss. Why throw bread at me?'

'He caught it in his right hand,' Rose said triumphantly.

'What has that got to do with Gawain's murder?' Vere demanded.

'Ask Bennett. He'll explain, but my brother is left-handed. He couldn't have struck the fatal blow.'

Pasco glared at Rose, curling his lip. 'She's off her head.'

'We should get these two back to Portmorna, Mr

Tressidick.' Scully made a move towards the door. 'The sooner they're in clink, the better.'

'We can't leave without Bennett,' Vere said, frowning.

'I won't go anywhere until I know what's happened to my brother.' Rose faced them angrily. 'He's the victim in all this.'

'That's true,' Vere said softly, 'but we're doing our best for him, Rose. It's a pity he ran off like that. It doesn't help his case.'

'What would you have done in similar circumstances? Billy is frightened and confused.'

'Bennett will make him see sense.' Vere turned with a start as the door burst open and Bennett entered the room. 'Where's Billy?'

'He had more than a head start. I lost him.'

'Thank the Lord.' Jenifry walked slowly down the stairs. She was fully dressed and smiling. 'You won't catch him now.'

'Are you completely mad?' Rose said angrily. 'Haven't you heard a word that's been said?'

'I dunno know what you mean, miss.'

'My brother is innocent, and we can prove it. He has to stand trial so that he can be acquitted honourably.'

'I don't understand.'

Bennett held the door open. 'The tide is on the turn and we need to leave now, or we could be stuck here for hours. Scully, you're in charge of Day, and I'll see that Pasco doesn't escape. You can look after the ladies, Vere.'

'I ain't going nowhere.' Jenifry clutched the newel post with both hands. 'I'm not leaving without Billy.'

'Do you think you're the only one who cares for him?' Rose turned on her like a fury. 'Billy has to give himself up, or he'll never be free, and you're not helping.'

'I love him,' Jenifry whispered.

'Then you'll return to Portmorna with us.'

'But Billy will follow.'

'That's what I'm hoping.' Regretting her sharp tone, Rose slipped her arm around Jenifry's shoulders. 'He'll be a fugitive for the rest of his life if he goes on like this. He must be made to see sense, and I think he'll listen to you.'

Bennett met Rose's anxious glance with a smile and a nod. 'Well argued, lady lawyer.' He grabbed Pasco by the collar and propelled him out of the cottage, following by Scully and Day, who needed little persuasion.

'It's time to go,' Vere said urgently.

'Jenifry?' Rose extended her hand. 'Trust me. You can't imagine the lengths to which my sister and I have gone in our attempts to help Billy. You and I are on the same side.'

'If you say so, miss.' Jenifry's shoulders drooped and she bowed her head, as if the fight had gone from her. She allowed herself to be led from the comparative warmth of the kitchen into the chill of early dawn.

*

367

The sun had risen by the time they reached Portmorna. Bennett and Scully marched the Penneck brothers off to the police constable's house, and a tearful Jenifry was reunited with her mother.

Mrs Tregony wrapped her arms around her errant daughter. 'You'm a daft little maid, Jenifry. Look what trouble you've caused.'

'I'm sorry, Ma, but I love Billy.'

'And now no decent boy will want to wed you. You've ruined yourself and us, maid.'

'No, Ma. Billy will marry me; he said so.'

'He'll be dangling at the end of a hangman's noose if they catches him.'

Rose had been about to take her leave, but she could not let this go. 'Billy is innocent, Mrs Tregony. We have a witness who will swear that it was Pasco Penneck who killed Mr Tressidick.'

Mrs Tregony's eyes widened. 'Is that so, miss?'

'It is so, ma'am, but Billy has to return and stand trial.'

'D'you hear that, Jenifry?' Mrs Tregony held her daughter at arm's length. 'You must make him see sense.'

'How can I, Ma? I dunno where Billy has got to.'

'He'll come for you, maid. If he loves you he'll be back, and then it's up to you. If you run away again that's how you'll spend the rest of your life.' Mrs Tregony handed her daughter a scrap of cloth. 'Wipe your eyes. You've got work to do.'

'I think we all need to get some sleep, but what your mother says is true, Jenifry.' Rose patted her hand. 'Billy won't let you down. He's a good man.' She glanced over her shoulder at the sound of footsteps and saw Vere standing in the doorway.

'Time to go, Rose. I sent Scully to the coach house with a message for Yelland. He's just arrived with the carriage to take us home.'

'You go with them,' Mrs Tregony said, giving Jenifry a push towards the door.

'But, Ma, I've lost my position at the big house.' Jenifry shot a sideways glance at Vere. 'I don't expect my behaviour to be overlooked, sir.'

'I have nothing to do with that side of things,' Vere said, shrugging. 'It's up to Mrs Vennor.'

'We can't manage on the small pension I gets from the mine, sir.' Mrs Tregony faced him with a steady look. 'It's little enough to keep me, let alone the two of us. Jenifry has to find work, no matter what she thinks.'

Rose moved to Vere's side. 'I'll have a word with Mrs Vennor,' she said in a low voice. 'She's hard-pressed at the moment, and I think she'll agree to give Jenifry a second chance.'

'You know more about these things than I do. I'll leave it to you, Rose.'

'Come, Jenifry.' Rose held out her hand. 'We need you at Portmorna House.'

Jenifry bobbed a curtsey. 'Thank you, miss.'

'God bless you.' Mrs Tregony's worried expression

melted into a tremulous smile. 'Mr Tressidick has chosen his lady well.'

Rose opened her mouth to protest, but Vere tucked her hand in the crook of his arm. 'We'll say good day to you, Mrs Tregony. I'll make sure that Jenifry is reinstated.' He tipped his hat and escorted Rose out to the waiting carriage.

'You should have put her right,' Rose whispered. 'I dare say it will be the talk of the village from now on.'

Vere handed her into the vehicle. 'Who knows? Maybe my luck will change and you'll relent and make a lonely bachelor happy. I haven't given up yet, Rose.' He climbed in beside her, leaving Jenifry to settle herself on the driver's seat beside Yelland.

'You know my feelings on that score,' Rose said carefully. 'Nothing has changed.'

'I live in hope, my dear.' Vere leaned out of the window. 'Drive on, Yelland.'

Maisie was waiting in the entrance hall. The news of their imminent arrival had travelled from the coach house to the servants' quarters in the blink of an eye, and normally stoical James could hardly contain his curiosity as he took their salt-stained outer garments and soggy headgear.

'Will there be anything else, sir?' he asked tentatively.

'We'll have breakfast as soon as it's ready, James. It's been a long night.'

'And a successful one, I hope, sir.'

'Moderately so.' Vere turned to Rose. 'I'm going to change before we eat. I'm afraid I reek of mackerel.'

'Me, too,' she said, wrinkling her nose. 'But perhaps I'd better speak to Mrs Vennor before I do anything else.'

'That would be kind, thank you, Rose.' Vere walked towards the staircase and Rose waited until he was out of earshot before turning to Maisie, who was hopping from one foot to the other.

'How is my sister?' Rose asked eagerly.

'Perking up nicely, miss. I didn't tell her what you was up to in case it made her worse, but this morning she woke up and is almost back to normal. She said she wanted a cup of tea and some toast, and now she's asking for you.'

'That's wonderful, and such a relief. I'll go and see her as soon as I've sorted things out below stairs, and I need to change out of these clothes.' Rose felt as though her feet barely touched the ground as she hurried after James. A great weight had been lifted from her shoulders now that Cora was on the mend. Billy might have taken flight, but he was still in Cornwall, and she was convinced that he would return to Portmorna, if only to see the girl he loved.

Having washed and changed, Rose went to the kitchen to find Mrs Vennor, but as she entered the room she was surprised to see Bennett and Scully seated at the table, enjoying a breakfast of fried bacon and hog's pudding.

Bennett rose from his chair. 'Have you come to join us, Rose?'

'I didn't know you were all here. It's Mrs Vennor I need to speak to.'

Flushed from the heat of the fire, Mrs Vennor lifted a pan off the flames and set it on the hob. 'I'm a bit busy, miss. As you can see.'

'And you need more help, Mrs Vennor,' Rose said tactfully. 'How would you feel about taking Jenifry back? Just for a trial period, of course.'

Kensa stooped to pick up a slice of bread that had fallen off the toasting fork. 'Jenifry should be doing this. I'm the parlour maid now.'

Mrs Vennor flipped her round the head with a drying cloth. 'You'll do what you're told, Kensa Penneck.'

Scully swallowed a mouthful of food. 'If that girl's related to them other Pennecks, I wouldn't trust her an inch.'

'Innocent until proven guilty, Scully.' Bennett resumed his seat. 'I take it that my cousin is giving Billy's ladylove a second chance.'

'If Mrs Vennor agrees,' Rose said tactfully. 'It's up to you, Mrs Vennor. Jenifry has done nothing wrong, other than try to help the man she loves. Mr Tressidick is happy for her to take up her old job, but you have the last word.'

'It ain't fair,' Kensa muttered, and received another swipe with the cloth.

'You're lucky I don't send you packing, girl,' Mrs

Vennor said angrily. 'You're idle and you've broken more plates than any other scullery maid we've had. Jenifry is welcome to come back, and I've already told her so, Miss Perkins. I sent her upstairs to change into her uniform. She'll be down in time to serve breakfast in the dining room.'

'Thank you for being so understanding, Mrs Vennor.' Rose was about to leave the kitchen, but she hesitated in the doorway. 'What will happen to the Pennecks now, Bennett?'

'They're in the hands of the local constable.' He rose from his seat. 'They'll be taken to Bodmin Gaol later today, and I'm putting a case for a retrial to the magistrate.'

'But we don't know where Billy is.'

'How far can a fellow get, barefoot and in his drawers? Scully is going to continue the search when he's finished his breakfast.' Bennett followed Rose out of the kitchen. 'How is Cora?'

'She's much better, according to Maisie. I'm going to see her now.' She was about to mount the stairs when he caught her by the wrist.

'How does the land lie between you and my cousin?'

She stiffened. 'I don't think that's any of your business.'

'Vere is a good man. I don't want to see him hurt.'

'I've told him how I feel. I'm truly grateful for everything he's done for us, but Cora and I will leave as soon as matters are settled here.' She met his intense gaze with a steady look. 'Please let me go.'

He released her immediately. 'I'm sorry, but I had to know. What will you do when you return to London?'

'If Cora is willing, we'll begin again as the Sunshine Sisters. The Grecian isn't the only theatre in town, and when we get work we'll settle your fees. I won't rest until the debt is paid.'

'I'm weary of telling you that the debt is non-existent, Rose. This has become even more of a personal matter to me, and I wouldn't touch a penny of your hard-earned money.'

'It's a matter of principle. Now, if you'll excuse me, I need to see Cora.' She negotiated the narrow staircase with as much dignity as she could muster. Exhaustion was enveloping her like a London particular, and it was hard to think. Every part of her body ached and she needed to sleep, but first she must see her sister and make sure that, as Maisie had said, Cora was on the mend.

Cora lay in the four-poster, staring up at the embroidered tester. She was deathly pale and her golden hair spread about the pillow gave her an ethereal look.

'How do you feel?' Rose asked gently.

Cora's thin fingers plucked at the coverlet. 'You should have let me die.' She turned her head away, avoiding Rose's anxious gaze.

'It's the illness talking, Corrie. You'll feel quite different when you've regained your strength.'

'No, I won't. You know how it will be if I return to London. Everyone will know what a silly fool I was to believe a man like Gerard. My reputation is ruined.'

Rose sat on the edge of the bed. 'He'll hardly boast about a conquest that ended with the person in question running away. It would be as good as admitting that he had taken advantage of you.'

'There might be other complications.' Cora turned on her side, face to the wall.

Rose could see that this conversation was going nowhere. 'If you'll stop thinking about yourself for a minute, I'll tell you where I went last night.'

'Maisie said you were tired and had an early night.'

'Far from it. In fact, I haven't been to bed.'

'Really?' Cora raised herself on her elbow. 'Why?'

'Because we crossed the bay in a smelly old fishing boat and landed in a cove, miles from the nearest village. Scully had followed Gryffyn Penneck one night, suspecting that he was going to meet his sons. He spotted a light high up on the cliffs and that made it seem even likelier. As it happens he was right.'

Suddenly alert, Cora sat up in bed, wrapping her arms around her knees. 'Go on.'

'We found the cottage and the Penneck brothers put up a fight, but they were no match for Bennett and Vere.'

'Did you find Billy?'

'He was there with Jenifry, but he escaped through an upstairs window and ran away. Bennett chased after him, but he couldn't catch him, so we brought Jenifry back to Portmorna.'

'Do you think that he'll come looking for her?'

'I'm sure of it. Besides which, Billy ran off barefoot and wearing only his drawers.' Rose chuckled at the image it conjured up of their serious-minded brother, running round the Cornish countryside, half-naked. 'Can you imagine what Papa would say if he knew?'

A weary smile hovered around Cora's pale lips. 'I don't know who would disgust him the most. We've all been a terrible disappointment to him.'

'Perhaps he set his standards too high, Corrie. We're all human and we make mistakes, but Papa expected us to be perfect.'

Cora lay back against the pillows. 'I've been so stupid, Rose.'

'I won't allow that. We were thrown into a situation that none of us could have imagined. We've coped as best we could, and if we've made mistakes, at least we've learned by them.'

'And you, Rosie,' Cora said tiredly. 'What about you? You have two men falling at your feet. Which one will you choose?'

'Vere asked me to marry him. Are you suggesting that Scully is going to propose next?'

'You know very well who I mean. Bennett has

been your devoted admirer from the moment you first met.'

'Nonsense, Corrie. It must be the laudanum talking.' Rose jumped to her feet and walked over to the window, throwing up the sash. 'It's a lovely morning. You need some fresh air, and this afternoon you ought to get up for a while. You'll only get weak and wobbly if you remain in bed.'

'You can change the subject as many times as you like,' Cora said smugly, 'but I know you, Rosie. You won't admit it, even to yourself, but it's Bennett who makes your heart beat faster.'

But Rose was not listening. She had seen a movement in the bushes where the green sweep of the lawn ended. 'There's someone out there, Corrie, and he doesn't want to be seen.'

Chapter Twenty

Tiredness forgotten, Rose left Cora's bedroom and raced downstairs. She did not stop running until she reached the dense shrubbery at the edge of the lawn. 'Billy, is it you?' She waited, hardly daring to breathe. 'Billy, I know you're there. Come out and talk to me. It's all right, we're all on your side.'

A sharp sound, the snap of a twig and the rustle of dry leaves underfoot, caught her attention, and she pushed her way through a thick patch of laurel bushes, coming face to face with her brother. 'Billy.'

'I saw you at the window, Rosie, and I thought I was dreaming. But it really is you.'

'Of course it's me, silly. You might have known that I'd do anything I could to bring you home, safe and sound.'

'Jenifry told me that you'd been staying at Portmorna House, but I thought you might have given up.'

'I'd never give up on you, Billy.' She threw her arms around him, but drew back almost immediately, covering her nose with her hand. 'What is that awful smell?'

'That's a nice welcome,' he said with a reluctant smile.

'You look like a scarecrow.' She stared in distaste at his filthy old shirt, and even dirtier trousers. 'No, you didn't, did you?'

'I'm afraid so. The scarecrow could go round next to naked, but I couldn't.' His smile faded. 'Is Jenifry here? I called at her mother's cottage, but there was no one at home.'

'Yes, she's here, but you need to wash and change before you see her . . . or anyone, come to that.'

He ran his hand through his tumbled auburn hair, which had grown long, and was curling wildly around his head. His face was smeared with mud and there were dark shadows underlining his eyes. 'I know what you're going to say, Rosie.'

She reached out to pluck a leaf from his hair. 'You're right, Billy. I'm going to tell you to give yourself up. It's the only way you'll ever be free from all this.'

'But they'll hang me for sure, Rosie.'

'The Penneck brothers aren't your friends,' she said gently. 'It was Pasco who killed Gawain. Your friend Edric witnessed the attack, but was too ill next morning to realise what was going on. By the time he recovered, the Pennecks had sworn that it was you. They'd set the whole thing up so that it looked as if you were the murderer.'

'Then it's their word against Edric's,' Billy said, frowning.

'As Bennett said, your friends are scholars and gentlemen. A jury would believe them and not the Penneck brothers. Even if that weren't the case, Bennett made Day confess to lying and Pasco virtually admitted his guilt in front of me, Vere and Scully. So you see, you have to go to trial, but you'll be acquitted for certain.'

'I'd like to hear it from Bennett himself. It's not that I don't believe you, Rosie, but I need to be certain that I won't be putting my neck in a noose.'

'Of course you do.' Rose linked her hand through his arm. 'Come into the house. We'll go in by the servants' entrance and I'll get Maisie to fill a bath for you. Perhaps Vere could lend you some clean clothes. You can't go round looking and smelling like a scarecrow.'

'You're a good sister.' He hesitated at the edge of the shrubbery. 'Does Pa know about this sorry business?'

'I'm afraid he does,' Rose admitted reluctantly. 'It wasn't possible to keep it from him.'

'And how did he react?'

'He left London and moved to Dorset. I believe he has the living of a small parish not far from Lyme Regis. I'm sorry, Billy.'

He shook his head. 'It's what I expected, but how are you and Cora managing?'

'Cora is here,' Rose said, evading the question. 'She hasn't been well, but is recovering nicely. She'll be overjoyed to see you, but not in this state.' She hurried him across the lawn and was about to guide him round to the servants' entrance when the front door opened, and Vere stepped outside.

'Is that you beneath the dirt and rags, Billy?' Vere took in Billy's dishevelled appearance with raised eyebrows. 'So you decided to give yourself up, after all.'

'Yes, sir. But if my being here is an embarrassment I'll move on.'

'We know you're innocent,' Vere said firmly. 'But the fewer people who see you, the better. Come inside.'

'Thank you.' Rose could have hugged him, but she managed to control herself. 'I don't know what we would have done if it weren't for you, Vere.'

He beckoned to James, who was hovering at the top of the steps. 'Not a word of this, James. Have one of the maids fill the bath in my dressing room. We have a guest, but I don't want this to become common knowledge.'

'Yes, sir.' James hurried off to do his master's bidding.

'You can trust him not to say anything.' Vere hurried Billy into the house. 'We're much the same size. I think I can find clothes to fit you a little better than the ones you're wearing.'

Rose followed them indoors. 'Thank you again, Vere.'

His expression softened. 'There's no need for thanks, Rose. Why don't you join Bennett in the dining room? Mrs Vennor sent him upstairs to finish his breakfast. You can tell him that Billy has returned. He'll know what steps to take next.'

'I'd like to see Jenifry,' Billy said anxiously. 'I want her to know that I'm all right.'

'There's plenty of time for that, old chap.' Vere patted him on the shoulder. 'Best get you cleaned up first.'

Rose nodded in agreement. 'No matter how much she loves you, she might find your present state less than attractive. Go with Vere and I'll speak to Bennett.'

Bennett stood up as Rose entered the dining room. 'I was sent out of the kitchen, but I'll gladly keep you company while you eat.'

She took a seat at the table. 'I'll have a cup of coffee, but I've no appetite.'

'Are you unwell? Are you going down with Cora's illness, or did you catch a chill on the water?' Twin furrows creased his brow as he gave her a searching look.

'No, nothing like that.' She reached for the silver coffee pot and filled a cup. 'It's Billy. He's here.'

'That's the best news I've had for some time.'

Bennett picked up the toast rack and passed it to her. 'You really should eat something. You've been nursing Cora and now this. We can't have you falling ill on us, Rose.'

She took a slice. 'I'm perfectly fine. It's Billy who needs looking after, and thankfully Vere has taken him in hand.'

'I see.' Bennett sat back in his chair, eyeing her thoughtfully. 'I must have a word with your brother. We can't have him running off again.'

'I don't think he'd be so stupid. He knows he must face trial.' Rose buttered the toast and took a bite.

'I'll go to Bodmin today and see what I can do. If his case could be heard at the summer assizes it isn't long to wait. We have our witnesses, but there's one person whose testimony could sway things in Billy's favour.'

'Who is that?' Rose asked curiously.

'Your father,' Bennett said gently. 'The jury must be made aware that Billy comes from a good family. Do you think you could persuade Mr Perkins to act as character witness?'

'I could try, but Papa made it very clear that he wants nothing to do with me or my sister, let alone Billy. We've disappointed him and let him down. He won't lie, nor will he dissemble. Pa will tell the absolute truth.'

'That's a pity, but try not to worry. I'll stake my reputation on getting Billy acquitted.'

*

Rose and Cora sat with Vere and Jenifry in the public area of the courtroom. Bennett was appearing for Billy in place of the circuit barrister, for which Rose knew she would be eternally grateful. She trusted Bennett above all people, and seeing him for the first time in his wig and robes she was struck by the sheer weight of his presence and personality. She had admired him before, but seeing him in his professional role took her breath away.

Vere had volunteered to be a character witness, and Toby Wilkes and Edric Kenyon had travelled down from Oxford to fulfil their part in the trial. Rose had written to her father, begging him to stand by his son, but had received no reply. She was saddened, but not surprised. Polly had sent her best wishes, and now there was nothing that any of them could do other than sit, listen and hope that the outcome of the trial would be in Billy's favour.

The Penneck brothers protested their innocence, and the solicitor who represented them did his best to convince the judge and jury that they had been cruelly maligned. But it was Bennett who dominated the courtroom, and his quick wit outpaced the prosecution, at times leaving the country lawyer floundering for words and temporarily speechless.

Gryffyn Penneck swore on oath that his sons had been at home when the murder took place, but under Bennett's clever cross-examination he crumbled and admitted that he might have been mistaken. Toby and Edric were called to the witness box and each gave his testimony in a loud, clear voice. Rose kept a close eye on the jurors, watching their reactions and willing them to come to the right conclusion. They seemed impressed by the two young under-graduates, and Bennett was quick to note their reactions and press home his advantage.

In his summing up, the circuit judge criticised Billy and his friends for their drunken behaviour on that fatal night. 'They are not,' he said firmly, 'the sort of young men whom I would expect to find in an ecclesiastical college of such repute. They let them-selves and their families down very badly, but they are young men, and we have character witnesses to bear testimony to their previous good behaviour. It is,' he said, peering round the courtroom, 'a pity that the defendant's father, who is a clergyman of some standing, has not chosen to support his son.'

'I am here, Your Honour.'

Rose turned her head to see her father enter the courtroom accompanied by Joshua Hart.

'Who are you, sir?' the judge demanded angrily. 'This is very irregular.'

'I've travelled a long way to be here today.' Seymour's voice rang out as if he were preaching to his congregation. 'But for the vagaries of the train timetable I would have been here at the correct hour.'

'Very well.' The judge inclined his bewigged head. 'We are running late as it is. Say your piece, and be done with it, sir.'

The clerk of the court escorted Seymour to the witness stand, and swore him in.

'My name is Seymour Perkins and I have come here today to tell the court that my son is a good man. His behaviour might have fallen short of that which might have been expected of him, but, given a second chance, William Perkins will make an upstanding citizen. He is honest and has a genuine desire to work for the good of mankind, whether or not he chooses to spread the Word of God. I can say no more than that, as I was not present when the tragic death took place, but I do know that Gawain Tressidick was my son's best friend, and that William would not use violence against anyone.'

'Thank you, Mr Perkins. You may stand down.' The judge turned to the jury, and, after summing up the case, he sent them off to deliberate.

Rose followed her father outside to the waiting area. 'I'm so glad you came, Pa.'

'I wasn't going to attend, but Joshua came to see me and persuaded me to change my mind.' Seymour held up his hands as Rose made a move towards him. 'That doesn't mean that I have forgiven your behaviour, Rose.' He glanced over her shoulder. 'Or yours, Cora. You girls have shamed me more than Billy could ever do. The Sunshine Sisters, indeed. Prancing about on stage and exposing your bodies for men to leer at is almost as low as it is possible for a woman to sink.'

'Don't say that, Papa.' Cora's voice broke on a sob. 'We only did it to raise money for Billy's defence.'

'I don't know how you have the nerve to look me in the face,' Seymour continued angrily. 'Don't resort to tears, Cora. I know your tricks only too well. You always managed to evade punishment by weeping when you were a child. It worked with your mother, but I am of stronger stuff. I know that you ran away with that libertine Gerard Barclay.'

'It wasn't her fault, Papa,' Rose protested. 'Cora thought he was in love with her.'

'That doesn't make it better,' Seymour raged. 'In fact, it makes it worse. A decent man would have spoken to me first. He would have sought my permission to court and marry my daughter, and if Cora had had any sense she would have seen him for the philanderer he is. Now her reputation, such as it was, is in shreds and the family name is tarnished by her sins.'

Cora broke down in tears and Rose enveloped her in a hug. 'How can you say such cruel things to her, Pa? She knows what she's done and she's deeply ashamed and sorry. What happened to love and forgiveness?'

Vere had been silent until this moment, but he stepped forward. 'I think this has gone far enough, Mr Perkins.'

'And who may you be, sir?' Seymour glared at him.

'This is Vere Tressidick, Papa,' Rose said hastily. 'It was his brother who was murdered. He's been the soul of kindness and consideration since all this happened, and the defending barrister is Vere's cousin, Bennett Sharpe.'

Seymour narrowed his eyes. 'So you have chosen to throw yourselves at the mercy of men who have doubtless taken advantage of your youth and vulnerability.'

'Mr Perkins, sir.' Joshua tugged at Seymour's sleeve. 'This is neither the time nor the place. We are attracting unwanted attention.'

'I agree,' Vere said angrily. 'You need to calm down, sir. I have every sympathy for your son and daughters, for now I can see where the blame lies.'

Seymour recoiled, staring at Vere in astonishment. 'How dare you speak to me in that tone? I'm a man of God.'

'Then act like one, sir.' Vere took a large white handkerchief from his pocket and gave it to Cora. 'This young woman has been through a terrible ordeal, and her health has suffered. These are your daughters; your own flesh and blood. Have you no compassion?'

Seymour stared at him, thunderstruck, and for once he seemed to have nothing to say.

'Oh, Cora, I'm so sorry.' Joshua touched her tentatively on the shoulder. 'If there's anything I can do to help, please tell me.'

'Thank you.' Cora's voice was muffled by the folds of the hankie.

'You're very kind,' Rose added. 'You're a good friend, Joshua.'

'I think the jury is about to return,' Vere said quietly. 'We should take our seats for the verdict.'

Rose beckoned to Jenifry, who had been hovering in the background. 'Come. I'm sure you of all people want to hear this.'

'Am I to be ignored?' Seymour demanded in a plaintive voice.

'Yes, Papa. I believe you are.' Rose turned to him, unsmiling. 'You've made your opinions clear, so I don't think there's much good to be served by you remaining, unless, of course, you want to congratulate Billy when they find him not guilty.'

'I'm staying.' Joshua proffered his arm to Jenifry. 'We haven't been introduced, but I'm a friend of the family, and I can see that you are very much involved.'

'I am, sir. Billy and me, we're going to be wed.'

'Has the world gone mad?' Seymour demanded. 'Rose, speak to me. Tell me this young woman is not my son's intended.'

'Billy loves Jenifry and she has stood by him all through this, which is more than I can say for you, Papa. I'm sorry to be so bold, but you've made it perfectly clear that we are an embarrassment to you.'

'Indeed you are.' Seymour rammed his hat on his head. 'I'm leaving now. I've done my duty, but from this day onwards I want nothing to do with any of you. I have no children.' He stalked off, leaving Rose to stare after him.

Vere took her by the hand. 'This is Billy's moment, Rose. Your father will come round eventually.'

'I doubt it,' Rose said sadly. 'He's a proud man and we haven't lived up to his expectations. He'll never forgive us.' She allowed Vere to lead her back to the gallery, where they took their seats just in time to hear the judge ask the foreman of the jury for their verdict.

There was a moment of complete silence. The suspense was unbearable, and Rose held her breath.

Then the foreman cleared his throat. 'Not guilty.'

'Is that the verdict of you all?' the judge demanded.

'Yes, Your Honour.'

'You may walk from this court a free man, William Perkins.' The judge's last words were drowned by boos from the Pennecks and their supporters.

As they left the gallery Rose realised that she was still holding Vere's hand. She released it with a murmured apology.

He flexed his fingers. 'Remind me not to get into an argument with you, Rose. You're stronger than you look.'

'I'm sorry. I didn't mean to hurt you.'

'I was joking,' he said with a wry smile. 'I seem to recall you used to think I was too serious.'

'I didn't know you then.' She met his amused gaze with a tremulous smile. 'We owe you so much. Without you and Bennett the outcome might have been quite different.' She glanced over her shoulder at the sound of footsteps and saw Billy hurrying towards them.

'I can't believe it, Rose. I'm a free man.' He gave her a hug. 'I owe you so much.'

Halfway between laughter and tears, she returned the embrace. 'I'm just so glad it's over.'

Billy turned to Vere and shook his hand. 'Thank you, sir. I owe you and Bennett my life.'

'Justice has been done,' Vere said calmly. 'It's Bennett you must thank, not I.'

'I have already done so.' Billy turned to Rose and gave her a hug. 'You are the best sister a man could have. None of this would have been possible if you hadn't gone to such lengths to save me.'

'It was a joint effort.' Rose nudged Cora, who had been deep in conversation with Joshua. 'We are the Sunshine Sisters, aren't we, Corrie?'

'Never mind that now.' Billy slipped his arm around Jenifry's waist. 'We should celebrate. My friends are staying at the George and Dragon, and they've invited us to share a meal with them. What do you say?'

Bennett had just joined them and he slapped Billy on the shoulder. 'I say, yes, by all means. You're a free man, without a stain on your character. If that doesn't call for a celebration, I don't know what would.' He turned to Rose. 'Congratulations, Miss Sunshine. Billy is right; without you and Cora none of this would have happened. We should toast your success in the best champagne, if they have such a thing in the local inn.'

Rose was about to reply when an all-too-familiar figure sidled towards them with his notebook at the ready.

391

Enoch Frayne doffed his bowler hat. 'A satisfactory verdict, no doubt, ladies and gentlemen.'

'Go away, Frayne,' Vere said angrily. 'There's no story here for you.'

Frayne smiled and tipped his hat. 'You think not, Mr Tressidick?' His glance slid round the group, taking them in with a sly smile. 'Ah, yes. I know the Tregony family of old. Miss Jenifry's father was always in the newspaper for one transgression or another, and his sudden death in the mine was supposed to have been an accident.'

'You mustn't speak ill of my pa,' Jenifry cried angrily. 'He was a good man.'

'I'm sure he was,' Frayne said smoothly. 'And now your name is linked with a man who might well have ended up dancing at the end of the hangman's noose, were it not for the smart-talking Mr Sharpe.'

'That's enough.' Bennett stepped forward, and grabbed Frayne by the lapels of his mustard-coloured jacket. 'You'd better leave, or do I have to throw you out?'

'Come, come, Mr Sharpe.' Frayne pulled away and adjusted his crumpled clothing. 'There's no need to take that attitude. The readers of the *West Briton and Cornwall Advertiser* are very interested in the lives, loves and scandals associated with the local gentry.'

Billy pushed Bennett aside. 'Leave Miss Tregony's name out of this. Write what you like about me, but if you mention her you'll find yourself facing a libel suit.'

'Harsh words, sir.' Frayne's smile did not waver. 'Your pa gave an interesting performance. I think my readers will enjoy the fact that a man of the cloth disowned his entire family.'

Bennett and Vere exchanged glances and without saying a word, they each took an arm and marched the protesting Frayne from the building.

The party was subdued after the encounter with Frayne, but their spirits rose during the meal at the inn, aided by copious amounts of beer, wine and cider. Billy sat next to Jenifry, and Rose was quick to note that Joshua took a seat beside Cora, who seemed to be enjoying his company. It pleased Rose to see her sister looking happy again, and it gave her hope that Cora was coming to terms with her disastrous relationship with Gerard Barclay. Joshua was an old and trusted friend, and Rose suspected that he had harboured tender feelings for her sister for quite some time. Perhaps Cora would see him for the good, kind man he was, and would forget her childish dreams of marrying a wealthy man.

Edric and Toby kept the company amused with their accounts of student life, and it was hard for Rose to imagine either of them as sober minsters of the Church. She was seated on a wooden bench between Bennett and Vere, and she could see that the latter was shocked by some of the escapades described by Edric, but Bennett was laughing heartily. Almost without thinking she moved a little closer to him, but Vere also shifted his position and she found herself sandwiched between the cousins, with each of them vying for her attention. At first it was amusing and flattering, but she began to feel uncomfortable and was starting to lose patience when Vere announced that they had a long carriage drive ahead of them, and it was time to leave.

It was late evening when they arrived back at Portmorna House. Cora was in a state of complete exhaustion and retired to her room immediately, with Maisie clucking round her like a small hen. Joshua had taken a room at the inn, as had Toby and Edric, who intended to return to Oxford next day. They had made Billy promise to resume his studies as soon as he felt able, and he had agreed, although Rose thought it unlikely in the circumstances. She loved her brother dearly, but she was not sure whether he was cut out to follow their father into the ministry. She did not doubt that he would marry Jenifry, but how they would live was another matter. For the moment, she was simply grateful to have Billy returned to them.

'Shall I take your bonnet and mantle, miss?'

Rose looked round to find Jenifry standing at her side. 'Thank you.' She handed them to her. 'You won't be a servant much longer, I think.'

Jenifry bobbed a curtsey. 'I hope not, miss. But I don't know what Billy intends.'

Rose waited until Jenifry was out of earshot before challenging her brother. 'You can't allow this to go on.'

He stared at her with a puzzled frown. 'What's that, Rose?'

'You took Jenifry from her home; you must marry her. It's as simple as that. That was your intention, wasn't it?'

'Of course, but give me a chance, Rosie. I might have ended up in the cells again, or worse. I haven't had time to think about marriage.'

'It's not right that she's waiting on us, Billy. I think she should return home tomorrow, and you can make the necessary arrangements. If you don't, she'll have all the gossips making up stories about her, and blackening her name. You can't allow that to happen.'

Billy leaned over to kiss her cheek. 'You are a worrier, Rosie. I'll do the right thing by Jenny. I just hope that you choose one of your suitors, and put them out of their misery.'

'I don't know what you mean.'

'I've only spent one evening in their company, Rosie, but any fool can see that both Vere and Bennett are smitten by you. You'll have to make one of them happy and the other miserable. Which one will you choose?'

'Don't be ridiculous,' Rose said hastily. She stood on tiptoe to kiss her brother on the cheek. 'It's good to know that you're a free man, Billy. Make the most of it and don't allow Papa to browbeat you into taking up a career that isn't of your choosing.'

'You mustn't worry about me. I can take care of myself, but I'll always be grateful to you and Cora for what you've done for me.' He enveloped her in a hug. 'Good night, Rosie, and think about what I said earlier. I'm turning in now. They've put me in my old room as if nothing has changed, but of course it has. I still feel guilty for what happened to Gawain. If we hadn't gone out drinking, none of this would have taken place.' He hurried off without waiting for Rose to comment.

She was about to mount the stairs when she heard the sound of voices, and she turned to see Vere and Bennett enter the house. They had chosen to ride, and a gust of cool night air followed them in, laced with the smell of horseflesh and leather. Rose was about to speak when she realised that they were in the middle of a fierce argument.

Bennett was the first to see her and he came to a sudden halt. 'We'll leave it there, Vere. I've nothing more to say on the subject.'

'You can offer her nothing,' Vere said bitterly. 'You have no home to speak of and a comparatively modest income. I can give her everything she could desire.'

'You've made your point.' Bennett jerked his head in Rose's direction.

Vere spun round to face Rose and his cheeks reddened. 'I'm sorry, I didn't see you there.'

Rose opened her mouth to answer, but Bennett spoke first. 'I won't stand in your way, Vere. I'll return to London.'

'It's probably for the best.' Vere turned to Rose

with a hint of a smile. 'I have something I want to say to you.'

Rose met Bennett's steady gaze and for a moment it seemed as though he was about to speak, but he brushed past her. 'Goodbye, Rose.' He took the stairs two at a time.

'Will you spare a moment to hear me out, please, Rose?' Vere's voice seemed to come from far away.

'You'll have to excuse me. I'm afraid I'm very tired. Perhaps we can continue this conversation in the morning.' She mounted the stairs, moving like a sleepwalker. Billy had been right, she thought dazedly, but if Bennett had really cared, surely he would have fought for her. His last words rang in her ears as she walked slowly upstairs. 'Goodbye, Rose.'

It seemed like a final farewell. She did not look back.

Chapter Twenty-One

Rose was exhausted, but she could not sleep. The feather bed, which had once seemed the height of luxury, now felt suffocating and too warm for comfort. She got up and went to open the window. The briny tang of the sea mingled with the scent of damask roses and mock orange blossom, but their cloying sweetness was suddenly too much for her. She found herself longing for the smoky, industrial smells of the city; the wet pavements glistening beneath gas lamps and the clatter of horses' hoofs on cobbled streets.

The silence was broken by the hoot of a barn owl, and the bark of a dog fox hunting in the woods, but these sounds were alien to her ears. In London she might have been awakened by the night soil collectors doing their rounds, or the tramp of booted feet as the night shift in the manufactories trudged home, and the recently awakened morning workers dragged their feet on their way to begin a new day of ceaseless toil.

Pale strands of light in the east heralded a summer dawn, and a gentle breeze ruffled the leaves of the ancient oak tree that stood sentinel at the end of the carriage sweep. Until this moment Rose had thought of Portmorna House as being the closest to paradise she was likely to reach, but she realised now that it was not for her. She was city born and city bred. Vere had offered her the chance to live a life of luxury, which would have been wonderful had she had any tender feelings towards him. The truth came upon her with the force of a thunderbolt, and it was not Vere whom she loved with all her heart and soul, but if Bennett had feelings for her, he hid them well. Even if it were true, it was not in her nature to set cousin against cousin. The rift in her own family was hard enough to bear, without inflicting such pain on people who had been good to her.

Billy was a free man, and well able to take care of himself and his bride-to-be. It was Cora who needed her now, and they were not going to hide away in Cornwall. The Sunshine Sisters would rise again. Rose giggled at the unintentional pun, but as far as she could see there was only one thing to do.

She dressed quickly and packed her belongings in the battered valise she had brought from London. She hesitated in the corridor outside her room, listening for sounds of movement downstairs, but it seemed that the servants were not yet up and about. She went to Cora's room where Maisie slept on a truckle bed.

'Wake up, Maisie.'

'What's the matter?' Maisie asked sleepily. 'Is it morning?'

'Don't make a noise. We're going home, but I don't want to wake the rest of the household.'

Maisie snapped into a sitting position. 'We're going home?'

'Get dressed and I'll see to Cora. If we hurry we might catch the road coach to Bodmin, and get the train from there.'

Maisie scrambled to her feet and Rose left her to get dressed while she awakened Cora.

It was early evening when they arrived in Old Street after a long and tortuous journey, having changed trains several times with long waits on draughty railway stations. Cora had been reluctant to leave the comfort of Portmorna House, but her mood had lightened when they met Joshua, Edric and Toby on Bodmin station. They had travelled together until their ways parted.

Rose held her hand out to Joshua, who had seen them to Aunt Polly's door. 'Thank you for everything. I doubt if Papa would have come to Billy's aid had you not taken the time and trouble to persuade him.'

'It was nothing, Rose.' He shot a sideways glance

at Cora, who was hammering on the knocker. 'I hope I will always be a friend of the family.'

'Of course you will,' Cora said, treating him to a bright smile. 'You are always welcome here. Isn't he, Rose?'

'Yes, of course.' Rose gave him a searching look. 'You must be tired, Joshua. Go home and get some rest.'

'I'll call tomorrow, if I may?'

'Yes, do,' Cora said casually. 'You know we're always pleased to see you.' She took a step backwards and the door was wrenched open.

Sukey stared at them, open-mouthed. 'Well, I never did!'

'Let us in, you silly woman.' Maisie pushed past her and dumped the valise at the foot of the stairs. 'I hope Ethel's got the kettle on, because I'm parched.'

Cora stepped inside, followed by Rose. She stopped for a moment, taking in her surroundings. Aunt Polly's shabby old house, with its peeling paintwork and flaking plaster, was a familiar haven where she felt safe. The faint smell of tobacco smoke wafted down the narrow staircase, and the sound of women's voices and babies crying seemed like a heavenly choir. No doubt it would pall after a while, but Rose felt that she had come home. Beautiful as Portmorna House was, she had been a guest, and although she had been made welcome she had not felt entirely comfortable within its elegant walls. She had a suspicion that the feeling might endure, even had she married Vere.

'I'm exhausted, Rose.' Cora's plaintive voice brought Rose abruptly back to the present.

'You must be,' she said sympathetically. 'Maisie, will you see that my sister has hot water sent up to her room?'

'And a cup of cocoa with lots of sugar,' Cora added with a weary smile. 'And perhaps a slice of bread and butter. It's a long time since we last ate.'

'Yes, miss. Right away.' Maisie disappeared in the direction of the back stairs, followed by Sukey.

'Do you need me to help you, Corrie?' Rose asked anxiously. 'You're very pale. Do you feel faint?'

'No, I'm just tired. Don't fuss. I'm quite all right, in fact I'm very much better, if you know what I mean. I can stop worrying.'

'You mean you're not in the family way?'

Cora blushed and averted her gaze. 'I had to ask Maisie what to expect if the worst had happened. Now I know that there will be nothing to link me to Gerard, and I'm glad.'

'As am I.' Rose patted her on the shoulder. 'Go to bed. I'll make your excuses to Aunt Polly, and I'll see you in the morning. Now that we know you're on the mend we'll have to start looking for another venue.'

'Are you serious about returning to the stage, Rosie?'

'Deadly serious. We have to support ourselves, and if I can repay some of the money we owe Bennett, then I will. I don't want to be beholden to any man, least of all him.' Rose left her sister to negotiate the stairs and crossed the hall, intending to knock on the parlour door, but it opened before she had a chance to raise her hand.

'Rose, I thought I heard your voice.' Polly flung her arms around her niece, enveloping her in a cloud of patchouli, tuberose and gin fumes.

Fancello appeared behind Polly, and his moustache quivered as a broad grin almost split his face in two. 'My Sunshine Sisters have returned. Come in and tell us everything, Rose. We've missed your company, haven't we, Paloma?'

'Do sit down, Sandro,' Polly said impatiently. 'Let the girl in, you silly man.'

He subsided onto a chair, eyeing Spartacus warily as the animal leaped off the chaise longue and stalked out of the room. 'I'm just pleased to see Rose. It's not a crime.'

Polly tugged at the bell pull. 'Have you eaten, dear? Would you like tea or cocoa? Where is Cora?'

'She's very tired and she's gone straight to her room.' Rose sank down on the chaise and braced herself to answer their questions, but she was granted a brief reprieve by Sal, who burst into the room, her face flushed and her eyes alight with curiosity. 'Maisie tells us you've had an exciting time, miss.'

'Don't listen to gossip,' Polly said sharply. 'My niece would like tea and cake.'

Sal's mouth drooped at the corners. 'Yes'm.' She left the room, head bowed and muttering something unintelligible.

'Wretched creature,' Polly said, sighing. 'It's time

she left and made her own way in the world. Now, where were we, Rose?'

Rose launched into an account of the events leading up to Billy's trial. Both Fancello and Polly were incensed by the treatment Cora had received, and Fancello declared that if duelling had not been made illegal, he would feel obliged to call the young man out. Polly treated this with contempt, but she was visibly moved.

'That unspeakable cad should be horsewhipped through the streets,' she said angrily. 'If I hear a word of scandal involving Cora I'll make it my business to let everyone know that Gerard Barclay is a rake and a philanderer.'

'At least Cora has recovered from her infatuation, and the best piece of news is that Billy is a free man. Papa travelled all the way to Bodmin to act as character witness, and that, together with Bennett's brilliant handling of the case, convinced the jury of Billy's innocence.'

'I'm so glad,' Polly said, frowning thoughtfully. 'But I wonder why Seymour had such a change of heart. Did he make his peace with you girls?'

'No, Aunt Polly, the very reverse. It hurts me to say it, but Papa wants nothing more to do with any of us. He can't forgive Cora and me for performing in public, and he was furious when he realised that Billy intends to marry a servant girl, whom I should add is a sweet creature and will make him a loving wife.'

'Seymour always was a sanctimonious fool,' Polly

said angrily. 'I pity my sister, but then she should have stood up to him years ago. Her compliance has created a monster.'

'That's a bit harsh, *cara mia*.' Fancello moved to sit by her side. 'Poor Eleanor is not as strong as you, and Seymour is a bully, despite his calling.'

'I intend to visit Mrs Harman as soon as I am able,' Rose said slowly. 'I'm sure she could arrange a meeting between me and Mama, even if it means deceiving my father. I need to know that she is well and happy.'

A tap on the door preceded Big Bertha, who lumbered into the room carrying a laden tray. She dumped it down on the tea table. 'Shall I pour, missis?'

Rose leaped to her feet. 'It's all right, thank you, Bertha. I'll do it.'

'Oh, very well.' Bertha stomped out of the parlour and slammed the door.

'They know that something is going on,' Polly said in a stage whisper. 'I won't be able to keep it from them much longer.'

Rose paused with the teapot in her hand. 'Is something wrong? What is it, Aunt?'

Polly and Fancello exchanged wary glances. 'The truth is, dear, that the lease on the house has expired, and the landlord refuses to renew it. I'm afraid we have to move out at the end of the month.'

'But that only gives us three weeks to find somewhere else to live,' Rose said dazedly, 'and what will happen to the poor women who live with you?'

'They are only here on a temporary basis. They know that.' Polly stood up and went to the chiffonier to refill her glass with gin, adding just a dash of water.

'But Ethel and Sukey have been with you for as long as I can remember, and there's Tommy Tinker, too. What will become of him?'

'I don't know, Rose.' Polly drank deeply. 'I wish I did.'

Rose looked from one to the other and saw defeat in their eyes. 'We'll manage somehow. I'll start looking for work tomorrow, and we'll find somewhere else to live.'

Fancello slapped his hand on his thigh. 'She's right, Paloma. We must stop bemoaning our fate and do something positive.'

'But how will we settle the bills?' Polly tossed back the contents of her glass in one gulp. 'The charity pays me a small salary, but without it I will be destitute.'

'What did you do previously?' Rose directed the question to Fancello. 'You were both successful performers in your own right, so why not form a double act. I've heard you singing together.'

Fancello's bushy eyebrows shot up to his hairline. 'I can think of nothing I would rather do.' He held his hand out to Polly. 'We could do it, *cara*.'

'We're too old. Who would want to watch a middle-aged man and woman making fools of themselves on stage?'

'You both sing beautifully,' Rose said, warming to the subject. 'You would take London by storm.'

'I suppose it's possible.' Polly stared into her empty glass. 'I was a star, but could I reach those heights again?'

Fancello went down on his knees in front of her and grasped her hands. 'We could do it, *cara mia*. You and I were always meant to be together. Now is our chance.'

'And we must find somewhere cheap to live,' Rose said firmly. 'Perhaps we could take Maisie, Ethel and Sukey with us. I doubt if they could manage on their own.'

Polly set her glass aside. 'You're right, my dear. We cannot give in when ill fortune strikes.' She leaned over to kiss Fancello on the tip of his nose. 'Tomorrow we will start rehearsing as Day and Fancello.'

'Fancello and Day has a better ring to it, *cara*.'

'No, dearest. It will be Day and Fancello.'

Rose left them arguing and went to her room.

Everything was packed and the rooms that once echoed to the sound of women's voices were empty and silent. Big Bertha and Sal had taken jobs in the Lying-In Hospital, which were poorly paid, but offered accommodation and free meals. Polly had worked tirelessly to find homes for the remaining four mothers and their babies. They were settled now, although perhaps not in the best of places, but at least they were not in the dreaded workhouse.

Their departures had been tearful affairs, but Polly had promised to keep in touch. Tommy Tinker had been taken on as a tea boy in the General Letter Office, and hoped one day to graduate to the sorting room. He was still sweet on Maisie, and Rose suspected that they had not seen the last of him, although Maisie herself feigned indifference.

Neither the Sunshine Sisters nor the newly formed duo, Day and Fancello, had found work, but by a stroke of good luck Fancello had discovered a house to let in Shorter's Rents, which he described as a narrow alley between Glasshouse Street and Dock Street.

Rose took a last look around but this was not home now. It was not quite as painful as leaving the vicarage, where she had been born and raised, but it was yet another broken link with the past. She smiled as the memory of two little girls practising their dance steps to Aunt Polly's somewhat erratic accompaniment on the piano came to mind. She could hear echoes of their childish voices as she and Cora had warbled the words to popular songs, with the ever-present chorus of babies wailing in the background. The infants were no longer here and the mothers had moved away. She sighed – it was time to move on.

The larger pieces of furniture had been sold to pay for the carter, who was to take the rest of their belongings to Whitechapel. Spartacus was confined in a wicker basket and his angry howls had given way to a deep-throated keening that was even more distressing. Polly had left him in the entrance hall, to be picked up at the last minute and placed in one of the two hackney carriages that Fancello had gone out to flag down.

Cora was last to come downstairs, having volunteered to check that everything had been removed from the upper rooms. She joined Rose in the hall. 'This is a sad day for Aunt Polly.'

'It's a sad day for us, too.' Rose picked up the cat's basket. 'I hope the poor animal doesn't decide to run away from the new house.'

'He's a horrible creature. I don't know why Aunt Polly dotes on him.' Cora glanced out into the street. 'There's the cab. Is that the first or the second?'

'The second. Ethel, Sukey and Maisie went in the first one with Aunt Polly. She wanted to make sure that the furniture was placed where she chose.' Rose followed her sister out onto the pavement. With one last look, she closed the door and turned the key in the lock.

'Hurry up, girls,' Fancello called from the cab. 'No time to lose.'

Rose placed the cat's basket on the floor of the cab, and was about to climb in when she heard the sound of running footsteps. She looked over her shoulder and saw Joshua hurrying towards them.

Cora's cheeks reddened. 'Oh, he's come to say goodbye. How kind of him.'

'Not goodbye, I think,' Rose said, smiling. 'Make sure he has our new address, Corrie.'

But she was speaking to thin air, as Cora had run to meet him, and Joshua's feelings were clear for all to see.

'That young man is smitten, I think.' Fancello leaned back in his seat. 'Cora seems to like him.'

'Joshua is a good man, and an old friend. He's just what my sister needs, at present.'

'Perhaps they will marry.'

'Maybe,' Rose said cautiously. 'I'd like to see Cora happy again, but you never know how she'll react. I'm not sure that she has recovered from her affair with Gerard.'

Spartacus began to yowl plaintively and Fancello prodded the cat basket with the toe of his highly polished boot. 'Be quiet, you ugly beast.' He shuddered. 'I cannot tell Paloma, but I dislike cats, especially this brute. He bites and he scratches.'

'Then I'm afraid the feeling must be mutual.' Rose leaned her head out of the window. 'Hurry up, Cora. We're waiting.'

Joshua handed Cora into the cab. He doffed his hat to Rose. 'I will call on you in Whitechapel, if I may?'

'Of course. You'll be most welcome,' Rose said, beaming. 'It was good of you to take the trouble to see us off.'

His gaze never left Cora, who had seated herself in the corner of the cab and was adjusting her skirts. 'I'll see you soon, Miss Cora.'

'I hope so.' She blushed prettily.

Fancello tapped the roof with his cane. 'Drive on, cabby.'

Their new home, as Rose soon discovered, was in a poverty-stricken area close to the London Docks, and a short walk from the Tower and the Royal Mint. With the Destitute Sailors' Asylum and the Sailors' Home nearby in Well Street, it was not the sort of place that she would have chosen to live, but Fancello had assured her that it was cheap, and the house just large enough to accommodate them all.

The first thing Rose noticed as she climbed down from the cab in Shorter's Rents was the almost overpowering aroma of chocolate. It was not what she had expected. The stench of the river mud at low tide, mingled with sewage, horse dung, soot and industrial effluent was, for a brief moment, blotted out by the sickly-sweet smell.

'It's the Peek Brothers and Winch cocoa factory,' Fancello said knowingly. 'I was surprised by it myself when I first came to Shorter's Rents, but I suppose one can get used to anything. It's better than most of the odours emanating from the docks.'

Cora joined Rose on the pavement. She thrust the cat basket into her sister's hands. 'Take the miserable creature. He put his paw out and tried to scratch me.' She glanced up and down the filthy, litter-strewn alley. 'So this is where we have to live. Heaven help us.'

Fancello paid the cabby. 'Come along, ladies.

411

Come inside and see your new home.' He marched into the house.

'I suppose anything is better than sleeping in a shop doorway,' Cora said, looking round nervously. 'Although, I'm not too sure about this place. It looks like a slum, Rose.'

Rose glanced at the crowd of small ragged boys who had gathered on the opposite side of the street. She smiled at them, but their pale, dirt-streaked faces remained set in expressions that varied from sheer indifference to overtly hostile and calculating. Several slatternly women had emerged from doorways, some of them with babes at their breasts, while others leaned against the wall with clay pipes stuck in the corners of their mouths. None of them looked particularly welcoming. A feral dog, covered in scabby sores, rushed at them yapping, which silenced Spartacus. Rose could feel the cat trembling inside his wicker prison. She had no way of knowing whether it was from fear or anger, and she hurried into the narrow hallway and slammed the door. She found Cora in the front room standing amidst a chaotic jumble of furniture and boxes that had been left higgledy-piggledy, wherever the carter had found a space.

Rose covered her mouth and nose with her hand. 'What is that awful stench?'

'I don't know, but it smells as if something has died in here and been left to rot.' Cora's cheeks paled and she sank down on a tea chest.

'I'll open a window.' Rose attempted to lift the

sash, but the window was wedged shut, and the panes were caked with mud on the outside and a thick layer of grime on the inside. The remains of dead flies covered the sill, and the yellowed net curtain crumbled to her touch. 'Whoever lived here previously was not very house-proud,' she said in an attempt at levity, but it was no laughing matter. The house, which was tiny by comparison with the one in Old Street, was in a truly disgusting state of neglect. She left Cora sitting disconsolately in the middle of the room and went to find Polly.

Cobwebs festooned the hallway and the floorboards were carpeted in straw, rodent droppings and carapaces of dead cockroaches. She found Polly and Fancello in the back room, where Ethel was attempting to light a fire. A sudden fall of soot crashed into the grate and smoke billowed out in a suffocating cloud. Fancello rushed to open the back door.

'This is a frightful place.' Polly blinked and mopped her streaming eyes. 'The chimney can't have been swept for years, and there's filth everywhere. I refuse to live like this, Sandro. How could you bring us here?'

Fancello's lips trembled and his moustache drooped. 'It was the only residence we could afford, *cara mia.*'

'There are only two bedrooms,' Polly continued angrily. 'The attic is barely large enough for a mattress, let alone a proper bed.'

'I've slept in worse.' Ethel scrambled to her feet.

'It ain't too bad, missis. All it needs is a bit of elbow grease.'

'There's no tap.' Polly moved to the back door and peered out. 'Not even a pump.'

'I saw one at the end of the alley.' Rose picked up two wooden buckets. 'If you can get the fire going, Ethel, I'll fetch some water.'

Fancello snatched the pails from her hands. 'Allow me.' He hurried from the room.

Rose suspected that his gallant gesture was motivated by a desire to escape Polly's simmering wrath, but with one person less in the room she was able to have a good look round. It was small, and without a range it would be impossible to cook a proper meal, but when the fire was lit they would be able to boil a kettle.

'I'll start unpacking,' she said, making an effort to sound positive. 'We'll need brooms and scrubbing brushes, and we'll have to pile the rubbish in the yard for the dustmen to collect.'

'It looks as though we have to share our privy with the neighbours,' Polly said, shuddering. 'How low have we sunk?'

Rose heaved a chair from beneath a pile of boxes. 'Sit down, Aunt. Leave everything to us. We'll soon make this house into a home.' She hoped she sounded more convincing than she was feeling.

Polly was about to sit when a loud howl from Spartacus made them all jump. 'My poor boy,' she cried. 'Where is he, Rose? I'd almost forgotten him.'

Rose fetched the basket and an indignant Spartacus was let loose in the house. Outer doors were kept closed, and as it was impossible to open any of the windows there was little chance of him running away. Oddly enough, he seemed to like his new quarters and he stalked about, examining each room in turn. He was busy exploring the upstairs when Maisie fled from the attic and arrived in the kitchen, pale-faced and trembling. It took some minutes to calm her down enough to tell them that she had seen something large and furry creeping about beneath the eaves, with yellow eyes shining in the darkness. 'It were the devil himself,' she whispered.

Just at that moment Spartacus strolled into the room with a large rat dangling from his mouth, which he presented to Polly, who shrieked in horror. Ethel picked up the dead rodent by its tail and threw it out onto the dust heap.

'There's your devil,' Rose said, chuckling. 'Don't tell him off, Aunt Polly. Spartacus is doing a fine job. We'll soon be free from vermin and we'll have him to thank for that. He's found his true calling at last.'

Spartacus rubbed himself against her legs, purring loudly.

'Well, I ain't sleeping up there,' Maisie said, tossing her head so that her mobcap tilted over one eye. She righted it with a dusty hand. 'I'll help get it cleaned up ready for Ethel and Sukey, but I'll sleep on the floor in here if needs be. There's barely room for two to stretch out side by side in the attic anyway.'

'I'm sure we'll sort everything out in time,' Rose said hopefully. 'I'll get Cora to help me make up the beds, and then we'll have to think about food. I think I saw a grocer's shop in Glasshouse Street.'

'We'll be living on pies and bread and cheese.' Polly shook her head. 'Even Ethel couldn't make a hot meal with just a small fire and a trivet.'

Ethel sat back on her heels as the flames began to lick around the kindling. 'You'd be surprised, missis. Given time I can make a good stew or a pan of broth. We won't starve.'

'We will if Sandro can't find work for us,' Polly said gloomily.

Rose delved into a basket they had brought from the old house and produced a bottle of brandy. She poured a generous tot into a teacup and handed it to her aunt. 'Drink this, Aunt Polly. We'll get your room ready first and you can have a lie-down. It's been a very trying day for you, but we'll make it better, you'll see.'

Polly drank the brandy in one gulp. 'You're living in a dream world, dear. We've sunk as low as we possibly can. We're doomed to end our days in the workhouse.'

Chapter Twenty-Two

An hour later they were still waiting for Fancello to return with the water. Rose had gone out to look for him on a couple of occasions, but he was nowhere in sight. Polly was agitated and growing more irritable with each passing minute.

'He's been murdered,' she said, clasping her hands to her bosom. 'I feel it in here. What will we do without him?'

'I'm sure there's a reasonable explanation,' Rose said, glancing anxiously at the clock, which had been unpacked and stood alone on the slate mantelshelf. She tried to sound positive but she was beginning to worry, and was just about to go out again when the door opened and Fancello breezed in as if nothing had happened. He dumped the buckets on the floor, slopping water over the filthy floorboards.

'I have some wonderful news, Paloma.'

'You stupid man. Where have you been? I was worried sick.'

'I'm sorry, *cara*. I didn't think I would be gone for so long.'

'I don't know why you are looking so pleased with yourself,' Polly said angrily. 'Look what you've brought us to.'

He went down on his knees in front of her, regardless of the muddy floor. 'I didn't mention it before, *cara mia*. I didn't want to raise your hopes, but the main reason I came to this area was because of business.'

She pushed him away. 'What sort of business? Do you want me and the girls to go on the streets to entertain drunken sailors and stevedores?'

'No, of course not.' Fancello raised himself to his feet.

Rose heard his bones creaking as he did so and was instantly sorry for him. He had tried his best, of that she was certain, but his efforts had not come up to expectations. 'Let him speak, Aunt Polly,' she said gently. 'He has something he wants to tell us.'

'Quite so.' Fancello shot her a grateful glance. 'I'm sure you have all heard of Wilton's Music Hall?'

'I ain't.' Ethel tossed a lump of coal on the fire. 'We need some more of this stuff if we're going to heat the water. That's all we got.'

'Never mind that,' Fancello said impatiently. 'We will have money to buy all the coal and kindling we need when we start work.'

418

'Work? What sort of work?' Rose asked curiously.

'At Wilton's Music Hall, of course. When I came here to inspect the property I called in to see the manager. Charming fellow, a little addicted to drink and laudanum, I suspect, but perhaps I caught him on an off day.'

'Do get to the point, Sandro,' Polly said, frowning. 'What are you saying?'

'We have auditions, *cara mia*. You and I and the Sunshine Sisters. Luckily the fellow had seen the girls performing at the Grecian and he liked them. He also remembers you, Paloma, dearest. But then who could forget you and your golden voice?'

'It's not so golden now. Why didn't you tell us this in the first place? Why did you allow me to suffer so?'

'I'm sorry, but it was not certain until this morning. I called in at the theatre when I went to fetch the water, although, come to think of it, I must have presented an odd sight carrying two pails. Anyway, to cut a long story short, we have auditions tomorrow afternoon. If successful we will be on the bill from Saturday for an indefinite period, depending upon box office receipts.'

Polly's face blanched and then a dull flush crept up from her neck to flood her cheeks with colour. She stood up and embraced Fancello. 'You are a darling man, but I could still flay you alive for putting me through this torment.'

'*Cara mia.*' Fancello kissed her soundly on the lips.

Rose retreated to the front room to pass the good news on to Cora, who was attempting to unpack a box of ornaments.

Wilton's Music Hall in Grace's Alley was to be their new venue. The auditions had gone well. Polly and Fancello and the Sunshine Sisters had been booked to appear on Saturday evening, and the whole of the following week, with the possibility of more work should they attract a large audience. They were to share the bill with a magician, a group of tumblers, a solo artiste known as the Canary, from Cheapside, and a sword swallower. Rose and Cora had two numbers, one in each half of the show. Polly and Fancello were to appear as the third act, which greatly offended Polly, who had been used to having top billing. She threatened to walk out, but Fancello managed to talk her round, and in the end she was persuaded that it was more important to put food on the table than to nurse her wounded pride.

They had only one day to brush up their acts, which had made Rose panic at first, but then she decided perhaps it was better that way. Cora was very nervous, but Polly and Fancello took everything in their stride like old troupers. They had to leave Ethel, Sukey and Maisie to make the house habitable, but the thought of being back in the limelight had taken Polly's mind off the discomfort they were enduring at home.

Rose was up early on Friday morning. She had

to share a bed with Cora, who was a restless sleeper, and Fancello's loud snores penetrated the thin walls, drowning out the seemingly endless noise from the docks. The creaking of cranes, and the rumble of barrels being rolled over cobblestones had continued throughout the night, accompanied by hoots of steam whistles from the ships coming into port. Rose washed in the small amount of water they allowed themselves, dressed and went downstairs. She put her head round the door of the front room and saw Maisie, fast asleep and curled up on the chaise longue with Spartacus. Rose smiled as she closed the door. Spartacus had at last found his true calling as an accomplished rat catcher and was a reformed character. His tendency to bite and scratch was now reserved for rodents, and scaring off the feral dogs that lingered outside, looking for scraps.

The kitchen was reasonably clean after the energetic application of lye soap and tepid water and much scrubbing, but the bare walls were in desperate need of fresh paint, and, despite Ethel's best efforts, the stone sink was stained with green slime. Rose picked up two buckets and left the house to walk to the end of the alley. It was quiet at this time in the morning and she was the only person at the pump. As the day went on she knew that queues would form, and the locals had been less than welcoming. During the years Rose had spent visiting the poor in her father's parish, she had never been exposed to such abject poverty. It was a shock to realise that most of the two-up, two-down houses were occupied by several families, existing in almost unimaginable cramped conditions.

She filled the buckets and carried them back to the house, taking care not to slop the precious water onto the pavement. Fancello had gone out the previous evening and bought more fuel, and even though it was stiflingly hot they had to keep a fire going in order to boil a kettle. They had managed this far on cold food, but Ethel had promised to attempt a stew with dumplings. Rose's mouth watered at the thought. Bread and cheese and pies bought from a street seller were all right in their way, but a tasty hot meal would be more than welcome. She managed to get the fire going at her first attempt, filled the kettle and set it on the trivet to boil. A quick sniff of the milk jug made her wrinkle her nose, but she remembered what Mrs Blunt had taught her about turning sour milk into cream cheese, and she set it aside to attend to later. If she wanted a cup of tea and some fresh bread she would have to venture out to the shop in Glasshouse Street. She put on her bonnet, took a clean jug from the cupboard, and let herself out of the house.

The alley had been relatively peaceful during the night, but it was beginning to come back to life. A queue was forming at the pump, mainly of ragged children, barefoot, and, Rose thought, probably running with fleas and lice. She realised that her clean grey poplin dress and straw bonnet made her stand out amongst the unwashed crowd, but she wished they would not stare at her as if she were an alien who had landed in their midst. Some of the older girls giggled amongst themselves, muttering comments that Rose suspected were anything but flattering. It appeared that they had been detailed off to take care of the smaller children, although they seemed to take their responsibilities very lightly. Babies and toddlers grubbed around in the gutter, shoving anything remotely edible into their pink mouths. Rose was tempted to scoop up a baby who was playing with a dead mouse, but she managed to stop herself, and the infant's mother detached herself from a group of women and older boys who were heading off to their places of employment. She boxed the ears of a girl who could not have been more than five, and thrust the baby into her arms.

'If little Alfie comes to grief I know who's to blame, and you'll be for it.' The mother rejoined the shuffling crowd and the small girl slumped down in a doorway with her baby brother clutched in her arms.

Rose was painfully aware that the women and boys would work a twelve- or fourteen-hour day for little more than a few pence, and, in the meantime, the children at home would be left to fend for themselves. She had been vaguely aware that such poverty still existed, but the reality was far more shocking. She wondered if any of the young children attended school on a regular basis. Ignorance and want were the real enemies, she thought sadly. She walked on, ignoring the jibes from the bolder children.

Glasshouse Street was thronged with horse-drawn wagons, brewers' drays and carts. The grocer's shop was busy, but she bought the necessities, and hurried back to Shorter's Rents taking care not to spill any of the milk. She placed the pat of butter on the table together with the fresh loaf of bread. There was no money for jam or marmalade, but things would be different when they were earning. The kettle was boiling and she made a pot of tea and set it aside to brew while she cut a slice of bread, and scraped it with butter. It was a frugal meal, but she knew she would get nothing more until the evening, and there was much to do. She took a cup of tea to Cora.

'We have a busy day ahead, Corrie. We'll need to go through our routines again and make sure our costumes are ready for tomorrow night.'

Cora yawned and stretched. 'Did you have to wake me so early? I was dreaming of Portmorna House. Vere was holding a ball in the grounds and we were dancing in the moonlight.'

'The only dancing you'll do today, my girl, is on the stage at Wilton's.' Rose pulled the bedclothes off her sister and tickled her feet. 'Get up, lazybones.'

On Saturday evening the theatre was packed, and Rose could feel the energy and enthusiasm of the audience, which was both encouraging and exciting. The orchestra played the introduction and the juggler was on first, but it became apparent that he had been drinking and he dropped the clubs several times before the audience finally lost patience and started hurling empty beer bottles at him. The smashing of glass was drowned out by their booing and hissing, and the defeated performer staggered off the stage, leaving one of the hands to sweep up the debris while the orchestra struck up a cheerful tune.

The magician was on next, but the audience were not in the mood to be fooled by sleight of hand. He received little better treatment than the juggler, and was pelted with rotten tomatoes, which made a mess, but were not as dangerous as shards of broken glass. The manager, who appeared to be slightly intoxicated himself, urged Polly and Fancello to go on stage.

'Good luck,' Rose said, blowing a kiss to them as they made their entrance.

'I hope the audience don't throw anything,' Cora whispered.

But the orchestra had struck up the intro for 'The Ratcatcher's Daughter', which, despite the jolly tune, was the tragic tale of a young sprat-seller from south of the river and her doomed love for the vendor of silver sand who lived in Westminster. Polly and Fancello rendered a touching version of the song, but a ripple of amusement ran through the audience, and tears of laughter instead of sorrow greeted the heart-rending conclusion when the heroine drowned in the river, and the hero killed himself and his poor donkey. Perhaps it was the emotion that Polly and Fancello put into the song, or, Rose thought, because Fancello was overdramatic. Whatever it was that caused the audience such hilarity, Polly and Fancello were troupers to the last. They took their bows and left the stage, but Polly was clearly upset.

'Why are they laughing at us, Sandro?' she demanded. 'It wasn't funny.'

Fancello hung his head. 'I don't know.'

Rose placed her arm around her aunt's shoulders. 'They're clapping, Aunt Polly. They're calling for an encore.'

'They're mocking us,' Polly said bitterly. 'I've never been so insulted.'

'They're not throwing things.' Cora stuck her head round one of the great steel pillars that supported the roof. 'They want more.'

'What are you waiting for?' The manager gave Fancello a shove. 'Go on. Keep them laughing. You're a great success.'

'I suppose we'd better,' Polly said, nervously. 'We don't want to upset the mob element.'

'Very well.' Fancello led her back on the stage. He signalled to the conductor. ' "The Daring Young Man on the Flying Trapeze", please, maestro.'

This brought a storm of applause, whistles and shouts of approval. Fancello sang the lyrics and Polly, getting into the spirit of the evening, joined in with the chorus while she danced around the stage. The audience needed little encouragement to join in, and they clapped enthusiastically, calling for more.

'That's a hard act to follow,' Rose said in an undertone.

Cora nodded. 'I know. Thank goodness we've got the tumblers before we go on. I'm afraid we might be an anticlimax after this.'

'Nonsense,' Rose said stoutly. 'We'll be fine.'

As they took their final bows, Rose had the satisfaction of having been proved right. The Sunshine Sisters had been a success. They had performed two encores and the audience were reluctant to let them go, but eventually it was all over; the stage make-up was removed and the costumes hung carefully on hooks in the dressing room they shared with Polly and the magician's young assistant.

As they left the theatre Cora gave a cry of pleasure at the sight of Joshua, who was waiting for them in the narrow alley. He came towards them, smiling. 'You were all wonderful. I think the audience would have rioted but for your act, Miss Day and Signor Fancello. I thoroughly enjoyed it.'

Polly pursed her lips. 'Hmm, it didn't go as planned.'

'But we were a hit, Paloma,' Fancello said softly. 'They loved us.'

'They laughed. We are not a comedy act.'

'It's better to laugh than to throw bottles.' Fancello

winked at Rose. 'Tell your aunt that she was wonderful, and the audience adored her.'

'He's right, Aunt Polly.' Rose nodded in agreement. 'Making people happy is a gift.'

'How true.' Joshua smiled shyly. 'Might I walk you home, Cora?'

'I don't think that's a good idea,' she said, shaking her head. 'The street where we're living isn't in a very nice area, and it wouldn't be safe for you to walk home from there unaccompanied.'

'Cora is right.' Rose nodded emphatically. 'Perhaps it would be better if you went straight home, Joshua. We would hate to place you in danger.'

'I'm used to venturing into troubled areas.' Joshua proffered his arm to Cora and then to Rose. 'I'd be honoured if you would allow me to walk with you.'

It was impossible to refuse, and they fell in step behind Polly and Fancello, but Rose's thoughts were far away as they returned to Shorter's Rents in the cool of a summer's evening. She was elated after their performance, but there was something lacking, and it was not just the comfort and security of the house in Old Street that she missed. She regretted leaving Portmorna without having said goodbye to Vere and Bennett. It had been a decision brought about by panic, and the realisation that she felt more for Bennett Sharpe than she had previously cared to admit. He was an enigma. At times she had thought he had feelings for her, but then he seemed to retreat, hiding behind the professional façade he presented in court. Vere loved her, or at least he thought he did. He was lonely, she knew that, and he needed a wife, but he did not really know her. She was not a quiet country girl who would be content to run the house, bear his children and ask for little more than a kind husband and a lovely home. She had come to know herself a little better since their old world had been torn apart, and she had discovered a spirit of independence she had not known she possessed. If she were to marry, her husband must be a man who would respect her as an individual and allow her the freedom to express herself.

Cora and Joshua were chatting together, and Rose was happy to keep her own counsel. Ahead of them she could hear Polly and Fancello going over their act in minute detail.

They arrived in Shorter's Rents to find a street fight in progress. Several men, very much the worse for drink, were throwing wild punches and their womenfolk crowded round screaming insults and encouragement. Their young children clung to their skirts, sobbing, and were in danger of being trampled underfoot.

Before any of them could stop him Joshua had waded into the fray. Cora turned to Rose, white-faced and trembling. 'He'll be killed.'

Polly hurried to their front door and rattled the knocker. 'Let us in.' She turned to glare at Fancello. 'Don't stand there. Do something.'

'Take Cora inside,' Rose said, thrusting her sister into his arms.

Fancello drew himself up to his full height. 'No. It is time that Alessandro Fancello showed his woman that he is a man.' He put Cora behind him and marched up to Joshua, who was fending off a couple of drunken men. 'Stop this now. There are women and children present. Are you animals or men?'

A startled silence was followed by grunts and groans as the injured fighters scrambled to their feet.

'Who are you, old man?' The oldest and most aggressive of the brawlers squared up to Fancello, flexing his muscles. 'Fight me, then.'

Rose caught Fancello by his coat-tails. 'Leave them. Come indoors.'

'No, Rose. I will deal with this.' Fancello turned to Joshua. 'Take her inside.'

Rose shook her head. 'Never mind me, Joshua. See if you can calm things down.'

Joshua moved to stand between Fancello and his aggressor. 'I beg of you to stop this, my man. It's not the way.'

'I ain't your man. I'm Malachy Woods and I run things round here. Go back to your church, holy man. There is no god in Shorter's Rents.'

Joshua opened his mouth to protest, but Fancello edged him out of the way. He threw back his head and burst into a heartfelt rendition of 'Ave Maria'. His fine baritone voice filled the night air and the crowd moved back. They stood in silence, some with heads bowed as they listened to him sing, even though none of them, except Joshua, would have understood the Latin. Even the children were silent, and then, with the voice of an angel, Polly joined in. Rose stood transfixed by the scene. Blood was running freely, but the men seemed to have lost the desire to fight. Fancello brought the aria to an end, turned and walked slowly into the house with Polly at his side.

Rose caught Joshua by the hand. 'Come in and wait until they've gone,' she said in a low voice.

'Thank you, but I'd better be on my way. That was quite incredible, Rose. I'll use that in my sermon tomorrow. As William Congreve so rightly said: "Music has charms to soothe a savage breast, To soften rocks, or bend a knotted oak." I feel humbled by the experience.' He walked away slowly, and left the alley unmolested.

Sunday was supposed to be a day of rest, but Ethel, Sukey and Maisie were intent on cleaning the house until it met with their high standards. Polly and Fancello had not risen from bed by the time Rose and Cora had eaten their meagre breakfast of bread and butter, washed down with weak tea.

Cora left the table and reached for her bonnet and shawl.

'Where are you going?' Rose asked curiously.

'I thought I'd attend matins at St Matthew's. Papa

would be horrified if he knew that I hadn't been to church for weeks.'

'Papa is easily offended.' Rose stood up and placed her plate and cup in the stone sink. 'I think I'll come with you.'

'I was hoping you'd say that.' Cora smiled mischievously. 'I've only a penny or two in my purse. Would you happen to have enough for the cab fare?'

Rose put on her bonnet and tied the ribbons into a bow. 'There isn't much left, but I can just about afford to get us there and back. It's too hot to walk that far.' She turned to Ethel, who was chopping vegetables to put in the stew pot. 'We won't be long, but would you tell my aunt that we've gone to church?'

Ethel nodded. 'Yes, miss, but be careful out there. I won't be venturing far from home, and that's a fact.'

It seemed odd to walk into the cool interior of St Matthew's church, with its familiar smell of musty hymnals, candlewax and sour communion wine. Rose kneeled to murmur a brief prayer before taking her seat on the narrow wooden pew. It was hard to believe that someone other than her father would be taking the service, and simply being here, next to the vicarage, was like stepping back in time. Memories of helping to clean the altar brass and silver, and assisting her mother in the arrangement of garden flowers in season, and greenery and berried branches in the autumn and winter, brought with them a sudden desire to be reunited with her parents. She would never completely understand her father, but he had come to Billy's aid in the end, and Mama had done nothing to deserve the loss of her family.

The congregation shuffled to their feet as Joshua announced the first hymn, and Rose dragged her attention back to the service. A quick glance at her sister confirmed her suspicions that Cora had an ulterior motive for coming to church. She was smiling at Joshua and her cheeks were tinged with pink. He had obviously just spotted her, and he lost concentration momentarily, but recovered quickly to lead the singing. There was the usual mix of quivering sopranos, gruff baritones and the exuberant efforts of those who were apparently tone deaf, but there was one voice out of the many that was achingly familiar. Rose glanced across the aisle and saw Bennett. He met her startled gaze with a smile.

The rest of the service passed without Rose taking in any of Joshua's heartfelt sermon, and she repeated the prayers like an automaton. Her mind had gone completely blank of rational thought. She had to wait until everyone filed out of the church before she had a chance to speak to him, and it was necessary to squeeze between groups of parishioners who had stopped to chat to their friends and neighbours. She thought for a moment that he had gone, but Bennett was waiting for her on the pavement.

'I wasn't expecting to see you here,' she said breathlessly.

He clutched his top hat in his hands and a gentle breeze ruffled his dark hair so that it curled around his head. 'I went to the house in Old Street, and was told that you had all moved away. I was going to ask your friend the vicar where you had gone, but you've forestalled me.'

'Joshua does know, as it happens, but why did you want to find us? Is something wrong? It isn't to do with Billy, is it? The jury found him not guilty.'

A slow smile lit Bennett's eyes and his stern features relaxed. 'Nothing like that, Rose. I wanted to see you and make sure you were all right.'

'Thank you. As you can see, I am quite well.'

'That's not what I meant, and you know it.'

She glanced over her shoulder to make sure that Cora was still giving her full attention to Joshua. Everyone, including her sister, would jump to the wrong conclusion if they realised that Bennett had taken the trouble to seek her out.

'Did Vere send you?' she asked suspiciously. 'I know we left suddenly, but it was a long journey home and we needed an early start.'

'You ran away.' Bennett fixed her with a penetrating stare. 'You didn't stop to think that it might upset my cousin. He proposed marriage, damn it.' He shook his head. 'I'm sorry. I apologise for the language, but you treated Vere badly, Rose. He deserved better from you.'

She raised her chin and looked him in the eye. 'Perhaps he did, but I refused him twice, and he wouldn't take no for an answer. I'm sorry if I hurt him, but he was taking advantage of my vulnerable situation.'

'Put like that it makes a difference. I didn't realise he had been importuning you.'

'No, I wouldn't put it as strongly as that. Vere was a perfect gentleman, and he is the kindest man I've ever met, but the truth is that I don't love him. I could never marry for wealth and social standing, and I tried to tell him that.'

'You were in a difficult position. I see that, but there's something else bothering you that has nothing to do with my family. What is it, Rose? You can tell me.'

'I suppose it was coming back here,' she said slowly. 'I was remembering happier times with my parents, and wishing that the rift between us could be healed.'

'It can't be insurmountable. I know your father to be a proud man, but I'm sure that deep down he cares very much for all of you, otherwise why would he take the trouble to travel all the way to Bodmin for Billy's trial?' He glanced over her shoulder. 'Your sister is advancing on us with a purposeful look on her face. I should take my leave.'

'You're going? Is that it, then?' Her heart was beating so fast she was certain he must be able to hear it thudding inside her breast. His expression was unreadable, and she was angry with him for not caring, and furious with herself for caring too much. 'I suppose that now Billy is a free man, you've done what you set out to do, and you are going to move on to your next case. You've said your piece concerning Vere, and now you're leaving.'

Chapter Twenty-Three

'Is that what you want, Rose?' Bennett fixed her with a look that would have turned a hostile witness to stone.

She was momentarily lost for words, but was saved from replying by Cora, who came rushing up to them. 'Bennett,' she cried happily. 'How lovely to see you, and what a surprise. How is your cousin? I was so sorry not to say goodbye after all his kindness when I was unwell.'

Joshua had followed her and he held his hand out to Bennett. 'I didn't have a chance to congratulate you personally on your performance at the trial, but you were magnificent. Billy is a lucky man to have had you on his side.'

Bennett shook his hand and he relaxed visibly. 'Thank you, Vicar, but it was almost a foregone conclusion. With the new evidence and the confessions that were more or less freely given, it would have been ill judgement indeed had the jury come to any other decision.'

'We really ought to be on our way, Cora,' Rose said hastily. 'We have a very busy week ahead of us—' She broke off, biting her lip. She had not told Bennett that the Sunshine Sisters had returned to the stage, and there was no need for him to know that they had been struggling to survive. She neither wanted nor needed his pity.

Cora stared at her blankly and then she smiled. 'Yes, we have such a lot to do.' She turned to Joshua. 'I'll see you next Sunday. I really must get back into the habit of attending church. Papa would never forgive us if we turned heathen.'

'I don't think that's like to happen,' Joshua said, laughing. 'I might call on you in Shorter's Rents before then. I sometimes visit that area.'

'Shorter's Rents?' Bennett raised an eyebrow. 'I know that place. Is that where you're living now, Rose?'

She nodded. 'Yes, but it's only temporary. I'm sure we'll move on to somewhere better soon. Now we really must go.' She managed what she hoped was a bright smile. 'It was nice to see you again, Bennett. Give my regards and apologies to your cousin when you next see him.' She grabbed her sister by the arm. 'Come, Cora. We've dallied long enough, and I'm sure both these gentlemen have much to do.'

Cora followed her, protesting volubly, but Bennett

caught up with them in long strides. He handed Rose a visiting card. 'You'll remember where this is, no doubt, but you can find me here if you need to talk to me. Should I be in court, just leave a message, and I will contact you.'

She was tempted to refuse, but she accepted it anyway. 'Thank you.'

'If there is anything I can do to help, you only have to ask.' He placed his hat on his head and walked away in the opposite direction.

'He might have found us a cab,' Rose said, tucking the card into her reticule. 'Men are such temperamental creatures.'

'Really, Rosie, are you completely stupid?' Cora heaved a sigh. 'The man is in love with you, you silly girl, and you've just sent him away thinking you don't care.'

'If he cares for me, as you seem to think, then why does he keep on about his wretched cousin?'

'Rose, that's not like you. It's not fair.'

'All right, I was being a bit harsh. Vere is a kind and generous man, but I don't love him. I would make him a terrible wife, and we would both end up frustrated and unhappy.'

'I think you'd be lucky to live in such a wonderful house with servants at your beck and call. You wouldn't have to worry about money ever again.'

'You don't mean that, Corrie. Would you choose Vere over Joshua?'

'There's a cab, Rose. Flag him down. I think it's going to rain.'

News of the Sunshine Sisters' return to the stage spread quickly, and Day and Fancello were billed as the latest comedy duo to hit the music halls. Their initial week at Wilton's was extended for another fortnight, and by that time the managers of the Royal Pavilion Theatre in Whitechapel, Lusby's in the Mile End Road, and the Theatre Royal, High Holborn, were showing interest in both acts. Rose and Cora decided to accept an offer to appear at the Pavilion, but Fancello decided that Lusby's was a more suitable venue.

Polly herself was pleased, but confused by the twist of fate that had turned what was supposed to be a serious double act into one that had the audience rocking with laughter. Rose sympathised with her aunt, although she was quick to point out the advantages of climbing towards the top of the bill, and reluctantly Polly had to agree. Fancello was sanguine about their success, but Rose could tell that he was secretly delighted. He walked with a swagger and his moustache was waxed and curled until it seemed to have taken on a life of its own. Rose found herself mesmerised by it each time she had a conversation with Fancello. He had even bought himself a special moustache cup to protect his pride and joy when drinking tea. Polly teased him mercilessly, but she had also indulged in their new-found solvency by purchasing a pair of sequin-encrusted dancing shoes for herself and a velvet collar for her cat. Spartacus himself was not impressed: he tried everything he could to rid himself of it, and ran round the room backwards in a futile attempt to shake it off.

Rose paid her contribution towards the house-keeping each week, but she saved as much of her wages as possible for her planned visit to Dorset. She had written to Mrs Harman asking if she would be kind enough to arrange a meeting between herself and her parents, but had not received a reply. She did not mention it to Cora, who was now seeing Joshua on a regular basis and attended church every Sunday. Joshua, for his part, came to the theatre at least once a week, sometimes more. Rose wondered how he could sit through their act time and time again without getting bored, but she supposed that a man in love would do almost anything to be close to the object of his affection. She tried not to think about Bennett.

On the night of their last performance at Wilton's, Rose and Cora had just finished their first number, and were taking their bow when Cora clutched her sister's hand, digging her nails into Rose's flesh.

'What's the matter?' Rose demanded as they danced off the stage, waving to the audience.

Cora's fixed smile froze. 'It's Gerard. I saw him on the balcony. He's come slumming with a group of swells. I can't believe you didn't see him.'

Rose peered round the edge of the curtain. 'I think you're right. Just ignore him, Corrie. We've only got one more number to do and then that's it. We start at the Pavilion next week, and I doubt if he'd follow us there. It might be a coincidence that he's here tonight.'

'I hope he doesn't make a scene and spoil everything. I didn't want to tell you, Rose, it's supposed to be a huge surprise, but Billy is here too. He's going to take us all out to supper and he's got an important announcement to make, although it doesn't take a genius to guess what it is.'

'Oh, my goodness. How exciting. I've been thinking about him and wondering how he was getting on in Cornwall.'

'Well, now you'll find out.'

After several encores, the artistes took their final bows, but amidst the applause Rose was startled to hear boos and catcalls. Then, to her dismay, she saw Gerard and several young men in evening dress advancing towards the stage. They were obviously the worse for drink and intent on causing trouble. The audience seemed to think it was part of the show and settled back in their seats to watch the entertainment. Rose caught her sister by the hand but Gerard leaped onto the stage, and, before either of them could do anything, he hefted Cora over his shoulder.

'This one's mine. Take your pick, gentlemen.'

Rose pummelled him with her fists, but someone seized her from behind and swung her off her feet. 'Let me go,' she cried, flailing her fists and kicking out in an attempt to break free.

Fancello rushed forward in an attempt to free her, and Polly used her furled parasol like a sword, aiming at any part of the man's anatomy that came within striking distance. Rose's assailant dropped her with a yelp of pain and she landed in a heap next to the magician's assistant, who had collapsed in a dead faint. The magician himself had disappeared, but the juggler and the tumblers launched themselves into the fray. The stage manager and the props men erupted onto the scene, and as Rose struggled to her feet she saw Billy step up onto the stage.

'Put my sister down.' He squared up to Gerard.

'I haven't finished with her yet,' Gerard said thickly. 'I haven't had my money's worth from this little baggage.'

Billy raised his arm and caught Gerard on the jaw with a left hook.

Cora was thrown to the ground and Gerard staggered backwards, clutching his hand to his cheek.

'You asked for that, old man.' One of Gerard's less drunken companions helped him to his feet. 'You've had your fun. Let's go before the coppers arrive.'

Billy lifted Cora to her feet. 'Are you hurt?'

She shook her head. 'I'm all right. Where's Rose?'

'I'm here.' Rose gave her a hug. 'Well done, Billy. I didn't know you had it in you.'

'I was boxing champion at school, although I didn't tell Pa. I knew he wouldn't approve.'

Polly hurried up to them, prodding one of Gerard's companions with the ferule of her parasol when he stepped in her way. 'Are you all right, girls? I never saw such bad behaviour from an audience.' She turned to Fancello. 'Make sure those ruffians leave the theatre, Sandro. We don't want them lying in wait outside.'

He nodded. 'We will, with pleasure.' He turned to the tumblers. 'Come, gentlemen. We will show them they cannot treat us like this.'

With Fancello in the lead they chased the embattled swells from the auditorium.

The stage manager rushed to the footlights, holding his hands out to the audience who had settled back into their seats, and had been watching the fracas with evident enjoyment. 'The show is over, ladies and gentlemen. I apologise for the disturbance. I would ask you now to leave the theatre in an orderly fashion.'

'What is it you have to tell us, Billy?' Rose asked as they left the stage.

'We'll discuss it over supper,' he said, grinning boyishly. 'I'm staying at the Three Tuns in Billingsgate. Bennett is going to meet us there.'

Rose stared at him, frowning. 'Why is he included? This is a family matter.'

'What's wrong, Rosie? I thought you liked him.'

'I do,' she said hastily, 'but it seems odd to include him in everything.'

'You'll understand when I tell you, but I want everyone together when I make my announcement.'

Rose could see that she was not going to get anything more from her brother. Billy, she thought, sighing, could be very stubborn at times. 'We'd best change out of our costumes. We won't be long.'

The supper room at the pub was hot and steamy and filled with the tempting aroma of fried fish and roast meat. Bennett was already there and he greeted everyone with easy bonhomie that surprised Rose. He seemed relaxed, and equally at home when chatting to Polly and Fancello, or when exchanging jocular remarks with Billy. Rose greeted him civilly, but she could not bring herself to look him in the eye. The sound of his voice and the touch of his hand still had the power to make her heart beat faster, and she moved away quickly.

They took their places at a table by the window. Rose had chosen to sit next to her brother, but Bennett took a seat opposite and each time she looked up she seemed to catch his eye. It was a relief when the waiter came to take their order, which took some time with people having difficulty in making up their minds, but eventually it was settled. Another waiter brought wine to the table, and under its influence the conversation grew more animated.

Cora was unusually subdued, but Rose put this

down to her most recent encounter with Gerard, and she gave her an encouraging smile. 'I doubt if he'll bother you again, Corrie,' she said in a low voice.

Fancello leaned across the table. 'If you're speaking of that fellow who tried to make off with Cora, I promise you he won't attempt anything like that again.'

'What happened outside the theatre?' Rose asked curiously.

'Let's just say that the toffs came off worst.' Fancello puffed his chest out, looking to Polly for approval.

'You're a naughty man.' Polly slapped his wrist with her fan. 'But I'm very proud of you, my dear. You showed those young swells that they can't come to the East End and behave like animals.'

Bennett raised his glass to Fancello. 'Well done, sir. Had I been there I would have joined you. As it is, if the person in question decides to sue, I will be pleased to defend you.'

Rose met his amused gaze and smiled. 'Stop teasing him, Bennett. You'll have Aunt Polly shaking in her shoes.'

'It would take more than that to scare me,' Polly said firmly. 'Anyway, we didn't come here to discuss the unfortunate events after the show. Billy has an announcement to make, so he should tell us now and put us out of our misery.'

Billy rose to his feet. 'Jenifry and I are to be married in two weeks. You are all invited to our wedding.'

'Congratulations, Billy.' Bennett was the first to

speak. 'I should add that my cousin has asked you all to be his guests at Portmorna House.'

'And,' Billy continued eagerly, 'I have decided that the Church is not for me, and Vere has not only given me a job at the quarry, but has also found us a cottage on the estate.'

'I'm so happy for you.' Rose smiled, but the prospect of revisiting Portmorna House left her with mixed feelings.

Not so, it seemed with Cora. 'I can't wait to visit Portmorna House again,' she said eagerly. 'Just wait until you see it, Aunt Polly. It's quite the most delightful place I've ever seen, and Vere is such a gentleman. He'll make us all feel welcome.'

Conversation came to a temporary halt with the arrival of the food, and Rose began to relax. When the meal was over, and everyone was mellowed by good food and wine, they left the table, forming small groups to chat before taking leave of each other.

Rose had just said goodbye to Billy when Bennett drew her aside. 'I have some news for you, Rose.'

'Really? What is it?'

'I took the liberty of travelling to Dorset, and I had words with your father.'

'Why would you do that?'

'I saw how upset you were by the way your father behaved after the trial, and with Billy about to get married I thought it time that someone intervened.'

'But why? What could you hope to gain by interfering in what is our business?'

'Perhaps that is a question you ought to ask yourself, Rose.' Bennett looked round as Billy tapped a wineglass with a spoon, calling for their attention.

'Before we all go our separate ways, I have something to tell you. I've been saving this for last.'

Cora clapped her hands. 'What is it, Billy? Do tell.'

'Our parents are travelling to Cornwall for the wedding. Pa has apparently forgiven me for dragging the family name through the courts, although I'm not sure what brought about this sudden change of heart. Anyway, it's the best news I could have had.'

Rose could feel Bennett's gaze upon her, but she could not look him in the eye. His timely intervention had made Billy happy and Cora was smiling again. Rose's cheeks burned and she turned her head away. She knew she ought to apologise, but somehow she could not bring herself to do so.

A flurry of congratulations followed Billy's announcement.

'I'll see you at the wedding,' Bennett said softly. He walked off to speak to Billy, and Rose found herself alone in the crowd.

After a buzz of conversation, Polly announced that she was tired and ready to go home, and in the midst of a flurry of goodbyes, Rose was able to avoid being alone with Bennett.

'What was that all about?' Cora demanded when they were seated side by side in a hackney carriage, travelling home to Shorter's Rents. 'I thought you were getting along nicely with Bennett, and then suddenly the atmosphere was as chilly as midwinter.'

'I'll tell you later,' Rose whispered.

'Are you all right now, Cora, dear?' Polly leaned over to pat her on the knee. 'You had a horrible experience on stage.'

'Yes, Aunt, thank you. Strange as it may sound, it was almost a relief. I knew Gerard and I would meet again one day, and now it's happened. He'll have a black eye to show for it and he will have been made to look foolish in front of his friends. I don't think he'll trouble me again.'

'He'd better not.' Fancello seized Polly's hand and held it against his heart. 'I won't allow anyone to harm one of my ladies.'

'You did well tonight, my love.' Polly kissed him on the cheek.

'I've been thinking, Paloma. If we're to travel all the way to Cornwall to celebrate Billy's nuptials, we ought to make it a double wedding. It's high time I made an honest woman of you.'

Rose held her breath and she felt Cora stiffen at her side.

'You're drunk, Sandro,' Polly said crossly.

'I'm dead sober, *cara mia*. Will you do me the honour of becoming my wife?' He attempted to kneel in the confines of the cab and became wedged between the seats.

'Get up, you silly man.' Polly leaned over to kiss

449

him on the forehead. 'Of course I'll marry you. Just get up before you do yourself an injury.'

The fracas at Wilton's was reported widely in the newspapers, which gave the Sunshine Sisters a certain notoriety. Polly predicted that it would be the end of their careers, but it seemed to have the opposite effect. The Royal Pavilion was packed from the first night and the Sunshine Sisters performed to rapturous applause. They were booked for the following week, and possibly longer.

Polly and Fancello had settled into their act at Lusby's and were proving equally popular. It seemed that hard times were over and their future was assured.

'We will look for better accommodation the moment we return from Cornwall,' Fancello announced grandly, one morning at breakfast. 'I already have my eye on a much larger property in Sekforde Street, close to Clerkenwell Green. We are coming up in the world, Paloma.'

'Never mind that,' Polly said impatiently. 'Have you found out the times of the trains from Waterloo Bridge station? We're leaving tomorrow and I have all the packing to consider, and I have an appointment with the dressmaker.' She glanced across the table at Rose, who was just finishing her bowl of porridge. 'Are you girls prepared for the journey?'

'Yes, Aunt.' Rose put her spoon down. 'We're ready. What time will we be leaving tomorrow?'

Fancello dabbed his moustache with his napkin, taking care not to spoil its shape. 'I intend to purchase a copy of Bradshaw's railway timetable, which will tell us everything we want to know. Our journey will be organised to the last detail. Leave it all to me, Paloma.' He rose from his seat and left the kitchen.

'Am I to go with you, miss?' Maisie hovered at Rose's side, preparing to clear the table.

'Of course you will,' Polly said grandly. 'No lady would think of travelling without her maid. Ethel and Sukey will remain here and keep house while we're away.'

Rose could see that they were not impressed. 'I have two tickets for the show at the Pavilion for tomorrow night's performance. Perhaps you would like to go?'

Ethel's dour expression was wiped away by a grin. 'Ta, miss. That would be lovely.'

'And I'll treat you to a fish supper afterwards,' Rose added. 'You've worked so hard to make this house habitable, I think you deserve something in return.'

'But don't think that allows you to entertain gentlemen callers in my house,' Polly said sternly.

'As if we would, missis?' Sukey cast her eyes down. 'Us would never think of such a thing. Would us, Ethel?'

'No, us wouldn't. I learned about men the hard way.' Ethel filled the stone sink with hot water from the kettle. 'I hope the next house has a proper range in the kitchen.'

'You heard what my betrothed said.' Polly rose from the table. 'We're going to take our rightful place in society, and that means running water and our own privy in the back yard.'

The journey to Portmorna House next day was uneventful. Fancello had studied Bradshaw's and had planned each connection with as little waiting time between trains as was possible. They travelled first class and there was a horse-drawn carriage waiting for them at Bodmin. Fancello announced with some pride that he had sent a telegram to Vere, advising him of the time of their arrival. He was patently delighted with himself, and even Polly was impressed.

Rose was looking forward to the weddings, but she found the thought of meeting Vere again unnerving. Her conscience still bothered her when she remembered her hasty departure from Portmorna House. It was, of course, unforgiveable since she had received nothing but kindness and consideration from Vere, and she intended to apologise the moment a suitable opportunity arose. Cora, however, seemed to have put the past behind her, and was bubbling with excitement. Polly and Fancello were acting like twenty-year-old lovers, and Rose found herself wishing that she could return to London, and sanity.

By the time they arrived at their destination, Rose

had her feelings well in hand, or so she thought, but as James handed her down from the carriage she saw Vere waiting to greet them, and standing at his side was Bennett. Her worst fears were realised – she would have to face them together.

Chapter Twenty-Four

'Rose, how delightful you look.' Vere came down the steps to greet her. He raised her hand to his lips and brushed it with a kiss.

'Thank you,' Rose said shyly. 'It was kind of you to invite us all to stay. I hope we won't be too many.'

'Not at all. I have taken your advice and hired extra staff. Portmorna House now runs more or less like a well-oiled machine.' He released her hand and extended it to Polly. 'Miss Day, it's an honour to welcome such a famous person to my home.'

Rose did not wait to listen to the pleasantries. She approached Bennett with a wary smile. 'I think I owe you an apology,' she said hastily. 'I shouldn't have said the things I did when we last met.'

'Tact has never been my strong point, Rose. If you're referring to my visit to your parents, I suppose I did take a lot on myself, but I did it with the best of intentions. However, I realise that I could have broken it more gently. I'm not surprised that you were angry.'

'It was a shock, I admit. I still don't know exactly why you took it upon yourself. I can't imagine what Papa thought when you turned up on his doorstep.'

'He was very polite, and he listened intently. He's a deep-thinking, serious man, Rose. I believe he has difficulty in sharing his feelings, but that doesn't mean that he is devoid of compassion.'

'It's a side of him I haven't seen for a very long time.'

'Nevertheless, it's there.' Bennett ushered her into the now familiar entrance hall. 'You must be tired after your journey. We'll talk again later. Kensa will show you to your room.' He beckoned to the young girl who was neatly attired in a plain grey gown with a starched white cap and apron.

She bounded forward and came to a sudden halt, blushing to the roots of her hair. 'Sorry, miss. I forgot to walk slow like Mrs Vennor showed me.'

'That's quite all right,' Rose said, smiling. 'It's not easy, but it will come to you with practice.' She turned her head to look for Maisie, and saw her struggling valiantly with their luggage, but just as Rose was going to ask someone to assist her, James went to her aid.

Cora was chatting to Vere, and Polly was walking slowly round the entrance hall, taking in every detail as if she were in a museum, with Fancello following her like a faithful hound.

'Come this way, please, miss.' Kensa walked slowly, measuring her tread across the polished floorboards, as if following a funeral cortège.

'What's the matter with the girl?' Polly came to a halt beside Rose. 'Is she a simpleton?'

Rose held her finger to her lips. 'Hush, Aunt Polly, she'll hear you.'

'What is that girl doing?' Cora joined them. 'Is it a country dance?'

Kensa came to a halt at the foot of the stairs. 'Did I do wrong, Miss Rose? Weren't I going slow enough?'

'You did extremely well,' Rose said, nudging Cora in the ribs as she started to giggle. 'Although you could, perhaps, walk a little faster.'

'It ain't easy being a maidservant,' Kensa grumbled, taking the stairs two at a time with her skirts bunched up above her knees.

'I can see some basic training is lacking.' Polly shook her head. 'This house needs a mistress, and that young man is in need of a wife.'

Rose hoped that her aunt's voice had not carried to the hall below. She quickened her step in order to keep up with Kensa. The next few days, she thought, were going to be challenging.

Kensa came to a halt outside Rose's old room. 'This one's yours, so Mrs Vennor said. I think that's right, and yours is just along there, miss.' She jerked her head in the direction of Cora's bedchamber.

'Thank you,' Cora said politely. 'I remember it well.'

'And where are we?' Polly demanded.

Kensa folded her arms across her chest, glaring at Polly. 'I don't see no wedding band, miss?'

'Are you daring to judge me, child?' Polly towered over her, but Kensa did not flinch.

'Mrs Vennor said you should have two rooms, miss.'

Rose stood with her hand on the doorknob, waiting to see how Polly dealt with the situation. She could feel Cora's silent laughter, but she managed to keep a straight face.

'We are handfasted,' Polly said grandly. 'You have no need to fret, child.'

'Oh, that's all right then. Come this way, missis.'

Polly seized a mystified Fancello by the hand and followed Kensa.

'Well!' Cora exclaimed, giggling. 'Handfasted! What on earth is that?'

'I believe it's something like jumping over a broomstick instead of going through a formal marriage ceremony. I thought for a moment that Aunt Polly was going to explode or strike the poor child dead.'

'It's lucky she didn't have her parasol with her.' Cora doubled up with laughter. 'I can't wait to tell Billy.'

'I wonder if he'll dine with us this evening.'

'I hope so. Anyway, I'm going to my room to change. I'll see you downstairs in the drawing room. Vere said he had a surprise for us, although I can't think what it could be.'

'We'll find out soon.' Rose entered her room. It was just as she had left it, although someone had thought to put a vase filled with her favourite sweet-scented roses on the washstand. Sunlight poured in through the open window and birdsong floated in on a gentle breeze. After the cramped confines of the room she shared with Cora in the London house, this was luxury indeed. She took off her bonnet and shawl and laid them on a damask-covered chair. If she had accepted Vere's offer of marriage all this would have been hers. She went to sit on the window seat while she waited for Maisie to bring her valise and portmanteau.

Half an hour later, leaving Cora to finish getting ready, Rose made her way downstairs. She had changed into sprigged muslin afternoon gown, and Maisie had arranged her hair, taming the wild auburn curls into a demure chignon. Rose hesitated outside the drawing room, feeling unaccountably nervous, or perhaps it was excitement that made her hand shake as her fingers closed around the doorknob. She braced her shoulders, telling herself not to be so silly. She was not about to go on stage – she was with friends and family. She opened the door and stepped inside.

'Oh, my goodness!' She came to a halt, hardly able to believe her eyes. 'Mama!'

Eleanor rose from the sofa where she had been seated between Polly and Fancello. She crossed the floor, arms outstretched. 'Rose, my dear girl.'

They embraced, hugging each other, halfway between tears and laughter. Rose was the first to recover. She held her mother at arm's length. 'I wasn't expecting to see you until the wedding.'

Seymour advanced on them, his stern features showing little emotion, but Rose thought she saw a hint of a smile in his pale eyes. He laid his hand on her shoulder. 'It's been too long, Rose.'

She nodded and swallowed hard. 'I don't understand.' She looked to Bennett, who had risen from his chair, and was standing with his back to the flower-filled fireplace. Vere had also risen, but he gave her an encouraging smile and resumed his seat.

Seymour followed her gaze. 'You have Bennett to thank for this, Rose. He spoke to me briefly after the trial, and then he came to visit me in Dorset.'

Eleanor sank down on the nearest chair, fanning herself vigorously. 'I've been looking forward to this moment, but where is Cora?'

'She'll join us directly.' Rose perched on the arm of her mother's chair. 'The roses in my room,' she said, thoughtfully. 'You know they're my favourite, Mama. It was your doing, wasn't it?'

'I've been helping Vere to put his house in order,' Eleanor said, smiling. 'I don't think I've ever enjoyed myself so much as I have these past two weeks while we've been settling into the parsonage.'

'Settling in?' Rose looked to Bennett. 'I don't understand.'

'Once again, you have Vere to thank. He used his

influence to recommend Seymour for the living when the former incumbent passed away.'

Vere rose to his feet and tugged at the embroidered bell pull. 'I think this calls for a small celebration. You are not averse to a glass of port or a sherry, are you, Vicar?'

Seymour inclined his head. 'I've been known to imbibe when the occasion merits it, sir.'

'I'm sure the ladies would prefer tea.' Vere looked to Eleanor for confirmation and she nodded.

'Don't I get a choice?' Polly said crossly. 'I need brandy after the shock I've had. I wasn't expecting to meet my dear sister under such circumstances.' She glared at Seymour. 'I didn't know you were going to conduct the ceremony. Does this mean that you are going to officiate at our wedding, should we choose to marry here?'

'I will be conducting the service, Polly. I could do the same for you and Signor Fancello, if you so wish, although you would have to remain here while the banns were read, or apply for a special licence.'

'Don't think you can push me into marriage.' Polly tossed her head. 'It just so happens that we have decided to wed, haven't we, dearest?' She turned to Fancello, who nodded eagerly.

'Yes, indeed. But perhaps it could wait until we return to London.'

'Are you backing out of it again, Sandro?' Polly faced him angrily. 'You said you wanted to marry me. Have you changed your mind?'

He ran his finger around the inside of his stiffly starched collar. 'No, of course not, *cara mia*. But can we afford to spend three weeks here while the banns are read? We would have to turn down the offer to appear at Lusby's.'

'You always were a difficult man,' Polly said, sighing. 'We will have to remain handfasted until we return to London.' She shot a sideways glance at her brother-in-law. 'Anyway, I don't think you would have your heart in it, Seymour. You and I never did get on.'

'Don't start a fight, Polly,' Eleanor said, wagging her finger at her sister. 'This is going to be a joyful occasion. We've come round to Billy's way of thinking and both Seymour and I approve of his marriage to Jenifry. She's a sweet girl and will make him a good wife.' She turned to her husband. 'Isn't that so, Seymour?'

He nodded. 'Yes, my dear. Quite so.'

Rose stared at them in amazement. She had never heard her mother speak up in such a manner, and in the past she would never have put her own opinion forward. She caught Bennett's eye and she knew instinctively that he understood.

Billy and Jenifry arrived in time for dinner, and Mrs Vennor had excelled herself. Luckily Kensa was not called upon to wait at table, and the new butler and parlour maid had been well trained. In an aside, Eleanor told Rose that Vere had entrusted her with the task of finding suitable servants, and she had wisely involved Mrs Vennor in their selection. Rose continued to be amazed by the change in her parents. Her father seemed much more human and less domineering and her mother was a changed woman. She had gained in confidence and regained her health and vitality. It was, Rose thought, little short of a miracle.

Later that evening, when Eleanor and Seymour had returned to the vicarage and Billy had taken Jenifry home to her mother's cottage, the rest of the party retired to the drawing room. Cora sat beside Vere on the sofa, playing backgammon, while Fancello accompanied Polly on the piano in a selection of the songs they performed on stage.

Rose was tired, but happy. She stood by one of the tall windows. The perfume of night-scented stocks and honeysuckle wafted in from the garden, where purple shadows had all but masked the lawn and the shrubbery had dissolved into darkness.

'Would you care for a stroll?'

She turned with a start at the sound of Bennett's voice. It would have been sensible to decline, but she was tired of being the level-headed, rational sister. She glanced over her shoulder at Cora, who was flirting outrageously with Vere. 'Yes, that would be nice. It's such a lovely evening.'

The tall sash windows opened onto the terrace

and as she stepped outside Rose was conscious of the warm summer air caressing her cheeks. Above them the stars twinkled like diamond studs in an indigo velvet sky and the lawn was suddenly bathed in moonlight. She took deep breaths of the scented air.

'It was you who persuaded my father to move here permanently, wasn't it, Bennett?'

He tucked her hand in the crook of his arm as they walked slowly along the gravel path. 'I'd discussed it with Billy. He was eager to heal the rift in the family, but he didn't think your father would listen to anything he had to say.'

'How did you do it? I know my pa; it can't have been easy.'

'It wasn't as hard as you imagine. I think Mr Perkins had had time to think, and he realised what he had lost. He's a good man, Rose, but stubborn, like someone else I know.'

She chuckled. 'I suppose you mean me.'

'You are like him in some ways, of course, but you are much prettier.'

'Now you're flattering me.'

'No, I meant every word.' He came to a sudden halt, taking both her hands in his. 'I've been hovering in the background for too long, Rose. I kept my peace because I knew that Vere had feelings for you, and he's a far better man than I.'

'I won't allow that,' she said fiercely. 'I admire

and respect your cousin, and at one time I thought I might grow fond of him, but then I realised my mistake.'

'Do you think you could grow fond of me?'

The question was not unexpected. The setting was romantic, and the barrier she had set up against heartbreak had been giving way, a little at a time. 'What are you saying?' she asked cautiously.

His eyes were in deep shadow, but his generous lips curved in a smile. 'I always said you would make a good lawyer. I'm trying to tell you that I love you, Rose. I've always loved you, but at every turn fate seemed to throw an obstacle in my way.' He drew her into his arms. 'I wasn't telling the entire truth earlier. Everything I've done has been for you, and you alone. Have I a chance, Rose?'

There was only one answer to this question. She slid her arms around his neck and closed her eyes. Her body responded to his as if they were two halves of the same coin, and they became one in a kiss that seemed to last for eternity, but was over too soon.

'You do love me, Rose?' His voice shook and he held her close. 'I can feel your heart beating against mine. I never want to let you go.'

She closed her eyes and laid her head against his chest. 'I do love you, Bennett. I just didn't realise how much until now.'

'I'm going to London first thing in the morning.'

Alarmed, she tilted her head to look him in the eye. 'You're leaving me so soon?'

'I'm going to get a special licence. If you agree we'll have a double wedding in your father's church. I'm not letting you get away this time. What do you say, Rose?'

She put her head on one side. 'What about the Sunshine Sisters?'

'I won't expect you to give up your stage career, if that's what you mean. I'm proud of your success and I'm not the sort of man who'll tie you to the home.'

'Really?'

'Yes, really. I don't want you to turn into a copy of your mother or your aunt Polly. I know very well that you have a mind of your own, Rose Perkins, and that's part of the reason I'm so in love with you.'

She ran her hands through his hair, pulling his head down so that their lips met again in a breathless kiss. 'I think a double wedding would be wonderful, Bennett.'

'Then let's go indoors and tell Vere and Cora.'

Rose glanced over his shoulder. She could see her sister and Vere with their heads close together as they laughed over something that had obviously amused them. 'I don't think they've even noticed that we've left the room. I'm afraid Joshua will be very disappointed if those two make a match of it, although I never did see Cora as a vicar's wife.'

'Did you see yourself as a struggling lawyer's wife?'

'No, but I see myself as your wife, Bennett, and one day you'll be a QC. You'll be twice as famous as the Sunshine Sisters, and I'll be so proud of you.'

'You will always make the sun shine for me, Rose.'

A Letter from Dilly

Dear Reader

With every book I write I become immersed in the characters, and getting to know them as the story evolves is a never-ending thrill. I admired the brave efforts of Rose and Cora as, with everything against them, they struggled to clear their brother's name. It's easy to forget the constraints under which Victorian women lived their lives, and that the freedoms we take for granted today were forbidden to them.

It took courage for women to rebel against the Victorian expectation that they would become the Angel in the House, and Aunt Polly would have been considered eccentric in the extreme when she opened her home for fallen women. That was purely imaginary but St Luke's Hospital for Lunatics and its neighbour, the City of London Lying-In Hospital, did exist, with the Vinegar Works in the next street. I always use authentic sites and study old maps of London, prints and photographs so that I can see the area in my mind's eye.

I can sympathise with stage-struck Rose – I was much the same as a child and attended ballet classes for seven years. My parents used to take me regularly to the East Ham Palace in East London, which was a variety theatre until it was knocked down in the late 1950s, and I think this inspired me as much as anything. I always fancied being in a singing and dancing sister act, but the trouble was I didn't have a sister and I couldn't sing.

But I did have one brief period of being on the stage – when I was 12 my dancing school provided a chorus line (six of us to be exact) to appear in a semi-professional pantomime. I remember one snowy January at a church hall in Peckham Rye, south of the river, when the explosive charge timed to go off when Widow Twanky's washing machine blew up, went off with such force that the metal plug shot through the ceiling. Our dressing room was filled with smoke and we were hurried on to the stage. There wasn't much attention paid to health and safety in those days – but I did get five shillings (25p in today's money) for a letter I sent to *Girl* comic, describing the experience. That was the start of my writing career.

I do hope you enjoyed *Ragged Rose* as much as I enjoyed writing it.

With my very best wishes

Dilly Court

Read on for an exclusive extract from
Dilly Court's gripping new novel

The Swan Maid

coming in summer 2016

Chapter One

Cheapside, London, 1854

'Lottie, you wretched girl, where are you?' Mrs Filby's strident voice echoed round the galleries of The Swan with Two Necks, and the ancient building seemed to shake on its foundations.

Lottie was in the stable yard of the coaching inn, and had been emptying chamberpots on to the dung heap as it lay festering in the heat of the late summer sun. She had been up since five o'clock that morning and had not yet had breakfast, but the rooms had to be serviced, and the guests had to be looked after. Their needs came before those of the inn servants, and the mail coach from Exeter would be arriving at any moment.

'Lottie, answer me at once.' Prudence Filby leaned over the balustrade of the first floor gallery, shielding her eyes from the sunlight. 'Is that you down there in the horse muck?'

'Yes, ma'am.' Lottie had hoped that the short-sighted landlady might not see her, but it seemed that her luck was out. It was better to answer, and receive a tirade of abuse, than to hide, only to be accused later of every shortcoming and misde-meanour that came to Mrs Filby's mind.

'That's where you belong, you idle slut, but I have need of you in the dining parlour. Come in at once, and wash your filthy hands.'

'Coming, ma'am.' Lottie hurried indoors, leaving the chamberpots in the scullery to be scoured clean when she could find the time. She washed her hands in the stone sink and was about to dry them on her apron, when she realised that this would leave a wet mark, and that would be enough to earn a swift clout around the head from her employer. Mrs Filby had a right hook that would be the envy of champion bare-knuckle fighters, and had been seen to wrestle a drunk to the ground on many an occasion. Her husband, who was by no means a small man, treated her with due deference, and spent most of his time in the taproom, drinking ale with his customers.

Lottie hitched up her skirts and raced across the cobblestones to the kitchen on the far side of the stable yard. The heat from the range hit her with the force of a cannonball, and the smell of rancid bacon fat and the bullock's head being boiled for soup made her feel sick.

She acknowledged the cook with a nod, and hurried on until she reached the dining parlour, where she came to a halt, peering at her hazy reflection in a fly-spotted mirror on the wall. Strands of fair hair had escaped from the knot at the nape of her neck, and she tucked them under her frilled mobcap. She straightened her apron, braced her shoulders and entered the room.

Prudence Filby stood, arms akimbo, by the sideboard. She glowered at Lottie. 'You took your time,' she hissed. 'Clear the plates and don't offer them more coffee. The Exeter mail coach is due any minute, and I want this lot out of here.'

'More bread, girl.' A portly man clicked his fingers. 'And a slab of butter. I paid good money for my breakfast.'

Lottie hurried to his side. 'I'll do what I can, sir.'

'You'll do more than that. Bring me bread and butter, and a pot of jam wouldn't go amiss.'

'Is there jam?' A woman seated with her husband at the next table, leaned over to tug at Lottie's skirt. 'Why didn't we get any jam? I don't like dry bread, and I'll swear the flour had chalk added to it. My mouth is full of grit.'

'No wonder this place is half empty.' Her husband turned his head to stare at Mrs Filby. 'This is your establishment, madam. Why have we been deprived of jam?'

Mrs Filby folded her arms across her ample bosom and advanced on him, eyes narrowed, lips pursed.

'You paid for bed and breakfast, sir. No one never mentioned jam. Jam costs extra.'

'Don't make a fuss, Nathaniel.' The man's wife reached out across the table to touch his hand. 'Suddenly I've lost my appetite.'

The City gentlemen at a table by the window had been listening attentively, and they too started demanding more coffee, and bread and butter: one went so far as to ask for marmalade.

Mrs Filby answered their requests by dragging Lottie from the parlour. She closed the door, and boxed Lottie's ears. 'That's what you get for nothing – see what you get for something. I've told you time and time again that bread, butter, coffee and the like should be given sparingly. We're here to make money, and you must wait until the last minute before the coach arrives to serve the coffee or soup. It has to be so hot that the customers have to leave it.' She caught Lottie by the ear. 'What happens then, girl? Do you remember anything you've been taught?'

'It goes back in the pot, ma'am.'

Mrs Filby released her, wiping her hands on her skirt. 'That's right. Then we can sell it twice over and we make more money. You do know, so why don't you carry out my orders?'

'I'm sorry, ma'am. It won't happen again.'

'Go and fetch hot coffee, and make sure the bread is straight from the oven. I heard the post horn. This miserable lot of complainers will be leaving in the time it takes to change horses and turn the coach around.'

'What about jam?'

'Jam?' Mrs Filby's voice rose to a screech.

Lottie fled to the kitchen.

The next mail coach arrived just as the disgruntled passengers from the dining parlour were boarding the one that was about to leave. The lady who had been refused marmalade climbed into the coach declaring that they would be travelling by train next time. Her husband followed her, saying nothing.

Lottie stood to attention, waiting to show the new arrivals to the dining room. London might be the end of the journey for some, but others would want to rest and refresh themselves before travelling on. It was a never-ending cycle of weary travellers arriving and departing, with only minutes to achieve a swift turn around. The ostlers worked with impressive speed and dexterity, and Jem, the potboy, raced about doing the jobs that no one else wanted to do. He nudged Lottie as he went to offload the luggage.

'Save us a slice of bacon,' he said, grinning. 'I'm starving.'

She nodded. 'I will, if I can.'

He dashed forward to catch a carpet bag thrown from the roof by the guard, resplendent in his livery of scarlet and gold. Trotter was a regular on this route, and Lottie had observed that he liked to show off his strength in front of an appreciative audience. She looked up, and sure enough, the other chambermaids, May and Ruth, were leaning over the balustrade on the top floor, waving their cleaning cloths in an attempt to attract his attention.

Jem followed her gaze. 'You're an old goat, Trotter,' he said, chuckling. 'How do you do it, mate?'

Trotter's answer was to hurl a leather valise at Jem, which almost brought him to his knees. 'Cheeky devil.' Trotter flexed his muscles. 'You could learn a thing or two from me, son.' He turned and waved at the maids before leaping to the ground, and swaggering off in the direction of the taproom.

'You'd best get that lot indoors before Mrs Filby sees you,' Lottie said hastily. 'She's already given me a clout round the head that made me see stars.'

Jem tucked two smaller cases under his arms and then lifted the heavier bags, one in each hand. 'She'd have to stand on a box to reach my head, but she punched me in the bread-basket last time I made her mad. She's a nasty piece of work, and that's the truth, but we're better than her, Lottie. Keep that in mind, my girl.' He strolled off, whistling.

Lottie looked up but May and Ruth had vanished, and a quick glance over her shoulder revealed the cause. Mrs Filby was standing in the doorway, glaring at her. 'Don't loaf around doing nothing, you lazy little slut. Get on with your work.'

'How does she do it?' Lottie muttered as she hurried into the scullery to take up where she had left off. 'She's got eyes in the back of her head.'

'Talking to yourself, are you? That's the first sign of madness.' Ruth edged past her, carrying two dangerously full chamberpots. 'You'd think the horses had pissed in these. I was all for emptying them over the balustrade, but May stopped me just in time.'

'That would have taken Trotter down a peg or two,' Lottie said, laughing. 'He wouldn't have been so cocky then.'

Ruth backed out into the yard, taking care not to spill a drop. 'Maybe I'll be in time to have a few words with him before the coach leaves. It's me he fancies, not May.'

'I expect he's got a wife and half a dozen nippers at home. I'd watch out for him if I were you, Ruth.'

'I will, don't you fret, ducks.' Ruth stepped outside, leaving Lottie to finish her unenviable task.

That done, she returned to the bedrooms, and made them ready for the next occupants. When she was satisfied that Mrs Filby could find nothing to criticise of her work, she went downstairs to help Cook prepare the midday meal.

Jezebel Pretty did not live up to her name. She was tall, raw-boned and ungainly with a lean, mean face and a fiery temperament. She had served a two-year sentence in Coldbath Fields prison, commonly known as 'The Steel', for inflicting grievous bodily harm on her former lover, and had been employed at the inn for almost a year. Lottie, Ruth and May had often spoken about her in the privacy of the attic room where they lay their heads at night, but it was not the fact that the Filbys had taken on an ex-convict that shocked them. What they found hard to believe was that anyone as patently ugly as Jezebel could have found a man who fancied her in the first place, or one who was foolish enough to take on a woman whose volatile temper simmered beneath the surface, erupting every now and then like a volcano.

Even so, Lottie had discovered a different side of Jezebel. Not long after the cook had started work at the inn, a small mongrel terrier had got in the way of one of the mail coach horses. The poor creature had been flung up in the air and had landed on the cobblestones in a pathetic heap. Jezebel had happened to be in the yard, smoking her clay pipe, when the accident occurred and Lottie had seen her rush to the animal's aid. She had picked it up and, cradling it in her arms like a baby, carried it into the kitchen. Lottie had followed, offering to help and had watched Jezebel examining the tiny body for broken bones with the skill of an experienced surgeon, and the tenderness of a mother caring for her child.

Despite two broken ribs and several deep cuts, Lad, as Jezebel named him, survived and they became inseparable, despite Mrs Filby's attempts to banish the dog from the kitchen or any part of the building other than the stables. Lad, quite naturally, had developed a deep distrust of horses and he refused to be parted from his saviour. Jezebel, who was a good cook and worked for next to nothing, was the one person Mrs Filby treated with a certain amount of restraint and respect, and Lad was allowed to stay.

Lottie entered the kitchen and received an enthusiastic greeting from the small dog, who seemed to remember that she was one of the first people who had shown him any kindness. Having been flea-ridden and undernourished when he first arrived he was now plump and lively with a shiny white coat and comical brown patches over one eye and the tip of one ear.

'Where've you been?' Jezebel demanded. 'The bullock's head is done and the meat needs to be taken off the bone, and the vegetables need preparing to go in the stew. I've been run off me feet. I was better off in The Steel than I am here.'

'I would have come sooner, but I had to wait on in the dining parlour and I hadn't finished the bedchambers, but I'm here now.'

'And where are those two flibbertigibbets? I suppose they're making sheep's eyes at that fellow Trotter. My Bill was just like him, until I spoilt his beauty with my chiv. Trotter had best look out, that's all I can say.'

Lottie lifted the heavy saucepan off the range. She knew better than to argue the point with Jezebel. It was easier and safer to keep her mouth shut and get on with her work; that way the long days passed without unpleasantness and everyone was happy in their own way. She had learned long ago that it was pointless to bemoan the fate that had brought her to The Swan with Two Necks. Born into an army family, Lottie's early years had been spent in India and when her mother died of a fever, which also took Lottie's younger brothers and sister, she had been sent to England with a family who were returning on leave, and left with her Uncle Sefton in Clerkenwell. A confirmed bachelor, he had little time for children and Lottie had been packed off to boarding school, although her uncle had made it plain that he considered educating females to be a total waste of money.

She had received a basic education until the age of twelve, when she returned home to find that her uncle had married a rich widow. Lottie's childhood had ended when her new aunt – acting supposedly with her best interests at heart – had sent Lottie to work for the Filbys. It was just another form of slavery: she worked from the moment she rose in the morning until late at night, when she fell into her bed.

'Are you doing what I told you, or are you daydreaming again Lottie Lane? D'you want to feel the back of my hand, girl?' Jezebel reared up in front of Lottie, bringing her back to the present with a start.

'Sorry, ma'am.'

'Get on with it, or you'll get another clout round the head, and I ain't as gentle as the missis.' Jezebel stomped out into the yard, snatching up her pipe and tobacco pouch on the way. Lad trotted at her heels, growling and baring his teeth at the horses.

Lottie set to work and dissected the head, taking care not to waste a scrap of meat. Mrs Filby would check the bones later and woe betide her if there was any waste. Parsimonious to the last, Prudence Filby ruled her empire with a rod of iron.

Minutes later, Jezebel marched back into the room. 'Where's Jem? The butcher has delivered the mutton. I want the carcass boned and ready for the pot. Go and find him, girl.'

'But I haven't finished what I'm doing.'

Jezebel moved with the speed of a snake striking its prey. The sound of the slap echoed round the beamed kitchen, and Lottie clutched her hand to her cheek. 'The bullock's going nowhere, but you are. Find the boy and tell him to get started or I'll be after him.'

Lottie found Jem in the taproom, serving ale to the newly-arrived male passengers, while Mrs Filby shepherded the ladies to the dining parlour where they would be plied with coffee, tea and toast, all of which were added onto the bill. Each day was the same, and everyone knew their part in the carefully choreographed routine designed to make the travellers part with their money in as short a time as possible. Jem had taken too long offloading the last coach and was now behind with his tasks. Normally cheerful and easy-going, he was looking flushed and flustered.

'Cook wants you Jem.' Lottie took the pint mug from his hand. 'I'll finish up in here. There's only minutes before the coach leaves.'

'I suppose she's in a foul mood, as usual.'

'You'll soon find out if you don't hurry up.' Lottie passed the mug of ale to a man seated at the nearest table. She had just finished serving when the call came for the passengers to board, and she heard the clatter of hoofs and the rumble of wheels as yet another mail coach pulled into the stable yard. She was relieved by Shem Filby who escorted the new guests into the taproom, enabling her to hurry back to the kitchen to prepare the vegetables.

Early mornings were always hectic and she was used to the rush, although by midday everyone was beginning to flag, but there was no time to rest. Private carriages made up most of their custom during the day. Filby was pleased to point out that some people preferred the convenience of being transported from door to door, a luxury not provided when travelling by train, and others feared that the speed reached by steam engines would have serious effects on their health. The railways, he said, would one day put them out of business, but that was a long way off – or so he hoped.

Lottie did not have time to worry about such matters. She alternated between the kitchen, the dining room and the bedchambers, as did Ruth and May. They met briefly at mealtimes, with rare moments of free time during the afternoon lull, and then it was time for dinner to be prepared and served. After everything was cleared away and the dishes washed and dried, there were beds to be turned back and aired, using copper warming pans filled with live coals. The constant need to provide washing facilities necessitated regular trips from the kitchen to the bedrooms, carrying ewers of hot water, and there was always someone who wanted something extra. Lottie had been sent out to buy all manner of things, mainly for ladies on their travels who had forgotten to bring a hairbrush or a comb. Sometimes it was a bottle of laudanum for pain, or oil of cloves for toothache, and these were always needed as a matter of urgency. Lottie had once been sent out to purchase a gift for a man's wife as he had forgotten her birthday. Sometimes guests tipped generously, while others gave nothing in return, not even a thank you.

The only time the girls had to chat was during the brief period before they fell asleep on their straw-filled palliasses, and even then they could be awakened at any hour of the night and called upon to serve travellers who stopped at the inn.

Such a call came in the early hours of the next morning. Lottie was in a deep sleep when she was shaken awake by Ruth. 'Get up. We're wanted in the kitchen.'

'What's the matter?'

'Soldiers,' Ruth said excitedly. 'I leaned over the balustrade and saw their red jackets. I love a man in uniform. Come on, they'll be in need of sustenance.'

Half asleep, Lottie made her way downstairs, still struggling with the buttons on her blouse.

The stable yard was illuminated by gaslight and filled with the sound of booted feet, the clatter of horses' hooves and men's raised voices. Above them the night sky formed a dark canopy, creating a theatrical backdrop to the dramatic scene. An officer was issuing orders and Shem Filby was standing in the midst of the chaos, bellowing instructions to the ostlers that seemed to countermand those given by the young lieutenant. It had become a competition to see whose voice was the loudest. In the end it belonged to Mrs Filby, who was wearing a dressing robe over her nightgown and whose strident tones were heard above all others.

'Silence.' She waded into their midst, seizing a young private by the collar and thrusting him out of her way. 'Gentlemen, have a thought for our other guests.' She faced the officer with a contemptuous curl of her lip. 'You will be more comfortable in the dining parlour, sir. Ruth will show you the way.'

'Thank you, ma'am.' As meekly as a schoolboy caught scrumping apples, he followed Ruth into the building.

'Take the men into the kitchen, May.' Mrs Filby marched up to two soldiers who were supporting a comrade who appeared to be unconscious. 'What's the matter with him? Is he sick? If so you can take him to hospital.'

The elder of the two privates stood to attention. 'If you please, ma'am, he's suffered a knock on the head. A cracked skull ain't catching.'

'I don't need any of your cheek, soldier.' Mrs Filby peered at the injured man. 'Has he been drinking?'

Only Adam's ale, ma'am. We've been working on the telegraph lines in the Strand for two days, but now we're heading for Chatham and then on to the Crimea. All he needs is a bed for the night and some tender care, such as would be given by a kind lady like yourself.'

'Well, then, I'm sure we can do something for one of our brave men who will soon depart for battle.' Mrs Filby spun round to face Lottie. 'Take them to my parlour. See that they have everything they need.'

'Yes ma'am.' Lottie made a move towards the doorway. 'This way please, gents.'

'One moment.' The lieutenant had obviously had second thoughts and returned. 'I'm grateful for your help, ma'am, but I am in charge of my men. Private Ellis needs medical attention.'

'What is your name, sir?' Mrs Filby bristled visibly. 'You are on my property now, not the battlefield.'

He doffed his shako with a bow and a flourish. 'Lieutenant Farrell Gillingham, Corps of Royal Sappers and Miners, at your service.'

'Well, Lieutenant Gillingham, if you wish to take your man to hospital, feel free to do so, but we cannot incur the expense of the doctor's fees, unless, of course, you wish to stump up for them yourself.'

'Perhaps we will wait until daylight, ma'am. If Ellis is not well enough to be moved, I'll think again.' Gillingham spoke in a tone that did not invite argument. He bowed smartly and followed Ruth into the building.

'Go with the men, Lottie,' Mrs Filby said in a low voice. 'You're a sensible girl, for the most part, anyway. See to their needs as best you can.' She lowered her voice to a whisper. 'But don't make them too comfortable. Their sort don't pay well.' She glanced round the yard, which was empty except for the ostlers who were attending to the horses. 'Filby, where are you? Speak to me.'

Lottie beckoned to the soldiers. 'Let's get the poor fellow inside.'

The Filby's parlour was dominated by a huge walnut chiffonier, upon which were set out Prudence Filby's treasured china tea set and small ornaments which had no intrinsic value, but must surely have a meaning for her. Lottie knew each piece intimately, having had to dust them every day since her arrival at The Swan with Two Necks. For some reason best known to herself, Mrs Filby had made the cleaning of her private parlour Lottie's responsibility, insisting that the hand-hooked rugs with vibrant floral designs be taken out into the yard and beaten daily, and the heavy crimson, velvet curtains and portière had to be brushed free from dust and cobwebs at least once a week.

Lottie held the door open, and while the soldiers settled Private Ellis on to the sofa she raked the glowing embers of the fire into life.

'What happened to him?' she asked curiously.

The younger of the two men eyed her up and down. 'What makes a pretty girl like you want to work in a place like this?'

'I think we should send for the doctor.' Lottie chose to ignore the compliment. 'Your friend looks very poorly.'

'You've got eyes the colour of the cornflowers in the fields at home,' he said earnestly, 'and hair the

487

colour of ripe wheat. I've never seen such a pretty face in all me born days.'

'That's enough of that, Frank. You're a sapper, not a poet.' The older man held his hand out to Lottie. 'Private Joe Benson, miss. Don't take no notice of my mate. He can't help hisself when he meets a young lady.'

Lottie smiled. 'I don't mind being called pretty, but I still think that your friend looks very unwell.'

Benson leaned over to examine the unconscious man. 'I'd say he's got concussion. I seen it afore, miss. We was undergoing training at the Electric Telegraph Company, working on the underground wiring in the Strand, and Ellis was on the ladder when it gave way.'

'He should have been taken straight to hospital,' Lottie said worriedly.

'He could die.' Frank moved closer to the fire. 'Is there any chance of a bite to eat and a drink, miss? We can't do much for young Gideon, but the living has to be taken care of too.'

Lottie turned on him. 'How can you be so heartless? If you're hungry go to the kitchen and Mrs Pretty will feed you.'

Frank's tanned features split into a wide grin. 'Does she take after her name? Is she good-looking like you?'

It was on the tip of Lottie's tongue to put him straight, but she changed her mind. 'The only way you'll find out is to do as I say.' She shot a sideways glance at Private Benson. 'You look as though you could do with some sustenance. I'll stay with your friend while you get some food, but don't be too long.'

Benson tipped his cap. 'Ta, miss. Much obliged. We ain't eaten since midday.' He pushed Frank towards the door. 'Hurry up, then. If we don't hurry we'll find the greedy gannets have ate everything in the kitchen.'

Lottie stared down at the inert figure on the couch. A livid bruise marked his otherwise smooth forehead, and his light brown hair was matted with blood from a cut on the temple. He looked young and defenceless, despite the army uniform, and if she hadn't known better she might have thought him to be sleeping peacefully. She left the room briefly to look for Jem, who was rushing about fetching food and ale for their new guests. She called to him. 'When you've done that, could you bring me a bowl of warm water and some clean rags? I daren't leave the poor fellow on his own.'

'What a to-do! But the officer is a toff,' Jem chuckled and patted his trouser pocket. 'He gave me a handsome tip, so I don't mind running after him and his mates. I'll bring the water as soon as I can.' He raced off towards the kitchen, balancing a jug of ale with the expertise of long practice.

When she had bathed the soldier's cuts and placed a cold compress on his bruised forehead, Lottie could do no more and she settled down by the fire. It was warm in the Filbys' parlour and the chair was comfortable. She was tired and very sleepy.

She awakened with a start at the sound of someone calling out in distress.

Keep up with Dilly